A STORY FROM THE FILES OF ALEXANDER STRANGE

STRANGE CURRENTS

J.C. BRUCE

Strange Currents

ISBN: 978-1-7342903-9-4 Hardback)
ISBN: 978-1-7342903-6-3 (Paperback)
ISBN: 978-1-7342903-7-0 (eBook)

Library of Congress Control Number: 2019920437

This is a work of fiction. Names, characters, places, and incidents are a product of the author's imagination. Locales and public names are sometimes used for atmospheric purposes. Any resemblance to actual people, living or dead, or to businesses, companies, events, institutions, or locales is completely coincidental.

Book design by Damonza.com
Website design by Bumpy Flamingo LLC

Printed by Tropic Press in the United States of America.

First printing edition 2020

Tropic Press LLC
P.O. Box 110758
Naples, Florida 34108

www.Tropic.Press

Books by J.C. Bruce

The Strange Files

Florida Man: A Story From the Files of Alexander Strange

Get Strange

Strange Currents

To Sandy, Kacey, and Logan

CHAPTER 1

Key West

I KNEW MY number was up when the flamingo stepped on my face.

It wasn't the bird's fault. That's what I got for falling down in the middle of Duval Street. And she and her feathery cousins wouldn't have stampeded if the shotgun-toting douche bag hadn't let loose.

To be fair, he wasn't shooting at the birds; he was aiming at me.

With certain death at hand, your life is supposed to flash before your eyes. Not sure who returned from the afterlife to report that. But what was passing before my eyes was a sea of magenta feathers, nasty little claws on webbed feet, and a steady spattering of flamingo doo-doo.

It's not pink, by the way.

Then came the humans dressed in boas, fake wings, and flip-flops. The flamingos were honking, the people were screaming. A fat guy wearing a lavender tutu plopped on top of me, rolled off, and fled. He had the right idea.

I jumped to my feet, ready to run as if my life depended on it. Because it did. At the same time, I couldn't help but marvel at the spectacle I'd become part of, and how a few days earlier I'd been minding my own business aboard my fishing trawler when a woman named after a precious metal showed up.

CHAPTER 2

Naples, Florida—Ten days earlier

THE WOMAN CROSSED the pier toward my trawler wearing cut-off jeans, boots, and a straw cowboy hat that struggled to contain a mop of thick gray hair. She stretched her tan and muscular legs over the gunwale of the *Miss Demeanor* and confronted me on the stern of the boat. "You're the weird news guy, right?"

That was annoying. I planned to spend the day brooding, and that's impossible while entertaining uninvited guests. *Broodus interruptus.*

"Where's the rodeo?" I asked.

She planted both fists on her slim hips, cocked her head, and stared up at me, squinting in the morning sun. She was a shade over five feet tall, fit, and about fifty. "Alexander Strange, right?"

"Ordinarily, people ask permission to come aboard. You know, like knocking on doors? It's a common courtesy."

She rolled her eyes. "You're him. You fit the description perfectly."

"Meaning what?"

"A friend of yours, he told me you might be a pain in the butt."

For a fleeting moment, I wondered if she meant my girlfriend. We'd had one of those mornings. Hence my plans for some serious brooding.

"Which alleged friend?" I asked.

"Brett Barfield. He called you a gigantic hemorrhoid. But he also said you could help me."

Barfield is a cop-turned-detective with Third Eye Investigators working out of Phoenix. We met when I worked at a newspaper there. "Don't believe everything Barfield tells you," I said. "I'm only a medium-sized hemorrhoid."

That earned me a smirk.

"So, why are you here, and what's your name?" I asked.

"Sally Ann McFadden. Most people call me Silver." She removed her hat, exposing the fifty shades of gray on her head, making sure I understood the origin of her nickname. Then she offered her hand. It was small, firm, and ringless. We shook.

She looked up at me curiously, her brows furrowed. "Silver McFadden. You've heard of me, right?"

I hadn't, but didn't want to be impolite: "You the new Mullet Festival queen?"

Her fists were back on her hips. "THE AUTHOR!"

"AUTHOR OF WHAT?" I could do the capital letters thing, too.

She ticked off her alliterative titles: *Werewolves in Washington, Vampires of Virginia, Lunar Landing Lunacy.* "You write about news of the weird. You should know my books."

"Afraid not. Reality's weird enough. And you know Barfield, how?"

She set her hat back atop her head and frowned, clearly disappointed her fame had failed to penetrate this corner of the Gunshine State. "He answered the phone when I called the Third Eye's 800 number. Said he was the duty officer or something."

Must not grind teeth.

"So, Barfield told a total stranger I'm a pain in the ass? And where I live?"

"Not a total stranger. He's a fan of my vampire books. And he offered to show me the place in the desert where they filmed the fake moon landing."

"I'm sure he did."

"Anyway, he said since I was heading to the Keys you'd be on the way. I didn't understand why I should meet with a journalist instead of a real detective. Then he explained you've worked with the Third Eye on cases, so he wasn't totally negative."

"How nice."

Silver took a deep breath and adopted a more conciliatory tone: "He also said you were tenacious. And that this would be right up your alley. And if you got killed nobody would much give a shit—his words—because you live alone and don't have any friends."

That wasn't entirely true. Spock would miss me. But it was the use of the word "killed" that captured my attention. I keep an updated to-do list and I didn't recall "expire" on it.

"And I might unleash my mortal coil, why?"

"Because solving this murder might be dangerous."

There it was.

She pulled a green checkered bandana out of her back pocket and blew her nose. She looked up and her eyes were bloodshot. She was either having an allergy attack, or she was about to cry.

Then I realized my eyes were burning, too. The breeze had shifted eastward from the Gulf. A large Red Tide bloom had been reported heading ashore. In addition to killing fish, the algae releases irritating toxins into the air.

"Any chance we could sit down and talk?" she asked, the tone of her voice now definitely more subdued.

Cynic that I am, my first thought was she'd led off with the bad-ass routine and now was shifting gears. A one-woman version of bad cop-good cop. But she needn't have worked so hard at it. The moment she stepped on the boat, I knew I'd hear her out. Her getup alone had aroused my curiosity.

"Let's sit on the poop deck," I said. "I was about to brew some coffee. You can tell me all about this murder. And your books and vampires, too, if you like."

"Got anything stronger?"

I glanced at my Mickey Mouse watch. It was only nine o'clock. Maybe it was after five in Transylvania. "Name your poison."

A few minutes later we were resting in deck chairs, she with a beer, me with a cup of Pike's Place. The *Miss Demeanor* gently rocked as passing watercraft churned the bay. My dog was resting in Silver's lap where she was patting his little head. "Don't ordinarily drink this early," she said. "But I've been behind the wheel since dawn-thirty. Drove down from Ocala."

She scratched one of my dog's enormous ears and asked, "What's her name?"

"Fred."

Fred's a Papillion, eight pounds of black and white fur with ears like butterfly wings. He rolled over on his back so she could scratch his tummy. Or maybe he wanted to prove he wasn't a girl. Not for the first time, I suspected Fred understood more than he let on.

She patted Fred a few more times then set him on the deck. But he didn't like that. Fred enjoys being petted, and he demonstrated his displeasure with a short, sharp bark.

"Fuck you, bitch!" the voice of James Earl Jones bellowed from a speaker on his collar.

Silver jumped out of her chair.

"What the hell?" she gasped, her eyes wide, her mouth open in disbelief.

"Universal dog translator," I said nonchalantly and took another sip of coffee. "It's an experimental model. Fred's the test dog. An inventor friend of mine asked me to try it out."

"Doesn't that frighten him?" she sputtered.

"Fred's hearing is almost gone. Ironic, I know, given the size of his ears. He doesn't seem to mind."

After a few moments, she resumed her seat and slugged down a prodigious gulp of Florida Cracker white ale. I waited patiently for her to recover her composure, taking another sip from my Green Lantern mug.

"Dog translator?"

"Uh-huh."

"Barfield said you were weird."

"Occupational hazard. Now tell me about this murder."

She tipped the can and guzzled some more beer. "It's my brother. My adopted brother. Somebody killed him."

Oh.

"Sorry for your loss," I said. And I meant it. I knew about losing family.

"Medical examiner says the cause of death was drowning, maybe nitrogen narcosis. But I know it wasn't an accident."

Silver wiped her eyes with her bandanna, then blew her nose again.

"Hold on a sec," I said. "You're saying the ME's ruled your brother's death accidental, but you believe otherwise?"

She nodded. "Let me tell you about Wilson. And why this can't be an accident. He is—or was—a marine biologist with the University of South Florida. He was in Key West on a project for a European phone company. I'd called him last week. Had some inheritance business to clear up. My mother died recently—dad went seven years ago. It's all the pesticides and GMOs. I've gone organic."

She crossed her legs and a small chunk of organic matter with the scent of equine excrement dislodged from the bottom of her boot.

"Oops," she said. "I breed horses. I'm around the smell all the time; don't even notice it anymore."

She bent over, picked it up, and flipped it into the water. Then she rubbed her fingers on her cutoffs.

"My parents, in their will, they gave Wilson a percentage in the farm, but he wasn't interested," she said. "But there was paperwork to sign. He told me to email it. He shared a few things about his big project, how he was working out of the community college down there in the Keys, and he promised to tell me more the next time we talked. But he never did."

"Never told you?"

"Never talked again. I sent him the documents, but he didn't return them. After about a week, I called and left a message. He'd given me the name of a woman at the community college who was helping him, so I called her, too, but school's been on spring break."

A fishing boat chugged by on its way to the Gulf, and the *Miss Demeanor* rocked in its wake. A kid onboard dumped a bucket of fish heads and entrails, and a flurry of seagulls and pelicans swarmed into the water from their nearby roosts and began squawking and fighting over the morning treat. Silver seemed oblivious to the commotion.

"At first, I said, fuck it, it was *sooo* Wilson. He pulled this disappearing shit all the time. Went off, joined the navy. Never said a word. Went back to school, didn't tell anyone. He sorta cut himself off. Maybe he never felt a part of the family. I don't know."

She paused for a moment, gathering her thoughts. I sipped my coffee and waited.

"So, I got a call yesterday from the medical examiner's office in Marathon. Fishermen found a body floating off a place called Dredger's Key. The man was wearing a wetsuit, and his dog tag identified him as Wilson. They contacted the navy and got my name as next of kin."

"Was Wilson still in the navy?" I asked. I didn't know anyone in the service who wore their tags after they mustered out.

"No. But last time I saw him, he still wore his tag. He was proud of his service."

"How long ago was it that you saw him last?" I asked.

She waved a dismissive hand. "Year, about," she said.

"Alright. You got a call from the ME, and he told you Wilson's death was an accident."

"One of his assistants. But that doesn't make any sense. Wilson was an experienced diver."

Even experienced divers drown, but I let it go. "So Wilson's work for this international phone company involved diving. What was it he was doing for them, exactly?"

"He said they have problems with their undersea cables between

Miami and Mexico, and they called him because his specialty was sharks."

"Sharks?"

She nodded but didn't elaborate.

"Help me out, Silver. What have sharks got to do with underwater telephone lines?"

"They eat them."

CHAPTER 3

Silver drained the rest of her beer and wagged the can at me. I took her empty into the galley.

"Things are getting weird out there," I mumbled to my shipmates, Mona and Spock.

Mona is a busty mannequin, dressed in a pirate outfit, her sword pointed toward the back door of the cabin, *en garde*. The current love of my life, Gwenn Giroux, believes Mona is evidence I'm emotionally stunted.

Spock is a cardboard cutout of the *U.S.S. Enterprise's* first officer in full Vulcan salute. We've been best friends since I was a kid. Oddly, that doesn't seem to bother Gwenn.

I snatched a can of Swamp Head Stump Knocker from the small fridge and returned to the poop deck with the brewski and my notebook in hand.

"I need to write a few things down," I said after handing Silver the beer. "Wilson was his name. Wilson McFadden?" I like to start with fundamentals: who, what, when, where, why, how—the questions we learned to ask in Journalism 101.

She shook her head. "Donald. Donald Wilson. My aunt and uncle were killed in a car crash when Wilson was two, and my parents adopted him. I was thirteen at the time. I kinda resented him. I was used to having my mom and dad to myself."

I knew something about being orphaned. Wilson was lucky to have a family to take him in. I'd been lucky, too.

"And you called him Wilson?"

"Yeah, he hated his first name. Said only a duck should be named Donald."

Fred wandered back over to us and sniffed Silver's boot. She would either give him a pat or ignore him. It was a test of character. She passed, bending over to scratch him. I wondered if Fred regretted that "bitch" remark.

"Wilson was genius-level smart, but kind of a wuss," Silver continued. "I used to kid him that God gave him the brains and me the balls. After his stint in the navy, he got his P, H, and D. I stayed home to help my parents run the farm, never went to college. I think that actually helps my work. My publisher says I write at a fourth-grade level." She said it without a hint of irony.

"You say your brother wasn't very brave, but it takes guts to swim with sharks."

She offered a weak smile. "I told Wilson that, too, but he said, no, like most animals they leave you alone if you don't bother 'em."

"So, what's with this sharks-eating-underwater-phone-lines stuff?"

She shrugged. "Wilson said it's a thing. Remember last year when the internet crashed on the East Coast for a day? It was an undersea cable that got bit."

"Wait. The internet runs through underwater phone lines?"

"Optical cable, yes. Wilson told me that. People think it's all through satellites, up in space, but it isn't. Mostly it's through wires."

I mulled that for a moment then asked if she had pictures and bio material on her brother. She emailed them from her phone. Donald Wilson was a nice-looking guy, dark skinned, close cropped hair, late thirties or early forties. He'd done undergrad at Florida State and earned his doctorate in marine biology at Duke. But his college career was broken by four years in the navy.

"Wilson's father was first generation American, from Nigeria, in case you were wondering," she said while I was scanning his curriculum vitae.

"Why'd he join the navy?" I asked.

"We grew up in Florida, but nowhere near the beach. He was always fascinated by the ocean. Watched pirate movies, even those World War II films about battleships in the Pacific. And, probably the real reason, that's how he could afford to go back to school. Spent two years on an aircraft carrier, the *Theodore Roosevelt*. Then he did two more years in Washington. Worked at the Naval Research Laboratory."

"And you call this guy a wimp?"

She smiled. "Trust me, Wilson was no hero. He spent his carrier time in the radio room and was a glorified file clerk at the lab. But, hey, the government paid for college."

"Okay, tell me why you think Wilson was murdered."

She was quiet for a few seconds. While she gathered her thoughts, I jotted some notes from our previous conversation. Finally, she started to speak, and when she did there was a catch in her voice. She looked up at me, and her eyes were puffy and I was sure it wasn't just fumes from the Red Tide.

I reached over, patted her arm, and said, "Hey, take your time. We're not in a hurry here." I'm not Mr. Touchy Feely, but even though I wasn't sure where she was going with her story, it was clear she was in pain.

She took a couple of deep breaths, rubbed her nose, then resumed: "This is completely fucked up. No way he would have drowned."

"You said something about nitrogen narcosis."

"Yes. I didn't know what that was until the medical examiner said it's a kind of poisoning scuba divers can get. The further down you go, the more the air's compressed. Nitrogen in the tanks, it can make you sick."

"Rapture of the deep," I said.

"That's what he called it. He said Wilson might have got disoriented during a dive. Maybe even stripped off his gear, which has been known to happen. What he called the *terminal event* was drowning. He also said something bit Wilson on his legs, but not enough to kill him."

"What kind of bite marks?"

"They couldn't figure them out. Said they were real unusual."

"Okay, but how do you get from a diving accident to homicide?"

"I'm telling you, there's something messed up about this. I'm going to get his body and take it back to Ocala and have another autopsy. This is stupid. His body showed no life-threatening injuries. He was in good physical condition. They're doing toxic tests—"

"Toxicology?"

"Yeah, that. Takes a while to get results. But they won't find anything. Wilson didn't drink"—she wagged her beer can at me—"unlike his sister, and he didn't do drugs."

"Alright, but..."

She held up her hand. She was on a roll and didn't want to be interrupted. "Wilson wasn't a risk-taker and he knew what he was doing. It was his career. And his body washed up on the north side of Key West at Dredgers Key, which is suspicious as hell. He told me he was doing all his work off the south side of the island. So how did it end up there?"

"What's your theory?"

"He was murdered. And it's being covered up."

"And why would anyone do that?"

"That's what I need you to find out."

My coffee was cold, so I stood up and tossed the remains overboard. "Silver, I don't want to sound unsympathetic. I can tell you're sincere. But you haven't offered one piece of evidence pointing to a homicide."

She took off her hat and ran her hands through her hair. "I'm not stupid. And I know what I know. There's no evidence because nobody's looked for it. That's why I need help."

It sounded like a wild goose chase. There was no reason to believe I could find anything the cops hadn't already looked for. She was a grieving sister unable to accept the truth. A woman who wrote books about vampires and lunar landing conspiracies, no less.

But then she said this:

"One more thing. Right when I finished talking to Wilson the last time, he said something really odd."

"What was that?"

"He said, and I think these are his exact words, 'Would you believe me if I told you I found a mermaid?'"

CHAPTER 4

Looking back, I realize I never actually said I would do it. Not in so many words. I think Silver took it as given once she dropped the word "mermaid." How could I pass that up?

I'm the Weird News Editor for Tropic@Press, an online news service. UFO sightings, morons dying to win Darwin Awards, dogs accidentally shooting their owners—that's my bread and butter. It helps that I'm located in Florida, the Candy Land of crazy.

And for the record, I don't believe in ghosts, space aliens, or government conspiracies to mutate our DNA. The real world is weird enough. And a scientist who said he discovered a mermaid then drowned while chasing sharks eating underwater phone lines crashing the internet—that was a story my editor would love.

I thought my friend Lester Rivers might find it fascinating, too. He was the agent in charge of Third Eye Investigators' southwest Florida office in Naples, which was where I was sitting.

"Let me see if I got all dat," Lester said, in his faint Cajun accent. "I try to recruit you to join the agency, and you say no way. You say you're a writer, you don't do the cloak and dagger, and you want to chill out on your scow, drink rum, and write about weirdos. Now, you want my help to solve a murder?"

"You owe me a buck," I said. Lester used the word "dat" a lot, a hangover from his childhood in New Orleans—Norlins, he would pronounce it—where "dat" is everyone's favorite word, as in "Who Dat?" He was trying to cut back, and I fined him a dollar every time he abused the pronoun.

As a kid, Lester hustled quarters on Bourbon Street playing the trombone. He'd moved up in the world. His Naples office was on Fifth Avenue South, the trendy main street of Naples. The picturesque avenue is flanked by swaying palms that offer skitterings of shade for the Bentleys, Maseratis, and Audis parked curbside. Turn right out his front door and in five blocks you're wading in the Gulf of Mexico, which, ordinarily, is where I would prefer to be. Not so much at that moment, though, with the Red Tide and the accompanying fish kill washing ashore.

"Why'd dat turd Barfield sic her on you?"

"Turd?"

"I don't like cops."

"Gimme a break. You were a cop in Afghanistan."

"Ixnay. I was a spy."

"So why don't you like cops?"

"I'm a private eye. Cops and private eyes hate each other. It's the code."

"But Bret's a private eye now."

"Once a flatfoot, always a flatfoot."

"Whatever." I knew perfectly well Lester didn't hate Brett Barfield. He starts these mischievous rants from time to time to provoke people. I'd known Barfield when he was a patrolman in Scottsdale and we played in a weekly poker game together. After his partner was killed, he quit the cops and joined the Third Eye.

"I called Brett before coming over here," I said. "He confirmed he was manning the phones when Silver called. She wanted the Third Eye to send a team down to investigate her brother's death."

"Barfield confirm he called you a hemorrhoid?"

"Said he was misquoted. Claims he called me an endless colonoscopy."

"A difference without a distinction."

I paused at that. "You surprise me sometimes, Lester."

He waved his hand in dismissal. "I took college."

"Anyway," I said, "there was a problem."

"Let me guess. Moolah."

"Yep. When Brett told her the firm's fees, she fell apart. She cried. Called it unfair. Said the Sheriff's Office blew her off when she told them her brother was murdered. She needed help…"

"Yadda, yadda, yadda."

"Right."

"So that's when dat turd Barfield suggested she get hold of you," Lester said. "Figured if cops were no help, and we weren't no help, maybe a hot-shot investigative reporter could dig out the truth?"

"Pretty much it. Of course, that would have required Brett to refer her to an actual investigative reporter."

"Underestimate yourself, you do," he said in a lousy imitation of Yoda.

"Whatever."

Lester leaned over and made an adjustment to his prosthesis. He'd lost his left leg below the knee to a roadside bomb outside Kabul. It irritated him sometimes. His was an old-fashioned plastic artificial leg, not one of the modern high-tech stainless-steel *Terminator 2* jobs. Since he was on the clock, Lester was wearing a suit. Catch him any other time, and you'll find him in atrocious Bermuda shorts, knee-high socks, Oxfords, and Hawaiian shirts. With a white belt, no less—the Full Cleveland.

"You're a diver. This nitrogen narcissist stuff, that make sense to you?" he asked.

"Nitrogen narcosis. And, no, that wouldn't be my first guess. Why assume he'd been deep diving just because he was found in a wetsuit? And, since he was an experienced diver, why assume nitrogen narcosis? He would have used trimix."

"Try what?"

"Trimix. It's a special combination of oxygen, nitrogen and helium used for deep dives. The helium displaces some of the nitrogen to counteract nitrogen poisoning."

"If you say so."

"Heck, I don't know, Lester. Not everybody who goes down comes up. Maybe he was deep and his equipment failed. Maybe a respirator gave out. But why'd he ditch his gear? And, like I said, there is no evidence—none that Silver shared, anyway—that's what happened."

"So, it's got you curious."

"A little."

"And she sold you."

"She's pretty worked up about it."

"Well, if she's this big-time author of all these famous books, which I've never heard of, by the way, why'd she balk at our rates?"

"Yeah, about that. I looked her up on Amazon. Turns out all her books are published by a company called American Conspiracy Imprints, which bills itself as a quote/unquote 'facilitator for self-publishing authors'."

"Which explains why we never heard of her."

"But Brett said he knew her."

"Don't you owe him money?" Lester asked.

"A small poker debt."

"Incurred right before you high-tailed it out of Arizona, never to return, if I recall correctly."

"I'll pay him back eventually," I said.

"I think he just paid *you* back."

CHAPTER 5

My next stop was the law office of Judd and Holkamp where my girlfriend, Gwenn Giroux, planned to get rich suing insurance companies. Before she went into private practice, she'd labored at the Collier County Public Defender's Office struggling to repay her law school loans while defending miscreants. Suing insurance companies was less fun but more lucrative.

I parked my car, an aging Toyota Solara convertible, under the shade of a sprawling live oak and took the elevator up to her second-floor office on Seagate Drive

"Alex, long time no see," the receptionist said, looking up from her smartphone as I exited the elevator car. I was relieved to be out of the suffocating confines of that death trap. I am slightly claustrophobic: Elevators, back seats, jail—none of them are my idea of a good time.

"Elizabeth," I said. "Fulsome as ever."

"Fulsome. Seven letters. I can use that." Her name was Elizabeth Warren—yeah, just like the famous U.S. senator. I'd never popped in when she wasn't playing Word Chums.

"Guinevere, she in?"

"Sure. Go on back."

I could hear Gwenn on the phone and lurked outside her door until she hung up. Then I peered around the corner and with my very best Snidely Whiplash impersonation said, "I say, I'm in a litigious mood. Could you sue someone for me?"

Gwenn looked up from a towering pile of paperwork, and her face opened in a huge smile. She was wearing a black suit with a salmon blouse and matching lipstick, which blended perfectly with her auburn hair.

"Hey there, big guy," she said, pulling off her black rimmed glasses, the ones that gave her the hot librarian look. "I wasn't sure when I'd see you after this morning."

She held my gaze for a moment, then her smile faded. "Oh, shit, what have you done?"

"Look, about this morning. I know you were trying to be helpful. I guess I don't take criticism well."

"Ya think?"

"And maybe I can be a little defensive at times."

Gwenn rose from her desk and walked into my arms. She was a tall woman, but still several inches shorter than me. And she was strong for her size, the result of regular Zumba and yoga classes. She gave me a hug, squeezing hard. A lesser man might have winced.

On her way out the door that morning, Gwenn mentioned—not for the first time—that while my column was popular, it was really only a part-time job. She was worried that I wasn't achieving my full potential, that I needed to find something more substantial to occupy my time.

I rebutted that not everyone was delivered into this world to be a workaholic, and that some people didn't need piles of cash to validate their sense of self-worth.

She hinted in return—also not for the first time—that maybe it wouldn't be such a bad idea to consider the Third Eye's offer to join the agency. That I could work for them while still writing for Tropic@Press, and that being a journalist was great cover for a snoop.

She said that even knowing it offended my sense of journalistic ethics, and a squabble ensued. But she wasn't wrong that I needed to ramp it up. Especially now that I'd rewatched the first three seasons of *Rick and Morty* for the second time.

She pulled back from her embrace and gazed up into my eyes. "You still have that look. What have you gotten yourself into?"

"Well, there's this big video game tournament and I thought I'd…"

She slugged me in the shoulder.

I plopped into one of her client chairs. The leather felt cool on the undersides of my thighs. I was wearing my customary work attire: cargo shorts, T-shirt, deck shoes, and ball cap. She returned to her desk chair.

"Actually, I'm cruising down to the Keys," I said. "Leaving first thing in the morning."

Gwenn leaned back, picked a yellow No. 2 pencil off her desk blotter, and began gnawing on the eraser. "Key West? On the *Miss Demeanor*? Can she make it?"

That was an excellent question. Until recently, the *Miss Demeanor* rested on empty oil cans and concrete blocks in the island town of Goodland, not far from Naples. It was my home for nearly a year, notwithstanding a large hole in her hull where my uncle—before he turned the keys over to me—had run her aground after three martinis too many.

I only recently came into the money to get her shipshape when a holding company bought the news service, creating a windfall for all of us who founded it.

The *Miss Demeanor* now floated—a useful feature for watercraft—but she still needed work. Bits and pieces kept falling off her—proving the adage about a boat being a hole in the water into which you throw money. This trip to the Keys would represent a serious test of her seaworthiness.

But I was confident in her ability to make the trip. "The *Miss Demeanor* will do fine," I said. "And besides, you said I needed to stay busy."

"Is this for a story?"

"Could be."

"Could be a story. Does Edwina know about it?"

The answer was no, I hadn't told my boss, Edwina Mahoney. Not yet. I thought I might drop a dime once I docked in Key West. She'd like the story, I knew. But she'd give me a ration of shit if it interfered with writing my column, *The Strange Files*, which, for reasons that defy logic and good taste, was a selling feature of the news service.

"Okay, here's the rundown," I said. "It all started a few hours ago when this woman, her name is Silver, showed up at the marina."

"Silver? As in Hi-ho?"

I nodded.

"A damsel in distress, huh?"

"An older damsel."

"Just how old?"

"Her hair is gray, that should tell you something."

I walked Gwenn through the events of the morning, Silver's story about her brother, her doubts about how he died, the weird reference to a mermaid, and my decision to cruise down to Key West and poke around.

"You think the cops and the medical examiner have missed something?" she asked.

I shrugged. "Could just be an interesting story about Wilson's job. How he was investigating sharks eating undersea telephone lines, and how his efforts ended tragically. Silver said her brother told her these shark attacks on submarine cables are unusual, but the very idea that sharks can screw up the internet is news to me. Whether he was murdered or not, who knows?"

"And you're cruising down, not driving?"

"Two reasons. Digging into this might take a few days, maybe longer, and it costs a lot less to dock at Garrison Bight than to rent a hotel room. You know how expensive it is down there. Also, there might be a chance I'll dive where Wilson was working, see what I can find."

"Do you know where?" Gwenn asked.

"Not yet. I'm guessing Wilson chartered a boat. I'll find out who took him out. Or maybe his friend at the community college that Silver mentioned can tell me. Silver has some business to take care of in Naples tomorrow, then she's driving down to collect his belongings and arrange to have his remains shipped back to Ocala. Maybe I can find something useful in his stuff."

"Silver. She's going to be there to help you, is she?" She gave me a look over the top of her glasses, pretending the presence of another woman would be a cause for concern.

"Very funny. But for the record, she's old enough to be my mother."

That probably was about right. My mom died when I was a kid. She was a drug-addled, but good-hearted hippie who staged a sit-in at a cave in Austin, Texas trying to save an endangered species of spider. Very noble. But in the Texas Hill Country flash floods can arrive suddenly. Hence the *flash* in flash flood. And one did, drowning her, and the spider, too, for all anyone knows.

Her brother, my Uncle Leo—Maricopa County Superior Court Judge Leonardo D. Strano to you—took me in, adopted me, helped me get through high school and college, and finally gave me the *Miss Demeanor* so I'd have a roof over my head.

Gwenn considered what I'd told her for a minute, then said, "Your mother." She tapped her pencil a few times. "This guy who drowned, Wilson, and you, you're both orphans. You've got a soft spot for that. And drowning victims."

"I've done okay."

"You have. And it sounds like Wilson did, too. Until now."

"Yeah."

"You believe her, don't you? That he might have been murdered. Her story got to you."

"A little bit, yeah. I'll grant you, she's a whack job with her conspiracy theories and such. But there's something about this. I can't quite put a finger on it. But something about it does seem a little funky. And she's alone. Nobody wants to help her. That doesn't sit well with me, you know?"

She shook her head, but she was smiling. "You were born six hundred years too late. You should be on horseback wearing a suit of armor."

"In this heat? Gimme a break."

She chewed on her pencil eraser some more. "So, the Third Eye's in on this, or are you on your own?"

"On my own," I said. "But Lester volunteered to come along for a couple days, said Duval Street is the next best thing to Bourbon Street, and he's a little homesick."

"Duval Street smells better," she said.

I agreed. "Less *eau de puke*."

She thought about that for a few moments then asked: "He's got a concealed carry permit, right?"

"All private eyes do. You thinking I might need backup?"

"If this Silver woman is right, maybe."

"I won't do anything stupid," I said.

That earned me the hairy eyeball.

"Have you considered asking your girlfriend along for this exciting cruise?" she asked.

Cleverly, I said, "Uh…"

Before I could say anything further, my iPhone vibrated and I reached into the pocket of my shorts to retrieve it. Saved by the buzzer.

I read the text message and looked at Gwenn.

"Lester. Says he's cleared some time off with his boss. He's good to go."

She nodded, her face neutral.

"Look, would you like to come along?" I asked, putting as much enthusiasm into it as I could. "I mean it would be great. Tracking this thing down won't take all my time, and we could…"

She held up her hand. "I couldn't go even if I wanted to. I'm up to my neck in work. In fact, no offense, but if you're out of town I can pull a few late-nighters and get caught up."

"Speaking of catching up," I said. "How about dinner tonight? Followed by a big sendoff for your favorite seafarer?"

She beamed. "Take me to The Capital Grille."

"Why there?"

"It's where we had cocktails before we, uh, set sail for the first time. I want to do it all over again."

We did.

CHAPTER 6

Ten Thousand Islands

LESTER WAS SITTING on the poop deck staring at a pelican perched on the prow of the *Miss Demeanor*.

We were half a mile due west of the Florida coastline heading south from Naples. Trawlers are roomy liveaboards and don't eat gas like outboards, but they are slow. At ten knots, it would take us all day to reach Key West. Which is why Lester and I embarked at dawn. During the first hour of our journey, we had choked on the fumes from the Red Tide outbreak. The *Naples Daily News* that morning featured a huge front page photo of dead fish covering the beach and wrote about tourists wearing surgical masks while sunbathing. Now, we were south of the bloom. The air was clear, the water sparkled, and the sky was cloudless.

Lester was catching some rays when the pelican alighted. They do that from time to time, hitch rides on passing watercraft. Pelicans seem unafraid of humans. Maybe that's because fishermen are always feeding them, or maybe it's because they're not the brightest of avians.

"You guys having a stare-down?" I asked. I was piloting the trawler from the flybridge, high above the deck, which gave me an unobstructed view of the Gulf of Mexico and the passing Everglades off our port side.

Lester looked up over his shoulder and squinted into the morning sun. "Why would a pelican hitch a ride?" he asked.

"To get to the other side?"

"I think he's an omen."

"Of what?"

"I don't know. My Jedi powers are failing me."

Lester curled out of his chair and disappeared into the cabin below me. I heard him rummaging around for a few seconds, then he re-emerged carrying Spock. "Okay," he said. "Do your mind-meld shit, Spock. What's with the bird?"

The pelican swiveled its head, glanced at Lester and Spock, then launched off the bow in an explosion of flapping wings.

Maybe pelicans aren't so stupid after all.

Lester returned Spock to the cabin, and in a few moments I heard the tinkle of ice in glasses. He climbed up to the flybridge and handed me a Diet Coke. I wasn't sure what he was drinking, but it sported a little paper umbrella.

"Are we there yet?" he asked.

I checked my watch. "Almost. Only eight hours to go."

He sighed. "Who's our featured band today?"

I turned and showed him. Ordinarily, I'd be in a T-shirt from my collection of obscure rock bands. I'd worn Jesus Chrysler Super Car all day yesterday. But this morning I'd thrown on an Albert Einstein, the one with his tongue dangling out like Mick Jagger.

"Nice. You think Albert ever got it on with Marilyn Monroe?"

"That's a myth. Einstein never met Marilyn Monroe."

"Huh."

Lester mopped his head and shoved his handkerchief into the back pocket of his madras shorts. Today he'd added a boater—a flat-top straw hat popular at political conventions—to his Full Cleveland getup. When I first met him, I assumed Lester's attire was calculated, a clever disguise that allowed him to blend in with the tourists—knee-high dress socks with baggy shorts are not unseen among those carrying AARP cards, of which Florida is blessed in abundance. But over time, I realized it was simply how he rolled. The socks covered his prosthesis and he dug white belts. And who am I to criticize? A guy who wears funky T-shirts and sweat-stained baseball caps is in no position to judge anyone else's attire.

"Here's something I bet you didn't know," he said. "If you take the first letters of Albert and Einstein, they spell alien."

I thought about that for a moment. "No, they don't. That would spell A-L-E-I-N."

"Well, you can't expect little green men to spell correctly, can you?"

Fred, who had been ignoring our conversation, began whining from the deck below.

"Dude, you can't be serious," I said. "We went for a nice walk before we cast off."

Fred whimpered again.

"What's with the doggie?" Lester asked.

"He's telling me he's got to go. I gave him some leftover steak last night and I think he ate too much."

"So why do you need that translator gadget if you understand him so well?"

"It only works when he barks."

I idled the engines, then Lester and I climbed down from the flybridge.

"What do we do?" he asked.

"Fred won't do his business on the boat. I've trained him well. We're gonna have to pull over and find a spot for him."

I'd plotted our course to stay near the coastline, and the waters off southwest Florida are dotted with small islands, sandbars and clumps of mangrove sprouting out of oyster beds. Look on the map and you'll see they're called the Ten Thousand Islands, although they really only number in the hundreds.

"The *Miss Demeanor* has a shallow draft," I said as we entered the cabin. "About two feet." I nodded out the port window to a series of sand spits. "I can pull up close to one of those and take Fred over in the dinghy." We were towing an eight-foot inflatable with a small electric motor. Mostly I used it to putter around Naples Bay, bar hopping.

Lester was gazing out the window. "What about that island over there?" he asked, pointing to a large mangrove-covered islet with a narrow beach only a hundred yards off the coastline. "We could all stretch our legs."

I settled in behind the cockpit steering wheel and navigated the *Miss Demeanor* in that direction, keeping a steady eye on the depth finder. "Lester, go back out and watch for any shallow spots," I said. "Or floating debris." We were well north of the Great Florida Reef, so I wasn't concerned about coral outcroppings, but I didn't fancy running aground or smacking into a floating log.

I guided the trawler to a small white sand beach on the north-western edge of the islet. As we neared, the depth finder showed six feet, then four, then held steady at three until the bow of the trawler gently kissed the sand. It was an unusually steep drop-off, which was fortunate, as it put us close enough to the beach that we wouldn't have to use the dinghy.

I cut the engines, walked out to the deck, and tossed the bow anchor onto the beach. I tightened the line until the mild current nudged the boat parallel to the shore. Then I lowered the rope ladder. I stepped to the bottom rung, Lester handed Fred to me, and we hopped ashore. I set Fred loose and offered Lester a hand as he lowered himself off the trawler.

"Come on, Pegleg," I said.

"Mr. Pegleg to you."

The sun was now directly overhead, so I hoped we wouldn't be pestered too badly by mosquitos, who are at their worst at dawn and dusk. Fred found a spot he liked, circled several times, and took care of business. He scratched the sand with his hind legs to cover his traces then bolted down the beach chasing a small flock of sandpipers at the water's edge.

Lester was bent over examining seashells. "This one's a beauty," he said, holding aloft an orange and white lion's paw scallop. "And look at this conch, it's gorgeous."

The air was still and the only sound was the metronomic lapping of small waves washing ashore. This was the kind of place Gwenn would love. She enjoyed collecting shells, too. I'd have to remember this island.

My reverie was interrupted by a rustling in the mangroves. Fred froze at the sound. "What's that?" Lester asked. I shrugged. Fred growled, then, barking madly, charged into the underbrush, his dog collar booming: *"Danger, Will Robinson! Danger!"*

Lester turned to me. "Danger, Will Robinson?"

"Hey, it's experimental. I didn't program it."

Lester dropped his seashells and walked toward the mangroves. "Here, Freddie, Freddie. Come on. Get out of there."

We couldn't see Fred. The mangrove roots were too thick. But his yapping and his translator—now bellowing *"Avast ye swabs!"*—indicated he was maybe a dozen feet in.

Suddenly his barking became a yelp and the mangroves erupted in a fury of screeching and thrashing leaves. Fred bounded out of the vegetation, blew past us, and bee-lined up the beach.

A furry gray head with a scarred pink snout poked through the mangrove leaves where Fred exited the underbrush. Several others joined Scar Face. Then one, then three, then six furry critters leaped out of the mangroves and began loping up the beach after Fred.

"Monkeys?" Lester shouted. "Fucking monkeys?"

"Get back on the boat, Lester," I yelled, and began running up the beach after them.

The monkeys were fast, but Fred was faster. He stopped near the water and turned back and began barking again: *"Bitch, bitch, bitch."*

I knew about this breed of monkeys. They were rhesus macaques. Another troop recently attacked tourists near Silver Springs, and I'd written about it. They stood only two feet tall, but were aggressive and carried the Herpes B virus, which can be fatal to humans—maybe canines, too, for all I knew.

"Get away from my dog, you fuckers!"

The monkeys whirled and stared at me.

"Yeah, that's right. I'm a primate, too. And I'm bigger than you. Whatcha gonna do about it?"

That might not have been the brightest question I'd ever asked as I now seemed to have captured the undivided focus of their hostility.

Fred spotted the opening and raced down the waterline. He zipped past the macaques, charged past me, and headed straight for Lester, who was now standing by the boat. Fred leaped into the air and Lester caught him. Holding the dog in one hand and the rope ladder in the other, he began clambering back aboard the trawler.

Which left me to confront the monkeys alone.

They got within ten yards of me, inching forward, then they stopped to regroup. Regrouping involved jumping up and down and making rude remarks in their own language.

I wasn't sure what to do in case of a monkey attack. I knew you never played dead to black bears because they like chewing on cadavers. And you were supposed to zig-zag when chased by gators. Monkeys I didn't know, so I started waving my arms at them and shouting. "Go away. Beat it. Scram."

They actually quieted down for a moment. Maybe it was my flailing arms. Or Einstein sticking his tongue out at them. Or maybe they were trying to translate English into Monkey. I kept it up and then for variety's sake yelled, "Vamoose."

Apparently, they understood Spanglish and didn't like it. They charged.

Running away seemed like a very good idea. I turned and sprinted toward the boat. But I quickly realized we weren't going anywhere with the anchor dug into the island. So, I veered in that direction, grabbed the anchor and wrenched it out of the sand. By then, the monkeys were almost on me, and I didn't fancy getting bitten or scratched and dying of encephalitis, one of the lovely consequences of a Herpes B infection.

So, I began swirling the anchor around me on its line, yelling and screaming, trying to look as dangerous as possible.

They stayed out of the anchor's arc, which was good, but it was heavy and I couldn't keep that up forever or before they figured out how to outflank me.

One of the monkeys grabbed the conch shell Lester had admired and hurled it at me, like that scene from *2001: A Space Odyssey*, when the ape flings the bone into the air, figuring out tools for the first time. These monkeys were smarter than they looked: They'd invented weapons.

I backtracked toward the *Miss Demeanor* at the water's edge, still swinging. Lester was at the rope ladder. "Come on, Padawan, hurry it up," he yelled.

I hurled the anchor over the gunwale onto the deck, leaped up and grabbed the rail, and hauled myself over and onto the boat just as the monkeys charged. Lester pulled up the ladder as the largest and loudest of the monkeys made a grab for it.

"No you don't," he shouted. "Stay off our boat."

I rolled to my feet and ran into the cabin and fired up the engines. The monkey population had grown to nearly two dozen, all lining the beach and making inhospitable comments.

"How'd they get out here?" Lester yelled, keeping an eye on the marauders.

"Probably escaped from one of the labs."

Monkey breeding farms were a growing business in Florida. They were highly sought after for medical research.

"Yeah, but how'd they get on an *island*?"

I pointed toward the stern. Several macaques were in the Gulf swimming after us. One of them, the overly ambitious male with the nasty scar on his snout, made a grab for the dinghy we were towing. He pulled himself aboard, then turned to signal his pals. A born leader.

Lester grabbed the tow rope, and gave it a huge yank, and the monkey toppled over backwards into the water. "Show off."

It took a few minutes for my racing heart to return to normal as I steered us away from the island, but as my pulse slowed and my head cleared, it dawned on me that Fred might have been injured.

"Lester, check on Fred," I said. "They didn't bite him or anything, did they?"

By then, Fred was curled up in his bed in my stateroom—his safe place. Lester retrieved him. "Looks fine to me. Don't see no blood or nothin'. How ya doin', puppy?"

Fred wriggled out of Lester's grasp and began rooting around for his chew toy.

"Guess he's alright."

I steered us back to our original course, due south, engines at full throttle, which isn't saying much—I could run faster, maybe swim faster, than the *Miss Demeanor* going full out.

Behind me, I heard Lester grumble, "Ow, what's this?" He held up a chrome-plated crank he'd stepped on.

"Dammit. It goes to that hatch above you. This scow's falling to pieces."

"As long as she floats."

Then Lester dug around the galley, found a dog treat, and gave it to Fred.

"I think Fred liked our little adventure," he said. "Not sure about Mona and Spock, though."

"Why?"

"Spock never seems bothered by anything, but Mona's looking a little peaked. I see you haven't repaired the bullet hole yet."

A Collier County sheriff's deputy accidentally shot Mona during a search of my boat a few months earlier. I'd put a Band-Aid over the holes the bullet made as it passed through her, and even researched mannequin repair kits online. But they weren't cheap and Mona never complained.

"Maybe you need to change her bandage," I told Lester.

"Hey, Mona, I get you a new Band-Aid, whaddaya do for me?"

"Mona, pay him no mind. He was attacked by a pack of wild monkeys. He's suffering from PTSD."

"It was a troop, not a pack," Lester said. "And those were some insane monkeys. But you know what? People are no better. We can talk, and we can print money, and we can invent shit like air conditioning, which I wish you would turn on, but, really, we're just as crazy as those monkeys back there."

I didn't disagree with Lester's assessment of humans. I've seen a lot of crazy. It's part of the job. Heck, it is the job: People who kill themselves exploding fireworks on their heads; cults who really, truly believe the Earth is flat; maybe a dead marine biologist who claimed to have seen a mermaid.

But it struck me that while the inhabitants of Monkey Island might have been annoyed with us, they behaved rationally. They were defending their home from invaders. And they were effective at getting rid of us. I didn't see anything crazy about that.

But we soon would be in Crazy Central—Key West, the oddest corner of the most bizarre state in America.

Of course, the denizens of Key West thought of themselves less as Americans and more as citizens of their own pirate republic. They'd actually seceded from the Union in the 1980s. That secession lasted about a minute, but the notion stuck.

"Monkeys got nothin' on the Conchs," I said.

Lester broke out a beer and raised it in a toast.

"To the Conch Republic."

CHAPTER 7

Key West

I WAS SWIMMING with a mermaid. Her long red hair swirled around her ample breasts, and she was about to slip into my arms when suddenly she pulled out a speargun and aimed it at my chest. That's when my iPhone began vibrating and I awoke, breathing hard and covered in sweat.

I picked up the phone, a little disoriented, and answered.

The caller was loud, frenzied, and sounding very unmermaid-like.

"Those damned blowtards have lost the body."

It was Silver. "Which blowtards?" I asked.

"The blowtards here at the morgue. I'm in Marathon. I came here to get Wilson's remains, and they've lost him."

I looked at my watch. Mickey's hands were on twelve and nine. I'd slept in. I glanced down from my berth aboard the *Miss Demeanor* and Fred was still snoozing in his little bed.

"What's in Marathon?" I asked, groggy.

"The medical examiner. It's where they took Wilson, did the autopsy on him."

"And he's not there?"

"No, dammit. Wake up. That's what I'm telling you. He's not here."

I could hear Lester snoring in the small aft cabin. After all the alcohol he'd swilled last night, it was a miracle he could still breathe. I'd been comparatively good, but I would need my morning coffee to bring the world into focus.

"I told you I didn't believe Wilson drowned. This is proof. It's a fucking conspiracy."

"Take a deep breath, Silver," I said. "He's bound to be somewhere."

That set her off. "Of course, he's somewhere. They've stolen his body for a reason. Probably Big Pharma's behind this. They've been killing off all the holistic doctors. And Wilson always said sharks have amazing immune systems. He probably found something that will put them out of business. This is..."

"Silver, Silver, that isn't getting us anywhere," I said. "How do you know he's not there?"

"The woman here, she checked. Went back and looked at all of them. No corpses with his name on their tags."

"Have you, yourself, seen all the bodies there?"

"No. She said that usually they show you pictures, they don't let people go back there. But their computer is down."

"Well, maybe you can persuade her to break the rule this once."

"I'll try. The guy in charge, the medical examiner, he isn't here. She tried to call him but he didn't answer. She kinda confided in me that she doesn't like him much. Apparently nobody does."

We hung up and I crawled out of my berth. All the chatter woke up Fred and he began his morning dance telling me he needed to go outside.

"Alright buddy," I said. "Let me put my shoes on."

Bayview Park is across Truman Avenue from the marina. I walked Fred there and let him wander around a bit on his leash until he finished his business. Key West is very dog friendly, and I found a convenient doggie waste station on our return trip to the boat. Back aboard, I fired up the Keurig and poured myself a cup of Starbucks French Roast. Black. I'd been cutting back on dairy products ever since I read a horror story about harmful growth hormones in milk.

And then there was Silver's theory about insecticides contributing to her parents' deaths. I mean, we can't be too careful with our health, can we? The rum in my Cuba Libres will kill only so much bacteria.

I carried my coffee out to the poop deck and enjoyed the pleasant breeze that wafted across the marina while I waited to hear back from Silver. It didn't take long.

"She let me in the back. Made me promise not to tell. Said her fuckhead boss would fire her."

"And?"

"And Wilson isn't here. She pulled all the trays out and let me look at their faces. One white guy, two Hispanic women."

"Hmm."

"She said the medical examiner is in hot water. His staff hates him. So does the sheriff and everyone else. There's all kinds of crazy shit going on here. So losing a body may be par for the course."

"Silver, did they offer any idea at all on where Wilson might have been taken? Surely, someone would have to sign for his remains or something."

"I thought of that, too. They said two cadavers were shipped out yesterday, both males, one down to Key West, one up to Key Largo."

"They say where they were being taken?"

"I just told you, Key West and Key Largo. You gotta start paying attention."

"I mean which funeral homes."

"Oh. Hang on." I heard some jabbering in the background, then she was back on the line.

"She can't tell me."

"Bullshit. Tell her it's public record."

"No, she literally can't tell me. I told you, their computer system is down. They've called a repair guy."

"Oh, for crying out loud."

"I'm telling you, Alex, this stinks. Something's wrong."

"Alright," I said. "Let's try this. I'll contact all the funeral homes here in Key West. There can't be that many. You call Key Largo. Let's regroup when we've made the rounds."

I looked up the names of local undertakers on my iPhone and started calling. I struck out with the first two, but at the third and final funeral home I learned something very important: They were busy helping other customers, but my call was important to them, and they would call back as soon as they could. I decided not to wait. I freshened Fred's water, left him some dry food, and swilled the rest of my coffee.

Before I could disembark, my phone rang again. It was Silver.

"This lady here, she's trying to help. Probably not part of the conspiracy. She can't get into the computer, but she told me they have closed circuit television by the loading dock and they record everything. It's on a different system."

"What's it show?"

"We're looking at it now. One hearse, it left at eleven o'clock yesterday and it has writing on the side. Branham Funeral Home, Key Largo. Okay, here comes the second hearse. Time stamp shows 3 p.m. The system is motion activated, so this isn't taking long."

There was a pause while Silver looked at the monitor, then she returned on the line.

"There a name on the second hearse?" I asked.

"No, but the video shows the plate on the back. You got a pencil?"

"Give it to me." She rattled off the letters and I wrote them down in my notebook. It was a custom tag, and the lettering didn't leave much doubt. But I needed to check.

Unlike in the movies and detective novels, I didn't have a contact at the Department of Motor Vehicles to call and look it up. But I did have a genuine licensed private investigator passed out inside my boat.

"Lester, get up," I said, rapping on his cabin door. "Time to do your shamus stuff."

I opened the door, and his head was under a blanket in the small berth. I heard him mumble something incoherent. "Rise and shine, party animal. The game's afoot."

Lester lowered the blanket and peered out with bloodshot eyes. "Can't. Move." He drew the blanket back over his head and rolled away from me. Useless.

It would be early back in Arizona, but I wasn't really bothered by rousting Brett Barfield out of bed. "Do you know Lester Rivers thinks you're a turd?" I said when he answered the phone.

"Whaddya want, Strange?"

"Need a favor."

"You owe me money."

"Okay, I'll owe you a favor, too. I need you to look up a tag for me."

"An Arizona tag?"

"No, Florida."

"But I'm not *in* Florida, in case you forgot. And it's still very early in the morning here. Get the Gimp to do it for you."

"He's, uh, under the weather. Come on. I know you can do this." I read him the plate. He said he'd call back in a few. It was more like thirty minutes, which gave me ample time to drink a second cup of coffee, snarf a protein bar, and check the news.

- A congressman from Texas had introduced a bill that would make taking a morning-after pill a crime.
- Another congressman, this one from Ohio and elected on a family-values platform, resigned after admitting an adulterous affair with a transsexual.
- *The New York Times* reported the millions the Pentagon spent on a program to investigate UFOs wasn't a complete boondoggle: They had one actual UFO sighting that couldn't be explained away as a natural phenomenon. Hello, E.T.
- In Pensacola, a vigilante calling himself Mister Manners struck again, this time taking a bottle opener to the side of a red

Porsche Panamera, headlight to tail light, for taking up two spaces in a crowded shopping center parking lot.

- And hospitals in Fort Myers and Naples were reporting an unusual number of people suffering from respiratory distress due to the Red Tide bloom in the Gulf of Mexico. The story in the *Naples Herald* said the outbreak of the reddish-brown algae was stronger than usual, apparently being fed by nutrients flowing into the Gulf from the heavily polluted Lake Okeechobee.

All of which reminded me that I was behind deadline on my column, and that I owed my boss at the Tropic◎Press a phone call telling her I was in Key West.

My iPhone buzzed and Caller ID showed it was Barfield. "The plate on the hearse is registered to a funeral home. Molton-Balsamo. So, what's this about?"

"This is about Silver McFadden and her dead brother. He's missing."

"Dead *and* missing?"

"Yeah, this is starting to get weird."

I heard him laugh. "Right up your alley, bro."

CHAPTER 8

THE MOLTON-BALSAMO FUNERAL Home was on Flagler Street, not far from the marina. Okay, it's Key West. Nothing's far from anything here, including Havana. I untangled the bungee cord that held my three-speed to the railing of the *Miss Demeanor* and manhandled it off the trawler.

Ten minutes later I was locking my bike to a palm tree outside the undertaker's. It was another warm day in paradise, but clouds were building and the wind was picking up. I wondered if I'd get rained on during the ride back to my boat. A couple of tourists on Mopeds scootered by as an American Airlines jet roared into Key West International. A rooster crowed in the crowded parking lot beside the funeral home.

Molton-Balsamo occupied a two-story, white Victorian wood-frame house with a wrap-around veranda. A blast of frigid air greeted me as I stepped inside, which I suppose made perfect sense. Morgues are chilly, too. I entered the reception area and looked around. Nobody appeared to be home. "Yoo-hoo. Hello. Anybody here?" I called out.

A door to my left opened, and a guy in an ill-fitting suit stepped out holding a finger to his lips. He was bald with a fringe of white hair, medium height, middle-aged, and built like a pot-bellied boxer. He wore a brass nametag that said "RUFO." I looked past him into the room beyond and realized a funeral service was underway. "Oh, sorry," I whispered. "You in charge?"

He gave me a cold stare and looked me up and down, as if I were the first person he'd ever seen wearing a Diarrhea Planet T-shirt. "May I help you?" he asked, in an accent I couldn't quite place, although it sounded vaguely French.

"Donald Wilson. Name ring a bell?"

He scrunched his face. "Who wants to know?"

I fished out a business card and handed it to him.

"Your name is Strange?"

"A guy named Rufo shouldn't judge."

He examined me again as if I were some vomitus mass befouling his parlor. "And what is this Diarrhea Planet?'

"Punk band. You know, *Aliens in the Outfield*?" The truth is, I'd never heard any of their music. But I like the shirts.

"So, about Donald Wilson," I said. "Medical Examiner's office up in Marathon said a hearse took a body out of there yesterday at 3 p.m. Got it on video. Was it Donald Wilson?"

"The only deceased we have picked up from the Medical Examiner's office is in there," he said, pointing to the door behind him. "His name is not Donald Wilson." He started to turn back to the chapel, and I pulled out my reporter's notebook.

"This the plate number of your hearse?" I asked.

He nodded. "Of course. Who else would have a tag like this?" The license plate was M-F FUN.

"And you were in Marathon yesterday, you picked up a body, but not Donald Wilson."

"Correct."

I was writing in my notebook. "Rufo? Is that a first name or a last name or an acronym for something?" He ignored me and opened the door to the chapel where it appeared the service was concluding. People were rising, hugging one another, drying their eyes. He glanced back at me and mumbled, "impetuous youth," then closed the door behind him.

I sat down on one of the sofas in the reception area and dialed Silver.

"You've got to be shitting me," she said when I told her. "No luck in Key Largo, either. The medical examiner is supposed to be in shortly, I'm going to wait for him, maybe he can straighten it out."

How do you lose a body? From a morgue? My Weird-Shit-O-Meter was vibrating.

The chapel door reopened and mourners began filing out. I watched from the sofa as they made their way through the parlor and assembled on the veranda, preparing for a ride to the cemetery, I assumed. The last person to leave was a young woman color coordinated in a black tank top, black shorts, and black flip-flops holding a tissue to her eyes. She joined the others outside.

I wandered into the chapel. Rufo was by the side door talking to another suit and a uniformed Key West police officer. I weaved my way around the folding chairs and approached them. But as I drew closer, I realized something was off. Something was missing. It took a moment—Hercule Poirot I am not—then it dawned on me: There was no casket. On the catafalque—that's the fancy name for the stand upon which the casket should have been resting—was a red can of Folger's coffee capped with a white plastic top.

"No fucking way," I blurted. The two suits and the cop turned to me. "Folgers? Really?"

The second suit walked over. "Were you a friend of the deceased?" he asked. His brass nametag said "GEORGE."

"No. Sorry. I'm here on another matter. The matter of the missing Donald Wilson."

The cop overheard that and looked over. The name badge on his uniform said "Paine." I was beginning to feel self-conscious. Everybody seemed to be wearing nametags today except me.

I set my backpack on a folding chair and fished out some more business cards. "I'm with the Tropic Press," I said. "I'm working with a woman named Silver McFadden. Her brother, Donald Wilson, drowned. His remains were up in Marathon at the ME's office. Yesterday, your hearse picked up a body there, but your homie, Rufo, said it wasn't him. So, we're trying to figure out where he is."

The cop walked over and introduced himself. His name was Harrison Paine. "I should talk to Miz McFadden," he said. "Is she in town?"

I shook my head. "She's driving down after she finishes up in Marathon," I said.

He gave me his card. "Have her call me."

"Key West PD doing something with his drowning?" I asked.

"Have her call." Then he walked out the door, leaving me with the two suits.

I looked at the coffee can, then back at them. The suit named George nodded. "It's a little unusual," he said. "Looked high and low before finding a metal coffee can. They're all plastic now, best I can tell."

"The deceased, was he a fan of the movie?" I asked.

"Yes. He told his girlfriend that if anything ever happened to him, he wanted a burial at sea and he wanted Jeff Bridges to preside. We didn't bother trying to find Bridges, but we found the can. They're sailing out into the Gulf shortly."

As for the missing body, George shrugged, but he gave me his business card and offered to help if he could. I walked to the side door, hoping to avoid the clutch of mourners on the veranda. But, no, by then they were gathered in the parking lot, and as I stepped out the door the woman in black was standing there.

"So sorry for your loss," I said reflexively for the second time in three days.

She looked up and offered a faint smile. "Were you a friend of Donny's?" she asked.

"No. I'm here on another matter." I was still holding my business cards and, on impulse, handed her one.

She glanced at it, then looked more closely. "Oh. This is really you? You write *The Strange Files*?"

I nodded.

"Donny loved your column. Said it was the only thing in the news that made any sense at all."

I suppose a guy who wanted to be buried in a coffee can might say something like that.

"Do you think..." She hesitated, then started again. "Do you think you could write something about Donny. He would love that."

THE STRANGE FILES

Another Donny in a Can

By Alexander Strange

Tropic Press

KEY WEST—Donny Westhaven loved the sea. Now he'll spend eternity there.

On a breezy, tropical afternoon, a funeral flotilla sailed out of here for the Gulf of Mexico where Westhaven's final remains were interred. He was 29 years old.

His girlfriend of three years, Mary Sue Flemister, 24, was at the helm of his 27-foot Boston Whaler, the *Beeracuda*. Donny rested inside a red Folgers coffee can in the cockpit.

Yes, a Folgers can, as in the movie *The Big Lebowski*, where Theodore Donald "Donny" Kerabatsos' cremated remains were tossed to the wind by his bowling buddies The Dude and Walter Sobchak.

"Donny loved that movie," Flemister said. "To him, it said everything about how futile life is."

Westhaven's life came to an unexpected end while he and Flemister were fishing off Smather's Beach. "It was hot, and I thought I'd jump in to cool off," she said. "But as soon as I did, Donny went nuts. He started screaming, 'We're drifting. We're drifting away.'" Flemister said her boyfriend grabbed the boat's anchor from the bow locker, but when he tossed it overboard his leg became entangled in the line and it pulled him under.

"Donny couldn't swim. He never came back up." Flemister managed to climb back aboard the *Beeracuda*, and called 911. But by then it was too late. Divers retrieved Donny's body later that day.

"It's so sad, so pointless," Flemister said. Westhaven told her that if anything ever happened to him, he wanted to be cremated and his remains scattered in the Gulf of Mexico.

"It was his wish that Jeff Bridges preside over the service," said funeral director George Molton. "We couldn't pull that off, but we were able to find a Folgers can at a local antique store. It should have a blue top, like in the film, but we couldn't find one. But white works. He won't be in there long."

STRANGE FACT: A cremated human body is light-to-dark gray with the texture of sand.

Weirdness knows no boundaries. Keep up at *www.TheStrangeFiles.com*. Contact Alexander Strange at Alex@TheStrangeFiles.com.

CHAPTER 9

TWO HOURS AFTER I filed my column, Silver showed up at the Key West City Marina at Garrison Bight where the *Miss Demeanor* was docked. We were sitting on the poop deck. I'd toweled off the seats after a brief shower swept through. I was sipping a Diet Coke. She'd started in on a beer.

"Okay, I think we finally figured it out," she said. "I called the funeral home when I got here, but they were closed. Guess we'll have to go over there tomorrow. But the good news is Wilson's definitely there."

"Really? I talked to the funeral director. He was adamant they didn't have him," I said.

"There was a mix-up."

I heard movement below decks and a few ticks later Lester emerged. He was unshaven and ashen, save for the crimson of his bloodshot eyes. He'd slept in his clothes.

"You must be the famous Silver McFadden," he said as he shambled onto the poop deck and stuck out his hand. "Lester Rivers."

"You're with the Third Eye, right?" Silver asked.

"Yes, I am."

Lester turned to me. "Uh, you got any aspirin or Advil? I think I may have been overserved last night."

I went inside the cabin with him and retrieved a bottle of Motrin from the galley. Spock was standing by the sink and I knew what he was thinking: Too much Romulan Ale. I relayed that to Rivers.

"Don't recall drinking anything blue," he said. "I remember green. Margaritas, I think."

"You remember the Jell-O shots?" I asked.

"I think I'm going to be sick."

Silver was giving me the stink eye when I returned. "We spent the evening on Duval Street," I explained, "talking up the locals when we could find any—mostly tourists—scouting out any scuttlebutt about the drowning. We were also on the prowl for mermaids."

"And alcohol, obviously."

"Said the woman drinking beer."

"I deserve one after what I've been through."

"Tell me about it."

"There were two corpses at the morgue, both with the first name Donald. Both with last names ending in the letter W."

"Don't tell me."

"Yeah, they shipped the wrong body here. Misidentified as a fellow named Donald Westhaven. It was really Wilson. Donald Westhaven is still up in Marathon."

"I told you not to tell me." I felt a migraine coming on.

"Are you alright?" Silver asked. "Don't tell me you have a hangover, too."

"Worse."

"Why are you looking at me like that?"

"Silver, did you see this other corpse, the other Donald?"

"Yes, they asked me to make sure it wasn't Wilson, why?"

"Give me a second." I walked back into the cabin and retrieved the business card George Molton, the funeral home director, had given me. It included a cell phone number and I dialed it. He answered on the third ring.

"Mr. Molton," I said. "Alexander Strange here. We met at your funeral home earlier today."

Molton: "Yes, Mrs. Strange. How can I be of service?"

Me: "You can answer two quick questions. The first: Did Donny Westhaven's girlfriend see his corpse before he was cremated?"

Molton: "No. Mr. Westhaven had no next of kin. Ms. Flemister handled the arrangements with my partner, Mr. Balsamo, and she gave us instructions to cremate his remains as soon as he arrived. She said they wanted to hurry up the process because the forecast called for rain and they needed to set sail as soon as possible."

Me: "Final question, Mr. Molton. Was Donny Westhaven black?"

Molton: "No. He was white. Didn't you see his picture when you were here earlier today?"

Me: "I didn't notice. But you're certain?"

Molton: "Well, of course I'm certain. What's this about?"

Me: "I think there's a chance the medical examiner's office sent you the wrong body."

There was a pause on the line.

Molton: "I'll call you right back."

Two minutes later, my iPhone buzzed.

Molton: "I just checked with my partner, Mr. Balsamo, and I don't understand this, but he confirmed what you were asking. The body we received from the medical examiner was indeed an African-American male. Are you telling me it was not Donald Westhaven?"

I walked back out and sat down next to Silver.

"Silver," I said, "we have a problem.

CHAPTER 10

"YOU SOLVE THE murder yet?"

I was sitting on the poop deck nursing a Cuba Libre and talking to Gwenn on my iPhone. Fred and Lester were below. Fred was snarfing his Alpo. Lester had crawled back to bed promising he'd be better in the morning. I'd put Silver in an Uber to take her back to her bed and breakfast, but not before she wiped out my beer supply, openly wept, screamed a few times, and threatened to burn Key West to the ground.

"Well, a funny thing happened on the way to the funeral home," I said.

"Oh, I can tell this is going to be good."

"It was a real donnybrook, you'll excuse the pun."

"It's you. So, it'll be weird, right?"

"They cremated the wrong dead guy."

"Say what?"

"Say you're the local coroner. And you got two dudes on ice both named Donald, both with last names beginning with the letter W, both dead by drowning. And say you're the local coroner with a reputation for screwing the pooch. Guess what happens?"

"You don't say."

"I do say. The morgue shipped the wrong Donny down to Key

West. He was cremated and buried at sea before anyone figured out the bodies were switched."

"You're saying Donald Wilson was cremated accidentally?"

"Before another autopsy could be performed by his grieving sister, who now is convinced it's all part of a massive conspiracy to cover up the real cause of his death."

I thought I heard a giggle.

I was laughing now, too. "This is not funny, goddammit."

"Only you, Alexander. You're a magnet for weirdness."

"It could be worse," I said.

"How so?"

"I was able to kill my column about the burial at sea of one Donny Westhaven before the news service sent it out, so now I don't have to write an embarrassing retraction."

"Well, that *is* good news. But how is your friend Silver taking all this?"

"She wants to sue the county, sue the funeral home, sue the United Nations. Know a good lawyer?"

"I know a lot of attorneys who are skillful. I can't say whether they are good or not. They are lawyers, after all."

"She have a case?" I asked.

"Not sure she can blame the funeral home if the body delivered to them was misidentified. She can certainly sue the medical examiner for negligence. State of Florida ordinarily limits damages to a couple hundred thousand when government is sued. Sovereign immunity and all that. But I'm sure I can find a lawyer in the Keys who would be happy to take her case. I'll send you some names."

"Thanks."

"What about this poor woman? The one who buried her boyfriend at sea. Has she been told yet?"

"George Molton, the undertaker, that's his job."

"You know, this could be an even better column now, not that you're the kind of guy who would capitalize on personal tragedy."

"Oddly, that thought did not elude me, but I think I'll hold onto this for a while. I've got a hunch this is going to turn out to be a bigger story than mixed-up dead guys."

I filled Gwenn in about our voyage the day before to Key West, our misadventure on Monkey Island, and Lester's big night on the town.

"Lester drunk?"

"I think it kind of snuck up on him," I said. "We decided to do the Duval Crawl, see how far we could make it. I knew we were in trouble when Lester insisted on checking out the drag queens at Aqua. He'd downed a couple Jell-O shots by then. I was lucky to get him back to the boat."

"And how was your head this morning?"

"I have the strength of ten because my heart is pure. And because I stopped drinking after my fourth beer."

"Well, if anyone deserves to blow off a little steam from time to time it's Lester, after all he's been through."

I agreed.

"Miss you," I said.

"Good to be missed."

CHAPTER 11

LESTER AND I met Silver at Sarabeth's Kitchen on Simonton Street the next morning. It was three blocks from where she spent the night at the Coco Plum Inn, and a somewhat longer—but healthy—hike for us from the marina. Lester seemed to have shaken his monster hangover. I'd not been able to shake the feeling that Wilson's untimely cremation was too convenient. Silver might be paranoid, but that didn't mean she was wrong.

Lester asked our server for a shrimp and bacon omelet. Silver had already eaten at her bed and breakfast—bacon and pancakes. I decided to stick with the bacon theme and ordered an omelet with duck bacon. I'd tried turkey bacon before, could duck bacon be so different? Spoiler alert: Duck bacon is much better than turkey bacon, but, really, there's no beating the original, cancer-causing nitrosamines and all.

"Got the names of several lawyers for you," I told Silver. "Check your email."

She signaled our server. "Can I have a mimosa, please?"

"No problem," our server said cheerfully and scurried off to the bar.

I must have given Silver a snarky look because she held up her hand. "I don't want to hear it." She turned to Lester. "How about you, champ? Care to join me in a little morning restorative?"

"I don't drink," Lester said.

"Since when?"

"Since starting today. I'm officially on the wagon."

"A private eye and a reporter and neither of you are drinking. You guys are wrecking your stereotypes."

"Stereotype? Such a big word for so early," I said.

"I do sign language, too," she said, and shot me the bird.

Our food arrived, and while Lester and I dug in, Silver scanned the names of local lawyers Gwenn passed along.

"Silver, I'd like to get over to your brother's place and see what we can find," I said between bites. "Have you been there?"

"No. But I've got his address." She was toting a turquoise leather purse big enough to hold a Fiat. "It's in here somewhere." She began rooting through the handbag and finally extracted a little notebook. She paged through it and read out the address: "1801 North Roosevelt Boulevard."

"You're kidding."

"No. Why?"

"That's the address of our marina," I said.

"Oh, didn't I tell you? He rented a houseboat. But I didn't know where."

"Is there a slip number?"

She read it off.

"As soon as we eat, we'll head back to the marina."

"So, you're in charge now, are you?" she asked, getting her snark on.

"That's what you're paying me for," I said.

That captured Lester's attention. "Paid? I want a cut. Fifty-fifty."

"Seventy-thirty."

He shook his head. "Sixty-forty, that's my final offer."

Silver barged in. "What are you two jackasses talking about. I'm not paying him."

"I still get forty percent," Lester said. "A deal's a deal."

Silver began tapping her empty champagne glass with her fingernail, drawing our server's attention.

"Another?" our server asked.

"Please."

I avoided eye contact with Silver lest I be misinterpreted again. None of my business when she started drinking. She was an adult. She could have sushi for breakfast for all I cared, as long as I didn't have to look at it.

"We also need to drop by the cop shop," I said. I told Silver and Lester about my brief conversation at the funeral home yesterday with the Key West police officer. I pulled his business card out of my shorts and set it on the table. Silver barely glanced at it. Lester picked it up and cocked his head when he read the name.

"Harrison Paine," he said. "How many guys with that name can there be?"

"Whatcha talking about, Lester?" I asked.

He waved the cop's business card at us. "In Afghanistan, there was this Marine CID, he got in serious hot water with the army brass."

"What's a CID?" Silver asked, pulling herself away from the list of lawyers on her phone.

"Basically, a detective in the military police. Stands for Criminal Investigative Division. He was looking for another Marine who'd gone missing." Lester set the business card on the table and tapped it with his forefinger. "If this is the same guy—what are the odds, but if it is—he punched out an Afghan commander who was molesting little boys. Tried to arrest him, but the army brass told him to ignore it, that *bacha bazi*—literally translated, *boy play*—was none of his business."

"You're talking pederasty?" I asked. "Like in the book, *The Kite Runner*?"

"Yeah. This guy Paine apparently didn't get the memo to look the other way. He clobbered the Afghan commander, put him in the hospital. This horrified the brass and it pretty much ended his career. He got a raw deal. Should have given him a medal, you ask me."

"That's horrible," Silver said.

"Yes, it is," Lester said. "It's a different world over there. And some of it is unspeakable."

"You ever run into him?" I asked.

Lester shook his head. "But it was pretty big news at the time. *Stars & Stripes* did a front page story on it. Lot of guys were pissed. Could be him. Lots of MPs leave the service and become civilian cops."

"It mean anything to us?" I asked.

"Hard to say. But if it's the same guy, I'd like to meet him, shake his hand. I think I'll wander over to the police department while you search the houseboat. It's right across the street from the marina. I'll see you when you get done."

Our server came by to clear the debris. I ordered another coffee. Silver tinked her empty champagne glass again with her fingernail. "Nobody joining me?" she asked. "Come on, it's Key West. It's illegal not to drink."

"I'll be the designated driver," I said. "We can take your car over to the marina."

"Not a car. A truck. And I can't move it."

"It's broke?"

"No," she said. "The B&B doesn't have parking, but they saved a spot for me across the street in a free-parking zone. If I move it, I lose it. That's why I cabbed it over to your place yesterday."

So we walked. Lester peeled off from our little caravan at the modern police building on Truman Avenue, and Silver and I continued across the street to the marina. Wilson's houseboat was docked at Sailfish Pier, and we found it right away.

Before we could board, however, my cell phone rang. Caller ID said it was my boss, Edwina Mahoney. "I've got to take this," I told Silver. "Maybe now would be a good time for you to call the funeral home again, see if they have any more information about the mix-up."

"Conspiracy, you mean."

I answered the phone. "Hey, Ed, what's hangin'?"

"Elegant African-American women such as myself do not have

parts that hang. And what the fuck are you doing in Key West?" One of Edwina's many charms is that she never beats around the bush.

"So, you saw my column before I spiked it."

"You didn't drive all the way to the Keys for that," she said.

"You are absolutely right. I didn't drive."

"Don't tell me you flew?" I could imagine her pounding an adding machine, worrying about my expenses account.

"No. Sailed down on the *Miss Demeanor*. Lester Rivers is with me."

"Rivers? Oh, crap. What have you gotten into now?"

I knew this would take a few, so I sat down on the pier and let my legs dangle over the water. Fifteen minutes later, I'd shared the complete rundown. I expected a volcanic reaction, Ed's usual lecture about making sure the column came first, but she surprised me.

"Sharks eating underwater phone lines. A mysterious death. Mixed up corpses. Mermaids. I totally see why you wanted to cover this. You need anything?"

"You're getting soft in your old age," I said.

"Nope. We both know you can write *The Strange Files* in your sleep. You need more to keep you busy. I like this story."

"You've been talking to Guinevere."

"She give you an earful?"

"Basically, the same thing you said."

"Trust the women in your life, Alex." She hung up.

One of the other women in my life at the moment was waiting aboard Donald Wilson's houseboat, the *Ship for Brains*.

"You call the funeral home?" I asked. "Any more on the mix-up?"

She shook her head. "They've clammed up. Guy I talked to said that on the advice of their attorneys they were referring any questions to the medical examiner."

"Guess that figures. Well, wanna look around? Got a key?"

Silver shook her head. "No, but maybe Wilson hid one."

There were two purple resin Adirondack chairs on the navy-blue deck flanking a pair of potted plants—a sprawling prickly pear cactus and another odd looking succulent. The houseboat was painted powder blue with purple and yellow trim. For all intents and purposes, it was simply a floating platform with a single-wide mobile home atop. It was one of the smaller vessels in the marina, many houseboats being two-story affairs, which meant Wilson probably got a good deal on the rent.

I lifted the pot containing the cactus, figuring its thorns would discourage interlopers, and, sure enough, there was a key underneath.

"*Voila*!"

I inserted the key into the door, but I needn't have bothered. As I pressed inward, the door opened on its own revealing, well, nothing.

CHAPTER 12

"It's empty. Like Wilson was never here," Silver said.

"You sure we got the right boat?" I asked.

She walked outside and pulled a cell phone from her purse. "Yeah, this is it," she said. "It's the right slip number. I asked him for his snail mail address to send him the documents I needed him to sign. He gave me this address, but then said it was stupid to use the postal service when I could just email them instead."

I joined her on the deck and sat down in one of the plastic chairs. She collapsed into the other one. "Whoever cleaned this place out, they left these chairs and plants," I said. "From the outside, you can't tell it's been stripped."

Silver stared through the doorway of the vacant houseboat, seemingly catatonic.

"Could he have moved?"

She didn't respond immediately, so I prompted her: "Silver?"

She shook her head. "I don't know. And I'm ashamed of myself for that. Some sister I am." She was quiet for a few moments, and I let her be. Finally, she said, "Maybe we should visit that woman over at the community college he was working with."

"We'll check with her," I said. "And we need to see if the ME listed an estimated date of death. Did you get his death certificate?"

She shook her head. "No. That would have been too smart for me, obviously."

"Hey, lighten up on yourself, a little," I said. "You're under a lot of stress. We need to focus on what we can do now."

"Such as?"

"Such as asking questions. For starters, if Wilson was still living here when he died, where's his stuff? You think the landlord would have moved it out already?"

"Doesn't seem likely, does it?"

"Not to me. Probably should check with the owner of the boat. We'll get his name from the dockmaster."

I dug into my backpack and fished out a map of Key West. "You said his body was found off a place called Dredger's Key, right?"

"Yes. Some guys out fishing found him. Called the Sheriff's Office."

"Do you know how far offshore he was?"

She shook her head. "Is that important?"

"Beats me. But in my line of work, if a question occurs to you, you ask it. You never know." Silver was giving me a puzzled look. Like I was screwing with her or something. "Look, if he was found a mile offshore, then probably he was out in the Gulf in a boat, right. If he was only a few yards from shore, maybe he swam out from there."

"Or he drifted ashore from further out," she said.

"Fair point."

I was looking at the map again. "Dredger's Key is right over there," I said, pointing across the marina. "There's a causeway leading over to it, according to the map."

"So, we go there. Then what?"

"I don't know. Better to be doing something than nothing."

She didn't respond to that. While I sat there, another thought occurred to me. "I'm going to check with the neighbors, see if they know anything useful," I said. I set my backpack on the chair. "Keep an eye on this for me, please. My camera and iPad are in there."

I worked my way back toward the entrance of the pier, across to the other side, then back toward Wilson's houseboat. I knocked on every cabin door, but nobody was home. My last stop completed a full circle of the pier and I found myself in front of a green houseboat next door to Wilson's. The lettering on the side of the boat said *Wet Dream*. An elderly man with bourbon breath answered with a scowl. His houseboat may have been the most unusual watercraft in the marina for two reasons. First, a tiki bar graced its roof. And, second, it was listing severely, clearly on its way to Davy Jones' locker.

"Hi," I said. "I'm trying to find a friend. Donald Wilson. He was staying on the boat next door. But we checked in on him and the place is vacant."

"Whaddaya mean vacant?" he asked.

"Empty. Completely. No furniture or anything. Did somebody come by and clean the place out?"

The old guy shook his head. "This Wilson guy, he about your age?"

"Older. Late thirties, early forties."

"Black?"

"Yes."

"I seen him around, but we never spoke. He seemed to have lots of diving gear. A boat came by a bunch of times and he went out in it, took his gear with him. Air tanks, fins, all that kind of crap. But I wasn't sure he was actually staying here."

"Why's that?"

"Cause that houseboat's been empty a good long while."

"Empty, meaning unfurnished?" I asked.

"That's right. If he slept there, he was sleeping on the floor."

"Did you see anything unusual going on?" I asked.

"Define unusual. This is Key West. Everything's fucking unusual."

"I mean, did you see any strangers lurking, maybe taking things off his boat?"

"Nah. But if anything like that happened, it would have been at night and I'm pretty much down for the count after sunset. Day drinking will do that for you."

I figured that was all the useful information I would get, but I was curious about the condition of his houseboat. "This from the storm?" I asked.

He nodded. Hurricane Whitney made landfall in the Keys. There were still signs of wind damage and debris piled up around the marina and elsewhere on the island.

"It's a hell of a story," he said. "My wife and I, when we realized the hurricane would blow through here, we packed up our stuff, all our valuables, pictures, papers, and evacuated. Took all day, the highway was bumper to bumper all the way to Miami. Spent a few weeks visiting relatives up north, waiting for all the chaos to die down. When we returned, we were thrilled. The boat was fine. We put all our stuff back aboard. Then last week, this happened. The boat started sinking. Must have been damaged below the waterline, maybe a small hole that's gotten bigger."

"Ah, geez, that's terrible," I said. "Got insurance?"

"No. You can't get insurance for custom-made houseboats like this. We're wiped out."

"Where will you go?" I was feeling sorry for the old guy.

He shrugged. "Maybe we'll stay, go down with the ship. We don't fucking know." He turned and shuffled back inside his floundering houseboat. I never got his name.

My diving gear was stowed aboard the *Miss Demeanor*. Maybe, if time allowed, I could go take a look at the bottom of his boat, see if it could be repaired. I disliked diving in marinas—the water is filthy. But it was necessary to maintain the *Miss Demeanor*, to keep the barnacles at bay. I could do it for this guy, too.

I walked back to Wilson's houseboat. Silver was still sitting there, but my backpack was no longer resting in the purple resin chair beside her. I must have looked startled because before I could say anything Silver waved me off. "Relax. I set it inside. Didn't want anything to happen to it. You kids. Always leaving your shit lying around."

She joined me as I stepped back into the houseboat, and I told her what the old man said.

"I don't see Wilson sleeping on the floor," she said. "But even if he was using an air mattress, somebody went in there and cleaned the place out."

We explored the interior of the houseboat thoroughly. Looking into every corner and cranny, hoping to find something—anything—that Wilson might have left behind. There was nothing. Except the dark splotches of fingerprint powder.

"Cops have already been here," I said.

"That what this is from?" she asked, wiggling her smudged fingers.

"Yes. But that's odd, isn't it?"

"What's odd?"

"If the official ruling from the medical examiner is accidental death from drowning, why bother to fingerprint his houseboat?"

She gave me a raised eyebrow. "Yeah, that's curious. That's really curious."

We walked over to the dockmaster's office, which was housed in a trailer planted in the marina's parking lot. I hoped he might have some answers for us, but a sign hanging on the door said he would be out until 3 p.m. The marina was not exactly a beehive of activity. A couple of boys ran along the pier chasing one another in some kind of game of tag. A sailboat was puttering back to its slip. The parking lot was deserted except for a man smoking a cigarette and leaning against a black SUV out by Truman Avenue. Maybe he was waiting for the dockmaster, too.

"Guess we'll have to come back later," I said.

It was warm, mid-80s, and sunny. Silver pulled a bandanna from the back pocket of her shorts and mopped her brow. "Is it nap time yet?"

"I was thinking our next stop would be the cop shop," I said. "Then maybe a hike over to Dredger's Island."

She shook her head. "I didn't sleep a wink last night. And the mimosas are kicking my butt right now. You go over, talk to that cop. You know everything I know at this point. I'll catch up with you bozos later."

I pulled out my iPhone and called for an Uber. The map on the phone showed four within half a mile, crawling about the streets of Key West like little ants on the phone's screen. I waited with Silver until the driver pulled up to the curb.

"Thank you," she told me. "For everything." She removed her cowboy hat and hugged me. "I know I've been a grouch."

That seemed out of character. One minute she was shooting me the bird and calling me a bozo. The next, she was passing out hugs. But then I never claimed to understand women. Of course the complete list of things I didn't understand would fill the *Encyclopedia Galactica*.

Silver climbed into the car and rolled the window down. "This is so fucked up," she said. "It's like somebody's trying to completely *disappear* Wilson. Make it like he never existed."

"Keep your chin up," I said. "We'll get to the bottom of this."

I tried to sound confident, reassuring. Don't know if that helped her or not. But it didn't fool me.

CHAPTER 13

I FOUND LESTER sitting inside a cruiser in the parking lot of the Key West Police Department talking to the officer I'd seen at the funeral parlor.

I tapped on the window. "Room for one more?"

Harrison Paine pushed the unlock button and I slid in, leaving the back door open.

"You're letting the air out," Lester said.

"I've been trapped in the back of one of these before," I said through the divider separating the front seat from the back where the undesirables were transported.

"Close the door and we'll head up the road and get some coffee," Harrison Paine said. "You can trust me. I'm an officer of the law."

"Swell." But I did it. In a few minutes we pulled into a Dunkin' Donuts, just past the turnoff on U.S. 1 to Dredger's Key, according to the map I'd been examining.

"The Tropic Press is buying today," I said when we entered the cool confines of the shop. The mouth-watering scent of sugar and lard drew me to the counter where I ordered three large coffees and a box of assorted doughnuts. I went for a glazed. Lester snatched a chocolate-covered. Paine thoughtfully considered his options for a moment then selected one with pink icing and sprinkles.

"Ooh-rah," I said.

"When others flee, Marines run to danger," Paine said, taking a big bite.

Paine was average height, buzz-cut blond hair, deeply tanned. He sprouted a full moustache that made him appear older than I guessed he was, maybe late twenties. His moustache now was home to a smear of pink icing. How does one mention such a thing to a Marine?

"You got pink shit on your 'stache," Lester said.

Question answered.

Paine rubbed it off with a paper napkin. "Where's this Silver woman Lester was telling me about?"

"Napping. I think the breakfast mimosas did her in."

"Lot of that going on around here," he said.

"Myself, I don't drink," Lester said.

That earned a curious look from Paine. "How'd you survive the army sober?"

"It's a new thing. I'm on the Brad Pitt diet."

"Okay, I'll bite," Paine said. "What's the Brad Pitt diet?"

"No alcohol, no Angelina."

I took a healthy bite of my glazed and washed it down with a mouthful of coffee. Doughnuts are better when there's cream in the coffee, but I was being disciplined.

"So what's the Key West PD's interest in Donald Wilson's death?" I asked. "I thought the sheriff was handling the murder investigation."

"What murder? He drowned."

"That's not what Silver thinks. Said he was too experienced a diver to drown. Now that they've cremated him, we might never know."

"Yeah, that's a real cluster fuck," Paine said. "The medical examiner's a tool. This is probably the final straw."

"But you seem to have an interest."

Paine nodded. "I know the detective in charge of the investigation over at the sheriff's. We're friends. There're few things about this that are curious."

"Like what?"

"Like the fact that he was ex-navy and he's found off Dredger's Key, for one."

"I'm not getting the connection."

Paine took a swallow of coffee and pointed at me with his finger. "Right. You're not from around here. Dredger's is navy. Lot of the real estate around here is."

"So?"

Paine shrugged. "Guy's found floating right off navy property. How'd he get there? Did he know someone there? Did he swim out from there? Or is it a coincidence?"

"My guess is you're not fond of coincidences," I said.

"You?"

I shook my head.

"What's the navy say about all dat?" Lester asked.

"You owe me a dollar," I said. Lester waved me off.

Paine looked confused for a moment, wondering what Lester and I were blabbing about, then got back to it. "Navy says they don't know anything about it. My detective friend, she's checked with the master-at-arms. He says it's not their problem."

"Even though Donald Wilson was ex-navy?" I asked.

"He was a civilian when he died."

"I was thinking about riding my bike over there to look around," I said.

He shook his head. "Not unless you can get past the Shore Patrol," he said. "Island's off limits to civilians. Base housing."

I took another bite of doughnut and washed it down.

"It's him," Lester said.

Paine looked back and forth between us. "We were talking about you, earlier," I said. "Lester guessed there couldn't be that many guys with your name and a law enforcement background."

He nodded and reached into the Dunkin's box and retrieved another doughnut, this time a glazed like mine.

I told Paine how Silver approached me to come down and look into her brother's death. I also told him about our discovery that his houseboat was empty. "Going back to talk to the dockmaster," I said.

"Yeah, I heard about that, the boat being empty."

I gave him a raised eyebrow.

"My detective friend found that curious, too."

"They printed the place?" I asked.

"I think so. Why?"

I showed him the smudges on my hand.

"Better wash that shit off. It gets on your doughnut you'll be tits up. It's highly toxic."

I could feel myself go rigid, and I looked down to see a dark smudge on my glazed.

Lester and Paine both snorted.

"Assholes."

I took another swig of coffee and asked Paine," You're detective friend, he got a name?"

"She." He pulled out his wallet and extracted a business card. The name on the card said Abby Kitchner. "She's going to want to talk to you and Silver."

Paine's radio crackled. The dispatcher said something about a Signal 22P—a disturbance. "Gotta go," he said. He snatched another doughnut out of the box and got up. "Afraid I'm going to strand you."

"After all this," Lester said, "we need the exercise."

"You guys run across anything interesting, call me." Paine strode out the door leaving Lester and me to stand guard over the remaining doughnuts.

"They go bad if you don't eat 'em right away," I said.

There were three left. I eyed Lester, wondering how we would divvy them up. He took a wooden stirring stick and cut the remaining pink doughnut in half, then took the last chocolate-covered, leaving me the remaining glazed.

"Excellent decision-making," I said.

Before Lester and I could polish off the doughnuts, though, my cell phone rang. It was Silver. "Where are you guys?" she asked.

"I thought you were down for the count."

"Not with all this noise. There's a fucking riot down the street. Some sort of demonstration. Figured I better call you. Might be newsworthy." She hung up.

THE STRANGE FILES

Cardboard Guns; Steel Handcuffs

By Alexander Strange

Tropic Press

KEY WEST—Seven demonstrators carrying cardboard cutouts of AR-15 assault rifles were arrested by police here today as they paraded outside the Monroe County Courthouse.

The marchers were protesting the recent action by the Florida Legislature authorizing teachers to bring semi-automatic rifles into classrooms in the wake of the most recent school shooting.

Police charged the demonstrators with disturbing the peace and "disobeying a lawful order of police" when they failed to disburse and take their cardboard guns with them. A Key West Police Department statement said: "The guns looked real. They were frightening people. We called out the SWAT team. When we asked them to leave, they became belligerent. That's when they were arrested."

Byron Garcia, an attorney for the American Civil Liberties Union, called the charges "ludicrous."

"We let people walk out of stores with assault rifles," he said. "We let teachers take them into classrooms. But carrying a cardboard cutout is illegal? The case against my clients is paper—er, cardboard—thin and a clear violation of their First Amendment rights."

In Tallahassee earlier this week, the State House of Representatives refused to let a bill out of committee that would reverse a decision to allow teachers to carry firearms, but did approve legislation declaring pornography "a public health threat."

"Maybe next time we'll march with cardboard dildos," said Stephanie Mace-Holcomb, one of the protestors who was released on her own recognizance shortly after "The Magnificent Seven," as they are now calling themselves, were arraigned.

STRANGE FACT: While the State of Florida allows guns in schools, firearms are not permitted in the state Capitol where the legislators meet.

Weirdness knows no boundaries. Keep up at *www.TheStrangeFiles.com.* Contact Alexander Strange at Alex@TheStrangeFiles.com.

CHAPTER 14

After filing my brief report on the riot outside the Monroe County Courthouse, Lester and I returned to the marina and caught the dockmaster as he was closing up shop.

"What the hell you mean you entered that boat?" he snarled when I told him we discovered it vacant. "That's private property. You can't do that."

Lester flashed his investigator's license. It was the first time I'd ever seen him do that. It immediately quelled the dockmaster's temper tantrum. "May we see the records on that watercraft, please," Lester said.

It took the old guy—his name was Cochran—a few seconds to find his file on the boat. While he scrounged through the top drawer of his file cabinet, I whispered to Lester: "That's a great Jedi mind trick, that flash your ID thing."

"Watch and learn you will."

The houseboat was owned by a man named Thomas Underwood. His home address was listed as St. Petersburg. Lester called his phone number, but it rolled over to voicemail. Lester left his name and number with a message asking him to call back as soon as possible. Otherwise, the dockmaster was of no help. He didn't know anything about Donald Wilson's disappearance. Although he'd seen the story about a body found floating near Dredger's Key, he hadn't connected the dots. He also hadn't heard from the owner about re-renting the houseboat. I tried to give him my card, but he waved it away.

"I got all your contact information already. It's here in the file. My assistant left me the forms." He rooted through his file cabinet some more and found the papers. "Says you paid a week in advance. Good. We like that."

"I'll bet you do."

The old man laughed. "Hey, got a question for you, sonny. What's with the name?"

I assumed he was talking about my surname. "What about it?"

"Why *Miss Demeanor*?" He waved the paperwork in front of me. "Says here you're a reporter or something. Why not *Miss Quote*?" He cackled at his own humor.

That was cute, but I wasn't going to let him know that. "The previous owner, he was a judge."

"You could change it," Cochran said. "I know a guy does a great job with lettering. My cousin, in fact."

"Bad luck changing a boat's name," I said.

"You superstitious, are you?" he asked, grinning like an idiot.

"I am. And I wouldn't want to make a *Miss Take*."

The old dockmaster thought that was hilarious and he was still laughing when we left his office.

It was Lester's last night in Key West. He'd booked a return trip to Naples on the high-speed Key West Express ferry leaving at 5 p.m. the following day. It would be a three-hour trip, much faster than aboard the *Miss Demeanor*. He'd been called back by his boss who needed him for a missing person's case. That was Lester's specialty—skip tracing. A banker was AWOL leaving her husband of fourteen years and two kids behind. They'd been having marital difficulties and—amazing coincidence!—her assistant at the bank was also unaccounted for.

"While I'm there, I'll run this guy Underwood down, see what I can find out," Lester said. "If I have to, I can swing up to St. Pete, try to corner him."

I'd agreed to buy Lester's dinner as a way to say thanks for all of his help, and we walked down to Duval Street. I'd heard about a place called the Smokin' Tuna Saloon I thought we'd try. We wandered past Jimmy Buffett's Margaritaville Café, Caroline's, Irish Kevin's, and Willie T's with its countless dollar bills stapled all over the restaurant. Many of the store and restaurant windows were plastered with posters advertising an event called the First Annual Flight of the Flamingo Parade and Dance Off. Duvall Street would be closed for the festivities. Hopefully, I'd be wrapped up and out of here by then.

At Bottom's Up Gentlemen's Club, Lester insisted we stop in for a drink. "You're on your own, cowboy," I told him. "I wouldn't set foot in a place like that without a full hazmat suit. I've never seen a strip join that wasn't full of creeps."

"Creeps are your business," he argued.

"Weirdos not creeps. Big difference."

In the end, he relented and settled for demolishing a couple of margaritas at the Gas Monkey. We were en route to our dinner destination when we spotted a couple of Wooks sitting on the sidewalk, just hanging out, not panhandling. A buck and a doe, maybe early twenties. Both wore their hair in dreads, both displayed a lot of ink. The guy was wearing a dashiki and holey jeans. The girl a flowered dress with buckskin boots.

"Dude," the Wook said as we approached.

"Dude," I replied. I stopped and considered the couple for a moment, then reached into the pocket of my cargo shorts and fished out my wallet. It's made of blue translucent plastic with a Superman emblem embroidered on the front.

"Whoa," the doe said. "Are you, like, him?"

"I smiled at her and failed to suppress a laugh. "No. I'm not like him. I'm taller and don't wear my underwear outside my pants."

They both nodded as if I'd delivered priceless wisdom from Krypton.

"I give you a twenty, can you guys do something for me?"

They looked at each other and nodded again. "You a trophy hunter?" the buck asked.

I laughed. "No, I don't bag and tag."

"Then what? We don't do kinky."

Lester had waited patiently during this idle chatter, but he finally couldn't help asking, "You gonna fill me in?"

I looked at the Wooks. "You wanna share?"

The buck was fondling the Jackson I'd handed him and he nodded, never taking his eyes off the money. "Sure. People like us, guys like him."—he nodded at me—"they call us Wooks, short for Wookies, man. Like from Star Wars, you know. The movie? Like, we have this long hair like Chewbacka." He grabbed his dreads and lifted them above his head in case Lester didn't understand.

"There's this website," the doe continued. "People take our pictures. Not just ours, a course, but Wooks from everywhere. And they post them. They call it bagging and tagging, like big game hunters." She turned to her boyfriend "You remember the name?"

He shook his head.

"Colorado Big Game Trophy Wook Hunters," I said. "And, for the record, I don't do that. I'm a reporter. This guy"—I gestured toward Lester—"he's a private eye. And I'm thinking maybe you can help us."

I kneeled down next to them and fished out a couple of my business cards. "My friend and I, we're investigating a suspicious death. We're with this lady. She thinks her brother was murdered. We need help."

The doe's eyes got wide. "How can *we* help?"

"You guys hang out on the street. Nobody pays any attention to you. They don't take you seriously, right? They see the dreads and the tats and they look right through you, am I right?."

They nodded.

"This may sound weird, but I've got this strange vibe here in Key West. A prickly feeling I can't explain. I need more eyes and ears on the street. Can you dig that?"

They looked at each other. The doe's eyes grew wider. "We get it.

We've been sensing something wrong, like electricity messing with our auras. Like something evil."

I nodded. "You got a phone?"

"Sure, man. Can't sell herb without one."

"I got more twenties. You keep an eye on things. You hear anything weird. Call me. My number's on the card. But keep it real."

"We can do that," he said. He paused for a moment then added, "We have friends."

"More eyes the better." I gave him a few more cards and another twenty.

I rose and rejoined Lester and we resumed our walk to the restaurant. "Eyes and ears only," I said over my shoulder. "Just observe."

They nodded.

At the restaurant, Lester ordered a Smokin' Tuna Melt and a Goombay Smash for dinner. I went for the Full Moon chicken sandwich and another beer.

"Wooks." Lester shook his head. "Learn something new every day. We used to call them hippies."

"Wooks are a subset of hippies, sort of," I said. "Hippies you find at Dead concerts. Wooks are outside the gates, panhandling the Hippies. Although that's a very rough overgeneralization."

"So, you done this sort of thing before?" Lester asked.

"Well, there's the Army of the Strange."

"Yeah, but those are vampires."

I have a number of Facebook followers who message me with tips for *The Strange Files*. A group of them have loosely banded together and call themselves The Army of the Strange. They identify themselves with vampirish nicknames such as Ermanno, Ponzio, Desponia, and Thanya. Hey, if you're into weirdness, might as well get in character.

But my impulse to recruit the Wooks had a literary genesis. "Actually, I'm inspired by the Baker Street Irregulars," I said.

"Sherlock Holmes's street urchins. His spies."

I nodded. "You're ex-army. Can you go to war with too many soldiers? I figure the more eyes and ears the better."

"Okay," he said. "But what's with this bad vibe? You really spooked?"

"I've been dreaming about mermaids. One attacked me with a speargun." I took a sip of my beer. "Lester, I never dream. Or if I do, I never remember them. It woke me up in a cold sweat. Yeah, something about this has me itchy. I have this weird feeling. It's been bothering me all day."

"Like what?"

"Like I'm being watched."

Instinctively, Lester scanned the restaurant crowd and glanced into the street. He turned back to me. "You know my history. You know how, when I was blown up outside Kabul…"

"Yes, you imagined that woman…"

"Not imagined, she was real. She was a light being. And she saved me."

This wasn't the first time Lester shared this story, how he lost his leg when a bomb blew up a bus he was traveling in, and how it caught on fire, then rolled over his leg. How he nearly died before help arrived and how this woman, glowing in the desert sun, stayed with him. And how she vanished as soon as the helicopters landed.

"I've told you before, Alexander. There's happenings in this world beyond our understanding. Like something just outside your peripheral vision. It's there, but you can't quite see it. You write about strange behavior. The world is stranger than you know."

"Meaning?"

"Meaning, if you feel something's off. Trust your gut. Your gut knows more than your brain. It's often the difference between dying and surviving in combat. You think something's weird, I believe you."

After we cabbed back to the marina, I took Fred for a walk. Lester said he was heading down to the Shipwreck Bar and Grill for a nightcap. He was still out when I hit the sack, but sometime in the middle of the night I was startled out of my sleep by the boat's rocking. Before

I could leave my berth, I heard Lester whispering to someone, then the door to his berth closed. Later there was more rocking and giggling.

I arose early after an uneasy night. When I returned to the boat after taking Fred for his morning walk, I was surprised to see Lester already up and sipping coffee on the poop deck. He wasn't alone. Lester was drinking from my Batman mug, wisely leaving my Green Lantern for me. His companion was sipping something, who knew what, out of a Wonder Woman mug.

It was Silver.

CHAPTER 15

Stock Island

SILVER AND I were in the back seat of an Uber on our way to Florida Keys Community College where we hoped to track down Dr. Tina Del Rio, Donald Wilson's former colleague.

We weren't exactly ignoring one another, but we weren't talking, either. Finally, I couldn't disregard the elephant in the Uber any longer.

"So, you and Lester," I said as we crossed the bridge to Stock Island.

She gave me a disgusted look, the one that said she'd seen a cockroach in her cereal or the plumber's butt crack was showing.

"What about me and Lester? Did I need permission to come aboard?"

It was Monday morning, and classes had resumed at the community college. We bailed out of the Uber and navigated our way through a bustling hallway to the office of Assistant Professor Tina Del Rio. We didn't have an appointment, but hoped to catch her between classes.

When we arrived, two students were sitting on the floor outside her door waiting to see to her. A third was leaning against the wall. I recalled doing the same sort of thing, not too many years earlier when I was a student at the University of Texas majoring in journalism and beer pong.

"Is Dr. Del Rio in?" I asked the kid holding up the wall. He was lanky, nearly my height, and sported a gold circular earring.

He shrugged. "Hope so." He waved a sheet of green paper at me. "I need her signature." The two female students sprawled on the floor didn't bother to join in the conversation, so I ignored them and turned to the door and knocked.

There was no response. I placed my ear to the door, thinking maybe she was on the phone, but I could not hear a voice inside. It was then that I noticed a yellow sticky note on the floor where it apparently had fallen off the door. I picked it up. In all caps in blue ink it read: DO NOT DISTURB. I stuck it back on the door.

"She doesn't have class now, does she?" I asked the tall kid. He pointed to the bulletin board by her door listing her office hours. I checked my Mickey Mouse watch. She was supposed to be in.

Maybe I'd knocked too softly, or perhaps she was ignoring the knocking, not wanting to be bothered, like her note said. Tough. I rapped on the wooden door again, this time with a lot more vigor. Still no answer.

But another door swung open down the hall and a small Asian woman in her forties peeked around the corner. She glanced at the students with an annoyed look on her face, then spotted Silver and me. "Are you looking for Dr. Del Rio?" she asked.

"Yes," Silver said. "Isn't she supposed to be in?"

The woman walked over to us. "Are you a parent?" she asked Silver. I was obviously too young to have the question directed to me.

Silver shook her head. "No. It's about my brother, Donald Wilson."

The woman's mouth went wide. She approached Silver and grabbed both of her hands. "I am so sorry." She and Silver were about the same height and they locked onto one another's eyes. "Tina, I think, no, I know, she cared about Dr. Wilson a great deal. This is so awful. I saw the story in the newspaper."

She let go of Silver's hands and rapped on the door herself. When there was no answer, she rummaged through a pocket in her slacks and retrieved a ring of keys. "Let me open her office for you and you can at least have a place to sit while you wait for her. If she's not here in a few minutes, I'll call her. I tried to reach her over the weekend but she didn't answer."

The woman inserted a key and turned the door handle. As it swung open, we recoiled at the hideous smell that boiled from the room. I held my breath and stepped past the women and entered the small office. Pale, shoeless feet protruded from behind a desk, a pair of abandoned flip flops a few inches away.

I walked over, certain of what I would find. And I was right. An Hispanic woman lay on the floor on her back, her eyes wide open in a mask of horror. Her abdomen was covered in dried blood, as was the carpet around her. A shiny shaft of metal protruded from her stomach. I recognized it immediately, and freaked out. It was like in my dream: A spear from a speargun.

The Asian woman screamed and ran out of the room back to her office. We heard her slam the door. Maybe she thought a killer was on the loose in the building. Maybe she was right.

Silver backed out of the room and collapsed on the hallway floor next to the sitting students and covered her face in her hands. The lanky kid stuck his head in. "Fuck me!" he shouted, turned and fled down the hallway. The girls on the floor watched him run off, glanced at one another with terrified looks on their faces, then they, too, skedaddled.

I stepped outside the office, took a deep breath, then dialed 911. The dispatcher told me to stay on the line, but I needed to make other calls. The first was to Lester. "Remember that dream I told you about? You aren't going to believe what I'm about to tell you…"

The next call was to Harrison Paine. "You told me to call if we ran into anything unusual," I said.

"Whatcha got?"

"A marine biology professor with a spear in her stomach."

"That *is* unusual. City or county."

"We're at the community college," I said. "Sheriff's jurisdiction, right?"

"Yeah. You call 911?"

"Just did."

"Don't touch anything."

"Of course not."

"Okay, I'm heading over. I'll call my friend at the sheriff's. The detective I told you about."

I hung up.

We could hear the growing wail of sirens now. We'd passed the entrance to the Sheriff's Office and the county jail off College Road when we'd Ubered over, so no surprise the response time was quick.

Despite my assurance to Harrison Paine, I knew this would be my only chance to check out Tina Del Rio's office. Could there be something in here that would help us get to the bottom of this? If I were careful not to disturb fingerprints and didn't step in the dried pool of blood on the floor, maybe I could find something.

And I did, but it wasn't what I expected. It was a framed photograph sitting atop a four-drawer file cabinet by her desk. It was a picture of a woman under water breathing from an air hose, the iconic image of a Weeki Wachee mermaid.

Mermaids are the highlight of Weeki Wachee Springs State Park, about sixty miles north of Tampa. Before Disney and Universal and the Museum of Holy Creation, Weeki Wachee was the hottest tourist attraction in the state, and to this day young women dressed in mermaid costumes perform for thousands of tourists each year in a four-hundred seat underwater auditorium. The woman in the mermaid costume in the photograph was clearly a younger version of the dead woman on the floor.

So this was the mermaid that Donald Wilson had mentioned to Silver. The Asian woman down the hall said they were close. Had Wilson told her something that led to this?

What did you know, Tina?

One thing that I knew for certain was that Silver's instincts—conspiracy nut or not—were correct. Until this moment, there'd been insufficient evidence to believe Donald Wilson was murdered, the premature cremation notwithstanding. But this eliminated any doubt.

And what about my nightmare? That could, of course, be nothing more than coincidence. In the dream, the mermaid was not on the receiving end of the spear, after all. But still. I felt my heart skip a beat—a premature ventricular heartbeat. I get them when I'm stressed. This definitely qualified as stressful.

Knowing my time was running short, I resumed my scan of the small office, holding my arm up to my nose trying, vainly, to filter the smell of rotten eggs, feces, and decaying flesh. Now this was where I *really* needed a hazmat suit.

Stacks of papers—tests from the looks of them—littered the desktop. A pad of yellow sticky notes and a blue gel-tip pen rested next to the papers. Otherwise, there was nothing remarkable. I did a slow three-sixty scan of the room, breathing shallowly, trying not to gag. It was just as important to notice what *wasn't* in the room that should have been. Was anything missing? I looked around for a purse or a backpack or a briefcase, which I expected to see. No dice. Maybe she tucked a purse away in a desk drawer.

I pulled a couple tissues out of a box on the desktop, wrapped them around the fingers of my right hand. For good measure, I grabbed two more and held them against my mouth and nose with my other hand. Then I leaned over the desk so I could slide the desk drawers open. As I did so, I found myself staring into Tina's ghastly frozen eyes and the hideous spear in her abdomen once again. I looked away and concentrated on the task at hand.

On the left-hand side of the desk was a large file drawer, but Tina's right leg was resting against that corner of the desk and I didn't dare disturb the body. I slid the shallow center drawer open and glanced in, seeing nothing unusual—pencils and pens, paperclips, rubber bands, more sticky notes, printer paper. The top right drawer slid open easily revealing a stapler and a roll of tape resting atop a campus directory. The middle drawer was home to envelopes and stacks of university forms. The bottom right drawer was my last chance to see if she might have stored her purse there. I slid it open. No purse. In fact, no nothing. It was empty, which seemed inconsistent with the rest of her desk organization. Her killer may have gone through the same routine. Maybe her purse had been there and now was in the hands of her assailant. I hoped I didn't smudge any prints.

I heard a clop of footsteps outside the office. I shoved the tissue paper into a pocket in my cargo shorts and turned toward the door as two sheriff's deputies materialized.

The taller of the two deputies drew his sidearm and demanded, "Hands up," like in the movies.

I reached for the ceiling. "I'm the guy who called 911," I said. "My friend, outside the door, she and I discovered the professor's body a few minutes ago."

The second deputy directed me to lean against the wall and he patted me down.

"You know we could do this outside," I said, suppressing a gag.

"Show me some ID," he said.

"Okay. I'm going to reach into my pocket here and remove my wallet. We cool with that?"

He rolled his hand, signaling me to get on with it, but never took his eyes off me.

The first deputy holstered his pistol and kneeled beside the professor's body. He coughed several times then said, "Jesus, Henry, you gotta see this. It's a fucking spear."

The deputy now identified as Henry returned my driver's license and told me to step outside the office. "Don't go anywhere," he ordered.

As I walked into the hallway, two more uniforms arrived. Silver was still on the floor, leaning against the wall. I squatted down next to her. "You okay?" I asked.

Her eyes were watery and bloodshot. She shook her head no. " I…I…I told you," she said, her voice weak.

"Yeah, you did, Silver. You certainly did."

The Asian woman, apparently reassured by the sound of all the commotion in the hallway, re-emerged from her office and walked over to us. She knelt down beside Silver and placed a comforting hand on her shoulder. Although it was clear from her own red-rimmed eyes she needed some TLC as well.

"I'm sorry I ran," she said. "I was frightened."

"Of course," I said.

The scene around us was chaotic, the hallway packed with cops. Neither Lester nor Paine had arrived yet.

"Could we step into your office for a few minutes?" I asked. "Get away from all this?"

She nodded.

I stood, towering over her, and extended my hand. "I'm Alexander Strange," I said. "This is Silver McFadden."

"Doctor Takahashi," she said. "Akari."

I helped Silver to her feet and we walked toward Akari's office. I was less interested in getting out of the crowd than having a few moments alone to talk to Tina Del Rio's colleague. Maybe she knew what Tina knew. Maybe she could help unravel this mystery.

Ever since I'd arrived in Key West I'd been pondering Donald Wilson's last words to his sister and what they meant. As we prepared to enter her office, I asked Akari, "If I said the word mermaid to you, would it mean anything?"

She looked at me curiously. "You know Tina used to perform at Wiki Wachee."

I nodded. "I saw the photo on her filing cabinet."

Silver said, "Wilson said something about a mermaid. Was he talking about Tina?"

Akari released the handle to her office door.

"Let's go to the lab. I think there's something there you'll want to see."

CHAPTER 16

Key West

"WELL, THIS IS another nice mess you've gotten yourself into," Gwenn said in an awful imitation of Oliver Hardy.

One of her many exceptional qualities was how clear-eyed she could be in the midst of confusion. Made her a terrific courtroom lawyer, no doubt, and a helpful sounding board for me when my Stress-O-Meter spiked. Finding dead bodies with spears embedded in their tummies may be all in a day's work for some guys, but it was not part of my ordinary nine-to-five.

By then, I was back at the marina, resting on the poop deck of the *Miss Demeanor*, sipping a Cuba Libre—another excellent stress reliever—and filling Gwenn in on the events of the past couple of days. The sun had set and a pleasant breeze was drifting in from the Gulf. The only sounds in the marina were the friendly clanking of halyards against the masts of sailboats and the steady lapping of small waves against the hull.

"I hoped to pull anchor before the end of the week," I said, "but I'm not sure now."

"I'm actually starting to miss you," she said. "Could it be love?"

"Pure lust. And who could blame you."

"That's probably it."

"You know, you could take the Key West Express down this weekend. There's supposed to be this hilarious festival, some sort of parade with flamingos. And I've heard rumors they serve alcohol hereabouts."

"And there are killers on the loose."

"Well, there's that."

She paused for a moment. "Seriously, are you concerned? Two people have been murdered and you're there investigating it with one of the victim's relatives."

"I'd actually have to know something incriminating to be a threat to anyone. I got squat. And, for that matter, neither do the cops. But I have to tell you, I've been bothered by this uneasy feeling ever since we got here. I can't explain it. It's like I'm being watched or there's something in the air. It's a little unnerving."

"Like how?"

"Like, the night before, I was being chased by a mermaid in a dream."

"Was she hot?"

"Volcanic. But she pulled a speargun and tried to shoot me."

"A speargun."

"Yeah, whaddaya think of that?"

She was quiet for a few moments. "What I think is that I'm regretting giving you grief for not staying busy enough. Why don't we pretend I never said that and you can come home and I'll cook us a nice dinner."

"That's a non-starter and we both know it."

"It's my cooking, isn't it?"

"There's that."

Again, silence on her end of the line. "Alright. But you have to promise me you'll be careful. I wish you owned a gun."

"Ironically, the only gun I have with me is a speargun. But it's kinda awkward walking down the street with one of those."

We were both quiet for a few moments, but it wasn't an awkward silence. Gwenn was good about thinking before she spoke. I was working on being more patient and less impulsive. She finally said, "Finish telling me about what this professor showed you in the lab."

I took another pull on my drink, not the first nor the last of the evening. Fred walked over with his chew toy and handed it to me. I tossed it across the deck and he chased after it then disappeared. A retriever, he is not.

It had been a long and, in some respects, tedious day after the initial shock of discovering Tina Del Rio's perforated remains. By the time Silver, Akari, and I returned from Wilson's lab to the scene of the crime, Lester and Harrison Paine were talking to Paine's detective friend from the Sheriff's Office, Sgt. Abby Kitchner.

Kitchner was easily the best looking sergeant I'd ever met. Medium height with an athletic build, short dark hair, and piercing blue eyes. She wore very little makeup and didn't need it. We shook hands and I glanced at Paine out of the corner of my eye. He caught it and his mouth twitched in a suppressed grin.

She interviewed Silver, Akari, and me separately and at length. I held nothing back save my poking around Tina Del Rio's desk and what Akari showed us in the college's marine sciences laboratory. Kitchner asked my opinion about the cremation of Donald Wilson, did I think it was an accident? I told her I didn't like coincidences, but it was not beyond the realm of possibility. Was I able to contact the owner of Wilson's houseboat, because she had struck out? I told her we left a message but hadn't heard back. She was thorough and professional, but my reporter's keen instincts told me she found the situation frustrating. My first clue came when at the end of our conversation she slapped her notebook shut and said, "Well, this is fucked up beyond all reason."

"Do me a favor, would you?" I asked her as she tucked her notebook into her pants pocket.

She gave me the stink eye, which was not unexpected. They teach a class at the police academy: How to Fuck with Newspaper Reporters.

"If you get prints on that speargun shaft, and you're able to identify them, would you let me know?"

She opened her mouth to say something—no doubt rich with sarcasm—but then stopped, looked at me for several seconds, then said, "What are you thinking?"

"Wanna make a bet?"

She cocked her head.

"I've got a twenty dollar bill that says if there are prints on that spear, they'll be Donald Wilson's."

"Why do you say that?"

"A speargun? Who has spearguns? Divers, that's who. Whose diving gear is AWOL? Donald Wilson's. Will you let me know?"

She chewed on it for a bit. "Yeah," she finally said. "That's interesting. Wilson's place looked like someone cleaned it out. Now this. Yeah, that's very interesting. I'm not taking your bet."

When Kitchner was finished, crime scene techs fingerprinted us to eliminate our prints from any others they might find in the office. A sheriff's detective wearing tan khakis, a blue dress shirt, and a Glock approached us and identified himself as Kitchner's supervisor, Lieutenant Barry Taylor. He asked where we were staying, how long we would be in Key West, and instructed us to be available for further questions.

I sat down with Paine and told him fundamentally the same story I told detective Kitchner, again omitting my extralegal poking around and our lab experience. He seemed less frustrated than bemused by the situation.

"I'm glad Kitch caught this one and not me. I got a feeling this will turn into a major time suck."

I asked, "You and the sergeant?"

He knew what I meant, but shrugged his shoulders and walked away.

Lester escorted Silver back to her B&B. He'd called his boss and got the okay to hang out in Key West a little longer. This wasn't the first time the Third Eye brass had let Lester off the leash to join me in a quest. "Colonel Lake sends his regards," Lester said of his boss, who, like Lester, used a water-themed fictitious last name, a holdover from their time together in Afghanistan in the U.S. Army Intelligence and Security Command.

"He says you have a knack for stirring up trouble."

"You tell the colonel that Brett Barfield deserves the credit for this one?"

"Dat turd Barfield can speak for himself."

It was late in the afternoon by the time I returned to the boat. Fred was a trooper but I could tell he desperately needed to do his business, so I leashed him up and we took a walk to the park. At one point during our stroll, I felt the hairs on the back of my neck rise and a chill roll down my spine. I whirled around, certain someone was behind me. But nobody was there. My heart was racing and I gave myself a minute to bring my breathing back to normal. Probably the after effects of discovering Tina Del Rio's body. Adrenaline aftershock.

When we got back, I fed Fred then I laced up my running shoes and headed out for a five-mile run. I needed to work off the jitters. My route took me down Truman Avenue to Whitehead Street then back on Olivia Street. I looked for my recent recruits to the newly formed Army of the Wook, but didn't see them. Then I jogged around the nineteen acres of the Key West Cemetery for a while glancing at the tombstones and historic markers as I ran past.

A few headstones stopped me dead in my tracks, you will excuse the expression. One was at the grave of B.P. "Pearl" Roberts with the inscription:

I Told You I Was Sick

Another read:

If You're Reading This,
You Desperately Need A Hobby

And for fans of Robert Heinlein:

GROK—Look It Up

Perhaps the saddest of all:

Down Below Lies Shakira Stokes
No One Laughed At Her Poor Jokes

By the time I got back to the boat I was sweaty, beat, and in need of liquid refreshment. I filled Gwenn in on my day including what we discovered in the community college's laboratory.

"Akari—that's her name, the professor—is a marine botanist at the school," I said. "She and Tina Del Rio were confidants. The lab for the most part looked like your normal college chemistry lab with all the test tubes, beakers, and microscopes. But what was really intriguing were the vats of water under artificial light where they were growing algae."

"Algae?" she asked with a tone of distaste. "I hope not Red Tide. It's getting awful here. Two dead manatees and a dolphin washed up on the beach yesterday, and the ER at Naples Community Hospital's overrun with people who can't breathe."

"No, not Red Tide. These are actually beautiful plants with pretty green circular tops on long stems. I've got the scientific name in my notebook, but commonly they're called mermaid's wineglass.

"Mermaid? Is this the mermaid Wilson was talking about?"

"That's a good question. Tina Del Rio was a Weeki Wachee mermaid when she was younger and I thought for sure that must be it when I saw that photograph in her office. But then I saw these plants, and now I'm not sure."

"Why are they growing them, did she say?"

"It's complicated. There are certain plant-eating fish that like this algae. And there are other carnivorous fish that like eating the plant-eating fish. And those fish, apparently are viewed as a delicacy for a rare kind of shark."

"And sharks were eating the phone lines, right?"

"Yes. And Wilson found these mermaid wineglass plants growing near the underwater phone lines where they became exposed."

"Exposed?"

"Close the shore, submarine cables are buried so they don't get damaged by boat anchors or fishing nets. But tidal action can expose them sometimes, and Wilson discovered a place where the lines were uncovered and this algae was growing, Akari told me. And some of the plants were discolored, and she's trying to figure out why."

"What would cause that?"

"We didn't have time to get into it, but I'm curious and I hope to have a chance to talk to her some more about it."

"So back to the sharks, the ones eating the phone lines," Gwenn said. "They were attracted to the phone lines by the fish eating the little mermaid plants, and maybe the phone lines getting bit was simply part of some feeding frenzy or something?"

"That could be. Or maybe the sharks are attracted to the lines independently of all that, maybe drawn to the electrical current. There are still more questions than answers, and now there might not be any answers ever with Wilson dead."

"So what got him killed?"

"Beats the shit out of me."

She laughed. "So, you know some more about what he was doing but not why anyone would want to murder him."

"Roger that."

Gwenn was quiet for a few moments digesting what she'd heard. She was blessed with a keen, logical mind, and I was hoping she might have a brilliant flash of insight that would clear all this up. I waited in anticipation until she was ready to offer her best thoughts on the matter.

"Well, fuck," she said.

"Exactly."

"What kind of sharks, by the way?" she asked.

"Oh yeah, that's the good part. You won't believe it."

"Try me."

"Vampire sharks."

CHAPTER 17

IF YOU WATCH enough crime shows on television, you begin to believe amazing things about forensic technology, not the least of which is the capability of CSIs to instantly analyze DNA samples.

The technology is getting better—and faster—but even rush jobs can take days, and with the backlog at the Florida Department of Law Enforcement's labs, even weeks.

But fingerprints? They're still the number one go-to for crime scene investigators. And they are fast.

So I wasn't surprised that the prints on the spear pulled from Tina Del Rio's body were identified overnight. What did surprise me was that Detective Abby Kitchner actually called me the next morning to share the news.

"Glad I didn't bet," she said.

"Donald Wilson's, right?"

"It gets better. We scoured the area around the building looking for anything resembling a clue, and got lucky. You know all that construction next door, that new building going up?"

"Yeah, I saw that."

"One of our guys dumpster dived over there and found something."

"You did not find the speargun," I said.

"We didn't? Sure looks like one to me."

"Well, damn. His prints on that, too?"

"Yes. But get this. His are the only prints."

"What does that mean?" I asked.

"It means our killer wore gloves, I suppose. But this is awfully curious."

"Like why use Donald Wilson's speargun in the first place, and why make sure his prints were undisturbed so we would know it was his?"

"Yes."

We were both quiet for a minute as we thought about that, then I asked her: "You know those are Wilson's prints, how? You got them from the navy?"

"FBI."

"And we know the corpse pulled out of the water at Dredger's Key for sure was Donald Wilson? You guys printed the corpse, right?"

"This is why they teach us to consult with journalists."

I guess she thought her sarcasm would put me off. "Well, did you or didn't you?"

I heard her chuckle, maybe settling a private bet with herself on whether I would be sharp enough to understand she hadn't actually answered my question. "It's complicated. Donald Wilson was in the water long enough to de-glove…"

"De-what?"

"De-glove. You know how your fingertips get wrinkly after you've been in the water for a while?"

"Yeah."

"Now imagine a corpse that's been submerged for a few days or more. Not only does that happen, but the layer of fat under the skin turns soapy and if the body isn't handled carefully, the entire skin of the hands can slip off, like a glove."

I felt my stomach churn. "And in Wilson's case?"

"The fishermen weren't careful. The corpse arrived at the morgue de-gloved. I don't know all the details, but apparently the ME couldn't pull prints off the underlying dermis. He sent it all off to the lab in Tallahassee along with DNA samples."

"Sent what off."

"The corpse's fingertips. They cut a few off for identification purposes."

I felt my stomach churn again and a cold sweat broke out on my forehead. Kitchner correctly guessed my reaction when I didn't respond right away. "Yeah. Been there, done that. Take a deep breath."

I took a moment to compose myself, then asked, "Well, you understand where I was going with all that, don't you?"

"Sure. Could Donald Wilson be Tina Del Rio's killer."

"It's all going to hinge on the time of their deaths, right?"

"No. Even if Tina Del Rio predeceased Donald Wilson, that doesn't mean he killed her."

"But he could have."

"Yes, technically."

"So, do we know about the time of their deaths?"

"We are off the record here."

It was a statement not a question, although she should have stipulated that earlier, but we shared common goals and I needed her more than she needed me. "I don't even know you," I said.

"Liar. Just don't say where any of this came from, okay?"

"Of course."

There was a pause on the line, and I wondered if she'd lost the thread of the conversation. "Uh, about time of death?"

"Oh, yeah, about that. No."

"No, what?"

"No, the medical examiner can't give us anything very precise right now. Both of them have been dead for at least four days. Tina Del Rio's body was well into decomposition. You knew that already from the smell. Same for Wilson. In addition to his fingertips, the medical examiner sent samples of Wilson's muscle tissue to the lab in Tallahassee for enzyme tests. If he was dead less than six days, they might be able to pin it down more closely. They'll do the same for Tina Del Rio. But, either way, all indications are that they died around the same time."

"But back up a minute," I said. "If I understand everything you've told me, there being no fingerprints or DNA and all, what hard evidence do you have that it was actually Donald Wilson who was pulled out of the Gulf?"

"You mean besides his dog tag, the fact that he was African-American, that he was a scuba diver, and his driver's license photograph we downloaded from the Division of Motor Vehicles?"

"Oh." I hadn't thought about the DMV photo. But then she said this:

"Actually, you're asking a fair question. Donald Wilson was very dark skinned. When he was alive, anyway. His DMV photo was not the best. Between the discoloration and the decay from decomposition, the medical examiner told us he was hoping to get a visual confirmation from next of kin."

"Yeah, right. Was that before or after they shipped his body off to be cremated?"

"I know, I know. It's a freaking disaster and the sheriff's assigned someone to look into it."

"My understanding is that they photograph all the bodies they receive as part of the autopsy process, that right?"

"Sure."

"Well then, Wilson's next of kin is here. Should she go take a look and confirm his identity?"

"That's up to her," Kitchner said. "We'll have fingerprints back soon, I hope, probably before the DNA results, but if she wants to, sure, it would eliminate a very small—and I should emphasize itsy-bitsy—chance the ID isn't right. But I gotta tell you I'm not losing sleep over that."

I thought about that for a moment and decided I'd ask Silver what she thought.

"One more thing," I said. "The note on Tina Del Rio's office door. Was that her handwriting?"

There was a long pause, then Kitchner came back on the line.

"What note?"

CHAPTER 18

I THOUGHT I'D run my conversation with Detective Kitchner past Lester, but his berth was empty. Then I remembered he hadn't returned last night after taking Silver back to her B&B. I pulled up his number on my cell phone and pressed the call button.

"How's Silver holding up?" I asked when he answered his phone.

His response was muffled, as if his mouth were full of food. "She's still in the room." I could hear him chewing.

"What's for breakfast?"

"Blueberry and banana pancakes with a side of bacon. Killer bee."

"Have her call me, would you? Got an idea she's not going to like."

"What you're really not going to like is the story in the *Key West Citizen* this morning," he said.

"They have something on Tina Del Rio's murder?"

"Lead story. Big pictures of both Donald Wilson and Tina Del Rio. Speculation that their deaths might be a murder/suicide. And you're in it, too, Padawan."

"Me?"

"You and Silver. Story quotes police reports that you guys found her body. Silver's identified as a horse rancher, author, and Wilson's grieving sister. You're identified as *The Strange Files* columnist who's in town investigating Wilson's death."

"Where'd they get that?"

"Apparently, it's in the police report. I'll look it up after breakfast. But it quotes some lieutenant in the Sheriff's Office."

"So much for keeping a low profile," I said. "Anyway, when you see Silver have her call me."

"Hang on," he said. "She's walking in now." He said something to her and then Silver's voice came on the phone.

"You have an idea I'm not going to like?"

"Yes. And I'm sorry to hit you with this first thing in the morning, but when you were at the morgue, did they show you a picture of Wilson's body?"

"Uh, no, actually. I saw all the bodies that were still there, like I told you. The woman who was in charge walked me back there where the corpses are stored. But she didn't have any pictures because her computer was down. Why are you asking?"

"So you've never actually seen Wilson's remains."

"What is wrong with you?" Her voice was stressed and a couple of decibels louder. "Are you seriously suggesting he might still be alive?"

"Sorry, Silver. I don't want to cause you any more headaches than you're already dealing with."

"A little fucking late for that now," she said, and hung up.

My life would be simpler if my mind worked in a more linear fashion—if A plus B always equaled C in my head. But I'm easily distracted, and I know I burn too much mental energy on stray thoughts. But I can't help myself. In this case, I was wondering if Wilson might have killed Tina Del Rio for unknown reasons. The answer was that he certainly could have if he were still alive at the time of her death. And there was at least one reason to consider that possibility: His prints were on the murder weapon. The extraneous thought related to that was this: Did we know for sure that Wilson was really dead?

Wilson worked in Naval Intelligence. And while Silver said he was a file clerk, who knew if that were true? If he were a spook, wouldn't he lie about that? What if this were all some elaborate plot to hide his real status? What if the stiff in the Monroe County Morgue had been a throw-down corpse and the feds were in on it, kind of like a witness-protection program for spies?

And what if the lunar landing had been faked? What if the Earth were flat? What if there really were ghosts and werewolves? What if, what if, what if. I knew I was being ridiculous. The far more likely answer was that whoever killed Wilson stole his gear and used his speargun to ice Tina Del Rio. Why? Who knows? Maybe so the police would be sidetracked. And like Abby Kitchner said, the possibility that the corpse wasn't Wilson was so remote that it didn't bother her.

But it wouldn't take much to put this worry of mine to rest: Go to the morgue, look at the picture, and then that would be that. A more rational person wouldn't waste his time, but I knew myself well enough that if I didn't settle this nagging detail it would pester me to no end.

So, I called Lester back.

"Can you put Silver back on?"

"She's not happy with you right now."

"She can take a number."

In a moment, she was on the line. "What?"

"Give me five minutes, let me explain myself, and if you still think I'm an asshole, we'll drop it. But this is straight out of your playbook."

"Meaning what?"

"Meaning, I suppose, that hanging around you has made me nervous about conspiracies." I walked her through my thinking, admitting that I was prone to chasing shiny objects and losing focus, but there was a simple way to lay this idea to rest. "So, what do you say?" I finally asked.

"I say you're still an asshole," she said, "but, yeah, I'll come by and pick you up and we can drive up to Marathon. But on one condition."

"What's that?"

"If I have to pay for parking after moving my truck, it's on you."

I agreed and asked her to give the phone back to Lester.

"Lester, do you recall seeing a yellow sticky note on the door to Tina Del Rio's office when you and Harrison Paine finally got there?"

"No, but it was pretty chaotic."

It was a circus, no doubt, but I also knew that very few details escaped Lester's attention at crime scenes. He might dress like a model from *GQ For Dorks*, and his Cajun drawl could lull people into underestimating him, but he was one of the smartest people I knew. It was not for nothing he'd achieved the rank of major in Army intelligence. I told him how Kitchner didn't recall the note.

"You say you found it on the floor by her door?" he asked.

"Yeah, I picked it up and stuck it back on."

"Could have fallen off again. Somebody might have stepped on it in all the confusion, walked off with it stuck to their shoe. Is it important?"

"No way of knowing," I said. "But I did wonder who put it there. There was a pad of yellow sticky notes on Tina Del Rio's desk next to a blue pen, which matched the ink on the note. I guess I was curious if she'd put the note on her door, not wanting to be disturbed while she was working in her office, or whether her killer did it, maybe thinking it would buy a little extra time before her body was discovered."

"Good is your thinking, Padawan. They got prints on the pen?"

"Kitchner said she'd call back."

"And if they find prints…"

"Three options. If Tina Del Rio's are the only prints, we can assume it was her note, which doesn't tell us anything useful. If the pen was wiped free of fingerprints, we can assume the killer put the note on the door, but it doesn't tell us anything about who he is. But if it's Wilson's prints…"

"It would be something, wouldn't it."

CHAPTER 19

Marathon

"WE'RE TALKIN' A SPECIAL kinda stupid there."

Lester was summing up our meeting at the Monroe County Medical Examiner's Office. Silver was behind the wheel of her black Ford F150 Super Cab heading east on the Overseas Highway. Lester was riding shotgun. I was zoning out in the back seat scrolling through the news stream on my iPhone trying not to think about how confined I was feeling.

- A high school assistant principal and a math teacher were wounded in a shootout in Jacksonville when they drew down on a student in a hallway carrying a cardboard cutout of an AR-15 assault rifle. Both men unholstered their weapons at either end of the hall and, according to witnesses, screamed at the student, who, showing vastly more intelligence than the adults, threw himself to the floor. The teacher and administrator began firing at the student, missing him, and shooting one another. Both were evacuated by helicopter to a local hospital where their injuries were said to be non-life-threatening.
- In Washington, D.C. a bill to criminalize the use of morning-after pills hit a snag when it was revealed by *Vanity Fair* that the author of the legislation, Rep. Percy Edwards of Fayetteville,

Arkansas, persuaded a legislative assistant on his staff to seek an abortion while they were having an affair.
- And in science news, more than one thousand astronomers signed a petition pleading with the billionaire inventor of Stealth Car Wax to stop sending radio signals to outer space in the hopes of contacting an alien civilization. "If they are out there, we need to hide, not put a bullseye on our planet," the petition said.

That billionaire, Dr. Omar Franken of Phoenix, was also the inventor of the Doggie Translator Fred was wearing. Reading that reminded me that I owed him an update on how the device was working. And I needed to ask him how to turn the damn thing off.

"Are you listening to Lester?" Silver asked me, interrupting my reverie.

"Um, sure. What was that again?"

"I was saying," Lester said, "that while I am not ordinarily inclined to conspiracy theories, this stupidity is tailor-made to arouse what we in the detection bidness call suspicions."

It should have been simple. Marathon is about an hour from Key West. Our plan was to check in at the morgue, confirm that the photograph of the corpse identified as Donald Wilson was indeed him, then grab some lunch at Herbie's Bar & Chowder House to sustain us for the return trip.

Remember that computer problem Silver ran into when she first arrived at the Medical Examiner's Office? The one that wouldn't let her discover where the two bodies shipped out of the morgue were destined? It still wasn't fixed.

The ME, himself, wasn't on site when we arrived, but the woman Silver talked to earlier, the one who showed her the video of the hearses leaving the day before—including the hearse from the Molton-Balsamo Funeral Home carrying the body misidentified as Donny Westhaven—she was there. She was a plump woman, with dull, dark brown hair curled into a bun, standing about five-feet-six and wearing a lab smock. Her name badge said "Samantha."

She shook her head when we made our request.

"Still on the fritz," she said.

"You're saying the computer holds all the photos of the cadavers and there is no other record of their images?"

She rubbed her chin and thought about that for a few seconds. "Probably on the memory card in the camera, I guess."

"Where's that?" I asked, giving her my best can-I-buy-you-a-drink smile.

"The camera?"

Must not grind teeth.

"Why, yes."

"Oh, good idea." She walked through a door leading to the storage area and returned in less than a minute carrying a Canon 5D Mark III, which was a bit of overkill in terms of camera horsepower for what they used it for, but that was between them and the taxpayers of Monroe County.

"Hmmm. She bit her lip and maneuvered the camera, looking at the bottom, then the top, then straight at the lens. "Not sure where it is."

"Let me help," I said, taking the camera from her. I opened the door on the side of the camera body that holds the dual memory cards. Closed it and handed it back to her.

"What?" Silver asked.

"The cards are missing."

"Well, fuck," Silver and Lester said simultaneously.

"What about backup?" I asked Samantha. "You guys have a cloud account or an external hard drive? You hooked up with the county's main computer system in Key West? These are public records, right?"

She looked at me blankly, as if I had just spoken to her in Mandarin.

"So what is the issue with your computer?" Lester asked.

That was a question she could answer. "Hacked."

"Someone hacked your computers?" Lester asked.

"That's what I said."

He smiled at her. "I guess you did, didn't you? But when you say hacked, did someone steal the data, screw up the system with malware or a virus, what was it?"

Mandarin again.

"Where exactly is this computer?" I asked.

"Oh, Nicky has it."

"What's a Nicky?" Silver asked.

"Nicky's Computer Repair and Softwear. Soft W-E-A-R. Get it?"

"No." That was all three of us simultaneously.

"Nicky's store's down the street." She pointed in an easterly direction up the Overseas Highway.

"Could you call Nicky and let him know we're coming to talk to him?" I asked.

She shook her head. "I know for a fact he's not at work today."

"How come?" Lester asked.

"Cause he got a little too drunk last night at his sister's wedding. It was her third. Wedding, that is. He was still sound asleep when I came to work this morning."

The three of us glanced at one another.

"Nicky lives with you?" I asked.

"Not regular. But he spent the night."

"Well, do you think we could talk to him at your place?"

She bobbed her head up and down, apparently happy to finally be helpful. She rattled off her address, I wrote it in my notebook. Samantha lived in a double-wide in something called the Mid-Keys Mobile Home Estates on Grassy Key, about ten minutes up the road.

CHAPTER 20

Grassy Key

THE ENTRANCE TO the mobile home park was surprisingly upscale and colorful comprising a wall of freshly painted white brick flanked by flowering red hibiscus and a tasteful sign in cornflower blue. It was downhill from there. After thirty feet, the blacktop drive morphed to dusty white crushed shell and dead-ended at a cross street. An upholstered maroon sofa rested in the weed-covered front yard of the single-wide facing us. A pot-bellied guy, shirtless, shoeless, and wearing a faded Texas A&M ball cap, was sitting on the couch trimming his toenails with a jackknife.

"I told you," Lester said to Silver. "Stick with me and I'll take you to the ends of the earth."

Silver braked the truck and rolled down her window. "Hey," she said to the toe-trimmer. "We're looking for someone at..." I reached over the front seat and showed her the lot number written in my notebook. "...lot number 32."

Nail trimming seemed to require intense concentration, and it took a few moments for Silver's question to trickle its way from the guy's ears to his auditory cortex. "What's that?" he asked in a high-pitched voice with an accent that screamed Deep College Station.

"Lot 32," Silver repeated.

"You be lookin' for Samantha. She ain't there. She be down in Marathon at the morgue."

"Yes, we know that," Silver said, showing uncharacteristic patience. "We left there a little while ago. She has a friend staying at her place that we've come to see."

"Ha! I'll bet she does." He resumed his focus on the big toe of his left foot.

"Sir, could you point us in the right direction?" Silver asked. Her voice now held a little edge.

Without looking up, the Aggie pointed his jackknife over his left shoulder and Silver wheeled the truck in that direction. Turns out, Mid-Keys Lane was a circle with trailers flanking it on either side of the street. Number 32 stood out both because it was one of the few double-wides and for its impressive collection of pink plastic yard flamingos crowding the flower bed.

"Will you look at that," Lester marveled. "This should be in the *Guinness Book of Records*. How many do you count?"

I took a brief gander. "At least forty, maybe fifty," I said.

"Take a picture."

As we stepped out of the truck, I dug into my backpack and retrieved my camera. I popped off the lens cap and shot a wide-angle of the birds.

"What a flock," Lester said.

"It's a flamboyance," I said.

Lester looked at me as if I'd been speaking in Mandarin again. "A flamboyance of flamingos," I said. "Not a flock. You know, like a pod of dolphins or a bale of turtles."

Silver was giving us the evil eye. "Or a truckload of dorks."

We walked over to the front door and I rapped on it. We waited a polite few seconds, then tried again, this time pounding with enough force that it rattled the door inside its cheap aluminum frame. Nothing. I signaled Lester to check out the right side of the trailer and I walked around to the left. I hammered the side of the mobile home a few times hoping to rouse Nicky from his slumber if he were still passed out. I could hear Lester shouting his name from the other side.

The racket attracted the attention of the next door neighbor, a middle-aged woman in a blue polka dot dress who stepped outside, shaded her eyes, and asked, "Y'all looking for somebody?"

I walked over to her. "Yes ma'am, we're acquaintances of Samantha and she said a friend spent the night here and we would like to talk to him."

"She sent you over here?" the woman asked.

"Yes ma'am."

"Well, that's funny."

I gave her a 200-watt smile, hoping the sunlight reflecting off my teeth wouldn't blind her, and said, "How's that?"

"Cause Nicky left here about a five minutes ago," she said.

I took my ball cap off, rubbed my forehead as if that idea were truly puzzling, and said, "That *is* funny, because Samantha told us she brought him home from a party last night. So, how'd he leave?"

"Big black SUV." She turned to re-enter her single-wide.

"Looks like you keep a good eye on things around here," I said. "You happen to notice who was in that car?"

She smiled at me revealing teeth that only a lifetime of smoking could render so yellow. "I do watch out for things around here," she said. "So what's your interest in Nicky? You feds, too?"

"Are you saying the SUV that picked up Nicky had U.S. Government plates?" I asked.

"No flies on you." She took a moment to eyeball me, from deck shoes to Cincinnati Reds ball cap. "You sure are a tall feller. What are you, like seven feet?"

"No, ma'am, not nearly that tall. Only a few inches over six feet. And to answer your question, no, we're not feds. That lady over there..." I nodded toward Silver who lingered at Samantha's front door. "...she lost her brother in a drowning accident. And the medical examiner's office took his picture, but their computer is down. Samantha told us

Nicky was trying to fix their computer. That's why we came to talk to him. We were hoping maybe he recovered the photo."

I shared more information than I might in ordinary circumstances, but I've learned that if you confide in people, often they feel obliged to return the favor. This was one of those times.

"Those feds, two guys in dark suits—who the hell wears suits in this climate, anyway?—they pounded on Samantha's door until Nicky stumbled outside. I saw them from my kitchen." She gestured to a small window facing Samantha's double-wide. "Nicky, he wasn't too happy, I could tell."

"How so?" I asked, just to keep her going.

"I could tell because he was yelling at the suits, and when I went outside and asked what the fuss was all about, one of the feds ordered me to go back inside and shut the door."

Now she was shaking her head. "I hope little Nicky is okay."

"Little Nicky? You guys are more than neighbors, from the sound of it, that right?"

She bobbed her head. "He's my brother."

"Your brother? Samantha told us that she was at Nicky's sister's wedding. Was that you? If so, congratulations."

"Nah. I wish. I'm destined to be a poor old maid living in a trailer, I'm afraid. It was my other sister, Camilla."

Her self-deprecation touched me. If a rich uncle hadn't rescued me after my mother died, I might be doing well to have a double-wide on a crushed-shell road. Not that the *Miss Demeanor* was a luxury liner.

"What, are you kidding?' I said. "Why, you can't even be forty yet. Old maid? Come on."

She smiled again at that. "Oh, go on, you."

I walked up to her and handed her one of my cards. "What's your name?" I asked.

She glanced down at my card then looked back up at me. "Camilla."

"Camilla? I thought you said your sister's name was Camilla."

She nodded. "Mom and Dad had three girls and a boy. All of us girls are named Camilla. That way if daddy needed anything, like somebody to bring him an ice-cold, he could yell Camilla and one of us would come a runnin'."

"That's either very clever or very weird," I said without thinking.

"Go for weird," she said. "You wouldn't believe the shit we put up with when we were kids."

I nodded. "I can imagine. I know a little something about strange names. Camilla, it's very important that we talk to Nicky. If you hear from him would you give me a call?"

She nodded.

I tipped my hat to her and met Silver and Lester at the truck.

"Looks like while we were having lunch, somebody got here ahead of us," I said. "The feds."

"How'd they know to come here?" Silver asked.

"They must have been right behind us," Lester said. "Probably stopped at the morgue like we did and discovered the computer problem, too."

"I told you we didn't have time to eat," I said.

"No, you didn't."

Silver pulled out her bandana and wiped her forehead. "Would you guys knock it off?"

I asked Lester, "Do you know if the FBI…"

"I'm looking it up now," he said, scrolling through his mobile phone. "The FBI's nearest field office is in Miami, of course, but they may have some space in the federal building in Key West. At least that's what Google says. That our next stop?"

"I'm open to suggestions."

"Where's the federal building?" Silver asked.

"On Simonton Street, not far from that place we ate breakfast," Lester said.

"So it's near Duval Street, then."

Lester nodded.

"And by the time we get back to Key West it'll be closing in on cocktail hour."

I looked at Silver. "Since when did you need an appointed hour to start drinking?"

"Good point. I'm thirsty. Let's roll."

CHAPTER 21

Marathon

It was only ten minutes from Grassy Key back to Marathon, and we were nearly there on our return trip to Key West when it dawned on me that we'd be driving right past Nicky's Computer Repair and Softwear.

"We need to stop here," I said to my compatriots in the front seat of the truck.

"Can't you hold it?" Silver asked.

"It's not my bladder. We should check out Nicky's computer store while we're here." I flipped open my notebook and read the address out loud. In a few minutes we pulled into a space in front of his store. A black SUV with federal government plates was already parked there.

"This should be interesting," Lester said.

We piled out of the truck and walked to the door. The shop was one of six storefronts in a small strip center facing the highway. To the left was a waxing salon called Bushwackers. To the right, a little Greek deli named Pita Pan. Several vintage computers and a rack of men's hoodies filled the window of Nicky's place. A sign under the clothes read "Duds for Nerds." If we solved no other mystery, we at least now knew why Nicky used the term "softwear" in his business name.

A CLOSED sign hung on the inside of the glass door, but Silver tried it anyway. To our surprise, she was able to pull it open, so we marched in. The front of the shop was a mishmash of computer gear and clothing displays. A door behind the sales counter led to another room and we could hear voices back there.

"Let's do this," I said. We barged in, surprising two guys in dark suits and a smallish middle-aged man with long greasy hair hunched over a workbench where he was inspecting a desktop computer. The nearest suit turned and scowled at us. "You're not supposed to be back here."

"Says who?" I asked.

The first suit was average height, slim, and Hispanic. He wore horned rim glasses, giving him an intellectual look. His partner was a white guy, a bit taller and heavier with one of those dark beards that shadowed his face even when clean shaven. Second suit joined his pal, forming a phalanx between us and Nicky. Neither responded to my question.

"How you doing, Nicky?" I said, ignoring them. "Samantha sent us over to talk to you. We need a picture." I took a step in his direction and Suit No. 2 held out his hand and pushed at my chest.

"Lester, better call 911," I said. "I've been assaulted."

Lester went along with the gag and reached for his phone. As he raised his Hawaiian shirt, he exposed a .38 holstered on his hip, which surprised me. The suits, too.

"Gun," Suit No. 1 shouted. Suit No. 2 whipped out a pistol and leveled it at Lester.

Nicky stopped typing on his keyboard. Silver let out a small gasp. The suits stood frozen for a moment. So did Lester and I.

"I have a carry permit," Lester said in an even voice. "I'm a licensed private eye with Third Eye Investigators. My permit and my license are in my wallet. Would you like me to show you?"

Suit No. 1 sidestepped me and fetched the pistol off Lester's waist. The suit ordered me to move aside to avoid blocking his partner's aim, then patted Lester down. He turned to me. I raised my arms, let him do his thing, then he waved Silver over.

"You lay one hand on me, motherfucker, and I will cut your balls off," she said.

Undaunted, the suit motioned for her purse. "Lemme see that."

Silver handed it to him and the guy poked through her handbag, which took a while since it was the approximate size of Toledo.

"Again, who are you guys?" I asked. Seemed like I should say something.

Suit No. 2 holstered his piece and they both pulled out wallets with IDs that said FBI. "I'm Special Agent Forester," said the white guy. "This is Special Agent Del Rio."

"Del Rio?" I asked. Suit No. 1's jaw clenched and his shoulders stiffened. "Oh, don't tell me."

Both agents glanced at each other. Being the keen observer of human nature that I am, I detected a certain nervousness. Maybe it was when Forester whispered "fuck" under his breath. He glanced again at Del Rio, who seemed riveted in place as if he'd been shot by a freeze ray.

I played a hunch. It was out of left field, but over the years I've learned the worst that happens when I guess wrong is that I get laughed at. I'm tough enough for that.

"You guys," I said. "You're not on the clock, are you?"

"Goddammit." It was Forester. He wasn't whispering now.

Lester took out his ID and handed it to Del Rio, which gave the agent something to do besides standing paralyzed. He looked Lester over, matching his face with his photo ID. "I've heard of you," he said. "You were involved in that Chitango deal."

"That's right," Lester said as Del Rio returned his revolver to him. "So was he."

I handed Del Rio and Forester my business cards. "This is Silver McFadden," I said, nodding in her direction. "We're investigating the death of her brother, Donald Wilson, and his friend, Tina Del Rio. Am I right that your last name is no coincidence?"

Forester spoke up. "Okay, that's correct. We are off the clock.

Hector, he couldn't sit around in Miami with his dick in his hand. He's taken a few days off. Me, too. We want to figure out what's up with all this."

"You checked in with the local cops?" I asked, deciding it wouldn't be a bad thing to make nice.

"I talked to Abby Kitchner," Del Rio said, his voice a little tight. "Over at the SO. She called."

"She know you're here?"

"Not yet."

I nodded. "There's also a cop over at the Key West PD you might want to touch bases with." I dug through my wallet and handed Harrison Paine's card to Del Rio. I'd already entered his info into my phone's contacts.

"Was she your sister?" I asked.

He nodded.

"I'm very sorry." Lester and Silver echoed the sentiments. "Silver and I were the ones who discovered her body. We came to see her, hoping she could help clear up some questions regarding the death of Silver's brother."

"I'm going to lock the front door," Lester said. "Meanwhile, why don't we all sit and talk a spell instead of pointing guns at each other."

"What do you think, Nicky?" I asked. "That sound like a plan?" I figured it would be bad manners to exclude him from the conversation.

He resumed clicking on his keyboard. "Anybody got an aspirin?"

CHAPTER 22

IT DIDN'T TAKE Nicky long to figure out the problem with the morgue's computer.

"See this," he said, pointing to the innards of the Dell desktop. He'd removed the black, metal cover and the inside of the box was filled with cobwebs, dust, and dirt. "This hasn't been cleaned in years."

"Not good?" Lester asked.

Nicky gave him a disgusted look. "Not good at all. It's fatal. All this dirt traps heat, causes the power supply to fry, can blow out the motherboard."

"What about the hard drive?" I asked.

"We're about to find out. I've pulled it and I'm going to hook it up." He fiddled with the silver drive case, ran wires to another desktop on his bench, and in a few minutes the contents of the hard drive were displayed on one of his monitors.

"So, it's intact," I said.

"Yep," Nicky said. "I'm going to blow out the box, replace the power supply, and hope the motherboard is okay. If so, I'll have this ready to return to the morgue shortly."

"Before you do that," Agent Del Rio said, "there's a photograph we need to see on that hard drive. Let's pull it up."

"You got a warrant?" Nicky asked. "This is county property."

Agent Forester put a meaty paw on Nicky's shoulder. "This is an FBI matter. You know it's a federal crime to disobey a lawful order from a federal agent."

Nicky spun around in his swivel chair. "Fuck you, man. You roust me out of my house, you drag me here against my will, and you ain't even officially working. How about I call the Sheriff's Office, ask them what they think of all this?"

I cleared my throat. "You're right Nicky. They don't have a warrant. But we can have a sheriff's detective here in a couple of hours with one, if you insist, but you'll be stuck here while we wait and we'll get what we want, anyway. It's a public record. We don't need a warrant for that. The county is legally required to share it. Samantha would have already shown it to us if the computer hadn't crashed. So why don't you be a sport, let us take a look, then I'm sure these FBI agents will be happy to take you home, maybe stop and get you some Advil on the way."

He fussed a bit more, but finally acquiesced. We waited anxiously while he sifted through the hard drive and finally located the folder holding the files of each of the cadavers processed at the morgue. I found myself holding my breath as he clicked on the file containing the name Donald Wilson in the heading.

Wilson's photograph was on the first page of the report. Silver gasped when she saw it. Drowning victims several days dead are not pretty. The face in the photograph was bloated, the tongue was black and protruded through his open mouth, and his skin was greenish-bronze. He looked like a space alien. I didn't see how anyone would be able to identify him.

Silver lurched to a nearby trash can and retched. I felt my own stomach churning, too. Didn't seem to bother anyone else. You can get used to anything, I suppose.

When Silver recovered, Lester put his arms around her shoulders and gently walked her back toward the computer screen. "Can you manage?" he asked her.

She swirled away and ran from the room. Lester followed her into the front of the store. In a few moments, I heard the outer door open. I peeked out through the storefront window and could see Lester holding Silver in the parking lot.

"I assume that's a yes," Del Rio said.

I shrugged. "We'll see."

"Assuming it is," Del Rio said, "and this is, in fact, a photo of the late-great Donald Wilson, what does that tell us?"

"Looks to me we were both trying to answer the same question. Am I right?"

Del Rio nodded. "Whether Donald Wilson, if he was my sister's murderer, is still on the prowl."

"Being dead doesn't mean he didn't do it," Forester, said.

"That may be true," I said, "but as we stand here, we have no idea what the motive would have been. Unless you guys know something we don't."

I looked at the FBI agents and they both shook their heads.

"And we still don't know whether Wilson's death was an accident or a homicide," I said.

"Possibilities," Del Rio said. He held up his hand and started ticking them off with his fingers. "One, Donald Wilson's prints on the murder weapon are conclusive and he killed Tina. Then he either took his own life—a murder, suicide—or he accidentally drowned, or he, himself, was murdered."

"Lots of variables there," I said.

He nodded and kept ticking off the possibilities. "Or, both my sister and Donald Wilson were murdered by some person or persons unknown for reasons unknown. Or, three, the timing of their deaths could be coincidental."

He looked up and saw me staring at him. "Okay, none of us believes in coincidences."

While we thought about that, Nicky finished replacing the power supply on the PC and fired it up. "The simplest answer is usually the right answer," he said.

At first, I thought he was joining our conversation, then I realized he'd gotten the computer working again.

"It was the power supply," he said. "Soon as I reinstall the hard drive, it will be good as new. Then you guys can take me home like your promised, right?"

Forester was staring at him and nodding his head. "Yeah."

"Yeah, you'll give me a ride home?"

"Yeah, the simplest answer is usually the best answer."

"Let me make a quick call," I said. "I might be able to help with that."

I pulled out my cell phone and punched Abby Kitchner's number. She answered on the second ring.

"Detective Kitchner," I said. "Alexander Strange here."

"I was wondering who was calling," she said. "You block Caller ID on all your calls?"

"Yes. Quick question. You find prints on that pen on Tina Del Rio's desk?"

"What's in it for me?" she asked.

"How about a positive ID on a photograph of a prematurely cremated corpse."

"By whom?"

"By Silver McFadden."

"What'd she say?"

"About those prints."

"Fine. Yeah, the pen looks like it was wiped clean. No prints."

"Thank you, detective. That helps a lot. I'm here with Tina Del Rio's brother."

"Where's here."

"Marathon."

I turned to Del Rio and Forester. "You guys heading down to Key West now?" Del Rio nodded. I told Kitchner.

"Put him on the phone," she said.

While they were talking, Lester returned and signaled me to come out to the front of the store to talk.

"How's she doing?" I asked.

"Not good. She's wishing she never came here. Seeing that picture. Says she'll be haunted the rest of her life."

I felt myself blushing. "You think I fucked up." It was a statement not a question.

He shook his head. "No. Not at all. It was necessary. But that doesn't make it any easier."

"She's sure it was Wilson?"

"Yeah. No doubt."

"How could she…"

"His left ear. Small golden earring. She gave it to him when he turned eighteen. Told him all pirates wore earrings. He was heavy into *Pirates of the Caribbean*."

Del Rio walked out and handed the phone to me. "We're heading down to Key West. Going to meet with Detective Kitchner."

Kitchner was still on the line. "You never answered my question. She ID him? It's Donald Wilson, right."

"I'm afraid so. You were right."

Nicky joined us outside carrying the repaired desktop computer.

"We'll take you down to the morgue to drop it off," Forester said. Nicky set the computer on the sidewalk in front of the store, reached into his jeans for keys, and locked up his shop.

I recapped for everyone what Kitchner told me.

"So," Del Rio summarized, "we can, for now anyway, assume that Donald Wilson was not the killer."

"I never did assume that," Silver said. There was no anger in her voice. She sounded dull, exhausted.

"Of course not," I said. "But it was important to consider all the possibilities. Were Donald Wilson the killer, he wouldn't have bothered to wipe the pen but still leave his prints on the spear and speargun."

"Odds are," Lester said, "it was designed to make us think he was the killer, send us in the wrong direction."

"Worked for a few hours," I said.

"It's gotta be like this," Forester said. "Donald Wilson was the first victim. That's how the killer got his speargun. Then he went after Hector's sister. We don't know why. If we can figure that out, we'll be on our way to finding our killer."

I turned to Del Rio. "Your sister. She talk to you about her relationship with Wilson?"

"Yeah." He took a couple of breaths before continuing. "Yeah, she was pretty much in love with him."

"You pick up anything from her that would cause you to believe there were problems between the two of them?"

"No."

"She say anything about his work?"

He started to answer, but Forester gave him a look. "It's been great talking to you Strange. But we've got to get a move on."

"What's the problem?" I asked.

"No problem. But our job is to ask the questions, not answer them."

Nicky was leaning against the black SUV and holding the desktop computer in his arms. "Come on guys, this thing's heavy." He pushed away from the car and walked around to the back, waiting for one of the FBI agents to pop the hatchback.

The sound of approaching laughter and scratching of polyurethane wheels on asphalt caused all of us to turn our heads. Five kids on skateboards were zooming through the parking lot doing tricks. The lead skater executed a cool kick flip and the others followed in suit. Some kind of skaters' follow-the-leader game. Then the kid up front attempted a heel flip, but messed it up and he sprawled onto the parking lot and the skateboard went flying.

Right into Nicky's face.

He stumbled backwards, blood spurting from his nose, and the computer tumbled from his arms and crashed on the pavement. The metal casing flew off and internal pieces of the computer scattered across the parking lot.

The lead skater jumped to his feet, yelled "sorry," grabbed his board, and hauled ass out of parking lot followed by his posse.

Nicky sat down in a heap holding his bleeding nose. "I need that fucking aspirin."

CHAPTER 23

Key West

"So, THE FEDS finally figured out they shouldn't be talking to a reporter and clamed up." It was my boss, Edwina Mahoney, and I was giving her a status update over the phone.

"Yeah. They were off their game for a little bit when we called them out for operating off the clock. Stupid me, I thought, okay, I've discovered feds who are real people, we can work together. I guess I'll never learn."

"We can arrange group therapy for you if you think that will help. Cynics Anonymous. Get you back in shape in no time."

"My name is Alexander Strange and I am naive."

"Admitting you have a problem is the first step to recovery."

Silver insisted she was able to drive us back to Key West, and for once, given her emotional state, I was happy to be crammed in the back seat where it was safer. She dropped me off at the marina, then she and Lester drove back to her B&B. No idea if she found a free parking space.

I took Fred for a walk and decided to rest on a bench in Bayview Park to collect my thoughts, figure out what my next moves should be. I looked around and didn't see anyone shadowing me, which was a relief. Must have simply been a case of nerves the last time I was here.

On the one hand, I got it that Del Rio and Forester decided enough was enough, talking with a reporter. They were cops with a murder to solve. And it was personal. What would I have to offer that could be of any possible help to them?

On the other hand, despite all the stereotypes in movies and novels about antagonistic relationships between police and reporters, I'd worked with a number of cops over the years. The key to those relationships always boiled down to one factor: I needed to be useful to them for them to work with me. An equitable exchange. Abby Kitchner being the most recent example.

Yeah, Kitchner. Fuck the feds. I'd work with Abby.

So, what could I do to be useful? And what did I want, anyway?

I could sit down right now and write a story about an ongoing murder investigation, two mysterious deaths, Wilson's sharks-eating-phone-lines stuff. It would be a good story. But it would be a story in progress, not a story with an ending. Act I. Maybe part of Act II. No Act III. That's what beat reporters do, write every day, incrementally advancing stories as they develop. It's important work, but not my thing. To me, there would be no story until I knew the answer to why all this happened.

But there was more to it than that. This wasn't just a story, another *Strange Files* entry, the primary purpose of which was to entertain our readers. Two people were murdered, after all. And the circumstances surrounding their deaths were mysterious. Who wanted them dead and why? What was motivating all this? Maybe hanging around Silver and her obsession with conspiracies had rubbed off on me a little, but this seemed more sinister than the usual stuff of police blotters.

Which is why I called Edwina. "I gotta figure out what to do now," I said. "Need to stay on top of this."

"So what are your options?" she asked.

"What the cops will be doing is talking to everyone who knew Tina Del Rio and Donald Wilson. The sixty-four-billion-dollar question is, of course: who would want them dead and why?"

Edwina didn't respond, which was typical. She's a great listener. In her day she was an amazing reporter. I knew she was waiting for me to work it out.

"Let's assume Wilson discovered something. Something that someone else did not want disclosed, wanted it kept secret badly enough to kill him. It might follow that the killer figured he needed to snuff Tina, too. That she might know what Wilson knew. Pillow talk and all."

"Go on."

"If Wilson found something, it would be out in the Gulf where he was diving."

"And you've got your boat," Edwina said.

"Yes. And I know Tina Del Rio's colleague, Akari Takahashi. She's the one who showed us Wilson's lab. Maybe she can help me figure out where he was diving."

"And then you'll go there. Dive and see what there is to see."

"And try not to get killed doing it."

Edwina was quiet for a bit, then she said, "You better tell Gwenn what you're thinking about doing. Remember, Alexander, this is only a story. No story is worth dying for."

"I'll take that under advisement."

My phone vibrated. It was an incoming call from a number I didn't recognize, so I ignored it.

"Also, Alexander, not to nag…"

"I owe you a column."

"Yes."

"And maybe I should file a few more in advance, just in case. Pull some items from my stack of evergreen stories I've already worked up."

"That would be nice."

"In the unfortunate event that I buy the farm."

"It would be helpful. Might take a day or two to hire your replacement. Paperwork, drug testing, it all takes time."

"Someone's been attending *her* Cynics Anonymous meetings, I see." That Edwina. Tough on the outside, cast iron in the middle.

I walked back to the *Miss Demeanor*, filled Fred's water bowl and gave him a treat. Then I fetched my laptop.

Ideas for my columns flow from various streams. Readers email me tips, often from stories they've read in their local newspapers. Those are the easiest columns to write because a reporter somewhere has already pieced together the basic facts. A phone call or two to confirm the information, to get fresh quotes and updated info, and I'm good to go. Many news services, such as the Associated Press, have their own "oddities" feeds, which can sometimes be useful as starting points for columns. But they also are competitors in the weird news space, as it might be called, so staying ahead of the competition has become a bit more challenging. My best ideas—where I get my original material—come from sources in government, academia, and law enforcement. The vamps in the Army of the Strange were a continuous source of tips, too.

I was scrolling through my email to see what my tipsters might have passed along when I came across a note from a dispatcher at the Hillsborough County Sheriff's Office. Dispatchers are the front line of law enforcement. When the 911 calls come in, they're the first to hear. I've invested time calling and keeping up with police and sheriff's dispatchers in big cities throughout south Florida, sending birthday greetings and including them on my mailing list of people who get first looks at my latest columns.

This tip exposed, you will forgive the expression, a weird slice of life:

THE STRANGE FILES

Don’t Ax Me That Again

By Alexander Strange

Tropic Press

APOLLO BEACH, Fla.—The sport of ax throwing is gaining popularity throughout America, pushed largely by taverns themed around the activity, such as TommyHawk’s here.

While most such establishments serve only beer and wine, the proprietor of this bar, Thomas Brunswick, secured a license that allowed him to sell hard liquor, as well. Then he sponsored his inaugural Toss an Ax, Toss Down a Shot night at his grand opening.

“Alcohol and sharp objects, the perfect combination for guys,” he told a television news crew on hand for the bar’s inaugural tournament. “And I should know, I’m an axpert.”

For the uninitiated, ax throwing is similar to darts. There’s a target. Score is kept. But instead of darts, large stainless steel cleavers are hurled at the targets. It began as a pastime for Canadian loggers.

At the Friday night opening, all was going well. There were only a few experienced ax hurlers among the competitors, but Brunswick offered helpful throwing tips. About two hours into it, the ax of one contestant missed the target and flew into the crowd of onlookers.

A man police identified as Horace Bixby, 27, of Riverside, Fla. ridiculed the thrower, Bobby James Simpson, 24, of Tampa. “What are you, a girl?” Bixby was reported to have shouted.

“Oh, yeah?” Simpson yelled. “Well, how’s this.” With that he hurled an ax at Bixby, missing the man, but smashing into a row of liquor bottles behind the bar.

Customers sitting at the bar were sprayed with flying shards of glass, became angry, and a fight broke out, police said. Three people were hospitalized with serious cuts. Bixby was arrested and held on charges of assault with a deadly weapon. Health officials have closed the bar pending a review.

STRANGE FACT: The handle of an ax is called a haft and traditionally is made of hickory, although wood of the Groot may be substituted.

Weirdness knows no boundaries. Keep up at *www.TheStrangeFiles.com*. Contact Alexander Strange at Alex@TheStrangeFiles.com.

CHAPTER 24

I'D JUST FILED my column when the phone rang. I was sitting on the poop deck and it was dark outside. The clock on the phone showed it was 11:04 p.m. and the Caller ID said it was from Gwenn's office phone.

"Burning the midnight oil," I see.

"I got a call a second ago," she said, her voice tense. "I'm still at the office, so I guess that's how he knew to find me."

"You don't sound good," I said.

"It was a man, I'm pretty sure, but his voice was mechanical sounding, robotic, like it was filtered through one of those voice-changer apps. He said he'd been watching you. He wanted me to deliver a message. He said get out of Key West. Or else."

"Or else? He really said that?"

"Yeah. Just like a line out of a bad movie."

"I wonder how he found you?"

"I don't know, but I'm a little freaked out. I locked the door to my office. I'm afraid to go down to my car, to drive home. What should I do?"

"Dial 911. Stay on this line and call from your cell phone."

"You think I should?"

"Yes. That's what it's for."

I heard her on the other line talking to the 911 dispatcher. She told her about the phone call. Could somebody come by, escort her home? After a few minutes, she got back on the line to me.

"They're sending a cruiser by. The dispatcher, she said she knew you, that they'd take care of me."

"Good."

"She told me to stay on the line with my cell phone until the deputy arrives."

My cell phone began beeping, signaling I had another incoming call. "Hang on a second, Gwenn. I need to take this call." It was a retired Collier County sheriff's detective named Jim Henderson, a friend.

"Hey, Jim," I said. "This can't be a coincidence."

"I'm rolling," he said. "Got a call from Angela in dispatch. She filled me in."

"Gwenn said they're sending a cruiser."

"Yes. I'm coming, too. I'll make sure she gets home okay. Somebody will watch her place tonight. I've already called the sheriff. He's called Naples PD, it's their jurisdiction."

Like I said before, not all my relationships with cops were in the toilet. Henderson took a bullet coming to my rescue when a couple of Russian thugs tried to gun me down in a Naples parking lot a few months earlier. I already owed him. Now even more so.

"Thanks," I said. "I'll get back there as soon as I can."

"Where are you, anyway?" he asked.

"Key West."

"You've done it again, haven't you. Stirred up another hornet's nest."

"So it would appear."

"You should have kept that piece." Henderson loaned me one of his pistols after the incident with the Russians, but I'd never used it and gave it back to him.

"I'd probably just hurt myself," I said.

"That Third Eye operator, Rivers, he there by any chance?"

"Yes, he is."

"Good. Call him. I checked his file through a buddy of mine in the Pentagon. He may be the best one-legged shot ever to come out of the army."

I switched back to Gwenn. "The cops there yet?"

"Yes. I see the cruiser outside. Now there's another car pulling up."

"Probably Jim Henderson. That's who called me."

"Oh, good. I'm going down. I'll have to hang up the office phone until I get there, need to stay on the cell phone with the dispatcher. I'll call you when I get to the car."

It was the longest two minutes that I could ever recall experiencing, but she finally called back.

"Okay, I'm in my car, and I'm heading home."

"Was it Henderson in the other car?"

"Yes. He said he'd clear my apartment when we got there, then stick around until Naples police show up. He said they'd protect me."

"Call me back when you get yourself locked in. Meanwhile, I'm going to find a rental car and come home. Any luck, I should be there before sunrise."

"*No!*" It wasn't exactly a shout, but it was emphatic. "I don't want you to do that. Please."

"Why?"

There was a pause on the line, as if she were gathering her thoughts or corralling her emotions. "I don't like feeling weak, okay? I hate it. If you come, I know you'll be doing it to protect me, but that will just make it worse. And if you come, he wins. Which means we lose. I don't like losing."

She was clearly agitated. And angry.

"Gwenn, I'm not going to let you…"

"I'm safe tonight. I'm caught up at work. Tomorrow, I'll take a little vacation. They'll never find me. Do what you have to do. Find the motherfucker who did this. I'm a big girl. I'll take care of myself."

She hung up.

I stared at my iPhone for a few moments, torn about what I should do. My first instinct was to rush back to Naples. But she was right. That would be a win for whoever called. And he'd still be out there, threatening her, threatening me. Gwenn might have been frightened, but she was tough. And smart. Time for me to be tough and smart, too.

It was then that I noticed I'd received a voicemail on my phone. I checked the time. It must have been the incoming call I'd ignored when I was talking with Edwina earlier.

"Came by to see you," the voice said. It was as Gwenn described, mechanical sounding, robotic. "You weren't home. Maybe I'll come back and visit later."

I called Lester.

"Can I borrow your gun?" I asked.

"You'd shoot your eye out."

I filled him in on the call Gwenn received and the message I'd received.

Lester was quiet for a few moments, then he said, "It's the newspaper."

"The newspaper?"

"Yeah, the story in the *Key West Citizen*. How else would this caller know about you and the fact that you're here poking around in Donald Wilson's death?"

I thought about that for a few seconds and finally came to the same conclusion. "But how would this guy know about Gwenn?" I asked.

"Yeah, that's a good question," he said. "Nothing comes to mind. But listen, I know this is a little unnerving, but this caller, the robot voice guy, he's trying to intimidate you, scare you away. If he wanted to pop you, he already would have done it."

"Wouldn't that be simpler?" I asked.

"Maybe not. Maybe he thinks the cops will go for the murder-suicide story, that the prints prove Donald Wilson killed Tina Del Rio. Killing you could be counterproductive. But if you're worried, call a cab. Grab Fred and find a place to crash tonight and we'll regroup in the morning."

It was midnight and I knew finding a pet-friendly room—any room—at that hour would be a challenge in busy Key West. I walked back into the cabin of the trawler, locked the doors, checked the window locks, and went below deck and rooted through my scuba gear. I retrieved a dive knife and my Mares Sten Mini Rigged Speargun, a small but powerful weapon with a pistol grip, complete with holster and leg straps.

In a few minutes, Gwenn called back. "I'm home now. I'm okay. Actually I'm feeling a little foolish. Maybe I overreacted."

"That's what that asshat wanted, to frighten you. Anyone would be scared."

"Even you, big guy?"

I was staring out the stateroom porthole, peering into the darkness, nervous about who might be lurking out there. I felt for the speargun by my side. "Not me, of course."

I doused the lights and lay down in my berth. I was certain I wouldn't be able to sleep, and I was right.

How could anyone connect Gwenn and me? From Key West? I was very careful about the information I revealed on social media. Gwenn and I lived in separate residences. We owned no property in common. And I didn't recall mentioning her to anyone here.

Then it struck me: I had written down her name and office number on the paperwork I filled out when I docked at the marina. One line of the form asked who to contact in case of emergency. I wrote down Gwenn's name and number without thinking.

I rolled out of my berth and threw on my shorts and flip flops. I strapped the speargun to my thigh and grabbed the dive knife. Then, with the interior lights in the cabin off, slipped out onto the trawler's deck and locked the door behind me.

The dockmaster's office was a short walk away and I headed in that direction down the pier, feeling exposed and vulnerable. In less than a minute, I was there. I scanned the area around the office. No one else was about. The lapping waves, the clanking lines against the sailboat masts—they no longer felt friendly. Every sound in the night air jangled my nerves.

I walked up to the door and peered in through the window. Lights out. Normal.

I tried the lock and it was secure.

The office was a single-wide trailer in blue and white trim resting on blocks in the marina's parking lot. Two windows flanked the door. I inspected each of them and both seemed secure. I heard a rustling sound behind me and whipped around, alarmed. But I saw nothing. I heard the noise again and realized it was a dead palm frond scraping the trunk of a tree beside the office in the growing breeze. The air smelled of rain.

I circled to the rear of the trailer. Another window was set into the aluminum siding. I walked over to it, but it was dark and I couldn't make out any detail. I risked firing up the flashlight app on my iPhone and aimed it at the window. Unlike the two windows on the front of the trailer, this one was not closed all the way. I approached it and my foot brushed against something on the asphalt. I aimed the flashlight toward the ground and spied a mangled aluminum-framed window screen leaning against the side of the structure.

I looked around. I was still alone. Even bad guys have to sleep. I dialed Harrison Paine's number.

"What is it," he asked. He seemed surprisingly alert.

"I'm at the dockmaster's office at City Marina," I said. "I believe it may have been broken into."

"So call 911."

"There's more to it." I gave him the *Reader's Digest* version of the situation. "I'll be right over," he said. "Stay there. Don't mess with anything."

When he hung up, I aimed my flashlight into the interior of the trailer and peered through the gap in the window. The dockmaster's desktop was still the messy pile of paperwork I recalled from the other day. But the top file drawer in the cabinet beside the desk was open. The same file drawer where the dockmaster—I recalled his name was Cochran—dug out my paperwork when Lester and I talked to him.

I was tempted to crawl through the window and see if my folder was missing, but knew that was not only risky, but stupid. If the office had, indeed, been tossed by the same guy who threatened Gwenn and me, he might have made a mistake. He might have left fingerprints. I couldn't risk screwing up evidence.

Key West is an expensive place to live, so I guessed it might take a while before Paine arrived, that he might live on one of the other islands as a lot of government employees do. But he surprised me by rolling up in a police cruiser.

"You on duty?" I asked.

"Lucky you."

I walked Paine to the back of the trailer and showed him the open window and busted out screen. He held his flashlight in his left hand leaving his right hand free to grab his weapon if necessary. "Look over at the file cabinet by the desk," I said. "That open drawer, that's where the dockmaster keeps files on the boats in the marina. My theory, and why I came here, is that's how the jerkoff who called got the information on my girlfriend."

Paine called in a possible break-in of city property on his radio, and in a few minutes the parking lot was alive with flashing lights and cop cars. It took the police nearly an hour to locate and drag Cochran back to the marina, and he wasn't happy about it.

A uniformed officer escorted him to the front of the trailer where Paine and I were standing. He took one look at me and shook his head. "I should have known you'd be trouble."

He unlocked the door to the office. We were told to wait outside while Paine and another uniform went in to clear the place. Then Paine escorted Cochran inside, warned him not to touch anything, but asked him to identify anything that seemed out of place. I stood by the open door and could hear him clearly.

"Goddammit. Somebody's been in my file cabinet."

Bingo.

In a few minutes a couple of CSIs rolled up. They spent about an hour inside photographing and fingerprinting.

"Why'd you come snooping around here, anyway?" Cochran asked me while we waited for the CSIs to do their thing.

I debated for a moment whether to tell him all the details, but then decided, for better or worse, that I needed all the allies I could recruit. I told him about the threatening calls Gwenn and I received and my hunch that only his files could have revealed our relationship to anyone here in Key West.

"I'm thinking I may need to pull anchor," I said. "I'm exposed here."

Once I confided in him, Cochran warmed up. "I can help you with that," he said. "Got a buddy has a slip over at Sunset Marina. His boat's in dry dock for a few weeks getting some work done. I'm sure he'll let you use it for a few days. I'll call first thing in the morning."

By then it was already technically morning, 3 a.m., but there were still a few hours until daylight. If we could confirm my file was missing or had been disturbed, I could sneak off and at least get a couple hours of shuteye.

The cops let Cochran back in after the CSIs were done. It didn't take him long to figure it out. "Your file is still there," he said, "but it's in the wrong place, out of alphabetical order. They put it in with the S's for Strange, but should have filed it with the M's for *Miss Demeanor*."

"I wonder why they didn't close the drawer," I said.

"File cabinet's not level because the floor's warped. Pops open all the time if you don't make sure it's clicked shut."

"What about the window?" Paine asked. "Wonder why he didn't close it completely."

"Cause it's jammed," Cochran said. "Frame got bent in the

hurricane. Tree limb hit the side of the building. It'll open all the way, but not close. It's on my to-do list."

Paine walked with me back to my boat, and on the way I told him how Cochran was going to find me another marina.

"Good idea," he said. "Or you could be a sissy and run back to Naples."

"Said the Jar Head who eats pink doughnuts."

CHAPTER 25

My iPhone buzzed me awake and Caller ID showed it was Gwenn. It also showed that it was 7:35 a.m. I snatched the phone out of its recharging cable.

"You okay?"

"I actually got a good night's sleep, and now I'm packed," she said. "Uber's on the way. I'll call when I get settled."

She was speaking in her all-business voice. She'd shaken off the anxiety of last night and was moving forward with her plan.

"You going to share your destination with your boyfriend?" I asked. I could hear her walking down the outside stairs of her apartment, which was over a restaurant on Fifth Avenue in downtown Naples.

"Car's here. I'll call you." Then she hung up.

I splashed some water on my face, leashed up Fred, and locked the door to the cabin behind me as we headed out to the park. I threw my backpack over my left shoulder. Inside was my dive knife and speargun. Of course, inside my backpack those weapons were not easily accessible, but I felt a little better knowing they were there. Plus, there was my dog. If I got ambushed by my mysterious caller, Fred could pee on him.

On our return trip, I stopped by the dockmaster's office. Cochran was hanging up the phone as I walked in. His face melted when he saw Fred in my arms.

"Fred, say hello to Mr. Cochran."

He curled out from behind his desk and gave Fred a pat on the head. "What kind of dog?"

"Papillon."

"Never heard of it, but he sure is cute. And look at the size of those ears."

"Papillon is French for butterfly. They named the breed because the ears look like butterfly wings."

"I'd have expected a big guy like you to have a Doberman, or something."

I laughed. "Fred and I have a lot of history."

He patted Fred again then said, "This is a funny looking collar. These holes, they look like a speaker."

"They are. It's a dog translator. When Fred barks, a little computer in the collar is supposed to interpret his tone and translate it into English."

"No kidding? Does it work?"

"It works at scaring the shit out of people, but otherwise, no."

Cochran chuckled and set Fred down. "Well, I was right. Got you in over at Sunset. You know where it is?"

I nodded. "Over on Stock Island, by the Sheriff's Office and the county jail."

"That's right. I'll write down the slip number for you. You're all set."

I started to leave, then paused as I remembered a question I meant to ask Cochran. "Say, you know that houseboat that's sinking next to where Donald Wilson was living?"

"What about it?"

"The old guy who lives there, said the hurricane did that. I asked him if insurance would cover it, and he said no. Is that right, all these cool houseboats in this marina and none of them have insurance?"

He shook his head. "That's not right. Houseboats are like cars. Factory-made boats, they got VIN numbers, like on cars. They're insurable. Some of these others, the homemade ones, nah, insurance won't touch them."

"Well, that's a shame. They look cool."

"They are. You ever want to get rid of your trawler and live on a houseboat, I'll set you up."

I called Lester as soon as Fred and I returned to the *Miss Demeanor* and filled him in on the commotion last night. "About to pull anchor and head over to another marina."

He was eating again. "You really should join us for breakfast over here," he said. "Best in town."

"So, you and Silver have a plan?"

"She's taking off. Gonna drive back to Ocala this morning. There's nothing more she can do here, and this whole scene has her seriously messed up in the head."

"How about you?"

"I figured you could use some company for a day or two until we get this sorted out. Why don't you hang out at the marina for a little while? I'll ask Silver to drop me off and then I'll go with you when you move the boat."

That was welcome news. But another idea occurred to me.

"Silver eaten her breakfast yet?"

"No, she's still packing."

"How's this sound. I'll cab it over there. Join you for breakfast and say goodbye to Silver, then we can wander back to the boat."

"We would be wandering, why?"

"I told you about this feeling that I've been followed. Looks like my instincts were right. I'm thinking, I walk back to the boat and you trail at a little distance, see if you can spot anyone tailing me. Whaddaya think?"

"I think you've watched too many movies, but I don't see how it could hurt anything. But you've got to carry my suitcase."

I filled Fred's water and food bowls, then I called Uber. By the time I'd walked from the pier to Truman Avenue it was waiting for me, and five minutes later I entered the breakfast room of the Coco Plum Inn. The inn comprised two white Victorian homes from the 1800s with a swimming pool and tropical courtyard between them. Silver was receiving her order of an omelet and buttermilk pancakes.

"Lynn," she shouted to someone in the kitchen, "that guy we warned you about, he's here and he's hungry."

A woman darted into the dining area, reached out, and shook my hand. "Hi." She looked me over for a moment then said, "You don't look strange."

"Appearances can be deceiving," I said. I introduced myself and ordered pancakes, scrambled eggs, and bacon. Lester was right—it might have been the best breakfast in Key West.

Afterward, I helped carry Silver's luggage out to her pickup truck parked at the curb across the street. She gave me a quick hug goodbye. Lester got a lingering embrace and a kiss.

She was about to climb into her truck when a light blue Ford Focus pulled into the parking space behind us and honked its horn. It startled me and I found myself reaching for my backpack with the knife and speargun inside.

The driver's door of the Ford opened, and a young woman stepped out. She was medium height, wearing jeans and a faded purple T-shirt, and carrying a reporter's notebook in her hand. "Hi," she said. "I'm Hermina Hermelinda Obregon with the *Key West Citizen*."

"Hermina Hermelinda Obregon?" I asked, slightly proud of myself for repeating that mouthful back accurately.

"You can call me Agua," she said. "Everybody does."

"Agua?" Silver asked.

The young woman smiled. "Yeah, my initials H.H.O. You know, H2O. Agua?"

"That's a stupid nickname."

"Said the woman who calls herself Silver," I said.

That got me an ugly look. Out of the corner of my eye I could see Lester suppressing a grin.

"What do you want?" Silver asked.

"I want to interview you, both of you, about the murder/suicide. You're Alexander Strange, right? And you're Silver McFadden? I've read all of your books."

Silver's demeanor instantly transformed. "Oh, really? What do you want to know?"

I intervened. "We have no comment. Silver, time to go."

She frowned at me and for a moment I thought she would put up a fuss, but Lester stepped forward, grabbed her elbow and helped her into the truck. "Safe travels," he said.

"A few words, please," Agua persisted. "I only have one or two questions."

I shook my head.

Silver rolled down her window. "I'll call when I get home," she told Lester. "Don't forget your promise." Then she drove off.

"What promise?" I asked as we walked back to the inn, ignoring Agua's pleas for a quote.

"I promised her I wouldn't get myself killed."

"You promise her I wouldn't get killed, either?"

"Funny thing. She didn't ask about you."

CHAPTER 26

WITH LESTER'S ROLLER bag in tow, I emerged from the small driveway in front of the B&B and turned right on Whitehead Street. I double-checked to ensure that Hermina Hermelinda Obregon wasn't lying in wait for us. The irony of telling her "no comment" wasn't lost on me, but there was nothing to be gained by having our names further splashed about in the local paper. Maybe I'd find a way to make it up to her later.

We plotted our route over coffee, giving ourselves time for Agua to, uh, evaporate. I would stroll up Whitehead to Caroline Street toward Mallory Square, hang a right, then head back on Duvall to Truman. From Truman, it would be a straight shot to the marina. It would be a hike, but if I were being followed, Lester should be able to spot my tail.

I put my earbuds in and slipped the iPhone inside my cargo shorts, Lester on the other end of the call. If I picked up a shadow, he'd let me know. It was overcast and the Weather Channel app showed a sixty percent chance of thunderstorms. If we caught the shitstick who frightened Gwenn before the rain came, that would be a bonus. If not, then we'd feel more confident that we could relocate the *Miss Demeanor* undetected.

The stroll up Whitehead was uneventful. As I approached Caroline

Street, I glanced back but didn't see Lester. "You still there, shamus?" I asked.

"Ten-Four."

"I can't see you."

"Then neither can the bad guy."

"I'm turning right on Caroline Street, so I'll be out of sight until you catch up on Duval."

"Check your nine," he said.

I looked left and there was a guy in Bermuda shorts, knee-high socks and a straw boater on a bicycle two blocks away at Duval and Front Street.

"Where'd you get the bike?" I asked.

"You didn't expect *me* to walk, did you?"

On the corner of Duval and Angela Street, I spotted the two Wooks I'd talked to earlier.

"Dude," the buck said.

"Dude. Anything for me?"

"No, man. We got friends watching, too."

"Thanks."

I kept walking.

At Duval and Olivia Street, my phone buzzed. I pulled it out and saw a call from an unknown number. "Got incoming on the phone, Lester. I'm putting you on hold."

I clicked on the new call. "Hello."

"Hey, dude, it's Anthony." I recognized the Wook's voice, but realized I'd never gotten his name.

"Dude, what's up."

"You got somebody behind you, he's, like, locked in and gaining on you."

"Not to worry," I said. "It's my friend. He's on a bicycle, right?"

"Bicycle? No, dude. No bike."

I switched off the call. "Lester. The Wook says I got a tail."

"I'm on him. I'm on foot now. He's a block away and closing. I'm thirty feet behind but I won't be able to keep up."

I was carrying my backpack on a single strap over my left shoulder, pulling Lester's roller bag with my right hand. I stopped and pretended to switch shoulders. When I did, I reached in and grabbed the handle to the speargun. A young guy, white, maybe early-20s, long blond hair, jeans, sneakers, light windbreaker, was approaching rapidly. His hand was inside his jacket.

I pulled the speargun out of my pack and leveled it at him. Behind him, Lester ordered, "Halt!"

The kid nearly face-planted trying to stop, threw his hands in the air, and screamed, "No, no, no, no!"

"No what?" I asked.

"No, don't shoot me with that thing. Jesus."

Lester caught up with him and pinned his arms. "Up against the wall," he ordered.

While Lester patted him down, I asked him why he was tailing me.

"My friend, she wants to talk to you. We saw you when you walked by."

A young woman who looked familiar ran up as Lester released him. "Hi, Alex," she said. "You remember me, right? Mary Sue Flemister."

I took a deep breath. "Of course. Donny Westhaven's girlfriend."

"Right, right."

I turned to the guy we'd rousted. "Hey, man, sorry about that. Didn't mean to alarm you. Somebody's been following me and we were trying to catch him."

"Whatever."

"I'm glad we found you," Flemister said, oblivious to our having roughed up her friend. "You heard about the mix-up at the funeral home, right?"

"I did. What a screw-up."

"Oh, no kidding. The funeral home, they've agreed to pay for everything, including the fuel to take Donny—the real Donny—out to sea. We're doing the service on Saturday. When I saw you through the window, I knew I had to invite you since you promised to write about it and all."

I'd already written about it, of course, but killed it when it turned out the body in the coffee can was really Donald Wilson. But she didn't need to know that. And the column would still be good once the real Donny's ashes were spread in the Gulf of Mexico.

"Did you give him the notice, Bobby?" she asked the kid who chased me down.

"They didn't exactly give me a chance," he said, all pouty. He handed it to her and she gave it to me.

"It'll be on Saturday. I hope you can make it."

Something about Saturday rang a distant bell and it took me a moment to pull it off my internal hard drive.

"Isn't Saturday the day of the big festival here, the flamingo parade and dance-off thing?"

"Yeah, like it says right here," Bobby said, pointing to a poster taped inside a storefront window.

"That's right" Flemister said. "After the service, we're all coming down to Duval Street to party. Maybe I'll see you there." She winked at me then grabbed her friend Bobby's arm and led him away, back in the direction we'd come from.

"Making friends wherever we go," Lester said. "Nice speargun, by the way. Seems a popular weapon around these parts."

The two Wooks shambled up, gave us head bobs, and the doe said, "So, we done good, right?"

I smiled. "You did." I pulled out my wallet and gave them each a twenty dollar bill. "Keep up the good work," I said. "We still haven't caught the guy we're looking for."

Without saying a word, they stepped to the edge of the sidewalk and sat down, back in full observation mode.

Lester and I continued our effort to spot a tail, but it was fruitless. If he were trying to keep tabs on me, I finally realized, he could simply hang out at the marina and wait until I returned. But it was still worth the effort, I thought.

The dockmaster, Cochran, came over to our slip and helped us release the lines. "Safe travels," he shouted as we pulled away. "Say hello to Naples for me." He shot us a big grin.

Hey, it could have worked. If the douchenozzle was within earshot, maybe he'd think he'd run us off.

It was a short cruise from Garrison Bight to Sunset Marina and we made it unmolested. No aircraft strafed us. No torpedoes slammed into our hull. No pelicans pooped on us either, for that matter.

The sky was darkening now and the rumble of distant thunder was drawing nearer. I put a call into Professor Akari Takahashi, but was forced to leave a message on her voicemail. I was hoping she might know the location of Donald Wilson's dive site and, if so, I also hoped to invite her along for the ride.

But with the weather, it would be pointless to attempt it today.

"Now what?" Lester asked.

Before I could respond, my cell phone rang. I listened for a minute then clicked the call off.

Lester gave me an inquiring look.

"We've been invited to early cocktails poolside at Southernmost House," I said. "Then I've been invited to a sleepover."

CHAPTER 27

Gwenn was sitting at the covered bar by the swimming pool wearing a cotton floral dress of reds, whites, and blues. Her flip-flops were white. Her auburn hair was tousled by the breeze exposing gold hoop earrings. Her right hand held what appeared to be a piña colada in a plastic glass. Her left hand rested in her lap, modestly holding down her dress in case of an unruly gust.

Sitting next to her was an older man, deeply tanned and utterly bald. He was dressed in an open-collared white shirt and a tan Banana Republic lightweight suit. An empty glass and a bottle of Perrier rested in front of him on the bar.

"Is that your boss sitting with my girlfriend?" I asked Lester as we strolled into the pool area through the back door of Southernmost House.

"I called him last night," Lester said. "Warned him I'd be down here for a bit longer."

"This isn't costing you, is it?"

"Not if you answer his questions correctly."

I had no idea what that meant, but it would have to wait. Gwenn turned in her chair, spotted me, and waved, flashing her high-wattage smile. Good thing I was wearing my polarized sunglasses. She hopped off the barstool, stood on her tiptoes, and gave me a big hug. "It worked," she whispered in my ear. "I knew I could lure you here with the promise of alcohol and sex."

Colonel Lake slipped off his barstool, shook Lester's hand, then mine. "Good seeing you again, Mr. Strange. You have a penchant for stirring up trouble."

"And isn't it funny how you show up wherever trouble is brewing," I said.

That earned a brief smile, a rarity in my short experience with Lester's old commander in Afghanistan and now the president of Third Eye Investigators.

"You, too, babe," I said to Gwenn.

"That guy rattled me, I'll admit it," she said. "But the more I thought about it, the madder I got. I'm a lawyer. It's *my* job to intimidate people."

How could I not love this girl?

Lake said, "Let's take a table, shall we? I think we'll be sheltered from the rain gods here."

The roof above the outdoor bar was actually a railed observation deck overlooking the Gulf of Mexico. The hotel marks the southern and less rowdy end of Duval Street where it dead-ends at the ocean's edge. The Southernmost House guest list included presidents, royalty, Ernest Hemingway, and now a personal injury lawyer harboring a grudge against a threatening dipshit with a mechanical voice.

The bartender walked over to our table and took our drink orders. Gwenn asked for another piña colada, Lake another bottled water, Lester a margarita, and I ordered a Cuba Libre. We had the place to ourselves. The overcast skies were discouraging sunbathers and other less courageous outdoor drinkers.

When our orders arrived, Lester held up his glass in a toast. "To liberty, justice, and the American way, whatever that is anymore." We clinked glasses.

"I'd like to tell you a story," Lake began. "When I joined the army, I didn't do it because I wanted to pull triggers or hurt people or certainly not for the money. It was old fashioned patriotism. The army, to me, represented being part of something bigger than myself. It helped give my life meaning. I know Major Rivers felt the same way."

Lester nodded and took a swig of his margarita.

"When I retired, I wanted to continue doing something with my life that continued to give it purpose. That vision was shared by several others like myself, and that's how we formed our agency. We've been financially successful over the past eleven years. We now have more than three hundred agents and staff people on our team, and offices in five countries, twenty-two cities, and the District of Columbia. Some of our profitability comes from work we do for large businesses, helping with their security, particularly overseas. And as you know, we do a great deal of work for the government.

"We also define ourselves by what we refuse to do. We do not engage in industrial espionage, nor opposition research for politicians." He took a swig of water and shook his head. "There's a lot of money to be made in digging up dirt on people and in stealing secrets, but that's not us.

"We've been very selective in whom we have taken on as clients, and it has paid handsomely. But, lately, as we've become better known, we've been approached by people, such as your Silver McFadden, who need help, but can't meet our financial requirements. We've decided to do something about that.

"So, long story short, we're creating a pro-bono program inside the agency. We've started a group that will evaluate requests for our services from people who are deserving and who may not have received the satisfaction they have a right to expect from traditional operators, like the police.

"To that end, Major Rivers is now officially on this case. He has kept me up to speed on all that you have encountered here, and I share his—and your—sense that something is terribly wrong. When I heard about the phone call Ms. Giroux received last night, that capped it. That is completely out of bounds. You never threaten families."

Lake took another drink of his Perrier and looked at me, waiting for some kind of reaction.

"That's admirable, Colonel Lake," I said. "But Lester could have told me all that. You must be here for another reason."

"Indeed. Much of what we do is never seen by the public, particularly our government work. But cases like this, they clearly are subject to public scrutiny. The police are involved. I gather we have a pair of off-duty FBI agents engaged, too. When this is resolved it will be a very public event and I know you will be writing about it."

I interrupted him. "I'm sure I will. But like I've talked to you before, I can't see my way clear to function both as a reporter and a private investigator," I said, anticipating that he was about to make another pitch that I join the agency. "Lawyers"—I nodded to Gwenn—"and you guys, you have clients you represent and you defend their interests. I don't pick winners and losers. My job is simple. I follow the facts. Journalism is different than advocacy."

Lake's face lit up. "Exactly. That's what I love about what journalists do. The search for the truth. Let the chips fall where they may. You're unstructured—the polar opposite of how Major Rivers and I have lived our lives. I envy you."

"So why are you here?" I asked.

"I absolutely have no intention of paying you to do anything," he said.

"Oh." Somehow that was deflating even though it shouldn't have been.

"In addition to our pro-bono unit, my partners and I have created a foundation. It is well funded by our firm and a few select clients who, like us, are concerned about the future of our democracy. Part of our philanthropy will be dedicated to funding investigative journalism, much like the foundations that support so many other news organizations, such as *Pro Publica* and the *Texas Tribune*. Indeed, *Pro Publica* is on our donation list as well as Investigative Reporters and Editors."

"Nice."

"Shortly before I flew down here—I was at our Miami office—I called your editor, Edwina Mahoney, and announced that we were writing a grant to Tropic Press."

"No strings attached?"

"Not entirely."

I looked at him, waiting for the other shoe to drop.

He looked at me, wondering if I would follow up and ask another question. Since I was clueless as to where this monologue was heading, I waited.

He spoke first. "We have agreed to sponsor the creation of an investigative team at the news service. I told Ms. Mahoney that we would be in a position to occasionally offer tips on story-worthy events that crossed our desk, and we would be able to offer our services to reporters engaged in investigations—as you know we have considerable resources."

I nodded.

"There are only two stipulations."

Here it comes, I thought. "Which are?"

"Which are, first, that at least one investigative project each year be dedicated to the protection of journalists. As I'm sure you know, journalists around the world are being threatened and murdered in increasing numbers. Major Rivers and I saw that firsthand in Afghanistan. Are you familiar with an organization called the Committee to Protect Journalists?"

I nodded.

"They report that in the past twenty-five years more than thirteen hundred journalists have been killed world-wide. Journalists are on the front lines of freedom. Kill or intimidate journalists, and our experiment in democracy is over." It was a corny thing to say, but he did so with utmost sincerity and conviction. He didn't need to convince me. A reporter friend of mine was nearly killed recently covering a story that I had assigned to her. The Third Eye was instrumental in saving her, which is how I became acquainted with Colonel Lake and Lester.

Generally speaking, journalists in America were far safer than our colleagues in other parts of the world where there isn't a tradition of a free and unfettered press. But the news media in the United States had come under increasing attack by politicians, creating an atmosphere far more threatening than even a few years earlier. The notion of having resources to help journalists do their jobs was appealing.

"What's the other stipulation?" I asked.

"I asked that you be given the opportunity to lead this team. But whether you choose to accept or not is entirely up to you and will not have any bearing on our grant."

Gwenn nearly jumped out of her chair. Finally her shiftless boyfriend would have a real job. If I accepted.

"Edwina hasn't called me about this," I said.

Lake nodded. "I asked her to allow me to talk to you first and she agreed. I wanted you to know from me, man-to-man, that you have my word that we will not interfere in any way in your work. I know you have been concerned about the ethics of my original proposal, that you work for us and your news service simultaneously. Upon reflection, I came to realize that your concern was valid. My hope, of course, is that you will agree that some of the people who come to us have stories worth telling. But it would be your call."

"Thank you for your offer, Colonel Lake. I'll need to think about this. I'll want to talk to my boss. How about we revisit the bidding when we wrap this mess up here?"

He raised his Perrier bottle in salute. "Absolutely. As I said, Major Rivers is on the case and you will have the full resources of the Third Eye behind you. Let us know what you need."

At that moment, what I needed was another drink.

CHAPTER 28

One of the advantages of having a well-heeled girlfriend is scoring the Southernmost House's Courtyard Cottage for the night. The Courtyard Cottage is a poolside bungalow off the hotel's main building, which makes it easy to slip out in the middle of the night and go skinny dipping. Which we were doing.

"Sounds like Edwina was amped about the grant," Gwenn said, sipping from a glass of champagne.

"Ed's a good editor, and one of her jobs is to keep the operation in the black. So this is mana from heaven."

"And she likes the idea of you heading this investigative team."

"Devil's in the details. A lot of investigative reporting involves database research. I'd rather have dental work. But shoe-leather reporting, that I like. When we're done here, I'll probably fly back to Phoenix and we can iron it out."

Gwenn smiled. "So you've decided?"

"No. As we sit here right now, I don't see a downside. But as we sit here right now I've drained half a bottle of rum, so I want to be clearheaded when I decide. And I want to think through all the ins and outs."

I expected that would draw a frown or maybe even a rebuttal, but

Gwenn was perfectly cheerful. Of course, it wasn't her first glass of champagne, either. "But you're thinking about it, right?"

"Sure. I could continue to write my column, and when projects come along that I find interesting, I could dive in. Kinda like I'm doing right now."

"And you'd be okay with supervising and editing, right?"

"I think so, especially since we don't operate like a centralized newsroom. We're distributed, if you will. Our staff isn't that large, but it's all over the country. Ed thinks we'll be able to hire four or five new reporters, which is terrific. We coordinate most everything by long distance, anyway, and we all chip in on editing and stuff when needs be. We'll take it one step at a time."

She drained her glass. "So are you excited?"

It was clear that she was. I took a swig of my Cuba Libre. We'd stayed at the hotel all afternoon and evening and ordered pizza for dinner. Figured it wouldn't be a brilliant move to wander the streets of Key West with a madman gunning for us.

"Yeah, I guess I am. It's flattering, of course. And a little intimidating. I've never done anything like this and I have no training, but other than that I'm the perfect candidate for the job."

"You'll do great." As if I'd already said yes.

"From your lips to God's ears."

"From my lips." She snuggled next to me and round two began.

The water was heated comfortably and the lightning on the horizon over the Gulf added a romantic and adventuresome quality. As if sex in a hotel swimming pool wasn't daring enough. At some point in the festivities, Gwenn screeched. We both started laughing. And our eyes darted around like a couple of teenagers afraid we'd been caught hooking up in the driveway.

We grabbed our beach towels, wrapped them around us, and darted back toward our cabana.

When we got there, the door was wide open.

"Uh, did we forget to close the door?" Gwenn asked, her voice hushed.

"Stay here."

I stepped into the little bungalow and reached around the door and flipped on the light switch. An empty suite yawned at me. "Give me a minute," I told Gwenn. The space was partitioned into an area dominated by a king size bed on one side and a bath and sitting area on the other. I walked to the bathroom and swung the door open. Unless an intruder had squeezed himself into the cabinet under the sink, it was empty. Back in the bedroom area, I checked the closet, and even peered under the bed. All clear.

I walked back outside where Gwenn was waiting by the door. She could see for herself that the space was empty. "I'm going to blame you for this," I said, "because otherwise it would mean I'm the one who forgot to shut the door."

"It's always the woman's fault."

As I closed the door behind us, I noticed it failed to latch. I checked the bolt, and it was stuck in the open position. I punched it with my index finger and it popped free. "Looks like this was the culprit," I said.

Gwenn was already in the bathroom. "I'm going to wash the chlorine off."

While she showered, I checked my phone. Lester, who was spending the night aboard the *Miss Demeanor* supervising Fred, Mona, and Spock, left a text message:

3 things. Fred's fine.
Silver made it to Ocala.
Nobody's blown up the boat.
LMAO.

Gwenn was still in the shower and I figured she'd be a while if she were going to wash her hair. I checked my Word Chums app. Gwenn's secretary,

Elizabeth Warren, scored a word worth 105 points and was now 63 points ahead of me in a game we were playing. That would take time and concentration to deal with so I switched out of the game and browsed my news apps.

- In Salina, Kansas, a woman who feared someone broke into her home found her ex-boyfriend's legs dangling from her living room ceiling when he fell through the attic. Her new boyfriend beat him up.
- Scientists in Bern, Switzerland announced that the rubber ducky in your bathtub can kill you. They cut open a selection of the bath toys and found "potentially pathogenic bacteria" in four out of five of the dissected ducks.
- A primate lab in Miami announced it was "utterly unsuccessful" in rounding up a troop of rhesus macaque monkeys that escaped the week before. They were offering a reward for information leading to their recapture.
- And meteorologists were predicting that conditions were ripe for the formation of a tropical storm in the Gulf of Mexico, which could be good news, on the one hand, because it might dissipate the growing Red Tide bloom that was spreading southward toward the Keys.

I heard Gwenn step out of the shower. "I'll be done in a minute," she said.

"Remember those monkeys Lester and I ran into? There's a lab offering a grand for their whereabouts."

"What would happen to the monkeys if the lab got them back?" she asked.

"My guess is they ran away for a reason."

"Poor monkeys."

"Yeah. I'm thinking live and let live."

"Good call."

"Guess what else?" I asked.

"What else?"

"The Red Tide. It's heading here. But there's a tropical storm and it may break it up."

"How do you know all this?"

"Well, I hesitate to use the word genius…"

She stepped into the bedroom wrapped in a white terrycloth towel. "Let me get this straight. Instead of enjoying post-coital bliss, you were working?"

"It's not work if you're having fun."

"*This* is fun," she said, stripping off the towel. "Red Tide is not fun."

"I stand corrected."

She sauntered back into the bathroom putting on a show, and it occurred to me that the gentlemanly thing to do would be to follow her.

"Don't even think about it," she said without looking back. "I'm caught up."

As I prepared to turn off my phone I noticed I'd received an email from a friend who covers Capitol Hill for the Associated Press. A Florida congressman was filing a bill the next day, she said, "that will be right up your alley." I made a mental note to follow up in the morning.

Gwenn and I had barely nodded off when a thunderclap nearly bounced me out of bed. Lightning strobed the windows and another crash of thunder rattled the cottage. Gwenn grumbled in her sleep, then was quiet. Ordinarily, I could sleep through a nuclear bombardment, but with recent events I was a little more on edge than usual.

I sat up in bed and watched the fireworks for a few minutes, and then, as a nearby lightning strike lit up the pool area, I could have sworn I saw the figure of a man silhouetted near our door. I blinked and he was gone.

I retrieved the speargun from my backpack and peered out the window. Nothing. Probably my imagination and raw nerves. But it added to my edginess and I stared at the ceiling for a while after I returned to bed and couldn't get back to sleep.

Finally, I slipped from under the covers and padded to the bathroom to get a drink of water. I grabbed a glass off the sink in the dark and held it under the faucet. I was about to take a big gulp when lightning once again illuminated the room and I saw two big eyes staring at me from inside the glass. It was a small anole lizard, probably as terrified of me as I was of him.

"Jesus," I sputtered and instinctively tossed the water into the sink. The lizard flew out of the glass with the water, landed on the faucet, then scampered out of sight. He must have snuck into the room when the door was open.

I wasn't about to drink out of that glass now, so I rooted through the refrigerator in the kitchenette and pulled out a beer, sat down at the little table, and allowed the ethanol replenishment to calm my nerves. Sleep came easily after that.

CHAPTER 29

"I NEED COFFEE," Gwenn said when we finally arose. The sun was well over the horizon. Mickey Mouse said it was 8:45 a.m. I threw on some clothes and strolled over to the main house, returning with two steaming cups—black for me, cream and sugar for Gwenn.

"You slept through all the fun last night," I said.

"Oh?"

"Yeah, first I ran off an intruder with my speargun, then I was attacked by a brown anole." I pronounced it "ann-o-Lee," which is how Floridians say it, but in the Caribbean you can also hear them called "Ann-ol" or "Uh-noll."

"What's an anole?"

"A lizard."

Gwenn was sitting on the bed and she curled her feet underneath her and looked around the room. "In here?"

I nodded.

"Did you kill it?"

"Of course not. They're harmless."

"There's a lizard running around our room?"

It occurred to me that this was the perfect opportunity for a little white lie. "No. No. No. He ran out the door this morning when I went to get coffee."

"Oh, okay." She uncurled her feet.

I looked around the room furtively, just to make sure the little guy wasn't lurking somewhere. Nothing to the left. Nothing to the right. Maybe he had sneaked out of the room on my way to get coffee, after all. It could have happened.

Then some instinct, some part deep inside my own lizard brain, told me to look up. I glanced toward the ceiling, and there he was. Dangling upside down, right over us.

"Um," I said, "you know, maybe there could have been more than one."

"More than one what?" Gwenn asked.

Just then, the lizard's grip on the ceiling broke free and it plummeted downward landing right on Gwenn's left knee.

She screamed. Her coffee went flying. The lizard went flying. She jumped out of bed and darted into the bathroom.

"Alexander Strange, get rid of that thing!"

"Huh. Looks like there were two of them." Quick thinking, right?

"Liar!"

The poor little guy was standing motionless on the bedspread, no doubt wondering what kind of strange world filled with hysterical giants he'd fallen into. Lizards are fast, but he must have been a little stunned since I was able to snatch him off the bed in a quick grab. I marched him over to the bathroom door.

"I've got him. You can see for yourself, if you like."

Gwenn cracked open the door and peeked out. I opened my hand ever so slightly and the little lizard poked his head out.

"Ugh. Get rid of him."

"Come on, pal," I said. "Party's over." I opened the cabana door and tossed him onto the grass.

"All clear."

Gwenn slinked out of the bathroom.

"No more lizards," I said.

"I seem to be out of coffee."

"I'll fetch some more."

She shook her head. "I'll get some at breakfast. So what's the plan for today?"

"First thing," I said, "I've got a column to knock out. It won't take me long. Only need to make one quick phone call. Then, I'm trying to call Tina Del Rio's colleague, Akari Takahashi. I'm hoping she can tell me where Donald Wilson was diving.

"We taking the boat out, then? You going to scuba down to where he was working, see what he was up to?"

I nodded. "That's the general idea. You up for that?"

"Sure. Otherwise I'd be cooped up somewhere all day hiding from assassins and lizards and forced to consume large quantities of margaritas. Lester's coming too, right?"

"I'll ask him."

While Gwenn tended to her morning bathroom routine, I called the press secretary for Congressman Dennis Levin, scored a couple of quotes, and finished my column.

THE STRANGE FILES

Gunning for Cardboard AR-15s

By Alexander Strange

Tropic©Press

It is perfectly legal to own an AR-15, a semi-automatic weapon styled after a military assault rifle that is favored by hunters and mass murderers in America.

Soon, however, it may be illegal to own a cardboard cutout of the gun.

U.S. Rep. Dennis Levin of Sarasota has filed a bill that has garnered 35 co-sponsors, that would make it a violation of federal law to "display in a threatening manner" any likeness of any firearm with the intent of "creating terror in the general population."

The bill would include cardboard cutouts of the rifle such as those recently carried by protestors outside the Monroe County courthouse in Key West. Seven anti-gun-violence demonstrators were jailed for failing to obey orders by police to disperse, among other charges.

More recently, two public school employees accidentally shot one another in a hallway in Jacksonville when they opened fire on a student carrying a similar AR-15 cardboard cutout mistakenly believing it was a real weapon.

"These replicas of real weapons are becoming a threat to national security," Levin said in a statement released by his office.

I called his press secretary, Roger Kintzel, and asked if the ban would also apply to toy guns and squirt guns.

"Absolutely," he said. "We can't have people carrying fake rifles around and terrorizing innocent people."

But what about real rifles? I asked.

"That's different. They're protected by the Second Amendment."

STRANGE FACT: The “AR” in AR-15 does not stand for assault rifle, as is popularly assumed, but Armalite rifle, named for the company that developed the weapon.

Weirdness knows no boundaries. Keep up at *www.TheStrangeFiles.com*. Contact Alexander Strange at Alex@TheStrangeFiles.com.

CHAPTER 30

Key West, Stock Island

I PUSHED THE SEND button on my column, then picked up my iPhone and dialed Akari Takahashi. Once again, it rolled over to voice mail. Gwenn stepped out of the bathroom, so I washed my face and brushed my teeth and had just sat down on the bed next to her when my phone buzzed. I hoped it would be Akari, but it wasn't.

"Twenty-four hours a day, seven days a week, this is Alexander Strange," I answered.

"And this is your favorite dog-sitter," Lester replied. "What's the plan?"

I told him about my idea to take the *Miss Demeanor* out into the Gulf and asked if he was up for it.

"Wouldn't miss it. You got hold of that Atari woman yet?"

"Akari. And no. I left her another message."

"Is it near here, the community college?"

I pulled out my handy map of Key West. "It's at the opposite end of Stock Island from the marina. But I get your drift. We should go over there and roust her."

"Nice if we scored some wheels," he said.

"You're on the clock now, right?"

"So are you."

"Okay, we'll do rock, paper, scissors."

"How in the name of Louis Armstrong we doin' that over the phone?"

"Honor system. Ready? One, two, three. Whatcha got?"

"Scissors."

"Oh, too bad. I've got rock. You get the rental."

Gwenn and I walked out of the hotel just as Lester pulled up in a lime green Chevrolet Spark he'd rented from Hertz at Key West International Airport. It was the size of a go-kart.

"How do you expect me to fit into that?" I asked.

"Next time, you rent the car," he said.

"Prick."

"Boys, boys, boys," Gwenn scolded. "I'll squeeze in the back."

First stop was the marina where we unloaded Gwenn's luggage. Two large bags, each weighing approximately eight hundred pounds. One of them sat on my lap during the drive to the marina and I could no longer feel my thighs.

"You hauling rebar in here?" I asked.

"Merely the essentials."

"Hope they don't sink the boat."

I checked on Fred, made sure he was stocked with food and water. This was totally unnecessary, of course, as Lester is an excellent dog-sitter. But we can't be too careful about our canine friends, can we? Then we piled back into the go-kart and drove to Florida Keys Community College. We parked near the Tennessee Williams Fine Arts Center, then wove our way through the familiar hallways leading to Akari's office.

Two female students were sitting on the floor outside Akari's door waiting for her, a chilling reminder of the scene we'd encountered outside Tina Del Rio's office before we discovered her perforated body inside.

"Dr. Takahashi in?" I asked.

One of the students looked up and nodded. "You in one of her classes?"

"No, I matriculated."

The other student rolled her eyes. "All primates matriculate."

The door to Akari's office opened and a lanky male student walked out. He was the same kid who'd been lingering outside Tina Del Rio's office when we discovered her body. He looked up, recognized me, and the color drained from his face. He scurried away without saying a word.

Akari appeared in the doorway, saw us, and raised a finger—the universal sign to wait a moment. She ushered both students in at once and closed the door.

"What's that about?" I asked.

"Those girls didn't look very happy," Gwenn said.

"Maybe they should matriculate more," Lester said.

A few minutes later the door reopened, and the young women left in a hurry, eyes downcast.

"What'd you do to them?" I asked Akari.

"I caught them cheating on a test and read them the riot act."

"You gonna flunk 'em?" Lester asked.

"No. I want them to learn from this. After all, that's what I do. I teach. This will be an important lesson for them to remember. Hopefully for the rest of their lives. Come in."

Akari's office was the same floor plan as Tina Del Rio's, which is to say it was a small cube with a metal desk, filing cabinet, and two guest chairs. Where Tina had displayed a photo of herself in mermaid regalia, a picture of two children rested atop Akari's filing cabinet. Photographs of undersea plants adorned her walls. I introduced Gwenn, and she and Lester sat down. I leaned against the wall.

"Donald Wilson was into sharks. Would I be right in assuming plants are more your thing?" Gwenn asked, gesturing at the photos.

"Yes. I'm a marine botanist. Plants don't ordinarily eat people. I like them better, but I should add sharks are widely misunderstood."

I nodded in agreement even though I'd yet to encounter a shark during any of my dives who looked remotely like he was in the midst of an identity crisis. "I want to thank you again for showing me Donald Wilson's lab space the other day. I assume by now you've done the same for the police?"

"Yes. I've been interviewed by that sheriff's detective, Kitchner's her name, I think. She wanted to know about my relationship with both Tina and Donald, whether there was any friction between them, if I knew anyone who might have a motive to kill them."

"She ask you about his work?"

"Only in general terms. I told her he was on leave from USF, working for an international phone company investigating damage to undersea cables. But she was more focused on people he might know."

Lester jumped in. "Pretty standard operating procedure. Both Dr. Wilson and Dr. Del Rio were likely killed by the same person, someone they both knew, perhaps."

Gwenn asked, "I'm curious, what did you tell the detective about their relationship?"

"They'd found a connection. Any thought that Donald killed Tina is way, way off the mark."

"Do you have any thoughts on who might be motivated to do this?" Lester asked.

She shook her head.

"Did either Tina or Donald ever express any concerns, any anxiety leading up to this?" I asked. We were tag-teaming her, peppering her with questions, but she didn't seem to mind.

"My conversations with Donald were entirely professional," she said. "When he found those algae samples I showed you, the ones growing near the undersea cables, he consulted with me about them."

"And Tina? You were close friends, right?"

"I was Tina's mentor when she came to the college last year. Every college and university has its bureaucracy to navigate, so new employees here are often assigned someone to help with that. I liked Tina. She was bright, energetic, and she cared about her students. Which is more than I can say about some of my colleagues. But we didn't socialize outside of work. Big age difference. And Tina was outgoing, an extrovert. Me, not so much."

"You don't strike me as shy," I said, trying to keep the conversation flowing.

She smiled. "I recharge my batteries curling up with a good book. I get all the human contact I need—and more—in the classroom."

"Did Tina talk about Wilson?" Lester asked.

"I could tell she was excited for him, but she said she couldn't discuss his work, that it was proprietary. But I do recall one thing she said."

"Yes?"

"She said she thought Donald was about to be famous."

"But she didn't say why?" Gwenn asked.

"No, I think she was teasing me, wanting me to beg for details, but I didn't bite. I figured I'd find out in due course. Actually, I was kind of annoyed with her for doing that."

"Let me throw an idea at you," I said. "It sounds like Wilson discovered something during his dives in the Gulf, something that excited his girlfriend. Do you think it's possible he might have run across something that his killer wanted kept secret?"

Akari frowned. "Sounds melodramatic, doesn't it?"

"There has to be a motive for these murders," I said. "Taking a spear to the stomach is pretty dramatic."

She blew out her breath and rocked back in her chair. "Yes, certainly."

"Another question, Akari. If we assume Wilson found something—as an operating hypothesis—do you have any idea how anyone would have known about it?"

She thought about that for a minute. "I don't believe it would have been from Tina. If she wouldn't tell me, I can't believe she would have told anyone else. I didn't know enough to tell anyone, in case you were reconsidering that possibility."

I was, but there was no point saying so.

"Was Wilson in contact with anyone else around here?" I asked.

She shrugged. "Don't know. Of course, he might have talked with the people at the telephone company he was doing his research for, or maybe his colleagues at USF. Or even his sister. Silver, wasn't it?"

I nodded.

"Did he charter a boat for his dives?"

She bobbed her head. "Yes. A local fishing charter. In fact, I think I recall the name. Tina mentioned it and it was amusing." She held up her index finger. "Let me think, let me think."

While she thought about it, I pulled out my iPhone and Googled the names of local charter boats. When the list came up, I handed my phone to Akari. "Maybe this will help."

She scrolled through the phone for a moment then said, "Oh, yes, here it is. How could I forget?"

She handed the phone back to me and pointed to the listing: "*Reel Time*."

Clever. Not as clever as *Miss Demeanor*, but then my guess is that whoever christened the boat wasn't a Superior Court judge.

One final question," I said. "Generally speaking—or more specifically, if possible—can you provide any guidance on where Donald was diving?"

"Yes," she said. "All the undersea cables are charted. He was examining the cable operated by Trans Europa Associated Telecom. I remember it because of the unfortunate acronym. Tina actually showed it to me on a map, where he was diving."

"Any chance the map is still there?" I asked, nodding in the direction of Del Rio's office. There was no police tape blocking access, so I assumed her office was no longer sealed for the investigation. But there was a wrinkle.

"All of Tina's things were taken away by the police," she said. "That detective, Kitchner, said it was all evidence. They took everything out of her desk, like they did with Donald Wilson's."

I glanced at Lester. "Makes sense," he said. "They would have printed everything in the room and would want to hold onto it for a while."

"Are you a diver?" Akari asked.

"I'm certified," I said. "But I don't do it all that often."

"Is it your intention to try to find Donald's dive site, to figure out what he might have discovered?"

"Yeah, that's what I was thinking. Honestly, Akari, I can't think of anything better."

She leaned back in her chair, steeped her hands, and smiled. "Sometimes the best course of action is the obvious one, isn't it?"

Deep.

"May I ask you a favor?" she said.

"Sure."

"May I come with you?"

I had hoped she would want to accompany us. "I take it you dive."

She gave me an eye roll, like how else would a marine botanist do her job?

"I'll take that as a yes. When are you free?"

"For this? Any time. I'll cancel classes if I have to."

CHAPTER 31

Stock Island

I CALLED THE number for Reel Time Charters that was listed on Google, but it rolled over to voicemail. The search engine said the boat was based at Hurricane Hole Marina on the other side of Stock Island from where we were docked.

"Sun's past the yardarm," Lester said. "I hear they have food and beer over there."

So we piled into the go-kart and in a few minutes found ourselves at a blue-topped dockside table ordering lunch at the Hurricane Hole Fresh Seafood Grille. Lester selected a shrimp po'boy with an Abita Purple Haze, a Louisiana lager. Neither Gwenn nor I were especially hungry after breakfast at Southernmost House, so we split a shrimp basket. She got a glass of Hogue Chardonnay. I ordered a Diet Coke.

When the server arrived with our vittles, I asked her about the *Reel Time*.

"She's usually docked right there," she said, pointing to an empty slip in the marina. "Her new owner, his name is Abner, Abner Daystrom, he doesn't take her out much. Seems like business kinda dropped off after he bought her."

"I tried to call but didn't get an answer," I said.

She shaded her eyes and glanced at the sun. "If he's out on a half-dayer, he'll be back soon."

"We can sit here and drink," Lester said, "or we can try Plan B."

"What's Plan B?" Gwenn asked.

"Working on it," I said.

Gwenn and I, for not being all that hungry, demolished the shrimp basket. Lester ordered another beer. Gwenn's wine glass was still half full. I ordered a second Diet Coke and the check.

While we lingered, I called Harrison Paine. He answered on the first ring. "You guys get any prints at the dockmaster's?" I asked.

"Yes. Mr. Cochran's and yours."

"Mine?"

"On the door knob and back window frame."

"Oh. Sorry about that."

"Gotta go. I spy a jaywalker." He hung up.

Next, I dialed Abby Kitchner. I might be lousy at reaching charter boat captains, but so far I was one-for-one with cops. Kitchner didn't break the streak.

"Got a question," I said when she answered.

"I live to talk to reporters."

"We just visited Akari Takahashi…"

"Who's we?"

"We would be Lester Rivers and my personal attorney and girlfriend Gwenn Giroux."

"You have a girlfriend?"

"Why, yes."

"Poor thing. Why are you bothering me?"

"Are you curious what Donald Wilson was working on out in the Gulf?"

"Dr. Hashataki said…"

"Takahashi."

"Yeah. She said he was working for a European phone company.

Looking at broken underwater data cables. Said something about sharks biting the lines."

"She tell you what kind of sharks?"

"No. Is it important?"

"Vampire sharks."

She hung up.

People have hung up on me countless times, so my sense of self-worth was not irretrievably damaged by this. But I guessed once Kitchner chewed on what I'd said, she wouldn't be able to help herself. And I was right.

My phone buzzed and I answered. "Twenty-four hours a day, seven days a week, this is Alexander Strange. Leave a message after the fuck you."

"You were serious, weren't you. I looked it up. There is such a thing, a vampire shark."

"Yeah, you see pictures."

"Yes. They're creepy, like out of the movie *Alien*. They have this mouth that comes out of their mouth, like its attached to a separate head. And those teeth. They look like needles."

"Do you recall that Donald Wilson's autopsy report noted unusual cuts through one of the legs of his wetsuit?"

"Yes. Said it was unidentifiable."

"I'm thinking vampire shark."

"Huh."

"Silver said they're the sharks nibbling the phone lines. Which is weird, because usually they aren't in shallow waters. I looked it up on Wikipedia, so I know it's true. But it turns out they are attracted to a kind of fish that likes to eat the algae growing near the phone lines, which also doesn't ordinarily grow there. So what Donald Wilson was doing is trying to figure out why all that was happening."

"Again, so what?"

"So, I want to know if you have any information on that. And if you know exactly where he was diving. You took all of Tina Del Rio's and Donald Wilson's stuff. Did you find anything about that?"

"I should share this with you, why?"

"Because you hung up on me and that was rude, so now you owe me."

"Jesus. But the answer is no. And I personally looked through every piece of paper that came out of there. There was nothing like that. Not that I was looking for it in particular. What does it matter?"

"Got nothing better to do. Figured I might go take a look."

"In the Gulf of Mexico?"

"Yes."

"What do you expect to find?"

"Not really sure. Akari did mention that Donald Wilson had planned to set up some underwater cameras to record the sharks. Maybe they're still down there."

"That could be interesting," Kitchner said. "Find anything, let me know."

Our server showed up with the check and I handed her my VISA card, the one with the picture of Darth Vader on it.

"What did that detective say when you mentioned my name?" Gwenn asked.

"She acted surprised I might have a girlfriend. Said quote 'poor thing' unquote."

"Hmmm. She's probably jealous."

"That's what I was thinking."

"Don't tell Paine," Lester said. "I think he's sweet on her."

Our server returned with the bill. "This card is so cool. I love *Star Wars*."

I get that a lot.

"Where'd you find it?" she asked.

I get that a lot, too. The answer is that it's issued through Disney, but what I told her was:

"Chewbacca gave it to me."

She laughed and put her hand on my shoulder, the universal sign she was ready to bear my children. Her touching me did not go unnoticed by Gwenn, who rolled her eyes.

"You do kinda look like that guy, the actor," the waitress said.

"Peter Mayhew?"

"Is he the one who played Hands Solo?"

"Han. And, no, he played Chewbacca."

I signed the check after adding twenty percent and was about to suggest to my companions that we take off when a fishing boat with the name *Reel Time* painted on the hull puttered into the marina.

"We're in luck," Lester said.

As we walked toward the dock, Gwenn elbowed me. "You love it when you get that attention."

"Jealous much?"

She wrapped her arm around me and tugged me next to her. "You're mine, all mine."

"Ten bucks says you don't know who sang that?"

"Dobby Dobson."

"Dammit."

We approached Captain Daystrom as he was tying up his boat. He was big-boned and about six feet tall with sun-bleached hair and a matching shaggy beard. I figured him for mid-forties. He wore a pair of mirrored shades that flashed as he turned his head, reflecting the midday sun.

"My name's Alexander Strange. This is Gwenn Giroux and Lester Rivers. She's an attorney. He's a private detective. We're interested in your relationship with Dr. Donald Wilson."

"Why?" he asked. "I heard he was dead."

"You took him out on your boat, right?"

He didn't answer right away, checking us out as if he were deciding whether he wanted to continue the conversation. He pulled a round, black and red can of Skoal from his back pocket and elaborately pinched off a piece and jammed it into the corner of his mouth.

"He was a customer. So, what's it to you?"

"So, where'd you go?"

He hooked his thumb in the direction of the water. "Not that it's any of your business, but due south. He gave me GPS coordinates."

"How many times you take him out?" Lester asked.

Abner thought for a moment. "You're asking a lot of questions, but I guess it ain't no secret. Seven or eight times. Always met him at his houseboat at Garrison Bight. He had a lot of gear. Scuba stuff. And a drone."

"Always the same place?" I asked.

"Yeah, his houseboat didn't move."

"No, I mean out in the Gulf."

Abner shook his head. "He gave me different GPS coordinates for each trip. Well, until the last few times. Then we went back to the same place."

"He find anything?"

"He was pretty tight lipped, didn't talk much. Said something about finding a shallow spot. Normal depth out there is around eight hundred feet. He said he found what he called a, uh…" He stopped for a moment, trying to recall. The bulge of snuff in his cheek seemed to move around while he did that. "Well, I don't exactly remember the technical name, but it a hill of sorts, like a big underwater sandbar, he said."

"He bring anything up?" Gwenn asked.

Abner nodded. "Several bags. Full of plants. Guess he was some kind of scientist. Said he was from Tampa but was working at the junior college."

"Anything else?"

He scratched his beard. "Nothin' comes to mind. Hey, did he leave a will or anything? He still owes me for our last trip."

"When was that?" I asked.

"About ten days ago."

I pulled out my notebook. "Can you give me the coordinates

where you took Dr. Wilson, that time he said he found that underwater sandbar, when he brought up the plants?"

He shook his head. "Man, we're at 24 North and 81 West. After that it's all decimal points. No, I don't remember the specific numbers. That's the same thing I told the cops."

"City or county?" I asked.

"City or county what?"

"The cops. Were they from the Sheriff's Office or Key West PD?"

"Sheriff's. A detective. A broad."

Gwenn bristled. "A broad?"

"A woman, okay? Her name, I can't remember it, but it sounded Jewish."

"Jewish?" Gwenn asked. "You can't remember the name of this Jewish broad?"

"Starts with a K, I think."

"Kitchner?" I asked.

Abner snapped his fingers in recognition. "Bingo."

Another question occurred to me. "You said Dr. Wilson dove on the site and he also had an underwater drone, right?"

"Yeah, that's what I told you."

"Sounds like he had a lot of gear with the drone and cameras and all. Did he leave his stuff on your boat, or did he offload it when you were done for the day?"

"He always took it with him. We'd tie up to his houseboat. And what cameras?"

"Dr. Wilson planted at least one, maybe more, down where he was diving. You didn't see them?"

Daystrom gave me a hard look then shook his head.

"You ever go aboard his houseboat with him?"

He shook his head again. "Look, you guys, I don't need any trouble. I've told you everything I know. The cops, too. But I still need to get paid for our last trip out, you know? Gas ain't free. So, do me a favor, can you tell the junior college or whoever he was working for I still need to get paid?"

"Good luck with that," I said, and we walked back toward the car.

"Broad?" I asked. It wasn't like Gwenn to get so huffy.

"I didn't like the way he was looking at me."

I hadn't noticed. "Like how?"

"Like I was a piece of meat."

"Well, you are a wonderful piece of…"

She started to elbow me, but I took off running and she gave chase. We circled around the car a couple of times until she caught me. I held her in my arms and whispered in her ear:

"Piece of work. What did you think I was going to say?"

CHAPTER 32

SINCE HE'D ALREADY downed a couple of cold ones, Lester handed me the car keys.

"Now what?" Gwenn asked.

"We're on a roll," I said. "Let's go back to the community college. I want to take another look at Donald Wilson's lab."

"But we were just there," Gwenn protested.

"Yeah, I know. I should have thought of this sooner. My hard drive needs a tune-up."

Thirty minutes later, we once again tracked down Akari and shortly after that were in Donald Wilson's work space, which consisted of a metal desk like those in Akari and Tina Del Rio's offices. But no filing cabinet and no guest chairs, only an isolated work station in the corner of the lab. I'd seen all that earlier when Akari showed Silver and me the algae growing in the laboratory's saltwater tanks. Then as now, his desktop was bare. Then, the desk drawers were locked. Now they were unlocked, but the drawers had been emptied by the police.

I looked around the laboratory, hoping to see something I might have overlooked the first time I was here. Our earlier visit had been cut short when a uniformed sheriff's deputy found us and asked us to speak with detectives huddled outside Tina Del Rio's office.

Gwenn wandered over to the saltwater tanks. "Oh, these are

pretty," she said. "They look like little green umbrellas." Gwenn turned to me. "Is this the algae you told me about?"

I nodded from across the room.

"Their scientific name is *Acetabularia crenulata*, but they are more commonly known as mermaid's wineglass," Akari said. "They are interesting for a number of reasons, but most fascinating is that despite their large size, each of these plants is but a single cell."

Lester and I joined the women at the tanks. "These specimens," Akari said, pointing to one of the tanks, "they were taken from shallow waters near the coral reef. We're growing them for a researcher at EPFL who's doing a study on circadian rhythm."

"Back up," I said.

"Akari laughed. "Oh, sorry. Circadian rhythm is…"

"I know what circadian rhythm is," I said. "It's our sleep cycle. But what's EPFL?"

"Sorry. It stands for *Ecole Polytechnique Federal de Lausanne*."

"Okay, that clears it up."

She laughed again. "It's a university in Switzerland. They're doing sleep research. They'll take these plants, deprive them of light, and see how that alters their natural circadian rhythm."

"Lester asked, "Plants have sleep cycles, too?"

"Indeed." Akari stepped over to another tank. "Take a look at these. Do you see a difference."

Gwenn peered into the tank. "There are only a few. But, oh, the stems. They're a different color. They're kind of reddish. So are the tips of the little umbrellas."

Akari's head bobbed up and down. "That's right. These are samples of *Acetabularia* that Dr. Wilson harvested near the undersea cable he was investigating. They are unlike anything we have ever seen before."

"You mentioned this before, when Silver and I were with you," I said. "What causes the discoloration?"

"I don't know. I've been trying to get them to multiply, but so far no luck. But there is one significant variable between the samples. The sand in which these plants are embedded was brought back by Dr. Wilson. And it is different in one important respect."

"How so?" I asked.

"It's mildly radioactive."

"Radioactive?"

"I didn't mention that to you before?" she asked.

"Uh, no. I think I would have remembered that."

She shook her head and frowned. "I've been forgetting things lately. Yes, mildly radioactive. Not to worry. Not enough to be harmful, but it is measurable."

"Is the radioactivity in the water, too?" I asked.

"Mostly in the sand. We added fresh seawater to the tanks and no doubt diluted whatever radioactivity was in the water. If only we'd known."

"Have you identified the cause?"

She shook her head. "Not yet. I've sent a sample of the sand off to a friend at the University of Florida to do an analysis. I don't have the equipment here for that."

"Any ideas?"

Akari shook her head again. "Good question, but I don't have enough data to form even a tentative hypothesis. There are too many possibilities."

Lester asked, "Such as?"

She began ticking them off with her fingers. "It could be naturally occurring deposit, although that would be unusual given the seafloor geology here. It could be a rare radioactive isotope of iron from an exploding supernova..."

"That happens?" Gwenn asked.

"Yes, but it, too, is rare. It could be manmade. Leakage from a nuclear power plant..."

"Like the nuke up in Turkey Point?" I asked. Radiation was leaking into Biscayne Bay off Miami and some crocodiles breeding in the nuke's cooling bonds may have mutated due to radiation exposure.

"Perhaps," Akari said. "But then we would expect to see it more widespread down here and that hasn't been observed. Or it could be radioactive material that has been dumped in the ocean. My point is, we need to know more about it before we make assumptions."

"When will you get results from the lab?" I asked.

"Any day, I hope."

While Gwenn and Lester spent more time examining the saltwater tanks, I took another look around the cluttered room. I noticed for the first time a small whiteboard attached to the pale green cement block wall near some lockers. I was sure that if I reviewed the photographs I shot of the lab the last time I was here, I would see it, but it meant nothing to me at the time.

There were several notes on the board in different colored marker ink, but one stood out. It was circled in blue and it read:

24.3501, -81.7889

"Was this here earlier?" I asked Akari.

She shrugged. "Couldn't tell you. But the only people who use this space, besides the students, were Tina, Donald, and me. That's not mine. I'd guess it was Donald's."

I pulled out my notebook and wrote the numbers down. Then I retrieved my iPad from my backpack, fired it up, and navigated to Google Maps. I punched the number in.

In a moment, a red pin was sitting in a sea of blue on the map. I zoomed in, tightening the perspective, until it showed the pin resting at what appeared to be ten miles due south of where Duval Street ends at the Gulf of Mexico.

I wasn't sure what those numbers meant, but in another box on the screen they were translated into what appeared to be GPS coordinates:

24 degrees, 21 minutes, 00.4 seconds North latitude; 81 degrees, 47 minutes, 20.0 seconds West latitude.

I showed the screen to my compatriots. "Looks like this is at least one of Wilson's dive sites."

"Let's go check it out," Gwenn said. She was amped.

It was too late in the afternoon to cruise into the Gulf, but I was as eager as Gwenn to start getting some answers. I clicked the Weather Channel app on my iPhone. "Forecast calls for rain tonight with clear skies tomorrow until late in the afternoon when there's a fifty percent chance of thunderstorms," I said. "We should pull out early. From our marina, it'll be about an hour's cruise, leaving plenty of time to dive and return before the weather."

Akari was looking at her phone, too. "No faculty meetings tomorrow and only one class in the morning, which I can cancel. Tell me where and when to meet you."

I gave her the details, then asked her, "You got a Geiger counter by any chance?"

"Yes, I do. And it is designed to work underwater. I'll bring it."

Gwenn, Lester, and I headed back to our rental car. The skies were already darkening as thick clouds rolled in from the southwest.

"Does it rain like this every day down here?" Gwenn asked. "We're not in rainy season up in Naples yet."

"Forecast says a tropical storm is brewing off the Mexican coast," I said. "Hopefully, we'll have this wrapped up before then."

I dropped Gwenn and Lester at the marina. "I'm going to find a dive shop and get a couple of extra air tanks, load them with trimix in case we have to go deep."

"I'll take the doggie for a walk," Lester said.

"Keep your eyes peeled for weirdos."

"It's Key West," he said. "How can you tell?"

"Stop by the grocery store, too," Gwenn told me. "There's nothing edible on the boat and we'll need food for tonight and tomorrow."

"Text me a list. I'll stop on the way back."

"Will do. Meanwhile, Lester and I will open the bar."

By the time I returned with extra air tanks and two bags of groceries, Lester and Gwenn were in the lounge sipping Cuba Libres. They'd repositioned Mona and Spock to make room.

"You find everything?" Gwenn asked.

"Coffee, cream, oranges, bananas, protein bars, and the fixin's for dinner tonight," I said.

I glanced at Spock. I knew what he was thinking: Had I scored any Romulan ale?

"Sorry, they were fresh out," I said.

"Out of what?" Gwenn asked.

"Romulan ale."

"You really asked for Romulan ale?"

"Of course. Mona doesn't drink, but Spock likes a nip now and then, right Spock?"

Spock said nothing. Probably pouting.

Gwenn looked at me like I was crazy.

Then she stepped behind Spock and in her deepest voice said, "Fascinating."

CHAPTER 33

WHILE GWENN AND Lester drank, I started dinner. I flattened three chicken breasts with a meat hammer then rolled them in whole wheat flower. The *Miss Demeanor's* galley has a small two-burner propane stove, and I heated a pan with a thin layer of vegetable oil and dropped the fillets into the skillet. In two minutes, I turned them, then drizzled fresh lime juice onto the fillets and sprinkled them with shredded cilantro.

While all that was going on, I prepped two cups of pre-cut broccoli florets and dropped them into a steamer and covered them with a thin coat of crushed garlic, red peppers, and a splash of butter.

A Spenser I am not, so my culinary repertoire is limited, but this is one of my go-to dinners. The trick is to finish the chicken at the same time the broccoli is just the right shade of bright green—in the Goldilocks zone between raw and overcooked. I sliced an Amelia tomato to add variety and color to the meal, then announced, "Dinner is served."

We filled our plates and carried them out to the poop deck. Rain was still threatening, but until the skies let loose we wanted to enjoy the fresh air outdoors. Lester opened a bottle of red wine, a Markham cabernet sauvignon that Gwenn had given me. While we ate and drank, Fred chowed down on a fresh doggie treat. The rain gods were forgiving, and we'd cleaned our plates before the first sprinkles descended from the heavens.

"Not it!" I said, and we scurried inside the cabin.

"Not it!" Gwenn echoed.

"What's this 'not it' stuff?" Lester asked.

"Means you do the dishes," I said.

"No fair," he protested. "I didn't know the rules."

"Okay, I'll help," Gwenn said.

While the two of them cleaned the galley, I grabbed a seat in the lounge. It was dark out now, and I guessed she'd be off duty, but I decided to call Abby Kitchner anyway. I got lucky. She answered on the fourth ring.

"What now?"

"And good evening to you, too, detective. I hope I'm interrupting something important."

"You are. I'm about to get a back rub."

"Tell Harrison I said hello."

"Who said Harrison's here?"

"I'm a journalist. I see all and know all. And among the things I know is that you held out on me earlier today."

"Held out, how?"

"We were talking on the phone about Donald Wilson, and where he dived. You failed to mention that you'd already interviewed the charter boat captain who took him out."

"Like I'm obliged to share everything I know with reporters. And how did you know I talked to this charter boat captain?"

"I know because Abner Daystrom spilled his guts when I used my Jedi powers on him. He said a sheriff's detective, to use his words, a broad with a Jewish last name, talked to him. Said her last name starts with a K. Is Kitchner Jewish?"

"Yes, and you better get to the point or I'm hanging up."

"So what would you say if I told you I found out the coordinates of Wilson's dive site?"

"I don't know. Are you likely to say something like that?"

"Very."

"Hold on." I could hear muffled conversation in the background, then she came back on. "I'm putting you on speaker phone."

"Hi, Harrison," I said.

"Hi, yourself."

Kitchner said, "So, you're going out to these coordinates? You're scuba certified?"

"Yes."

"And these coordinates, did Abner cough them up?"

"No."

"Are you going to make me beg?"

"I think you just did. The answer is that we found a note Donald Wilson made in his lab at the community college."

"A note? Where?"

"On a whiteboard by the water tanks filled with radioactive algae."

"Where exactly?" Harrison Paine asked.

"By the tanks in the lab, like I said."

"No, where in the Gulf?"

"About ten miles due south of Key West. Mostly the water that far out is around eight hundred feet deep, according to Abner, but he said Donald Wilson discovered an underwater mound of sorts. That's where Wilson was diving."

"An uncharted mound?" Paine asked.

"That's what he said."

"And you're going to see what's down there?" Paine asked.

"That's the plan."

I could hear Paine and Kitchner saying something to one another in muffled voices. I expected them to ask for the exact GPS coordinates, but they didn't go there.

"Back up a second," Kitchner said when she came back on the line. "Did you say something about radioactive algae?'

"I thought you'd like that." I filled her in on what Akari told us about Wilson's discovery near the submarine cables.

"Okay, appreciate the update," Kitchner said. "But I'm guessing you didn't call just to tell us how clever you are."

"Not just. Look guys, we all want the same thing. We want to find out who's behind these murders and who's been threatening Gwenn and me. I want you to be successful, okay? It's in my self-interest. So I'm sharing what I know. It's really that simple."

It wasn't entirely that simple. I wanted them to owe me. I might need a favor in the future. But close enough.

Paine jumped into the conversation. "I've been thinking about that call you got and the break-in at the marina office. And I've been wondering what led this guy to you. You figure it was the article in the paper?"

"I've thought about that," I said. "I retraced my steps and who I talked to since I've been here. And, yeah, that story rises to the top of my list."

"How about Silver?" he asked. "This robot-voice guy, he call her, too?"

"She didn't say anything about that. At least not to me. Hold the phone."

"Hey, Lester," I said. "Got a second? It's about Silver."

He walked into the lounge with a towel in his hand and a quizzical look on his face. I muted the phone. "Got Harrison Paine and Abby Kitchner on the line. Trying to figure out who down here knew what we were up to that could have led to somebody stalking me, threatening Gwenn."

"What's that got to do with Silver?" he asked.

I put the call on speaker. "Lester's here. Tell him what you're thinking."

"Hey, Lester," Paine said. "We were trying to sort out how anyone got wind of Alex poking around in the Wilson murder, and the only thing we can figure, so far, is that article in the newspaper."

"Okay."

"So, Silver was also mentioned in the story. Did she say anything to you about getting any threats?"

Lester's face turned red. "No. And I'm sure she would have told me. She's left Key West. Already returned to Ocala. But I'll call her to make sure she's okay."

Lester shook his head after we broke off the call. "That never occurred to me," he said. "I'm an idiot."

He dialed her number and after multiple rings the call rolled over into voicemail.

CHAPTER 34

A LIGHT FOG blanketed the marina when I awoke the next morning, the kind of early mist that burns off quickly after sunrise. It was what artists and photographers call the blue hour, the twenty minutes or so before the sun breaks the horizon, when indirect light tints the sky in a soft shade of azure. A peaceful, soft time of day. Relaxing. But it doesn't last long.

Lester was on the phone much of the previous evening with the Marion County Sheriff's Office. The SO dispatched a deputy to Silver's ranch outside Ocala, and he reported back that her place was locked tight, lights out, no sign of disturbance. But her truck was missing.

Lester was agitated, pacing the trawler's cabin, every so often rubbing his shiny scalp with his hands. If he wasn't already bald, he would have pulled all his hair out. "I'm seven times a fool. It never occurred to me she could be in danger, not once she left Key West."

"Take it easy," I told him. "She probably went out to dinner with her Ocala boyfriend."

That earned me heat vision.

"Hey, the cops are on it. Nothing you can do for her right now." Easy for me to say. When Gwenn got that threatening phone call, I was bolting out the door for Naples until she called me off.

"I should fly up there," he said.

"Her truck's not there. She's not home."

"I could look around."

"Where?"

It went on like that for a while, Lester castigating himself, me trying to calm him down. Gwenn jumped in, and after a while she seemed to mollify him.

"Lester," she said, "how could Silver be a threat to anyone? She's clueless about what happened to her brother."

"So's hotshot here," he replied, nodding to me, "but that didn't stop him—and you—from getting threatened."

"Yes, that's true. But the idea behind that was to make him run away. Silver already left on her own. I'm sure she's fine."

Gwenn's line of reasoning made sense at first blush. And it seemed to help Lester calm down. But there was a potential flaw: What if Silver did know something and she hadn't shared it with us, something that Wilson's killer wouldn't want disclosed? Of course, were that the case, why didn't he take a shot at her while she was in Key West?

Still, it reminded me that I really didn't know that much about her. Or Wilson, for that matter. Was Wilson as sanguine about giving up his inheritance as she let on? Family members were always suspect in murders. Was I making a mistake extending her too much trust? Then again, why would she drag a journalist along for the ride if she had something to hide? That made no sense. Why was I even bothering with that line of thought? I needed to stay focused, keep my boundless and annoying imagination in check.

Still, what if she knew something—or had access to something—that could be threatening to the killer? And what if she wasn't even aware? And *why not* snuff her in Ocala instead of Key West where maybe it would take time for the cops in different jurisdictions to connect the dots? Stray thoughts like that haunted me for a while until Gwenn and I finally hit the sack around midnight. Twice during the night my sleep was disturbed by the beeping on Lester tapping the keypad on his phone. No telling when he finally crashed, but he was still conked out, as was Gwenn, when the sun finally peeked over the horizon painting the tops of the masts in the marina in a pale orange glow.

I fired up the Keurig and burned two K-cups on a large, double-strong mug of black French roast. The coffee maker's gurgling roused Lester and he stepped up to the galley from his berth, holding his phone.

"You sleep with that thing?" I asked.

He nodded.

"No word?" I asked.

He shook his head.

"She'll call back. Her phone's probably turned off. I do it all the time." I handed him my coffee and began brewing another mug. Lester's daytime getup, with his knee-high socks and Bermuda shorts—the Full Cleveland—is disturbing enough, but his sleeping attire warranted an entire special edition of *GQ For Dorks*: He wore a genuine Medieval sleeping gown—not a robe, mind you, but a floor-length black satin nightshirt—with matching tasseled cap. It was straight from the pages of a Dickens novel.

"You've *got* to tell me where you shop," I said.

He ignored that and took a swig of coffee. "Damn, that's hot. And strong. I like it."

I'd finished filling the second cup when Gwenn climbed the stairs and ambled into the galley. "I'll have the usual," she said.

I added cream and sugar to the cup and gave it to her, then I refilled the Keurig's water reservoir and began brewing a cup of coffee for myself. As the life-giving caffeine gurgled into the cup, Fred pranced up to the galley from below and started his morning dance, his signal that it was time to go outside.

"I'm never going to get a cup of coffee, am I?"

Gwenn and Lester ignored me. Mona, per usual, offered no comment. Spock seemed lost in Vulcan dreamland. I picked Fred up, grabbed his leash, and opened the door to the aft deck to take him for a walk. That's when two guys in dark suits stepped over the gunwale and confronted me.

"Doesn't anybody ask permission to come aboard anymore?"

"Very funny, Strange." It was the two FBI agents from Miami, Forester and Del Rio.

I heard footsteps behind me, then noticed Lester out of the corner of my eye. His arms were folded across his chest, his hands hidden inside his sleeves.

Forester stared at Lester suspiciously. "What you got in there?" he asked.

"You got trust issues?" Lester asked.

"I'm from the government. I trust no one."

"Relax guys," I said. "Don't let his crazy get-up fool you. He's practicing to be a wizard."

Forester nodded, like that made perfect sense. "We're coming with you today."

"Says who?" I asked.

"We invited them," said a female voice on the dock. I turned and there stood Abby Kitchner and Harrison Paine. They were both wearing shorts and T-shirts, ready for a day at sea.

"And who invited you?"

Paine said, "We're from the government, too. We're here to help."

They stepped over the gunwale and Kitchner looked around. "Good God, is this really our ride? Have you ever heard of paint?"

This was turning into a carnival, and I wasn't sure what to do about it, so I figured I should take them up on their offer to help.

"If you're done with your critique of this outstanding example of American watercraft, I could use some help since you asked. My dog needs a walk. And there's a convenience store over there. We could use some doughnuts."

Forester and Del Rio looked at each other for a moment, then Del Rio shrugged. "An agent's got to do what an agent's got to do."

They took Fred's leash and turned to leave.

"Don't forget this," I said, handing them a plastic doggie waste bag.

"They don't pay us enough," Forester said. But he took the baggie and they lifted Fred onto the dock.

To Paine I said, "And I could use a hand unloading the air tanks from the back of my go-kart."

"Go-kart?"

"You'll see."

"What about me?" Kitchner asked.

"Coffee. I need coffee."

Gwenn wandered out to the deck. "This party's getting bigger by the minute."

I introduced Kitchner and Paine to her. "So you're the girlfriend," Kitchner said. "I feel your pain, and I've only known him for a few days."

"He grows on you."

"Do you live on this scow with him?" she asked.

"From time to time. The *Miss Demeanor* grows on you, too."

"If you say so. Got any coffee inside?"

"Yes. Come on in. But don't be alarmed by Mona. She doesn't like cops very much. The last time one was aboard he shot her."

"Mona?"

"Come in, I'll introduce you."

By the time the feebs came back with Fred and the doughnuts and Paine and I had unloaded the rental, Akari showed up at the dock pulling a cart filled with gear.

"I love trawlers," she said. "They're so roomy."

"We're going to need the space," I said. "The Police Benevolent Association is holding a convention."

Akari paused and gave the boat a more thorough look-see.

"I see you have some deferred maintenance issues. Teak needs oiling. Your radio antenna seems off center. You're missing a cleat over there. Is that capstan…"

"Hey, until a few weeks ago she didn't even float," I protested. "These things take time."

Lester introduced the FBI agents to Akari—she already knew Paine and Kitchner—and we began preparing to cast off.

"Any of you guys dive?' I asked.

They all shook their heads.

"You got something to wear besides suits?" I asked the feds. "It's going to be warm out there." By then, they'd already stripped off their jackets exposing their weapons. Del Rio carried a pistol on his hip; Forester did the James Bond bit with a shoulder holster.

"Afraid not," Del Rio said.

"I've got some spare trunks you're welcome to borrow."

He waved me off. "We'll be okay. But thanks."

I pointed them to the cleats on the dock. "When I give you the signal, untie those ropes and hop back aboard. Try not to drop your guns in the drink."

I disconnected the water and electrical lines at the dock, then climbed up to the flybridge and started the engines, letting them idle. Fuel tanks were full. Weather Channel radar on my cell phone showed clear skies out to sea. Once we were beyond cell phone range, we'd have to rely on our eyes to gauge the weather as the *Miss Demeanor* did not have all the latest, greatest gadgets like Sirius XM Marine Radar—or any kind of radar, for that matter. I didn't share this with my crew, but this would be the furthest from shore I'd ever piloted the trawler. No need to worry them about anything as inconsequential as that, right?

I was about to rev the engines when there was a loud metallic crash. "What was that?" asked Lester, who had joined me up top on the flybridge

"Looks like something fell off the boat," Harrison Paine said. He reached down and lifted an eight-foot-long antenna off the deck. "What is it?"

"Christ. That's our VHF radio antenna," I said. "We need to reattach it."

"Can we do it while we're underway?"

I didn't see any reason why not. "Sure," I said. "You're in charge. There are tools down below in the engine compartment. Gwenn can show you where."

I signaled the FBI agents to release the dock lines. "Any word from Silver?" I asked Lester while they unraveled the lines from the cleats.

"Talked to a deputy at the house. Said a Mexican guy who works in the stables said Silver told him she'd be gone for a few days, that he should tend to the horses."

"Wonder why she didn't let you know?"

Lester shrugged. "At least she's okay."

He was wearing dark sunglasses and I couldn't see his eyes, but there was something in his voice that made me wonder if Silver not calling maybe hurt his feelings a little bit. But that was probably just my imagination. After all, they'd only been hooked up a few days, how intense could their relationship be? And asking him about it would violate several provisions of Man Law.

So, instead, I revved up the *Miss Demeanor's* engines and we slowly pulled away from the dock. In short order, we were cruising through Cow Key Channel into the Gulf of Mexico, our destination an uncharted mound two hundred feet below the surface ten miles south and, with any luck, the answer to the question of why Donald Wilson was targeted for murder.

CHAPTER 35

Gulf of Mexico

Once we cleared the channel, I called down to Gwenn from the flybridge and asked her to join me. The *Miss Demeanor* has controls both inside the cabin and on top of the boat. I like the extra elevation of the flybridge as it provides a more commanding view of the water. In the summer, the breeze up top is cooling, and the Bimini top keeps the sun off.

"Okay," I told her when she joined me. "You've got the helm."

"Uh, you know, Alex, I've never done this before," she said.

"Just keep us pointed due south on the compass."

"What if there's a boat or something or a sandbar?"

"We're in the channel now, so you needn't worry about sandbars. And we'll keep a lookout. I'll take over in a little bit when we get closer. You'll do great."

I signaled Paine to join me. "I need somebody on the bow keeping an eye out for floating debris. Don't want to punch a hole in the hull. How about you take the first watch, then I'll get someone to spell you in a bit until we hit deep water."

"I see pirates, can I shoot them?"

"Watch your ass if it's Jack Sparrow."

While Gwenn steered us south into the Gulf, Akari and I sorted our gear. On the assumption that Wilson's dive took him deep, I'd decided to start with a tank of trimix, just to be safe. Akari agreed. She showed me a portable underwater Geiger counter she'd brought. Then she uncrated a small yellow drone with a camera mounted in its nose.

"Oh, that's cool."

"I suggest we send the drone down first to scout before we dive," Akari said. "GPS coordinates are good to within a few dozen feet, but it might be hard to spot what we're looking for. Might save us a lot of time."

I agreed. "What's its range?"

"It's good to a hundred meters deep and a hundred meters range," she said. "If this mound is, in fact, two hundred feet deep, it will be more than ample."

"Say, this isn't the drone Wilson was using, is it?"

She shook her head. "No, he used his own equipment. At least that's my understanding from what Tina told me. I wanted to dive with Dr. Wilson at some point after spring break, but, well…"

"Yeah."

We'd picked a clear morning for ocean cruising. Winds were under four knots and the sky overhead was cloudless. The forecast for later in the day was not so pleasant, but by then I expected we would be safe and sound back in the marina. We'd been cruising for about twenty minutes. Looking due south, the horizon was empty. There was a shrimp boat about a quarter mile off our port, but otherwise we had the ocean to ourselves.

I was startled when my iPhone began buzzing in the pocket of my cargo shorts. Who knew you could still get a signal this far offshore? I recognized the number. It was from Anthony, the Wook.

"Anthony, my man. What it is?"

"This Dr. Strange?"

"No. Dr. Strange carries a time stone. I wear a Mickey Mouse watch."

"Dude. You're hilarious. I got something for you, I think."

"Talk to me."

"Some fisher dudes last night, they were wrecked and talking trash over by Captain Tony's."

"Wrecked?"

"Yeah, man, they were DEFCON ONE, shitfaced. And pissed. Their day got totally fucked up."

"How's that?"

"They were chasing a school of gag grouper, at least that's what I think they called them. That a thing?"

"Yeah. It's a kind of game fish."

"Gag grouper. I thought it might be a joke, you know? Gag. Anyway, they were saying some ass hats in a Zodiac ran them off, said they were trespassing on a private dive site, like they owned the ocean or something weird like that."

"That's random."

"Yeah, and these drunk fisher dudes, they said the ass hats in the Zodiac, they threatened them with guns. Said they'd shoot them if they didn't leave."

"They call the cops?"

"Don't know, man. But they were out of their minds. I thought about selling them some herb to chill them down, but then I remembered I was under cover."

"Where'd this happen in the Gulf, did they say?" I asked.

"Dunno, man. But I figured it was the kind of thing we should report to you."

"Anthony, this is great. You done good. I'll catch up with you later. Keep your ears open."

"Ten-four, my commandant."

I scanned the horizon over the bow and it was still clear. At sea level, you can see about three miles out. Men with guns in Zodiac boats? Sounded like drug runners, and they could be anywhere. But we needed to stay alert.

"Yo, all you heavily armed cops, FBI agents, and private dicks. We could have company out here. Unfriendly. Keep your eyes peeled."

I pulled a piece of diving gear from my bag then climbed back up to the flybridge. "You did great, babe. I'll take over now."

"What was that about unfriendlies?"

I told her about my conversation with the Wook. "We see anybody out here, I need you and Akari to get below."

"Why us? Because we're women?"

"Because you're the only people on the boat without a weapon."

"What about you?"

I patted the holster strapped to my thigh. "Have speargun, will travel."

"Huh?"

"It was the name of an old western on TV."

"They used spearguns out West?"

"No, it was *Have Gun Will Travel.* Uncle Leo had a whole collection on VHS."

"VHS?"

"Stop it."

"And you're gonna take a speargun to a gunfight?"

"I've done dumber things. The Wook said the unfriendlies were driving a Zodiac. Maybe I'll shoot a hole in their boat."

"Or they'll shoot a hole in you. You think this is real?"

"Let's hope not."

And it wasn't.

"Our destination's about a mile out, dead ahead," I told the crew. "I don't see any other boats from here to the horizon."

"I wanted to fight pirates," Paine said.

"Maybe we'll find some on the way back," Kitchner said.

I kept the trawler at full throttle for another ten minutes, then slowed it down as we began to draw closer to the dive coordinates.

"I see something," Lester said from the bow where he was taking his turn on watch.

"Oh, crap," I said.

"What is it? I don't see anything," Gwenn said, shading her eyes. "There aren't any boats or anything."

"Not *on* the water," I said. "*In* the water."

"What's that smell?" Kitchner asked. "Jesus."

My eyes began tearing up. Both Paine and Forester began coughing.

"Dead fish ahead," Lester said. "A lot of them."

"Is this what I think it is?" Gwenn asked, covering her mouth.

"I'm afraid so."

No wonder we had this part of the Gulf to ourselves. There were no pirates. No gunboats. Just a sea of red-brown scum and poison gas. We'd cruised into the heart of a Red Tide outbreak.

CHAPTER 36

THE WIND WAS out of the southwest, blowing the algae bloom in a northeastwardly direction toward the uppers Keys. I reversed the *Miss Demeanor's* course, north, back toward Key West, then after a few hundred yards turned to a westerly heading hoping we might circumnavigate the outbreak.

"Any idea how big this is?" I asked Akari.

"Likely goes on for miles," she said. "How many miles is impossible to tell from sea level. If this is part of the bloom that's been drifting down the west coast, it will be very large. But I don't think it is."

"How come?"

"The wind is coming from a southerly direction, up from Cuba. This is likely a different bloom, perhaps blowing up from the coastline near Havana."

"All this Red Tide, is that normal?" I asked.

"Red Tide occurs naturally. The algae, *Karenia brevis,* feeds off nutrients in the water. Agricultural run-off into the ocean encourages it to grow larger, however, and the toxins the algae gives off are deadly to marine life. But I have to say this year does seem to be worse than usual. All those releases out of Lake Okeechobee, all that polluted lake water flowing into the Gulf, it has to be feeding this outbreak."

We continued in a westerly direction for a few minutes until Akari suggested, "Why don't you try heading south again. Let's see if we can get past its western edge."

I steered the trawler to port and we resumed our southerly course, now well off the line to take us to Wilson's dive coordinates. In a few minutes we were back in the soup again.

"I'm going to be sick," Lester said. "This is awful."

"Everybody below decks," I commanded. "Gwenn, Lester, button up the cabin and I'll turn on the air conditioner, maybe that will make it easier to breathe."

While the crew scrambled below, Akari began grabbing sample bottles out of a case she'd brought aboard.

"Slow us down, please," she said. "I want to scoop some of this up, take it back to the lab and examine it."

I idled the trawler and she dipped globs of the algae out of the Gulf and poured the samples into jars that she tightly sealed. When she was finished, I asked, "You've got the Ph.D. Any suggestions?"

Akari peered through the windows at the crew below. "They're still alive," she said. "Guess the AC is helping."

"Them, anyway." My eyes and lungs were on fire. It was as if some demon had mixed dead fish and Mace into an obnoxious aerosol and sprayed it into the air.

"Why don't we keep heading south, see how deep this bloom is," Akari said. "Sometimes it strings out, we might punch through the other side. Maybe we can approach our coordinates from south of the dive site."

I was tempted to put on a dive mask and tanks to keep the fumes out of my eyes and lungs. But if Akari could handle it, I had to man up.

We were lucky. After another ten minutes, we pushed through the reddish-brown glop and dead fish into clear, open ocean. I gave it a few more minutes then turned eastward, back toward our original line. With the winds off starboard, the fumes were no longer an issue and Akari gave the all-clear to the crew below.

Gwenn was the first on deck. "Thank God that's over," she said. "Where are we?"

"South of the Red Tide outbreak," I said. It's now between us and the Keys. I'm going to head this way for a bit, then turn north, see how close to our coordinates I can get."

Lester resumed his watch on the blow, this time armed with a pair of binoculars that he found in the cabin. In a few minutes, he shouted, "I can see the line of Red Tide ahead. About a hundred yards."

I brought the engines to idle.

"How close are we to our destination?" Akari asked.

"GPS indicates we're about a quarter mile away," I said. "It will be difficult to hold this position in the wind. It's starting to pick up."

She looked over the stern at the dinghy we were towing. "What about that? You and I could take the drone out toward the coordinates. Wear our dive gear. Even if we don't go down, it will protect us against the fumes."

"Why didn't I think of that?"

"It helps to have a Ph.D."

"Of course."

"If we see something, then, we'll go take a look," she said.

"Through the algae?" I was incredulous.

"You're not a fish," Akari said. "Oxygen depleted water won't kill you. And it's not deep. It'll get our gear messy, but we can dive through it. It's only a problem for us near the surface."

Having piloted the *Miss Demeanor* through the bloom once already, the cleanup of our diving gear was the least of my worries. I envisioned hours below deck washing out the bilge and the inboard engines.

"Should have brought a submarine," I said.

CHAPTER 37

It took a few minutes to wriggle into our wet suits and assemble the equipment. While Harrison Paine and Hector Del Rio held it snug to the hull of the trawler, I lowered myself into the dinghy, then Akari began handing down the gear: air tanks and regulators, weight belts, masks, fins, the underwater drone and its controller, Geiger counter, portable GPS navigator, walkie talkies, and one handy-dandy speargun. My dive knife was already strapped on my left thigh.

The wind was picking up and the swells were growing. A line of clouds was building to the southwest. The Weather Channel forecast had indicated we should have clear sailing until the afternoon with winds under seven knots, but in the brief time we had been afloat, conditions deteriorated. Not unheard of in the Gulf of Mexico.

"We need to get going," I told Akari as soon as she settled into the dinghy. In minutes we were deep into the Red Tide bloom and the *Miss Demeanor* was receding behind us.

I left Gwenn in charge of the trawler with instructions to keep it pointed into the wind and to try to hold position. "Whatever happens," I told her, "don't lose sight of us. If you can see us, we can see you." I didn't want to expose the entire crew to the Red Tide's noxious effects, so the plan was for the trawler to remain safely outside the bloom if at all possible. "Worse case, you may have to come get us if something goes wrong."

"I won't lose you," Gwenn said. "Finding a new boyfriend is a pain in the ass."

While I steered, Akari read out the GPS coordinates as we neared the dive site. We'd put on our masks to keep the fumes out of our eyes, but breathing was still painful. Dead fish surrounded our little craft, and as the dinghy pushed though the bodies, I worried about fouling the electric motor's props. I wouldn't want to get stuck in this soup.

We were approaching the dive site when Akari shouted, "There's something ahead." I saw it, too. As we got closer, we realized it was a bottlenose dolphin, struggling in the reddish-brown glop.

"Oh, no," Akari said. "He's in trouble. We have to help him."

The dolphin blew water out of its air hole. It was brownish red. I hoped that was the discoloration of the water from the algae and not blood.

The cetacean saw us approach, but didn't try to flee. Maybe it was my imagination, but I swear there was a look of panic in its eyes. Then we saw why.

The dolphin's dorsal fin was caught in what appeared to be a clump of fishing net. It was struggling to keep its head above water, but the net was dragging it down. I couldn't see the lower half of its body for the algae bloom, but I worried about further entanglement below the waterline.

Sure enough, as if reading my mind, the dolphin flopped over on its side exposing more netting wrapped around its tail.

"Flipper, you got yourself into a real mess."

"What are we going to do? Akari asked.

My first instinct was to grab hold of the net and try to motor out of the bloom into clean water, taking the dolphin with us. But when I reached over the side of the dinghy and pulled on the netting, it was unmovable. It was also clear it was not fishing net, which is thin, lightweight and usually made of nylon. The strands on this net were thick, heavy-duty cargo netting.

"It's either snagged on something," I said, "Or it is so heavy and waterlogged, it won't budge."

"I wonder how he got caught in that?"

"Yeah, and what kind of asshole would leave him out here like this."

"Now what?" she asked. "He needs our help." The dolphin joined in the conversation, trilling its frustration in a series of squeaks and grunts as it continued to thrash about.

"I need to cut him loose from this net," I said. "But I can't do it from inside the dinghy, he's flailing around too much, I might hurt him or I might capsize us. I'm going to have to jump in."

Akari put a hand on my arm and shook her head. "That's too dangerous. You could get tangled up, too. And the dolphin, he's panicked. He could hurt you."

Bottlenose dolphins are big animals, growing to around eight feet in length and weighing upwards of 600 pounds. People love them for their playfulness and the upward turn of their mouths, which humans misidentify as a grin. Crocodiles have the same shaped mouth and nobody thinks they smile—except maybe after a tasty meal of *homo sapiens* tartare.

And bottlenose dolphins are smart. They are second only to humans in the ratio between their brain and body size. And since the time of the ancient Greeks, there have been tales of dolphins saving humans at sea from drowning and even shark attacks. There are even documented cases of dolphins rescuing dogs who fell overboard.

I wasn't about to let this poor creature die like this, and the only way to save it was to jump into the Gulf with my knife and try to cut it free. I would count on the dolphin to understand that I was there to help and hope for the best.

"I'm going in, Akari. But I'm not putting on any other gear besides my mask. I don't want to get tangled up in that net."

She nodded. "Be careful."

I leaned out of the dinghy and pulled on the net, dragging us as close to Flipper as possible. For a moment, the dolphin looked into my eyes. Then it wriggled its way even closer to the boat. I rested my hand on its head and spoke to it:

"I'm coming in. I'm going to help you."

Flipper squeaked in what I interpreted as approval.

I slipped into the awful red sludge and dog-paddled my way around to the rear of the cetacean. I took a gulp of polluted air and dove.

The problem was instantly apparent. A square of netting had slipped over and wedged itself tightly onto the tail of the dolphin, which, unhelpfully, was still wriggling about. I reached out and touched the dolphin's body, hoping it would understand to calm down. As it turns out, the dolphin and I spoke different languages. It slapped its tail and struck me in the chest, but I grabbed on with my arms, then wrapped my legs around its lower body.

And we sank.

I've strong lung capacity, but I now wished I'd brought an air tank. I didn't have much time. I pulled my dive knife from its sheath and began hacking at the net. It was thick and didn't give up easily. Thank God my Uncle Leo taught me to keep my knives sharpened. The blade sliced through.

And I was out of air.

We'd descended about a dozen feet, and as I looked up toward the surface, I discovered that my path topside was blocked by the very netting I'd sawed off Flipper.

Nothing for it, I began kicking my way upward. But the dolphin, its tail now liberated, decided to escape by going deeper. And in so doing, it drug the net down that was still attached to his dorsal fin. And me with the net.

I'm not afraid of the water. I swam for the University of Texas, and I've free-dived the coral reefs off Key Largo. It was no time to panic. But I couldn't dawdle, either. My lungs were starting to scream for air, but I knew that as long as my head was clear, I was okay. But there's a limit. Once, during swim team practice, I decided to see how many laps I could swim underwater in the Olympic-sized pool. I've got a stubborn streak, and even though my lungs were clawing at me I kept going and going until finally I blacked out. Fortunately, I had teammates to pull me up. This time, I was on my own.

I grabbed the net and began rolling it away from me, all the while kicking upward against the dolphin's descent. My peripheral vision began narrowing. I desperately needed to take a breath. Kick, I told myself. Kick.

Flipper noticed my distress. We were well below the Red Tide now and while the algae blocked much of the sunlight that otherwise would have penetrated to our depth, the water was clear enough to see Flipper. And, more importantly, for Flipper to see me. He looked at me and reversed course.

In moments, he was underneath me and pushing me upward. I broke the surface and took a huge gulp of air. Noxious Red Tide fumes or not, it was the best lungful I've ever gulped. Flipper kept nudging me and I leaned on him, using him stay afloat. In a few seconds, I'd recovered sufficiently to grab the netting entangled in his dorsal fin and cut it away.

The dolphin immediately rocketed downward.

I thought momentarily about hauling the net up into the dinghy to get it out of the Gulf lest some other creature become entangled in it. But it was too massive.

"We shouldn't leave this net out here, Akari," I shouted up to her. "Any ideas?"

"Is it heavy?" she asked.

"Very."

"What's keeping it from sinking?"

"Me. And I can't keep this up much longer."

"So, don't. Let it go. But first, cut off a piece for me. I want to test it."

I thought about Flipper. I didn't want him to get snared again. But then I saw him about fifty feet away curling out of the water.

I sliced off a square foot of the netting, then pushed off from it and the remaining net slowly disappeared beneath the waves, hopefully all the way to the ocean floor where it would no longer pose a danger.

Akari extended a hand to me and I flopped back into the dinghy.

"You did it," she said. "You saved him."

Or her. Who knows? But Flipper, by whatever gender, got it, totally groked what had happened. He/She/It rocketed out of the water curling in a huge arc, then dove down again.

"He knows," Akari said. "He knows you saved him."

The dolphin gave us an encore performance, then swam in the direction of the trawler, which by now was maybe a half-mile away.

"How far are we from our coordinates?" I asked Akari.

She checked her GPS navigator then shook her head. "We drifted quite a way while we were dealing with the dolphin."

Oh. It wasn't the *Miss Demeanor* that had been carried by the current, it was us.

I looked back again toward the trawler and noticed that the boundary of the algae bloom was approaching us and that outside the discolored water whitecaps were forming. The clouds that had been hovering on the western horizon were now slipping overhead. I heard the muted rumble of thunder in the distance.

"Looks like the storm is almost on us," I said.

She nodded. "We need to leave. We can come back tomorrow. The Red Tide is bound to have moved on by then,"

We hadn't come any closer to solving the murders of Donald Wilson and Tina Del Rio, but we saved Flipper. All things considered, I felt pretty good about that.

CHAPTER 38

I PILOTED THE little dinghy toward the *Miss Demeanor* while Akari retrieved her small underwater Geiger counter, preparing to run it over the section of net I'd liberated.

"You think it might be hot?" I asked.

"Let's take a look." She turned on the device and it began clicking wildly.

"As soon as we get to clear water, you need to wash yourself off thoroughly," she said, a look of concern on her face.

"How dangerous is it?"

"It's in the same range as the soil samples Dr. Wilson brought back from to the lab," she said. "Nothing too alarming, small millirems."

"What about on me?" I asked. "Am I as hot as the net?"

She waved Geiger counter over my body, and to my relief it was nowhere near the level of snap, crackles, and pops of the net.

"What does this mean?" I asked.

"It means, I think, that this cargo net was used to haul something radioactive off the bottom of the seafloor," she said. "And not just mermaid's wineglasses."

"Something radioactive? Like what?"

She shrugged. "We knew there was radiation at the site. I thought, perhaps, it might have come from the nuclear plant up the coast. Or some naturally occurring phenomenon. Now I'm not sure." She placed the section of netting in an opaque rubber bag and zipped it shut.

"Will it be safe there?" I asked.

She smiled. "Lead lined."

"How'd you know to bring that?"

"I have a Ph.D."

Our walkie-talkie crackled. It was Harrison Paine. "We've been trying to reach you. Did you fucking wrestle a dolphin? We've been taking turns watching with binoculars, taking bets who would win. My money was on the fish."

"It's not a fish, it's a cetacean." I handed the radio to Akari and she filled the crew in on our adventure while I guided our dinghy back toward the trawler.

Gwenn's voice came over the radio. "You saved Flipper!"

Akari keyed the microphone for me. "I hesitate to use the word hero…"

We heard the crew laughing and it wasn't over the radio. We were now only a hundred yards off the boat.

Gwenn came on again. "From here, it looks like the algae bloom has drifted closer to shore and away from us. We might be able to motor over to the dive site now if you still want to try it."

"How about the weather?" I asked.

"A line of showers is approaching. It will be here pretty soon.. There's lightning, too. Whether we stay or head back to shore, we're going to get hit."

"You thinking we should stick it out, then get back to business?"

"Hey, we've come this far."

I looked at Akari and she gave me a thumbs up.

"Okay, then. Toss us a line when we get close enough and we'll come back aboard. But first, I'm taking a bath."

With that, I handed Akari the tiller and rolled off the dinghy into the clear Gulf water and washed off the slime from the algae bloom, and, I hoped, any lingering radioactive remnants from the net. I hung off the side of the little boat as Paine and Forester pulled us in and muscled our gear back on board.

Everyone was in an ebullient mood while we huddled in the cabin as the thunderstorm washed over the trawler. I briefly stepped out into the downpour to allow the rainwater to rinse off the salt and any lingering isotopes, but darted back inside when lightning cracked off the starboard bow. Lester handed me a towel from down below and I dried off as the storm rendered visibility to near zero. Gwenn was at the helm inside the cabin and she aimed the trawler into the wind, barely moving, doing an admirable job of keeping us as stable as possible in the stormy seas.

In a few minutes, the squall passed and then, to oohs and aahs from the crew, a rainbow blossomed over our dive site.

"It's an omen," Abby Kitchner said.

"It's ominous," Harrison Paine replied.

"A rainbow is ominous?" Gwenn asked.

"No," Paine said. "What's ominous is that boat out there."

I followed his gaze out the windshield and saw what appeared to be a shrimp boat—a large shrimp boat—heading toward us, maybe a half-mile off. At our relative speeds, we would arrive at the dive site at about the same time.

"We've got company after all," Lester said.

Behind me, I heard the unmistakable metallic clack of a round being loaded into a semi-automatic pistol. I turned. It was Harrison Paine fiddling with his Glock.

"Finally, pirates!"

CHAPTER 39

If this turned out to be same boatload of gunslingers Anthony the Wook warned me about, it could get ugly fast. My protective instincts kicked in. After all, the *Miss Demeanor* was carrying defenseless women, dogs, and journalists aboard. Not to mention a Vulcan. Of course, not all the women were defenseless and there was only one dog, and he was small and an unlikely target. And journalists are a dime a dozen these days, many unemployed.

Still, why take chances? The Coast Guard's Rescue 21 system monitored channel 16 on the Marine VHF radio. While VHF radio is line-of-sight and the shoreline was no longer visible, the Coast Guard's enormous radio tower in the Keys gave it an effective range of more than a hundred miles.

"I'm going to radio the Coast Guard," I said. "See if they know anything about marauding pistoleros out here."

"You're hoping all they got is pistols," Lester said.

"Yeah, we're kinda fucked if they got grenade launchers."

Paine joined us at the helm.

"Tell me you fixed the antenna," I said to him.

"Problem with that," he said. "The base of the antenna is rusted out. I can't see any way of reattaching it. You're going to need a new one."

"So we got no radio with bad guys approaching." I said, stating the obvious. I would have looked around for someone to blame, but there was no mirror in sight.

I scanned the trawler, checking on the rest of the crew. Gwenn and Abby Kitchner were standing outside on the bow, watching the shrimp boat as our distances closed. Akari was in the stern, reorganizing our diving gear. Del Rio was sitting in the lounge, his earbuds in place, lost in his own world. He'd been there most of the cruise.

Forester noticed me staring at Del Rio. "He's pretty much out of it," he said. "This is killing him. We still don't know how the bodies got mixed up at the morgue, whether it was plain stupidity or something else. But they did get results on the tissue samples they sent to the state crime lab. Your friend Silver was right. Dr. Wilson was clean—no alcohol or drugs in his system. Tissue samples from both Tina and him indicate time of death was pretty much coincident, like we figured."

"How long you guys hanging out down here?" I asked.

"Today's our last day, for now anyway," Forester said. "The medical examiner has released the body. We're taking Tina home tomorrow for the funeral."

"You and Del Rio, you veterans by any chance?" I asked.

He shook his head. "Did firearms training at Quantico, of course, but both Hector and I are accountants by training. We don't do a lot of field work, mostly analysis. Why?"

I turned to Lester. "Looks like you and Harrison are the only combat veterans here," I said nodding toward the approaching shrimp boat.

"Abby, too," Paine said.

I didn't know that.

"Army. She retired out as captain. Chopper pilot."

"We could use an Apache gunship about now."

"That would be sweet."

"Any combat suggestions?" I asked.

"Yeah, try not to get shot."

Lester was peering at the shrimp boat through his binoculars. “It’s stopped moving and they’re lowering an inflatable into the water,” he said. “It’s big. Looks like a Zodiac.”

“They armed?” Paine asked.

“Can’t tell.”

“Who’s jurisdiction is this?” Lester asked. “We still in the county or are we in international waters yet?”

“We’re just shy of international waters,” I said. “By about two miles.”

“Not my jurisdiction,” Kitchner said. “Florida stops three miles out. These are federal waters.”

“So it looks like the FBI is in charge,” Lester said. “You guys got any bright ideas?”

Forester and Del Rio looked at one another. “He’s senior,” Del Rio said.

“Can we outrun them?” Forester asked.

I shook my head.

He looked at me. “This is your boat and you’re the captain. You got any bright ideas?”

I cut the engines. “Yeah. Let’s not do the O.K. Corral thing just yet.”

I was standing on the foredeck with my back to the Zodiac as it approached. Abby Kitchner aimed my digital camera at me as if she were making a live recording. In fact, she could have been as I used the Canon 80D to shoot occasional video for the news service.

“How do I make it work?” she asked.

In the rush—and let’s face it, panic—to set up this ruse, I hadn’t even thought about actually filming the encounter. I stepped over, switched the camera on, and showed her the button to push when she was ready to start recording.

I glanced inside the cabin. Gwenn was at the wheel keeping the trawler pointed into the breeze. I'd asked Akari to stay inside and keep an eye on Fred, in case shooting broke out. He hates loud noises. Mona, too.

The rest of the crew was stationed in a rough semi-circle facing the approaching Zodiac, an arm's length between each of them, their guns hidden in their waistbands at their backs, their cellphones in their hands, pretending to shoot video, too. I hoped that's all we would be shooting.

When the Zodiac cut its engine, and before any of the three men aboard could say boo, I started my spiel in my very best booming radio announcer's voice:

"This is Alexander Strange streaming live via satellite from GPS coordinates 24 degrees, 21 minutes, 00.4 seconds North latitude; 81 degrees, 47 minutes, 20.0 seconds West latitude about ten miles south of Key West in the Gulf of Mexico.

"We are here today to celebrate the thirty-fifth anniversary…"

"Hey, you," the man behind the wheel of the Zodiac shouted. "What the hell are you doing here?"

I held up my finger, the universal sign to hold on. "The thirty-fifth anniversary of one of the most daring rescues at sea ever undertaken. It occurred in the midst of a devastating tropical storm at the height of the Mariel boatlift…"

"Hey, asshole, I'm talking to you."

I ran my index finger across my throat, signaling Kitchner to cut the recording, and turned around to face the loudmouth. He was average height, all muscle and sinew, with a shaggy black beard. He was also working on becoming a world-class melanoma victim. Apparently pirates don't use sunscreen.

"Yo, butthead, you're in our shot. Get the fuck away from us. You wanna be on television go rob a 7-Eleven."

I turned back to Kitchner to resume, and the guy began yelling again. "You see these?" He and his two buddies held up the weapons they'd hidden on the floor of the Zodiac. Looked like a shotgun and a couple of AR-15s.

Kitchner continued her videography, recording the morons with their guns held aloft.

"Yes we see them, you simpering clump of anal fungus. You see these cameras? You morons are live, on the internet, on the Tropic Press streaming channel right now via our satellite uplink."

That, of course, was total bullshit, but my hope was these idiots wouldn't know that.

"The Coast Guard Cutter *Resolute* is four miles out and heading this way. We're about to interview the crew. The *Resolute* rescued three dozen Cubans during the Mariel boatlift right at this spot. Now would you please get out of our shot, you are fucking up our production. Or would you like to explain to the Coast Guard why you are harassing us?"

Bigmouth turned to his two companions and they held a brief but spirited conversation in a language I didn't understand. Bigmouth then got on a walkie-talkie and yakked some more, presumably to their mothership. Again it came across as gibberish.

"Did any of you guys understand what they were saying?" I asked the crew.

"No," said Harrison Paine, "but if Abby recorded it, maybe we can translate it later."

"Alex," Gwenn yelled from the helm. "I got the Coast Guard on the radio."

That was a nice touch.

"Mayday, mayday, mayday," she yelled into the mic.

Bigmouth heard her, jabbered some more in the radio, then cranked the Zodiac's engine and one-eightied back to the shrimp boat leaving a huge wake that rocked the *Miss Demeanor*.

What a prick.

I watched them recede for a moment, then yelled into the cabin: "Nice touch, Gwenn."

She shook her head. “No, really, I got the Coast Guard on the line.”

“How?”

Then I noticed Akari on her knees, holding the antenna in her hands. She grinned at me. “Better hurry. This won’t stayed glued together for long.”

CHAPTER 40

"This is Chief Warrant Officer Jon Sebaly of the Coast Guard cutter Tillson," the voice on the radio said. "Are you declaring an emergency?"

"Mr. Sebaly," I replied. "We are not, repeat not, in immediate danger. But we do need to report a situation." I went on in detail, explaining our confrontation with the goons in the Zodiac, how they threatened us with their firearms, how we head-faked them, how their presence matched the reports Anthony the Wook told us about.

He asked for our coordinates and the direction the Zodiac and the shrimp boat were heading. The Zodiac had zoomed past the shrimp boat traveling in a northeasterly direction, toward the Upper Keys. The shrimper was following rapidly, leaving a substantial wake behind it.

"We are en route to a distress call about seven nautical miles south of you," Sebaly said. "I would advise returning to safe harbor as soon as possible. We are getting reports of gale-force winds and heavy seas moving in your direction."

"We've been hit by some heavy rain already," I said.

"Yes, it's coming in bands. The next one will be much stronger."

"How much time we got before it hits?" I asked.

"Less than an hour, I'd…" His transmission began breaking up and finally died.

Akari yelled, "Sorry, I couldn't hold it in place any longer. The wire's too corroded."

"Now what?" Lester asked.

Before I could answer Del Rio jumped in. His earbuds were gone and the confrontation with the asshats in the Zodiac had animated him. "We came here for a reason. We got an hour? Let's use it. Let's see what's down there." I looked around at the rest of the crew and their heads were bobbing.

"Let's give it a try," Akari said. "We can at least send down the drone."

Gwenn echoed the sentiment. "Let's do this thing."

What a crew!

In ten minutes we were over the GPS coordinates and Akari was lowering the drone over the gunwale. I returned the wheel to Gwenn and climbed down from the flybridge to slip back into my wetsuit. Akari was already in hers.

Our plan was simple. Akari would stay topside and maneuver the drone. I would be in the water prepared to follow the drone's control wire down if she found something interesting to examine up close or to retrieve. Paine would be with Akari and she would instruct him on the controls so she could follow me into the water if need be.

Before I lowered myself into the Gulf, Akari pulled me aside. She was blushing. "I'm embarrassed that I haven't mentioned this earlier," she said. "It's something Donald Wilson gave me. He asked me if I could translate it." She showed me a slip of paper with what looked like Chinese characters.

美人鱼

"So what is this?" I asked.

"That's what I asked Donald when he showed it to me," Akari said. "He assumed because of my Japanese heritage that, naturally, I would be able to read Chinese, which, to be honest, I found a little offensive. I was born in America and grew up in Seattle, for crying out loud. What if I'd asked him to translate something in Yoruba."

"Your what?"

"It's the language of Nigeria, where his father was born."

"Yeah, okay, can I go now?"

She grabbed my arm. "I'm telling you this because I didn't know what it meant until last night. I ran across it while I was packing my gear and I finally got around to translating it. I didn't think much of it, even then. But now that those awful men threatened us, I realize it must be important."

"So you do speak Chinese?"

"No I speak Google."

"And you're telling me this, why?"

"Remember what you asked me when we first met. About Donald's last words to Silver before he disappeared?"

"Of course. He said he found a mermaid. I assumed he meant Tina since she worked at Wiki Wachee. Then you showed us the mermaid's wineglasses, and that kind of muddied the water."

"Well, it gets muddier," she said.

"How's that?"

"These symbols translate to the word *mermaid*."

"Really?"

She nodded her head and lowered her eyes. "I should have done this sooner."

"Hey, better late than never. But Wilson must have figured it out on his own, right?"

"Assuming the mermaid he was referring to was this," she said waving the slip of paper.

"Let me see that," I said, taking the slip of paper from Akari's hand. It wasn't ordinary copy paper, but thinner. Tracing paper. The gears in my head were starting to mesh. "It looks like he traced these characters from something else. Perhaps a photograph? Or maybe an image on a computer screen? You think maybe wherever this came from could be below us?"

"Possibly."

Maybe this was finally the right mermaid. We'd know soon enough.

I splashed into the Gulf, cleared my mask, and descended about a dozen feet to ensure my gear was working properly. Then I returned topside.

"Anything yet?" I yelled up to the trawler when I surfaced.

"Not yet." It was Paine.

"No more visitors?" I asked.

"All clear," Gwenn shouted from the flybridge.

I could hear Akari now. "The camera is working. Visibility is good. I'm turning on the drone's lights now."

I tread water for a few minutes, waiting. There was no point in pestering her. If she found something, she'd let me know. Maybe there'd be a Chinese mermaid lurking on the ocean floor.

I dove again to have something to do and tried to follow the direction of the control wire as it dipped into the deep water. I could see it for only a dozen yards until it blurred out of sight. As Akari said, the water was reasonably clear, not crystalline, but not bad, but with storm clouds overhead the light wasn't the greatest. I caught a glimpse of a spotlight moving in the darkness below me, the drone's headlamp.

I resurfaced about forty feet from the *Miss Demeanor* to hear Paine yelling at me. "Hey, you got a visitor." His arm was extended and pointing to a spot in the water behind me. I thought for a moment he might be signaling that the Zodiac was returning, but when I turned my head I found myself facing an approaching blue-gray triangle, the unmistakable dorsal fin of a tiger shark.

Instinctively, I reached for the speargun holstered on my thigh, pulled it out of its holster, and aimed it in the shark's direction. There are two strategies when initially encountering a shark: go big or go small. Making yourself big in the water by spreading your arms and legs is supposed to discourage a shark that may be in attack mode. Going small, by curling up in a ball, is supposed to discourage attention if a shark is only passing through.

Since he appeared to be heading straight for me, I guessed this shark wasn't a tourist. I spread my arms and legs keeping the speargun pointed in his direction.

If a shark actually attacks, the best defense allegedly is to jab him in the eyes. This is easier said than done, of course. Sharks are fast and you're both moving in the water. What are the odds of hitting a target that small?

Statistically, shark attacks on people are rare. That's because, statistically, the vast majority of people will never encounter a shark in the water because statistically the vast majority of people are never ten miles offshore in the Gulf of Mexico. They're in their living rooms watching Mark Cuban on Shark Tank. So much for statistics.

But the most important thing to know about shark encounters is not to panic. Sharks have a terrific sense of smell and, like blood in the water, they can sense if you've pissed yourself. It's like ringing a dinner bell to them.

Another important tip, experts will tell you, is to never take your eyes off a shark. They're ambush hunters and they don't like being stared at. Sharks, generally speaking, are actually shy critters, they say. Not so much for tigers, however. Or great whites. Combined, they've recorded nearly five hundred attacks on humans.

I stared at the tiger as he circled me, turning my head with his movements to ensure he knew I had my eyes on him. Maybe he'd go all introvert and swim away.

With my right hand aiming the speargun at Jaws, I used my left hand and flippers to slowly paddle my way back toward the trawler. I wanted to get my back up against the hull to limit the shark's angles of attack. But Jaws wasn't cooperating, and he circled between me and the boat—and any chance of rescue.

I looked up and saw Paine and Lester aiming their pistols into the water.

"Jesus, don't shoot him," I yelled. "You'll only make him mad." It would also spill blood in the water, which would likely attract his nieces and nephews, and that was not a family reunion I wanted to attend.

The shark swam away from the trawler and seemed to be enlarging his circle around me. Maybe he figured I didn't look that tasty. Or maybe he wanted extra space to build speed for an attack.

Suddenly, three more dorsal fins appeared nearby.

Oh, great.

But these weren't shark fins. They were the dorsals of bottlenose dolphins and they began circling our boat, putting themselves between me and the tiger shark.

"Please, somebody get a picture of this," I yelled, but nobody was paying the slightest bit of attention to me at that point.

One of the dolphins changed course and swam toward the shark. He was just a ripple under the water, but I could see him dart in the shark's direction then veer away. Another dolphin surfaced briefly then curled under. The third dolphin followed suit.

And then the shark's dorsal fin vanished.

The dolphins circled the Miss Demeanor a few more times, curling in and out of the Gulf, blowing water out of their air holes, apparently enjoying themselves.

No way of knowing if the leader of the pod was Flipper, but since nobody can say otherwise, that's my story. It was Flipper. And he saved my life.

The dolphins vanished by the time I heard Akari's voice topside.

"I see something, Alexander. We need to take a first-hand look at this."

CHAPTER 41

As Akari and I kicked downward, following the submerged drone's control wire, it became increasingly dim as stirred-up sediment obscured our view and the light faded. Nevertheless, the water was still calmer than on the surface. The wind had picked up and swells of several feet were rocking the trawler when we dove. We'd have a seasick crew by the time we returned, I guessed.

The *Miss Demeanor* is a terrific watercraft to live aboard and is a perfect cruiser close to shore. With her shallow draft, she skims over sandbars that would cause many large boats to run aground. And, as we discovered a few days earlier, she can pull right up to deserted islands even if they are full of monkeys with anger-management issues. But that shallow draft also means she isn't the most stable craft in rough seas. With the approaching storm, time was not on our side.

The Gulf was alive with colorful angel fish, blue tangs, chubs, and the occasional barracuda as Akari and I descended. Off to our left, several nurse sharks cruised by paying us no heed. As we neared the sandy bottom, we could see the exposed line of the data cable that Wilson was investigating. At first glance, it appeared intact. But as we swam closer, I noticed that the exterior casing of the cable was exfoliating and that the sand on both sides of the cable exhibited a faint orange tint.

A hedge of mermaid wineglasses gently undulated in the current along the cable's discolored path. Something about the exposed telephone line, perhaps the mild electrical charge it gave off or the deteriorating coating on the cable's protective outer layer, seemed to draw the odd unicellular plants. If there were fish feeding on the plants, they weren't in evidence, although our presence might have scared them off. If so, their absence may also have discouraged the presence of any vampire sharks and their needle-like teeth, for which I was grateful.

I looked at my wrist and my Scubapro Digital Depth Gauge indicated we'd descended only 175 feet in an area of the Gulf that nautical charts showed to be substantially deeper. I wondered what force of nature could be responsible for this. I wriggled my hand into the sand near the cable and it sunk in to my elbow before I withdrew it. If I could drill down, how far would it go before hitting bedrock? Perhaps hundreds of feet of sand were piled up here, maybe the result of a gigantic storm that pushed up this mountain from the seafloor below. And it had gone undetected as it was still too deep to pose a navigation hazard. Undetected until a nosey marine biologist started poking around.

As I withdrew my hand from the sand, I noticed several small stones hidden among the mermaid's wineglasses. As I looked more closely, I saw they were translucent black rectangular crystals. They were pretty. I imagined they could be polished into gemstones. I took two of them and slipped them into my dive bag.

The crest of the undersea mound was only a hundred yards wide, then the hillside sloped dramatically downward, where Akari had directed the drone. We continued to follow the descending control wire. The drone's searchlight was painting the waterlogged and barnacle encrusted bow of an old shipwreck protruding from the sand. The stern of the ship was completely buried somewhere behind us, but the bow pointed downward, poking out of the underwater mound, and it appeared that someone recently cleaned off a small nameplate near the prow, a greenish metal, perhaps brass. It read:

美人鱼

We'd found Wilson's mermaid.

Akari signaled that we should circumnavigate the tip of the wreckage, check out the perimeter. She pointed to her undersea Geiger counter and I swam closer to inspect the readout. Underwater, I couldn't hear any of the familiar static, but a digital readout was flashing numbers the meaning of which eluded me, but I couldn't imagine them being good.

As we circled the vessel, the numbers on the Geiger counter rose slightly as we neared a massive rectangular hole in the hull on the starboard side, perhaps three feet by four feet, large enough to swim into. The edges of the hole were freshly sawed, so this was not the cause of the wreck. I ran my fingers over the edge and the wood felt surprisingly solid, not spongy or waterlogged. Probably teak. The new opening was large enough to remove contents from the interior of the ship, which is what I suspected happened as the plant life around the opening was damaged and there appeared to be scars in the sand as if something heavy was dragged out of the sunken vessel.

With the drone's searchlight shining on the other side of the ship, this side was in shadow, so I flicked on my headlamp and illuminated the inside of the wreck through the hole. It appeared to be empty. I was tempted to swim into the interior of the ship to check it out, despite my aversion to confined spaces. Akari must have read my mind. She grabbed my arm, shook her head, and pointed to her dive watch. We were both wearing AL-80s, aluminum air tanks holding 80 gallons of air compressed to 3,000 pounds per square inch. For recreational dives at moderate depths, that's enough air for about an hour underwater. But the deeper you dive, the more the air in your lungs becomes compressed, meaning you use more air from your tanks to keep your lungs inflated. We were now at about 180 feet. We'd planned our dive to be at this depth for only about fifteen minutes, and built into our schedule at least two decompression stops during our ascent. Those stops were essential to allow the dissolved gasses under pressure in our lungs and bloodstream time to dissipate. Otherwise, we risked getting the bends—or worse, an air embolism, which can be fatal.

Akari snapped photos of the hole, a matching brass nameplate on the starboard bow, and the profile of the wreckage while I shined my headlamp on it. Then we swam back to the port side where the light from the drone continued to illuminate that side of the shipwreck. Akari continued to photograph the hull and surrounding seafloor where much of the plant life was trampled. A cargo net lay abandoned beside the hull, the same kind of netting that had trapped Flipper. Most likely, the shrimp boat we saw topside was salvaging the contents of the wreck.

While Akari continued her photography I swam toward the undersea cable that drew Wilson to this site in the first place. I was less interested in the phone line, per se, than hoping to spot the cameras Wilson might have left behind. I assumed they would be motion activated and near the cable. If they were still here, and if they were aimed in the right direction, maybe they recorded the treasure hunters at work. Maybe even what happened to Wilson.

Had he stumbled onto the divers during their salvage operation? Is that what got him killed? Would be good to know what was so valuable about the contents of this ancient shipwreck that it would be worth a man's life.

Rediscovering the cable was easy, as a line of mermaid's wineglasses flanked it as it snaked off in both directions, back up the undersea mound from which we'd descended and down into the murky depths of the deepening ocean floor. I figured I would follow the line of plants for a bit, and I hoped it would lead to a camera that I could retrieve, although one wasn't evident in either direction.

But that plan was cut short when Akari tapped on my shoulder. It was time to go.

As much as I wanted to find one of Wilson's cameras, I knew better than to risk running out of air. Scuba diving is safe if you follow the rules. Break them, and you can be in a world of hurt very quickly.

As if on cue, the propellers of the drone began spinning and the little device began retreating topside. We followed its course upward, stopping for a few minutes at twenty meters, then again at ten, and finally at five. The most important decompression stops are nearer the surface, where the bulk of the dissolved gases dissipate.

We were staring upward at the underside of the *Miss Demeanor.* To my chagrin, barnacles once again were homesteading her hull, so a cleaning dive was in my future. We were getting bounced around now that we were closer to the surface as the waves were kicking up. I was feeling anxious, and signaled Akari that it was time to go. She checked her watch and shook her head. She held up two fingers, signaling we needed to wait a couple more minutes.

Ever get the bends? Me neither, and I don't intend to. I followed Akari's advice. She actually could have stayed down much longer than me. At about half my size, she used much less air on a dive than I did, so her concern about returning topside was largely for my benefit. Good to have a considerate dive partner.

Paine and Forester pulled Akari out of the drink first, tanks and all. While they did, I unharnessed my gear, weight belt first, and handed it up before being assisted aboard. The boat was rocking and the skies were angry. Thunder boomed nearby.

Gwenn was at the controls inside the cabin now. She gunned the engines and the trawler began its slow but steady course back to Key West. One hand on the wheel, she turned to speak to us when something very unfortunate happened:

The steering wheel came off in her hands.

CHAPTER 42

Gulf of Mexico, Stock Island

"ALEXANDER!" GWENN SHRIEKED, shoving the steering wheel toward me. "Is it supposed to do this?"

"Oh, great," I said. "You broke my boat."

"I didn't break it, it just came off!"

"Women drivers," Paine said. "No survivors."

"What the fuck is that supposed to mean?" Kitchner said, scowling.

"Yeah," echoed Akari, who walked over to stand beside Gwenn. "What the fuck is that supposed to mean?"

"Did you drop the F bomb?" Lester asked.

"No, not me, it was that other Asian woman."

It went on like that for a few minutes until finally I said, "Let me see if I can fix this."

The trawler was making lazy circles in the water, the rudder evidently yanked to starboard when the wheel spun off. Unlike the steering wheel of an automobile with its myriad built-in electronic components such as horns, volume controls, and whatnot, this was a simple mechanical rudder control and it reattached easily without any complicated connecting electronics. Which was a relief since I didn't fancy piloting the boat back to the marina from the flybridge in a raging squall.

"Could somebody fetch my tool box from the engine room?" I asked. "I need to tighten the Jesus nut."

"What's a Jesus nut?" Akari asked.

"Ordinarily, it refers to the nut attaching the rotors to a helicopter. If it falls off, the next person you meet is Jesus."

Forester laughed. He and Akari, apparently, were the only two people on the boat who'd never heard that joke before. And Akari still didn't get it.

"This isn't a helicopter," she said. "So why do you call this one a Jesus nut."

"Because it wouldn't be funny if I called it Buddha's nut."

Paine snorted. "Might be."

"Are you insulting Buddha?"

"Yeah," Kitchner said. "Are you insulting Buddha? And what the fuck do any of you know about helicopters?"

It went on like that again for a few more minutes.

"Is it my imagination or is this scow falling apart?" Forester finally asked.

"You're right, Forester," I said. "It's probably safer if you swim back to Key West."

He raised his hands in surrender. "Fine, fine. What do I know? Maybe shit falls off boats all the time. Where's the liquor?"

"Right here," Lester said. "Just opened a fresh bottle of rum."

We got lucky. The storm didn't hit until right before we pulled into Sunset Marina. Akari and I, by then out of our west suits but still damp from our dive, secured the boat to the dock cleats in the driving rain. The rainwater felt good coursing over our skin, washing off the salt. We luxuriated in it for a moment, laughing in the rain like little kids, until a nearby flash of lightning sobered us up. Akari scurried to the cabin while I hooked up the water and electrical connections. Then I joined the rest of the crew in the lounge where everyone was on their second or third drinks.

After toweling off, Akari fired up her laptop and went online to begin researching the shipwreck. She was consulting some databases, and she said a friend at East Carolina University who specialized in shipwrecks might help us identify the boat.

While she did that, I removed the SD card from her underwater camera and loaded it into my PowerBook. I clicked on the icon when it popped onto the screen, then opened a folder with the pictures Akari took of the shipwreck.

"Holy Moly," Gwenn said as I scrolled through the photos for the crew. "What kind of ship is that?"

"Looks Oriental, like a Chinese junk or something," Del Rio said. "Look at the way the front of the boat curls up like that."

"Very observant, agent Del Rio," Akari said, looking up from her laptop. "They don't teach Americans this in school, but Chinese sailors explored the waters off the New World long before Christopher Columbus."

"Really," Gwenn said. "Is the shipwreck that old?"

Akari shook her head. "I don't think so, and I'll tell you why." She motioned to me. "Alexander, can you find the picture I took of the hole that was sawed into the hull?"

"Sawed?" Lester asked.

Akari nodded. "Somebody has been salvaging the contents of this ship—and I definitely think it is a junk—and they cut a hole in the hull to do so."

"Here's the picture," I said.

Akari stepped over and pointed to the edge of the cut. "Do you see how fresh this looks?" she asked.

We all nodded.

"Shipwrecks aren't my specialty, but I have a longstanding interest in Asian maritime history. The junks used by Chinese explorers and pirates—"

"Pirates?" Lester, Gwenn and Paine all blurted.

"—Yes, pirates. China was home to thousands of pirate ships. And I'll get back to that in a moment. The hulls of Chinese junks during the time of Columbus were constructed of soft woods, such as pine. It would have deteriorated dramatically over the centuries. This wood was still fairly solid."

"Looked like teak to me," I said.

"Exactly," Akari said. "Chinese shipbuilders switched to hardwoods like teak near the end of the 18th century."

"And that's why you think this ship is more modern," Forester said.

"Very good, Agent Forester." Akari was in full professorial mode. She'd probably give us all a quiz afterward.

Her laptop dinged and she stepped back to it, looked at the message she'd received, and laughed. "My colleague in North Carolina doesn't believe us," she said. "He thinks I'm making a joke. He says I'm punking him."

"About what?" I asked. "That we found a Chinese shipwreck?"

"Not that so much. It's the name."

"What name?" Kitchner asked.

I explained how Donald Wilson asked Akari to translate a set of Chinese characters and that we'd discovered those same characters on a brass plaque on the shipwreck.

"So, the name of the ship is The Mermaid?" Gwenn asked. "Yet another mermaid?"

"Not only that," Akari said. "My friend, the reason he thinks I'm punking him is precisely because of the name."

"What's so special about it?" I asked her.

"Well, according to my colleague, it was the flagship of a small fleet sponsored by none other than Ching Shih."

CHAPTER 43

Stock Island

"CHING WHO?"

Del Rio asked the question. I'm glad somebody else did because the way Akari said the name it was clear she expected us to know who she was talking about. Instead she found herself staring at a collection of blank faces.

"Seriously?" she said. "You don't know about Ching Shih? Not even you Officer Paine?"

"Not so much. And why are you picking on me?"

"Because you've been talking about shooting pirates this whole trip."

"Ching Shih's a pirate?"

"The greatest pirate who ever lived."

"So how come we never heard of this guy before?" Paine asked.

"She. Not him."

"Shih's not him?"

"Shih's a she."

"You saying the greatest pirate who ever lived, who we've never heard of, was a chick?"

"Not an ordinary chick, detective," Akari said. "Ching Shih was a prostitute who married cleverly and inherited the largest pirate fleet the world has ever known. She commanded more than three hundred junks and forty thousand pirates. The great Red Flag Fleet. She was the terror of the China Sea. She died in 1822, but there have been rumors that long before then, around the turn of the century, she assembled a small fleet led by the junk, *The Mermaid*, to steal treasure from the New World."

"Chinese pirates were here?" Del Rio asked.

"Indeed they were," Akari said. "We know Spain operated its treasure fleet transporting precious gems and metals to Europe until around 1790. And we know that the Spanish used Havana as major port for its fleet. Speculation has long been that she ordered her pirates to raid the treasure ships, perhaps even the port of Havana itself."

"So if this is her fleet's flagship…" I began.

"Yes," Akari said. "If this is, indeed, the flagship from that expedition, it would be a great historical find."

"Minus the treasure, it sounds like," Paine said.

"Maybe not," I said. "If they've finished looting that shipwreck, why were they harassing us?"

Akari nodded. "Chinese junks from that period were very large, hundreds of feet in length. They were way ahead of the Europeans in terms of their marine engineering with water-tight compartments that gave their ships extra structural strength and protection from storm damage. Alexander, you and I only saw a few meters of the bow sticking out of the sand. That is a very large mound of sand on top of the wreck. *The Mermaid* could go for a hundred feet or more underground. There could be a great deal of treasure still aboard."

"Which could be worth a fortune," Del Rio said. "Enough to kill for."

I glanced at Lester. The expression on his face was strained.

"I'm sure Silver's okay," I said. "No word?"

He shook his head. "I informed Colonel Lake of the situation, and he's mobilized agency resources to try to locate her. Dat turd Barfield, he should be flying in today to help."

"Barfield's coming here?"

"That's your friend from Phoenix, right?" Gwenn asked.

I nodded.

"Don't you owe him some money?"

"A small poker debt."

I walked back to the galley to pour myself another drink when I felt the *Miss Demeanor* rock slightly. Fred began growling and charged to the back door of the cabin. I looked out the rain-streaked window and saw a man in a raincoat stepping over the gunwale onto the deck of the trawler.

As the figure approached the door, I entertained the notion that it must be Barfield, entering on cue.

The figure flung the door open and stepped inside the cabin.

CHAPTER 44

"For Christ's sake, doesn't anybody ask permission to come aboard anymore?" I said as the stranger flung the cabin door open.

Then I realized it wasn't Barfield.

"Quite a party," he said through the ski mask he was wearing. "Good thing I got lots of bullets." He swept open his raincoat, like a gunslinger in a B-grade Western, exposing an assault rifle dangling beside his left leg.

It was a terrifying moment. But only for a moment. The shooter made at least three tactical errors, and even in that adrenaline-filled instant they were obvious. First, his gun was pointed down. Which meant he had no advantage in getting the first shot off. Of course, he probably hadn't reckoned on facing a boat filled with heavily armed cops, FBI agents and private eyes. That was his second mistake. His third was his choice of weapon. Even with no combat experience, I knew that a long gun is not the best in tight quarters—it's too hard to maneuver, too easily deflected. Especially a rifle with a sound suppressor at the end of its barrel which made it even longer and more unwieldy.

What happened next unfolded in milliseconds.

Fred began barking madly and his universal dog translator began booming: *"Fuckhead. Fuckhead. Fuckhead."*

It startled the stranger and he glanced down at the distraction, another mistake on his part. He said something to Fred, but I couldn't hear him over the barking, and when his gaze returned to the crowded cabin he saw the hands of my crewmates reaching toward holsters and pistols tucked into waistbands.

The gunman's eyes grew wide behind his mask and he began to raise his weapon, his index finger already inside the trigger guard.

My speargun was already in my right hand. I'd retrieved it off the counter in the galley when the gunman walked through the door.

With my left hand, I grabbed Gwenn by her shoulder and pushed her down while raising the weapon.

The gunman's AR-15 was coming up. Everyone on the boat was moving, hands with guns drawn taking aim, bodies diving to either side of the gunman, trying to avoid his sights.

I pulled the speargun's trigger.

The assault rifle spat out three shots in a short burst as everyone else in the cabin with a gun let loose. The intruder staggered backwards through the still-open doorway and fell flat on his back, bullet holes pockmarking his shirt and a spear protruding from his right thigh.

Then Spock toppled over. He'd taken the full force of the assault rifle's blast, three holes in center mass, three pass-through bullet holes in the windshield of the trawler.

The crew swarmed through the cabin door toward the shooter who lay still on the deck.

"Check the perimeter," Forester yelled, and he and Del Rio leaped onto the pier, sweeping the area with their guns in case there were other shooters.

Abby Kitchner kneeled down beside the fallen gunman and placed a hand on his neck searching for a pulse. She looked up at Harrison Paine. "He's alive."

Paine bent down and ripped off the front of the guy's shirt. Underneath, he was wearing body armor. It had saved his life, but the impact of the bullets crashing into his chest and the fall must have rung his bell. Paine patted him down for other weapons, but found none.

The shooter started coming to and Paine put a hand on his face and shoved him back down. Hard. "Stay put, asshole."

Then Paine retrieved the AR-15 from where it had fallen on the deck and began unloading it. "Fucking bump stock," he said, referring to a device that allows semiautomatic rifles like the AR-15 to fire like machine guns.

A pool of blood was forming on the deck underneath the shooter. "He's going to bleed out if we don't get a tourniquet on that leg," Kitchner said.

The gunman moaned and tried to grab his injured thigh. Kitchner shoved him back down again. "Stay put or we'll shoot you some more."

I helped Gwenn to her feet. "You okay?" I could barely hear my own voice for the ringing in my ears from the gunshots. The cabin was filled with smoke. I looked her over and didn't see any damage.

She bobbed her head. "Thanks. I think." She shook her head and massaged her shoulder. Then she looked out the door of the cabin.

"Holy fuck."

She seemed disoriented, and I was concerned that she might have banged her head when I shoved her out of the way.

"You look a little woozy," I said.

"She nodded. Maybe I should sit down for a minute."

I helped her to our stateroom. Fred was already there, whining. He hates loud noises.

"Hold me for a second," she said. I could feel her tears on my cheek.

She wiped her eyes. "You acted so fast. You shoved me out of the way. I was standing right in front of Spock."

In all the confusion, I hadn't put that together.

"You saved my life."

I drew her to me and held her until I could feel her breathing return to normal. Finally, I said, "I hate breaking in new girlfriends, that's all."

She nodded, then gave me a brief smile. "I'll be okay now. Except my shoulder hurts, you big bully." I picked Fred off the floor and held him. He stopped whining.

"Take it easy for a minute," I told Gwenn. "I'm going back topside."

Akari was back at her computer when I returned to the lounge, which was still cloudy with gun smoke despite the open cabin door.

"Back at work already? You are one cool customer," I said.

"Nothing I can do out there," she said without taking her eyes off the computer screen. Then she looked up and saw Fred in my arms. She stopped typing and reached out. "Poor puppy. You were so brave barking at that bad man."

She nuzzled him and Fred wagged his tail. "My dog, Charles, passed away two weeks ago."

I was anxious to go outside and check out the fallen gunman, but I paused. "I'm sorry."

She smiled and set Fred down beside her. "I think you're right, by the way," she said. "Why try to kill us if all the treasure is gone? I'm trying to find out what Florida agency administers the Historical Resources Act."

"What's that?"

"The recovery of any treasure within ten miles of the Florida coast requires permits by both the state and the federal government under Florida law and the U.S. Abandoned Shipwreck Act."

"You know this how?"

"That Ph.D. we've been talking about."

She really was a cool customer. "So you're thinking the pirates are in trouble for not having a permit? It wasn't enough they were waving guns at us?"

"I'm thinking the state and the feds need to get out there and guard that site."

"Ah. Gotcha."

I reached down and uprighted Spock. "Looks like you took one for the team, buddy," I said. "Good thing he missed your heart." Vulcan hearts are located where humans have livers.

Akari looked at me curiously. "He ever answer?"

"He's actually kind of shy."

I stepped outside and Kitchner was on her phone calling for an ambulance. Paine was rooting through the gunman's pockets. He didn't find a wallet, but he did score a set of car keys. Kitchner had buckled a belt around the shooter's leg to staunch the bleeding. He was still on his back, but his hands were zip-tied in front of him. It would have been inhumane to roll him over on his back and cuff him from behind with a stainless steel spear protruding from the front of his leg.

Paine looked up and saw me. "For future reference, try aiming at the center of body mass," he said.

That's where I was aiming, but Paine didn't need to know that.

This was the second time in a matter of days that I'd witnessed a spear sticking out of a body. Seeing Tina Del Rio's gruesome remains had been a shock, but this was different. I'd done this. I didn't feel guilty, nor did I regret it. But it made me feel deflated somehow.

Gwenn joined us on the deck, and I heard her gasp. She turned to me, saw the look in my eyes, and reached for my hand.

Forester and Del Rio returned to the boat. "Looks clear," Del Rio said.

Forester looked down at the shooter. "A vest? Was he expecting trouble?"

"Probably ex-military," Paine said. "Standard operating procedure."

"Lucky for him," Gwenn said. She squeezed my hand. "Good thing somebody got a piece of him."

"Yeah," Del Rio said. "Nice shot, Strange." He examined the shooter, utter contempt in his eyes. "You shoot my sister, asshole?"

Forester edged over, stepped between the shooter and his partner. "Keep it professional," he said.

Paine turned to Del Rio and Forester. "I'm going to go find his car. Can you guys help Abby keep an eye on him? You okay to do that?"

"Yeah," Del Rio said. "Maybe we'll get lucky and he'll try to escape."

Lester, Gwenn, and I disembarked with Paine and followed him into the marina's parking lot.

"It's a Ford," Paine said, looking at the key. He clicked the remote. The lights on a black F150 pickup truck blinked.

"Lester, is that Silver's?" I asked. But he was already sprinting toward the truck.

He flung open the driver's door, peered inside, then stepped back and opened the door to the crew cab. On the floor between the front and back seats was a body.

The silver head of hair was unmistakable.

CHAPTER 45

Gwenn, Paine, and I were standing in the marina's parking lot as the ambulance pulled out. It would be a short run to the emergency room at Lower Keys Medical Center. Lester insisted on accompanying the medics, and the EMTs didn't argue with him.

The rain was taking a break, but the air was misty and it held the glow of the ambulance's receding red flashers. More flashing lights would be coming. Blues for the sheriff's deputies who had been summoned. Reds for a second ambulance, the one for the gunman lying on the deck of the *Miss Demeanor*.

He was safer there, even with a spear in his leg, if only marginally with Del Rio hovering over him. If he'd been anywhere near Lester when he discovered Silver in the back of the pickup truck, the shooter would have been a dead man.

When the first ambulance pulled up a few minutes earlier, the driver climbed out and asked, "You got a shooting victim?"

Lester was cradling Silver in his arms. She had a huge bruise on the side of her face. Lester had already removed the gag and untied her wrists and ankles. The good news was that she was breathing. But, while conscious, she seemed incoherent, no doubt from the blow she suffered to her head.

"Forget that," Lester told the EMT. We need to get this woman to the emergency room. Now."

They wasted no time debating the issue. You might think that a one-legged man dressed in Full Cleveland couldn't be intimidating. If so, you would be mistaken. The EMTs went straight to work, bundled Silver onto a gurney, and off they raced to the hospital.

Until that point, I'd only seen the personable, lighthearted side of Harrison Paine, not at all the guy who famously beat up an Afghan military commander for molesting little boys. He turned to us, grim faced.

"I'm going to check on our prisoner, have a word with him before the medics arrive. You guys stay here, point them in the right direction." Then he stomped off back to the boat.

"Word?" Gwenn asked. "He's going to have a word with that asshole?"

"Define word."

"I think I'll take him up on his suggestion and hang out here for a minute," she said.

"I'm sure he just meant he was going to read him his rights."

"Uh-huh."

A few minutes later, two sheriff's cruisers with lights and sirens roared into the parking and skidded to stops on the rain-slicked asphalt. Gwenn and I walked over and filled them in on the situation.

"We'll take you to the boat," I said. "Follow us."

But before we got to the pier, Harrison Paine returned showing his Key West PD badge. "Detective Abby Kitchner is having a conversation with the gunman as we speak," he told the deputies.

"I thought that was your job," I said.

"We're tag-teaming. Good cop, bad cop."

There was an anguished cry from the boat. "Stop!"

We all looked in that direction, then turned back to Paine.

"I'm the good cop."

The deputies glanced at one another, quizzical expressions on their faces.

"It's a very earnest conversation," Paine said. "He's been read his rights."

The taller of the two deputies, a young black guy, said to the other deputy, a mid-size Hispanic man with graying hair: "We don't want to miss this." They picked up their pace to the boat.

As we approached, we could see Kitchner kneeling beside the gunman, one hand on his throat, another holding the spear protruding from his thigh. "Deputies, I'm glad you're here," she said without looking up. "This man is having a seizure. Give me a hand, would you?"

"Seizure," the Hispanic deputy said.

"Looks like a seizure to me," the other one replied. "She's seizing something. Is that a fucking spear?"

CHAPTER 46

Silver was resting in a private room by the time Gwenn and I got to the hospital. We'd driven over in the tiny rental car after packing overnight bags and agreeing to allow Akari to keep Fred for the night. I was in no mood to wrestle her for the dog, and she'd become so attached to him it might have come to that.

Silver was sitting upright in bed sipping orange juice through a straw. The usual tangle of tubes and drip bags dangled from a stainless steel stand by her side and a heart monitor flashed red pulses above her head.

Lester was sitting at the foot of her bed in a chair, his prostheses removed, rubbing what remained of his lower left leg. It was probably sore from his sprint to Silver's truck. I hadn't seen him move that fast since we were attacked on Monkey Island.

"How's our girl doing?" I asked.

"Your girl needs some vodka in her orange juice," she replied.

"Back to normal, I see."

Lester shook his head. "Not quite. They MRI'd her. Afraid she's got a concussion. They're holding her overnight for observation."

Gwenn lowered the bedrail and sat down beside her. "I'm Gwenn Giroux," she said. "I've heard a lot about you."

Silver eyed her suspiciously for a moment, no doubt trying to recall where she'd heard the name. Then she smiled. "You're the girlfriend," she said. "Poor thing."

"Why do people keep saying that?"

"They're all jealous," I said.

Silver looked at me and smirked. "Yeah, that's it."

Gwenn picked up Silver's hand, the one with all the tubes poking into it. "Alexander's told me all about your brother. I'm so sorry."

"You're a lawyer, right?"

"Yes, that's correct."

"When we're done with this, I'm going to sue the living daylights out of everybody in Key West. You want the job?"

Gwenn smiled. "It's what I do. Suing the living daylights out of people."

Silver handed Gwenn the empty glass then asked her to recline the bed. "I feel a nap coming on." It was growing dark outside. She needed a good night's sleep.

Lester reattached his prothesis, rose from his chair, and leaned over Silver's bed and kissed her on the forehead. "Get some rest. I'm gonna talk to these guys."

We settled in at the hospital's coffee shop, but it was too late for caffeine. Sadly, in an egregious example of thoughtless customer service, the Lower Keys Medical Center did not sell cocktails. Of course, if an aspirin cost eight bucks, I could only imagine what they would charge for a beer.

Lester updated us on what he'd learned from Silver. She'd arrived back at her ranch in Ocala after dark and entered the house, as she usually did, through her garage. She slept in, exhausted from her drive the day before, but eventually headed out the front door to fetch her mail. That's when she discovered a soggy UPS package sitting on the porch. The shipping label showed it had arrived from Key West. The sprinkler system had been watering it for several days. She assumed it contained printouts of the documents she had asked her brother to sign, to turn the ranch over to her after her parents' deaths.

But the contents were a surprise.

"There was a small camera inside," he said. "It was one of her brother's underwater rigs that he'd planted at the dive site. There was a note with it. Something along the lines of 'if anything happens to me…' That kind of note."

"Was she able to review the memory card?" I asked.

"She was afraid to. Worried she might accidentally erase it or something. She figured the smart thing to do was bring it back to Key West. Show it to us. Then the police. She called the guy who manages her stable, told him she'd be gone for a few days, then headed straight back here."

"So how come she didn't call you back?" I asked.

"She forgot her phone. In the rush to get back here, she left it in the charger by her bed. Said it drove her crazy the entire trip. She'd planned on driving straight through, but couldn't hack it. So she crashed at a cheap motel someplace south of Tampa. And when she tried to call the next day from the motel phone, best I can tell from the timing, we were already out to sea."

"So where's this camera now?"

"It's missing. Before she left Key West, I told her where we were moving the *Miss Demeanor*, so she drove straight to the marina. She was carrying it when she went down to the dock, but we were gone by then. She was walking back to her truck when two guys jumped her. It happened so fast she didn't get a good look at them. Something hit her in the head and she blacked out. Next thing she remembers was me pulling her out of the truck."

"Two guys?"

"Yeah. The other one must have been the driver. Probably skedaddled when he saw his buddy getting shot."

"And there's no sign of the camera?"

"Abby Kitchner was here, just left before you showed up. She said they searched Silver's truck. It wasn't there."

"She tell you what she got out of the shooter?" I asked. I'd already heard Harrison Paine's version and wondered if they'd match, but Lester shook his head.

"She stuck around here long enough to get a statement from Silver, basically what I told you. Silver didn't hold anything back. Then Kitchner took off, said there was someone else she needed to question, didn't say who."

I told Lester what Gwenn and I saw when we returned to the boat from the marina parking lot with the two deputies.

"Kitchner? She was torturing the guy?" Lester asked, incredulous.

"Torture might be too strong a word."

"What would be a better one?"

"I'd say it was an aggressive interrogation."

"Torture would be too good for him," Lester said.

Gwenn and I glanced at one another. "We're seeing different sides of our friends on this trip, aren't we," she said.

I rolled my eyes.

"Not that I blame anyone," she hastily added. "If someone hurt Alexander, I'd be first in line to waterboard them."

"That's the spirit," Lester said.

We looked at each other and she rolled her eyes to let me know she had only said that for Lester's benefit.

I think.

"The shooter didn't want to talk," I said. "They read him Miranda and he demanded a lawyer. But they did get one thing out of him. According to Paine, Kitchner was asking the shooter who his pals on the Zodiac were, and he kept telling her he had never been on a Zodiac in his life. It finally dawned on her that he might be telling the truth, that he wasn't one of the boat people."

"Then who is he?"

"We don't know for sure. He wasn't carrying an ID. He's actually somewhere else here in the hospital right now."

Lester perked up, and I realized it might have been a mistake to mention that.

"Look, Lester, you need to stay away from him. This is for the police. You'll just get yourself in trouble."

He waved me off.

"But I have a theory," I said. "I think this guy, or maybe his driver pal, is the butthead who tried to scare Gwenn, who tried to run me out of town. We're pretty sure they were keeping tabs on us, so they might have recognized Silver when they stumbled across her in the parking lot. Why else jump her?"

Lester nodded. "Go on."

"I think it's a fair bet that either he or his pal iced Wilson and Tina Del Rio, too."

Lester gave me a hand roll, signaling me to continue.

"This guy, he's got to be wrapped up in whatever the hell is going on in the Gulf. But, maybe he's telling the truth. Maybe the boat people, they're a different crew. Maybe the Zodiac assholes and the guy down the hall all work for the same outfit, but are separate parts of whatever this operation is all about."

Gwenn scrunched her face in confusion. "Same outfit, but unaware of each other?"

I shrugged. "Technically, he didn't say he didn't know the other guys, he said he was never on a Zodiac."

Lester asked, "How is it that we go from a marine biologist exploring busted undersea cables to treasure ships all in the same place? That's too much of a coincidence. And why would people get all homicidal about that?"

"I'm thinking it's not a coincidence at all," I said. "Look at it like this: We've got this buried treasure thing. If there's any treasure. Who knows? And, we have the reason Donald Wilson was in Key West in the first place—trying to figure out why those phone lines are broken. That undersea mound where the data lines were exposed, it's not supposed to be there. It's not on the charts. If you look at the angle of the bow of the buried Chinese junk, and if you assume that Akari is right that the shipwreck might extend a hundred feet or more under the mound, then the data lines run right over the buried portion of the junk."

"So?" Gwenn asked.

"So it's not a coincidence, it's causal."

Lester ran a hand over his bald pate. "You're hurting my brain. What's the difference?"

"What Alexander is saying," she said, "is that the shipwreck is the cause of the data lines failing. It's not an accident they are both in the same place."

"Because we have all sworn a solemn oath, right?" I said. "One of the tenants of Cynics Anonymous: There's no such thing as a coincidence."

"But, Alexander," Gwenn said. "how would the shipwreck hurt the underwater phone lines? I mean, the shipwreck has been down there long before the phone cables were laid."

"Exactly."

"Exactly what?" she asked.

"Exactly the right question to ask. And when we find out the answer, we may have this mystery solved."

"And how are we going to do that?"

"We have two avenues of inquiry," I said. "First, we got the shooter somewhere in this hospital. If Kitchner can get him to talk, he might be able to clear things up. We need to know who he's working for. Maybe she can make him turn, offer him something."

"You think that's where Abby went after visiting Silver?" Gwenn asked.

"Almost certainly."

"She shows up in that asshole's room, he'll be shitting beignets when he sees her after what she's already done to him," Lester said.

"Beignets?"

"Bricks. Whatever."

"What's the other avenue?" Gwenn asked.

"I go back out and see what's inside that shipwreck."

CHAPTER 47

Key West

GWENN AND I were drinking Cuba Libres at The Green Parrot, a block down Whitehead Street from the Coco Plum Inn where we'd decided to spend the night. Lester reserved a room there, too. The idea of sleeping aboard the *Miss Demeanor* freaked Gwenn out. And, I'll confess, I didn't put up much of a fuss. My clever plan to switch marina's hadn't fooled anyone and the trawler felt like it had a giant bullseye painted on it.

Of course, the asshole we were trying to avoid might now be in a hospital under police guard. Or not. Silver had been accosted by two men, and one was missing. Who was the other guy and where was he lurking? It was clear to all of us aboard the boat that the shooter didn't seem surprised to see the large number of people aboard the *Miss Demeanor*. He even joked about bringing lots of bullets. And his weapon, an AR-15 with a bump stock that turned it into a machine gun, was designed to kill lots of people very quickly.

What appeared to startle him was the fact that the crew was so heavily armed. He wasn't expecting that. It was as if he were anticipating a bunch of videographers returned from filming a documentary at sea, the story we'd given the Zodiac assholes. We knew the Zodiac crew had been talking on the radio to somebody because they got orders to leave us. Maybe their boss told the shooter what to expect based on their account.

Whoever was behind all of this killed two people already. Shooting up the trawler would have increased the murder and mayhem exponentially. The stakes must be huge to attract that kind of attention.

What were those stakes? The answer remained on an undersea sandbar ten miles south in the Gulf of Mexico. And it had to have something to do with those undersea cables Wilson was investigating. I guess there was a part of me that still found it incredible that a shark could shut down the internet. If not sharks, what? Maybe land sharks. Two-legged sharks. The kind who had no compunction about killing to keep their secrets.

Gwenn and I caught a ride to the bed and breakfast after running into Abby Kitchner in the hospital lobby. I'd left the rental car for Lester.

"You get anything more out of that dickhead?" I asked her.

Kitchner closed a call on her mobile phone and shoved it into her pocket. "No. He's zonked out after surgery. He lost a lot of blood. Apparently your spear nicked his femoral artery."

"Or, perhaps, he might have experienced additional trauma after I shot him," I said.

She nodded. "Could be."

"Who is he?" Gwenn asked.

"This is where it gets weird. Let's step outside. Harrison's meeting me. Should be here any second."

In fact, his cruiser was idling outside the door. We piled in and he took a circuitous route to our hotel to give us time to talk.

"It's like this," Kitchner said. "The FBI identified his prints. Quick work. Name's David R. Bishop. Formerly with the navy. Division of Motor Vehicles lists his address as Key West, on Farragut Road."

"So let's go check it out," Gwenn said.

"Not so easy," Kitchner replied. "Farragut Road is on Dredgers Key."

"So?"

"Dredger's Key is navy housing. Not easy for civilians to be cleared through the checkpoint. We're going to have to get NCIS involved, get a federal search warrant."

NCIS, as fans of the television series know, stands for Naval Criminal Investigative Service. While its primary mission is to investigate crimes involving the navy and Marine Corps, since 9/11 its mission has broadened to include national security and counter-terrorism. Most of its investigators are civilians.

"You said this guy is ex-navy? So why is he living on base?" I asked.

"And why is he shooting at people?" Gwenn said.

"And Dredgers Key. That's where Wilson's body was found." Paine added.

"Like I said, this is where it gets weird," Kitchner said. "Those are all good questions. I talked to my boss. He agrees it's time to bring in the feds."

"Forester and Del Rio are in town until tomorrow, then Del Rio has to take his sister up to Miami for the funeral," I said.

"Yeah, I called them. They have to get back. My boss is reaching out to the SAC in Miami in the morning to get the ball rolling.

"So in the meantime, what's the game plan?" Gwenn asked.

"The game plan is that the civilians let the law enforcement professionals do their jobs," Kitchner said.

That was pretty blunt. Gwenn started to say something snarky in rebuttal, but I put my hand on her thigh and shook my head. That earned me a brief—but, fortunately, nonfatal—death stare.

Kitchner wasn't wrong about what she said, the part about the cops needing to throw their combined resources at this, at least. And I was glad the Sheriff's Office was asking the FBI for help. Maybe the NCIS, too. But the entire situation was such a cluster fuck, there was no way we "civilians" were going to curl up in a fetal position and wait for the cops to sort it out. But we didn't need to share that with them.

Paine dropped us off at the Coco Plum Inn. We signed in and then wandered down to The Green Parrot for drinks.

My iPhone buzzed. "We have a visitor on the way," I said.

Gwenn looked at me curiously.

"Remember that Third Eye investigator from Phoenix, Brett Barfield?"

"Yes. The one you owe money to. Lester said the agency was sending him down."

I nodded. "He's arrived. Should be here in a few. He's already dropped by the hospital to check in with Lester. Just got a text."

"What's he going to do?"

"Not sure. Maybe I'll have him watch the boat while I head back out into the Gulf with Abner Daystrom. I've reserved the *Reel Time* for the whole day."

"You're going out with Abner? You're not taking the *Miss Demeanor*?"

I nodded. "I'm thinking I should leave her at the marina. If she's gone, somebody might get the right idea that we've gone back out to the dive site. Maybe this way I can get out there and back undetected."

"Have you asked Akari to go with you?"

"I texted her, but she declined. Said she's had all the excitement on the high seas she can stand for a while. She was pretty cool after the shooting—nerves of steel, is what I thought—but now I don't know. I think it scared her pretty badly."

"She's not the only one."

"Look, Gwenn. If you'd like…"

She put a finger to my lips. "I'm a big girl."

She finished her drink, and I signaled the bartender for a pair of refills.

"And I assume you have plans for me, or do you want me to hide in a hotel room and watch *Love It or List It* all day?"

She was trying to be lighthearted, but it was a serious question.

"Well, I guess you could start filing lawsuits for Silver."

"That's for later."

"Okay, how's this." I told her my idea.

"That's going to take some research."

"I called Colonel Lake. He says he has a handful of geeks at your disposal."

She looked at me thoughtfully for a few moments. "You had this all figured out, didn't you? You were just waiting for me to ask."

I shrugged.

"You're not a dumb as you look."

"Yeah he is," said a voice behind us.

We turned on our barstools to see a deeply tanned man in his late-thirties, about six-feet tall, rangy, and wearing a cowboy hat and a crooked grin. A toothpick dangled from the corner of his mouth and bobbed up and down as he spoke.

He stuck out his hand to introduce himself to Gwenn.

"Brett Barfield," he said. "And the Gimp is right. You are one fine looking filly."

CHAPTER 48

Gulf of Mexico

THE FIRST THING you learn in scuba training is to never go down alone. And the deeper you dive, the greater the risk if something goes haywire. But if you absolutely, positively must make a solo dive, equipment redundancy is the key. An extra mask, extra regulator, extra air tank, at least two cutting devices, and an ascent line are essentials.

Of course, lots of solo divers don't take all those precautions, and almost always everything turns out okay. Almost. Since I would be below one hundred feet for up to half an hour at my maximum depth, I wanted to minimize any unnecessary risks.

At eight o'clock the next morning, Barfield and Lester joined us for breakfast at the inn. I'd given Brett the keys to the *Miss Demeanor* and he spent the night on board. I figured if the bad guys took another run at the boat, it would be good to have it staked out. And Kitchner arranged to have a pair of deputies shadowing the marina to back him up in case things got exciting.

But they hadn't.

"Were you able to relocate our shipmates?" Gwenn asked Barfield when he sat down at the table.

He nodded. "I disassembled the pirate lady to get her into my rental. Where you want 'em?"

"We'll put them in our room after breakfast," Gwenn said.

"You want to clue me in on this?" I asked.

Gwenn smiled. "Just looking out for your friends," she said.

When breakfast was over, I summoned an Uber and we drove to Divers Direct on Greene Street. I already possessed two AL-80 tanks filled with trimix, but I needed to fill the tank I'd drained on my dive with Akari. I also purchased a dual-tank harness, an extra mask, and flares. It occurred to me that it wouldn't be the worst thing to find some actual treasure to pay for all this equipment.

Next stop was Hurricane Hole and Abner Daystrom's dive boat. He was waiting for me at the dock and stood around useless, dipping snuff, not volunteering to help, while I unloaded all the dive gear from the Uber and onto the *Reel Time*.

When I was finished, he looked at the pile of equipment and laughed. "You planning on living down there?"

"Might be wet for a while. You got a book to read so you don't get bored?"

"Book?"

"Yeah, you know, rectangular in shape, has pages, some even come with pictures and small words."

He gave me a look that if translated from Abner into English would have been, "Whatever, dude. I get paid by the hour."

We pulled away from the dock, and I told Abner the GPS coordinates of the dive site. The water was rough and the wind was coming out of the south at 12 knots. While the brunt of the storm blew through overnight, thunderstorms were in the forecast for the afternoon.

Abner's boat was much faster than the *Miss Demeanor* and cut through the waves at what seemed like light speed compared to the trawler. But it was a teeth-rattling ride as it crashed over the swells, and I got the sense that Abner was enjoying making the trip as miserable as possible. But it could have been worse. We could have been plowing through a Red Tide bloom. But it seemed to have been blown apart by the storm.

"Yup," I said, scanning the empty horizon, relieved when we'd finally stopped. "This looks like the right spot."

Abner shook his head. "It all looks the same to me, but these are the coordinates."

My plan hinged on getting in and out of the dive site undetected. Akari had notified both state and federal authorities of the shipwreck, and given its historical significance and the fact that treasure hunters were looting the ship, we expected somebody—the Coast Guard, maybe the navy—to show up and chase off interlopers. I wanted to be long gone by the time that happened.

And that assumed that the authorities and not the Zodiac thugs would be the biggest challenge our expedition would face. But I couldn't bank on that, which is why I'd cooked up a backup plan. I hoped I wouldn't need it.

While I was taking my second—and, likely, final—look at the shipwreck and submarine phone cables, Lester's job was to bodyguard Silver and Gwenn. Assuming Silver was able, the idea was to relocate them for the day to the community college, where Akari promised Gwenn the use of an office and, critically, its computer and internet connection.

Kitchner arranged to keep a deputy staked out at Sunset Marina all day on the chance the bad guys made a return visit. I asked her to have the deputy surveil the *Miss Demeanor* from a location as close to the water as possible. This was based on an idea that had been, you will forgive the expression, floating around in my head ever since I'd visited the bourbon-breathed owner of the *Wet Dream*, the houseboat next to Wilson's at City Marina.

The old man said his boat began sinking months after Hurricane Whitney blew through. That was odd. Hurricanes aren't subtle. If his houseboat were battered by the storm sufficiently to spring a leak, it seemed to me that it wouldn't have taken so long to begin listing. My first instinct was that the old man was sinking his houseboat for insurance, but when I'd asked him if the boat was covered he said it couldn't be. And the dockmaster confirmed that.

I would have to dive under the boat and take a look to be sure, but I couldn't help but wonder: What if the real target had been Wilson's houseboat? Maybe to ensure that any useful evidence aboard would be lost? Or to scare him away? And what if the wrong boat was sabotaged?

It was pretty farfetched, I knew, and there was no evidence whatsoever to support the idea. But on the crazy chance someone might want to scuttle *The Misdemeanor*, or blow it up, or set it on fire, or shoot it full of holes, maybe the deputy could stop them. After all, she wasn't merely a boat, she was my home.

Fortunately, my dog was safe with Akari, and Gwenn and Barfield had conspired to ensure no harm would come to Mona and Spock. That's what all the mysterious jabber was about at breakfast. Gwenn knew something about my childhood that few people did—Spock had been my steady companion since I was a kid, a gift from my mother the Christmas before she drowned. He traveled with me everywhere: From Texas, after mom died, to Phoenix, where I lived with Leo. Then back to Austin to attend the University of Texas, where I refused to join Delta Tau Chi Beta unless they also admitted Spock. (They did.) Then a return trip to Arizona where I got my first job at the *Phoenix Daily Sun*. And now here to the Gunshine State.

I was touched that Gwenn had made the effort to ensure his safety, wounded though he was. And somewhat surprised she included Mona in the deal. When we first met, Gwenn didn't like having a reminder of a former girlfriend aboard the boat. She actually wasn't a girlfriend, but she had been a friend, although that was no longer the case, and to Gwenn it was a distinction without a difference, as Lester would say. But Mona was part of my crew and she kept Spock company when I wasn't around. I guess Gwenn had finally acquiesced to all that. Perhaps it was a milestone in our relationship, a sign of trust. Or maybe she'd simply resigned herself to the fact her boyfriend was destined to live up (or down) to his last name.

While Abner and I motored to the dive site, I asked him again about Wilson's underwater cameras.

"I helped him load all his gear back aboard every time. Never saw any of those cameras," he said.

Yet Wilson had retrieved one of them, the camera he shipped to Silver. Either it escaped Abner's attention, or Wilson had returned to the dive site and retrieved it on another boat. Given the timing of the package's delivery, I wondered if it might have been on Wilson's last trip out here, the one before he drowned.

Were the others still down there somewhere, and what secrets might they reveal? That was my first target on this dive. My hope was I could discover at least one of the cameras then still have time to poke around the shipwreck some more. The idea of swimming through the hole in *The Mermaid's* bow into the dark confines of the sunken ship gave me the heebie-jeebies, but I knew I needed to at least shine a light in there and see what there was to see.

I strapped on my dual tanks, organized my extra tank and gear in a dive net, then slipped over the side of the *Reel Time* into the Gulf of Mexico. This time, I didn't have the control line of Akari's underwater drone to follow down, but I did attach a line to a cleat on Daystrom's boat to find my way back. Visibility was even worse today than the day before and I had no choice but to head straight down and hope for the best.

As I descended, tropical fish flashed past my facemask then vanished into the turbid water. The visibility range was no more than twenty-five meters. While that's not horrible, it was far cloudier than my handful of previous dives in the Gulf. Perhaps the current here was especially turbulent, a spinoff from the Gulf Stream keeping the sand stirred up. Maybe that was the genesis of the undersea mound.

As I did when I dived with Akari, I made several pauses during my descent to clear my sinuses by holding my nose and swallowing. Called the Toynbee Maneuver, it equalizes the pressure in the sinus cavity and helps avoid the dreaded "ear squeeze," the most common injury divers experience.

I was also mindful of sharks, my most recent encounter still fresh in my memory, but they all seemed to be terrorizing innocent scuba divers elsewhere in the Gulf today. Or maybe Akari was right and they're simply misunderstood. Maybe the tiger that harassed me yesterday was just having a bad day. It happens.

Fifteen meters from the bottom, I spotted the faint outline of the shipwreck off to my right and I kicked in that direction. As I continued to kick downward, the seafloor came into sharper focus and I realized the landscape looked unfamiliar.

The undersea mound seemed to have shrunk, as if the inexorable force of gravity was sucking the sand back into the deeper ocean depths. Perhaps the storm had stirred up the water sufficiently, even at this depth, prompting the erosion. I was scanning the area for the telltale growths of mermaid's wineglasses, but they were nowhere to be seen. It was as if they'd been scraped cleanly away.

But the far more dramatic change in the submarine landscape was the unexpected presence of the stern of *The Mermaid*, which now poked through a previously undisturbed section of the sand. I was curious about the size of the shipwreck and swam in the direction of the bow until I could see it through the cloudy water. It was about two hundred feet from the stern and now was hanging over the edge of the undersea mound as if poised to take a nosedive down to Davy Jones' Locker.

As I swam back to the stern, I wondered how much longer it would be before erosion and gravity conspired to send the entire ship into the depths. The situation looked precarious. I certainly wouldn't want to be poking around inside the wreck when that happened.

The stern was horseshoe shaped with a high poop deck. And while only a few yards of ship protruded from the sand, the wood was in surprisingly good condition. At least, it surprised me. I'd read somewhere that shipwrecks found in deep ocean were better preserved. Something about less water movement and lower levels of dissolved oxygen that sea creatures who feast on the wooden hulls need to survive. But this was comparatively shallow water, which struck me as curious, but I was clearly out of my depth, if you will, when it came to evaluating that sort of thing.

And while it was evident that worms, crustaceans, and other creatures were making their homes in the hull, and while chunks of the stern were simply missing, the Chinese origin of the shipwreck was unmistakable even to my layman's eyes.

I weaved my descent line through the net bag holding my spare tank and other gear, and tied the line to the ship's sternpost. At this depth, the hull of the *Reel Time* was no longer visible, and when it was time to ascend I didn't want to waste precious minutes finding my line and extra gear.

I snapped several photographs of the sunken ship's stern with Akari's underwater camera, which I'd kept. Then I swam upward a few yards to get a photograph of the poop deck from above. But when I did so, I spotted what at first I thought might be a sea snake, and for a brief moment I thought my heart would jump out of my chest. But on closer inspection I realized it was a section of undersea cable uprooted by *The Mermaid* as she shifted on the sandy bottom.

I kicked my way along the route of the cable as it draped over the stern of the junk then back down into the sand. I continued along that trajectory for about thirty yards, when I spied another exposed length of the phone line terminating at something entirely unexpected. It was a mound of rocks, piled together in the form of a pyramid about three feet high. It was clearly manmade. Had Wilson anchored his cameras in rockpiles to protect them?

I checked my dive watch. I'd been down fifteen minutes. At this depth, I would have maybe another fifteen minutes of air before I would need to begin my ascent. My extra tank would buy be some more time if necessary, but I didn't want to take any stupid chances.

I began dislodging the rocks, starting at the top and working my way down, anxiously looking for a camera.

But what I discovered wasn't a camera. In fact, it wasn't like anything I'd ever seen before. It's black reflective surface shined in my headlamp. I grabbed Akari's camera and began taking pictures.

What on earth would a large metallic claw be doing on the ocean floor? And why was it pinching the data cable, like a hungry lobster?

CHAPTER 49

I SWAM BACK toward the stern of *The Mermaid* and floated over the deck. It might have been my imagination, but there seemed to be more exposed wood than a few minutes earlier. Perhaps the current was brushing sand off the surface of the shipwreck.

There was a hole in the deck near a deteriorated structure that at one time might have served as the captain's quarters. I was the furthest thing from an expert in Chinese shipbuilding, but it struck me that the hole was about the right size for a mast. It was round, fitting that hypothesis, but too tight a fit to swim into with tanks on my back—not that I was so inclined. I aimed my headlamp down into the hole to see what this opening into the shipwreck might reveal.

The darkness seemed to eat the beam of light, so I edged closer, my face nearly on the worm-eaten planks. I peered into the darkness, hoping perhaps to see the glint of pieces of eight or other treasure. There was a slight movement at the edge of the light and before I could react an orange tentacle shot from the hole, grabbed me around the head, and pulled me down.

It was an octopus, and a large one at that. His arm covered my mask and his suckers were in my hair, which, luckily, prevented him getting a secure grip. But he kept tugging on my facemask and it continued drawing my head down into the dark hole where he was hiding.

My plan for the day did not include becoming lunch for an octopus—do they even eat people?—so I grabbed the tentacle with both hands and began prying him off my head. But as I yanked on the sucker-covered arm, my mask snapped off and disappeared into the hole along with the tentacle that gripped it.

My heart pounded and my breathing accelerated, burning more of my limited air supply. This dive was turning into a calamity. Is this how Wilson bought the farm? Lost a fight with an eight-armed mollusk fifteen stories underwater? Oh, the indignity.

Fortunately, I was prepared for emergencies, and I kicked off the deck and dove down toward the sternpost of the shipwreck where I'd tied off my emergency gear in my net bag. I brought my dive watch to my eyes. There was no reason to panic. I had time and an extra dive mask and air tank waiting. I took a big breath, let it out slowly, and controlled my breathing. Panic kills, I told myself. Stay calm.

I have good vision, but without a mask the saltwater made everything blurry, so I wasn't alarmed when I couldn't see the dive bag right away as I approached the stern of the sunken ship. Finally, it came into view, however unclear, right where I left it, my ascent line snaking lazily upward to the surface. I felt a wave of relief course through me.

Suddenly, the ascent line grew taut and the sternpost, which at one time held the junk's rudder, creaked from the strain of the rope's tension. Then it broke free from the sunken ship carrying my dive bag and supplies with it toward the surface. I grabbed for bag and missed, then tried to chase after it kicking as hard as I could, but it was no use. In moments it was out of sight in the cloudy water.

Another shot of adrenaline blasted through my veins and my chest felt like it would burst. Abner had taken off and dragged my gear with him. Why the hell hadn't he untied the line? That was sloppy. It could get tangled up in his propellers.

Was he fucking with me? Or had he tried to signal me we had visitors? I'd arranged with him to tug on the descent line if he needed me to return. But in the excitement of seeing the stern of the *Mermaid* poking out of the sand, I'd forgotten and tied off the line.

My first impulse was to blame Abner. But I realized this could be all my fault.

Even though my situation was tense, it was still not Panic City. I'd hired Abner and his boat in the hope that by leaving the *Miss Demeanor* in port I could get back out to Wilson's dive site undetected. But when I told Gwenn and Brett Barfield about it over drinks at the Green Parrot they were uneasy. Especially Gwenn.

"What if those pirates in the Zodiac come back?" she asked.

"Daystrom will signal me and we can skedaddle."

That didn't mollify her, so I'd given Gwenn the phone number of the dockmaster over at City Marina, Cochran. "You guys get nervous, call him," I said. I'd also jotted down the GPS coordinates.

"I'm calling him first thing in the morning," she said. "Just in case."

I'd thought she was overreacting. Now I hoped she'd made that call.

With no mask and no spare tanks, it was time to head topside. I had more than enough air for two decompression stops, if I were reading my watch correctly—no mean trick without a dive mask.

As I began kicking upward in a slow ascent to the surface, I felt, rather than heard, a vibration behind me. I turned to see the stern of *The Mermaid* slowly rising from the undersea mound, unleashing a cloud of sand that began enveloping the shipwreck. An orange blur shot out of the deck as if propelled by a cannon. I wondered if the octopus still had my mask.

The shipwreck tilted upward a few more feet. Maybe Abner's tearing off the sternpost upset the delicate balance that held the ship on the eroding sandbar. I could not see the bow from where I was, but I imagined it nosing down, sliding off the sand dune to the seafloor hundreds of feet below.

In the movies, sailors too close to their sinking ships were often sucked into the depths by the undertow. No idea if that same force of nature applied to ships already submerged, but I didn't want to find out.

But before I could flee, the junk stopped its upward tilt. Through the blurry water I spotted the undersea cable pulled upward across the stern of the junk. The cable was uprooted all the way back to the mysterious black claw and appeared to be tethering *The Mermaid*, braking its slide toward the edge of the undersea mound.

Then it snapped. And the junk turned on its nose and plummeted downward. I began kicking with all my might, racing my bubbles upward lest I be sucked into the depths. At fifty feet, I stopped and looked back toward the wreck, but could see nothing, the sea mound now obscured by an eruption of sand. But I was certain *The Mermaid* was gone and likely broken apart by the descent to the deeper waters below.

I made my last decompression stop at fifteen feet. The saltwater was really doing a number on my eyes by then and my vision had deteriorated. But I gazed toward the surface in every direction, looking for boats above me. I would have loved to have seen Cochran's boat. But I was more concerned about seeing the profile of a Zodiac or a shrimper. Within the narrow range of visibility it looked all clear, so I began my final ascent.

CHAPTER 50

As soon as I surfaced, I turned in a full circle keeping my head just above water as the wind whipped the whitecaps. Oddly, the sun was still out, but a storm was coming. I could see it building on the horizon to the south.

I hoped to spot Cochran's boat, but it was nowhere in sight. However, I was not alone. Off to the east, about two hundred yards away, was the *Reel Time*, a shrimp boat, and a Zodiac, all huddled together. There were two men on the Zodiac wearing wetsuits as if they were preparing to dive down to the shipwreck. Were they ever in for a disappointment.

I could also see Abner in the cockpit of his boat gesturing at them with his hands. It looked like he'd made a run for it and got caught. I wondered how long he had tried to signal me before giving up. There was some kind of conversation going on, but at that distance I couldn't make out any words. Then the men in the Zodiac gestured toward Abner, and he clambered off the *Reel Time* and onto the shrimp boat and went below.

I stared at this mysterious scene for several seconds until it dawned on me that if the divers turned in my direction my bobbing head could be easily seen. I was still weighted down with air tanks and my dive belt, so I stopped kicking and allowed myself to slip under the waves for a few feet to avoid detection.

My situation was, as they like to say in the military, suboptimal. Not only was I exposed and at sea on my own, it seemed likely that if Cochran were out here and he spotted those other boats, he would be keeping his distance.

I wasn't sure how much air remained in my tanks, but there ought to be enough to put at least some distance between myself and the Zodiac, I figured. I could remain below the surface and swim away underwater for as long as my tanks held out. But which way to go?

I kicked back to the surface and blinked the saltwater out of my eyes. The divers were aboard the *Reel Time* now, and it appeared they were dousing the boat with gasoline from a red plastic container. They weren't looking my way, so I carefully did another three-sixty, scanning the horizon hoping against hope that Cochran's boat would be visible in the distance.

I got lucky. To the northwest, I spotted a motorboat, about two miles away and barely a speck on the water. It had to be Cochran. Just had to be. But even if not, better to swim in that direction, anyway, as it would bring me closer to shore.

I slipped back under the waves and began kicking. If I'd estimated correctly, my target was about two miles out, call it three thousand meters. Sixty laps in an Olympic-sized pool. How fast could I swim? The world record for the 1,500-meter freestyle was about just under fifteen minutes, set in 2012. While I swam for the University of Texas, I was not Olympic caliber. At my best, in a pool, it would have taken me no less than seventeen minutes. Double that for two miles and that's thirty-four minutes. Add a fatigue factor for the extra distance, add time for the fact I was older and not training four hours a day anymore, add time for waves and wind and current, and I didn't see how I could reach Cochran's boat in much less than an hour even with fins. The odds of the boat staying put for that long were nil.

Where was Flipper when I needed him?

I stayed under water as long as the tanks held out, hoping to put enough distance between me and the Zodiac so that when I finally surfaced I would be less noticeable. My air gave out after about fifteen minutes, not nearly long enough.

I slipped out of my harness and watched my depleted air tanks sink below me. Then I stripped off my weight belt and it, too, dropped out of sight. I looked behind me and the *Reel Time* was in flames, a thick plume of black smoke erupting into the air then quickly dissipating in the rising wind. The waves were pounding now, which on the one hand was good—it would make spotting me harder for the Zodiac killers. But it also would make it difficult for my friends to find me.

I rose on a wave, and to my relief Cochran's boat was still in sight, and a bit closer. I began swimming again.

CHAPTER 51

"YO, ALEX, YOU getting tired?"

My face was planted in the water and I was fully into the rhythm of my freestyle stroke, lost in my own world, my breathing steady and strong, when the sound of outboard motors startled me out of my reverie. I looked up, and there was Gwenn in the stern of a large Boston Whaler.

"Am I ever glad to see you," I said as Cochran and Barfield helped me aboard.

"Was that the *Reel Time*?" Cochran asked. I turned to look where he was pointing and the boat was no longer visible and the smoke had cleared. Unfortunately, the shrimp boat and the Zodiac were still lurking, and while I'd put some distance between us, Cochran's boat was now drawing their attention.

"It was," I said. "You guys see the fire?"

"Yeah," said Barfield. "She went down fast."

By then, the Zodiac had cranked up its engines and was heading straight for us.

Without a word, Cochran, spun the wheel on the fishing boat and jammed the throttle to the stop. The bow rose out of the water, and the roar of the engines split the air. We rocketed away in a northwesterly direction, the Zodiac about three hundred yards off our starboard stern effectively blocking a path that would take us back to our marina.

"Can we outrun them?" I yelled at Cochran, while holding onto Gwenn with one hand and the gunwale with the other as the boat jolted airborne then slapped back down sending cascades of water crashing over us.

"We'll find out."

Cochran's boat was a thirty-five foot Boston Whaler Outrage equipped with triple Mercury 250-horsepower outboard engines. It was rated for a top speed over fifty miles per hour. I didn't know the specs on the Zodiac, but it seemed to be falling behind, if ever so slightly. Maybe we could get ashore in time to avoid getting shot.

Up ahead, we could now see the westerly tip of Key West growing larger.

"What kind of weapons we got?" I asked Brett.

"My Glock and your speargun," he said.

I looked down and noticed the Mares Sten Mini Rigged Speargun still strapped to my thigh. I'd completely forgotten about it.

Cochran was holding the steering wheel in one hand and the radio mic in another. "Mayday, mayday, mayday," he shouted into the microphone.

When the Coast Guard responded, he gave our approximate location, and a quick rundown of what we had witnessed, including how they had set the *Reel Time* on fire and that its captain was being held on the shrimper.

"We're aiming for the docks at Mallory Square," he said. "Can't imagine them shooting at us there, but we'll see."

It was as if the Zodiac were listening in. Maybe it was. Suddenly the inflatable slowed, turned away from us, then resumed full throttle back toward the shrimper.

Cochran stayed on the radio, updating the Coast Guard on the Zodiac's maneuvers.

Barfield was now on his cellphone, calling it in to Harrison Paine. He looked up from his call. "Paine will coordinate with the sheriff. They got harbor boats and will be on the lookout for them," he said.

With the Zodiac heading away from us, Cochran dropped the Whaler's speed and the bow dipped back into the water. "We might as well take it back to Garrison Bight now," he said. "The Coast Guard and the cops are on it."

While we rounded the bend at Fort Zachary Taylor on Key West's southwest shoreline, Gwenn filled me in on what she'd learned that morning.

"You're hunch was right," she said. "The only record I could find for a Trans Europa Associated Telecom is an LLC registered by the Florida Secretary of State's Office. The registered agent is a law firm in Delray Beach, and the owner is another limited liability company, also registered in Florida, which, in turn, has a separate registered agent and another LLC listed as the owner. Also, Trans Europa has no online presence whatsoever. No website. No social media account. No references when I went searching on Google. It's clearly a made-up entity."

"And not a European company."

"Right. Colonel Lake's people at the Third Eye could find no record of a firm by that name anywhere in the European Union, so, yeah, it looks like a cover for something else."

"Which raises questions about this guy Wilson," Barfield said.

"Yes." I replied. "What did Donald Wilson know? Was he duped? Or was he in on this?"

I told Gwenn, Brett, and Cochran about what I'd discovered near the shipwreck, the mysterious claw-shaped device attached to the undersea cable and how *The Mermaid* tumbled off the underwater mound to an uncertain fate below.

"You got attacked by an octopus?" Barfield asked.

"A big one."

"Of course it was."

Gwenn asked, "You get pictures?"

"What, you don't believe me?"

"Not of the octopus, of this claw-like thing you were talking about."

I dug Akari's borrowed underwater camera out from my wetsuit's thigh pocket. "Right here. We'll take a look as soon as we get back to the *Miss Demeanor*."

"Or maybe we should give it straight to the Coast Guard," Gwenn said.

I thought about that for a few moments. "Okay, I get it. The more the cops have, the sooner we can get this resolved, and that makes good sense. What say we load it into my laptop, make copies, email it to everybody including ourselves, then take the SD card to the cops. That way we can be sure it doesn't get lost."

Barfield and Gwenn both nodded. Cochran turned and looked at us. "I knew you were trouble."

We rounded the Key West Ferry Terminal and were on a straight shot toward Garrison Bight and the City Marina, where Cochran docked his boat.

"I owe you," I told Cochran. "This is the second time you pulled my bacon out of the fire."

He glanced over his shoulder at me and laughed. "I ain't had this much fun since I drove those goddamned Swift Boats in 'Nam," he said.

"So could I ask another favor?" I asked.

"Now what?"

"Can you drop us off at Sunset Marina? I need to download this camera's memory card."

"Sure. But I already told the Coast Guard and the cops we're heading for Garrison Bight. You want me to call them again?"

"Give us a little head start, would you? I want to get this card downloaded before they show up."

"You got it, sonny." He throttled up the boat and we accelerated past the entrance to the bight, passing an outgoing fishing boat with half a dozen people on board. I checked the name on the side and it read *Beeracuda*. "There goes Donny in a can," I said.

Both Cochran and Barfield gave me what-the-fuck looks.

"It's a long story. And it ain't over yet."

CHAPTER 52

Stock Island

Lester and Silver were aboard the *Miss Demeanor* when we arrived. "How's our girl?" I asked.

"This *woman* is fine and she would be a lot better if my babysitter would pour me a drink," Silver said.

"Doctor's orders," Lester said. "No booze for forty-eight hours."

"I'm going to have to find me a new boyfriend," she grumbled. "One who knows how to ignore orders from headquarters."

It was the first time I'd heard Silver refer to Lester as her boyfriend. I glanced at Gwenn and she winked at me.

I sang the first few lines of John Paul Young's *Love Is in The Air* before everyone in the cabin began hooting and hollering. "Please fucking no. Jesus Christ. Stop that. Where's my gun?"

Everybody's a comedian.

I introduced Cochran and Silver, then popped the SD card from the camera, loaded it into my MacBook Pro, and opened the folder. The images of the rock pile, the claw-like device, and the stern of *The Mermaid* were clear.

"That is one weird looking whatever it is," Barfield said. "It's like one of the Transformers lost a fingertip or something."

I copied the file onto my Mac, then into my iCloud and Dropbox accounts. Then I emailed copies of the files to myself, to Gwenn, Kitchner, Paine, and Akari. I'd just ejected the SD card when I felt the boat rocking as Paine and Kitchner clambered aboard. Gwenn and I walked out onto the deck to greet them.

"I thought we agreed the civilians would let the professionals handle this," Kitchner said, clearly irritated. Paine, who was standing a step behind her gave me an eye roll. Years of practice at the gaming tables served me well as I maintained my very best poker face.

"You're absolutely correct, detective," I said. "Which is why we involved only professional attorneys, professional private investigators and professional journalists in today's activities."

"You think you're funny, don't you."

"Abby," Gwenn said, "you really need to hear what we've learned today. We don't have time for posturing."

Kitchner gave her a cop's dead-eye stare and Gwenn gave her a lawyer's heat ray right back.

"Come on," I said. "We're wasting time." And Gwenn and I walked back into the cabin giving Kitchner and Paine no real choice but to follow.

"I'm going to tell you what happened out in the Gulf this morning," I said. "Then Gwenn will share with you what she's learned."

Kitchner pulled out her smart phone and said, "I'm recording this." It wasn't a question, but there was no reason to object.

When I finished my part of the story, both Kitchner and Paine were, if not exactly wide-eyed, certainly in a more receptive frame of mind.

"You got pictures of this claw thing?" she asked.

"Yes. And I've emailed the file to both you and Harrison.

Pained checked his phone. "Yep. Got it."

Gwenn then shared what she learned about Trans Europa Associated Telecom.

"Run that past us again, would you?" Paine said. "Not sure I caught all those various holding companies."

"Sure. There's no European record for Trans Europa Associated Telecom. Best we can tell it's a Florida registered limited liability company. The registered agent is a law firm in Delray Beach. That law firm does lots of corporate registrations, so nothing unusual there. But the owner of record is yet another LLC." She glanced at her notes. "Consolidated Industrial Affiliates."

"Is this some kind of joke?" Kitchner said.

Gwenn gave her a raised eyebrow.

"The initials. The first one is T-E-A-T. The second one is C-I-A."

"Then you'll really like the third one," Gwenn said. "According to the Secretary of State's records, Consolidated Industrial is, in turn, owned by yet another Florida LLC, Federer, Underwood, Claybern and Kirk."

"Oh for fuck's sake."

"Wait a minute," Cochran said. "Underwood?"

"Yes, why? That ring a bell?"

"Thomas Underwood?"

Gwenn looked at her notes again. "I did look up the company. The name sounded like a professional association of some sort. It purports to be a law firm, but there is no record of it with the Florida Bar, so I assume it's another smokescreen. But, yes, Underwood is a Thomas Underwood in the records. Who is he?"

Cochran looked at me. I shook my head. "I don't believe it," I said.

"What is it?" Silver asked.

"Thomas Underwood," I said, "is listed as the owner the houseboat your brother was renting."

Lester, who'd been standing next to Silver, collapsed onto the couch with her. She looked at him. He didn't say anything, and I figured it would be up to me to explain the implication, but Abby Kitchner spared me.

"This is damned curious," she said. "Donald Wilson was supposed to be employed by a transatlantic cable company. But that company only exists on paper, and he was here living aboard a boat owned by a so-called lawyer involved in hiding the ownership record of this phony company."

"What are you saying?" Silver's voice was a whisper.

"I'm saying the same thing I've said from the very beginning," Kitchner said. "This whole business is a cluster fuck."

CHAPTER 53

PAINE WAS ON his cell phone talking with the commander of the Coast Guard cutter that responded to our mayday call. Mostly, he listened, then he finally said, "We've debriefed them and have it recorded. Let us know where and when, and we'll meet you."

"What?" Kitchner asked.

Paine turned to me. "Well Mr. Weird News Guy, your story is definitely getting stranger by the minute. That was the Coast Guard. They found the shrimp boat. It was abandoned. Not a soul onboard."

"Any sign of violence?" Kitchner asked.

"No."

"So we don't know Abner Daystrom's status." I said.

"Affirmative."

"Any trace of the Zodiac?" Cochran asked.

Paine shook his head.

"Could the shrimp boat crew have escaped on the Zodiac?" Gwenn asked.

"We don't actually know how big that crew was, do we?" I replied. "Did any of you get a head count?"

Cochran, Barfield, and Gwenn shook their heads.

"Which means they could be here in town right now," Gwenn said.

Paine said, "Yeah, that's a possibility. I need to call this in."

"Me, too," Kitchner said. She turned to Gwenn. "Sorry, no hard feelings."

Gwenn nodded.

"We'll keep a deputy here overnight," Kitchner said. "Make sure you guys are okay."

"Thanks," I said. But spending the night on the boat was a non-starter after all we'd been through. I'd already called Akari, and Fred was doing fine. She insisted he stay with her until we cleared this up, which was a blessing.

Paine, Kitchner, and Cochran left and the rest of us sat down in the lounge and stared at one another for a minute, absorbing it all.

"Beam me up, Scotty," Barfield said.

"He never said that, you know," I said.

"What?"

"'Beam me up, Scotty.' It's like 'Play it again, Sam'. Never happened."

"Huh."

Lester was holding Silver's bruised hand, the one where the doctors poked her with all those needles and tubes in the hospital.

"I can't do this anymore," she said, quietly. She looked at Lester, tears running down her cheeks. "Can you take me away from all of this? Please."

Her truck was still in the marina parking lot. She dug through her purse, and handed Lester the keys.

He opened his mouth to say something then shut it.

I put up my hand. "We'll hitch a ride with you back to the hotel. You should get your things and go. She needs you."

I turned to Gwenn. "You know, they've got room in the truck…"

"Don't even."

"Right."

Barfield said, "And don't worry about me. Why, I'll just hang out here on this scow. Keep the doors and windows locked. Hope a team of assassins doesn't show up and kill me."

I knew Barfield well enough to know he wouldn't fritter away the remaining hours of the afternoon doing nothing. My guess is he'd either prowl the streets looking for anything that struck him as out of the ordinary—and was he in for an eye-opening experience, this being his first trip to Key West. Or he'd stake out the *Miss Demeanor*, maybe along with the deputy standing watch, and hope to catch the bad guys if they made a return trip to the marina.

"On the off chance you're assassinated," I said, "I wouldn't want you to die while I still owe you money." I dug out my wallet, the translucent blue plastic one with the Superman emblem embroidered on the front.

Barfield raised his palm. "Nah, that's okay. I like that you owe me. Gives me something to badger you about. Besides, lots of people owe me money. Yours is a drop in the bucket."

"A drop in a bucket, huh. You sure?"

"Yeah, I'm good. Hang onto it."

As we disembarked the boat and walked to Silver's truck, Gwenn tugged at my sleeve.

"How much do you owe him, anyway?"

"It's a small poker debt."

She laughed. "Yeah, that's what you always say. But how much?"

I told her.

"Five bucks? Five fucking bucks?" She was shouting. "All this blabber about poker debts since I've known you and it's about five fucking dollars?"

"I told you it was a small debt."

"So why does he make such a big deal out of it."

"He's lonely. Doesn't have any friends. Nobody cares if he lives or dies."

"Didn't he say that about you?" she asked.

"He was projecting."

CHAPTER 54

Key West

"Now what are we going to do?"

Gwenn was sitting on the bed in our room at the Coco Plum Inn, her legs crossed with both of her feet resting on top of her opposing thighs, her hands on her knees palms up and open.

"Which one's that?" I asked, dodging her question for the moment. I could never remember the names of the various yoga poses she practiced. She got annoyed when I got them wrong. One day, she was in Downward Facing Dog position and I called it the Talking Dog. She threw a pillow at me. That's what our fights are like.

"Full Lotus. You're never going to remember, are you?"

"I think my hard drive's been damaged."

"That could explain a lot."

I checked my watch. "As for your question, I'm guessing we'll hear back from Paine or Kitchner and we'll have to meet with the Coast Guard, give them a formal statement or something."

"You want to hang out here until then?" Gwenn's tone indicated that wouldn't be her first choice. Nor mine. Not that it wasn't a lovely room, and we could always catch some rays around the pool, but we were both too amped for that.

"Why don't we go for a walk?" she suggested.

I picked up a copy of the *Key West Citizen* that I'd found lying on a poolside table en route to our room. The top story was an analysis on rising sea levels. Key West could expect continued flooding, and someday soon you'd need a snorkel to do the Duval Crawl.

In cheerier news, there was a story about today's First Annual Flight of the Flamingo Parade and Dance Off bylined by reporter Hermina Hermelinda Obregon, a.k.a. H2O, a.k.a. Agua.

"Or how about we go to the parade?" I said. "Starts in a little bit."

"Parade?"

"Yeah, we can see the flamingos."

"Live flamingos? Really?"

"That's what Agua says."

"What's an Agua?"

I told her how Hermina Hermelinda Obregon cornered us outside the inn on the day Silver left for Ocala, how I refused to answer her questions about the murder of Tina Del Rio, and that I felt slightly guilty about that, her being a fellow reporter and all.

"Don't feel guilty," she said. "It was the smart thing to do."

Nice to have affirmation.

"But I want to know more about this parade and the flamingos."

"All I know is what I read in the newspaper. Sounds like another excuse to party on Duval Street. Apparently, the birds in the parade have all been injured and can't fly. They're from some sort of flamingo sanctuary and proceeds from the parade will go to help them."

"Oh, that's nice."

"Yeah, but the animal rights people are pissed about it. They're staging a protest, saying the birds are being exploited or some such. But, anyway, there'll be like a herd of fifty or so birds there."

"Not a herd," Gwenn said. "A flamboyance. Don't you know anything?"

"Go back to your Talking Dog position."

She threw a pillow at me.

"You see that Spock? I've been assaulted."

Spock, with his fresh bullet holes, and Mona, reassembled, lurked in the corner of the room. Neither of them responded. I was pretty sure Spock was jealous I saved Gwenn from the shooter instead of him. Nothing worse than a resentful Vulcan.

"Let's get our shoes on and go," I said to Gwenn. "Stay here and sulk, Spock."

CHAPTER 55

THE PARADE BEGAN at the end of Duval Street near the Southernmost House where we spent our first night in Key West together. We turned left out of the inn and took Whitehead Street south. Our route would take us past Ernest Hemingway's old house and continue until Whitehead dead-ended at Southernmost Point and its gigantic red, black, and yellow concrete buoy marking, as the name implies, the most southern tip of the continental United States.

That was inaccurate, as it turns out. The beach at nearby Fort Zachary Taylor Historic State Park is, in reality, five hundred feet further south. But we seemed to be living in a post-truth era where even the president lied so routinely nobody knew fact from fiction anymore. So what the heck? It's Key West. Drink up and don't sweat the small stuff.

We'd been holding hands as we strolled, but Gwenn shook hers free for a moment and wiped the perspiration off on the side of her shorts. The temperature was hovering near ninety, and with all the rain the relative humidity was about two thousand percent.

Gwenn was wearing white Bermuda shorts, matching white flip-flops, and a sexy semi-transparent pink top through which I could see the shadow of her black bra against her lightly tanned skin. I was in my usual uniform of cargo shorts and deck shoes, and my T-shirt *du jour* was from the punk band Fang Boy and the Ghouls. My backpack was slung over my left shoulder.

"I feel so sorry for Silver," Gwenn said. "This looks very bad for her brother."

"She told me Wilson was adopted by her folks when she was a teenager," I said. "He was only two at the time. I got the sense she pretty much ignored him, even resented him. His death, I think it brought out her sense of guilt about that negligence. She felt she owed it to him to find out what happened even if they never were close."

"You believed her story right from the beginning."

"I believed she was sincere, even if she is some kind of world-class conspiracy nut. Turns out she was more right than she knew. Kitchner is right, too, this has turned into a major clown fiesta."

"Well, your suspicions about the undersea cable company turned out to be right. That was impressive."

"Even a stopped clock is right twice a day."

"Okay. But don't forget your nightmare. The one about the mermaid and the speargun. That was prescient."

"I talked to Lester about that. He's kinda weird on the subject, what with his experience in the desert, the day he lost his leg and that mysterious light being, as he calls her, appeared and kept him company."

"He's mentioned that to me, too. He swears she wasn't a hallucination."

I nodded. "He thinks there's something about all this stuff, something paranormal. He keeps telling me that my job will turn out to be weirder than I know. That there are phenomena out there, forces outside our perception.

"I guess it makes him and Silver a perfect match."

Gwenn pulled me to a stop. "I agree with Lester, by the way. I think we only experience the world through a very narrow window. I think there's lots we don't see and more we don't understand."

"You too?" I was trying to make light of it, but I could tell she was being earnest.

"You also thought you were being followed," she said. "And it turns out you were."

"Well, that could be explained..."

"Sure. Maybe you noticed someone more than once and it didn't register consciously and your subconscious was speaking to you. It happens. It's a survival instinct. But it's good to have those instincts."

I stepped closer to her, drawing her into my arms. I saw the back of her head reflected in the storefront window behind her. I liked how she'd drawn her big mop of auburn hair into a ponytail. With her freckles, it gave her a girl-next-door kind of innocence.

"Speaking of instincts," I said and leaned down and kissed her gently on the lips.

"You're an animal," she said, smiling.

We'd come to Southernmost Point where about a dozen tourists were queued up waiting to take selfies in front of the buoy. We hooked a left toward Duval where a gaggle of parade-goers was mingling with a flamboyance of flamingos anticipating the start of festivities.

"Look at all the birds," Gwenn said. "They're so pretty. But some of them only have one leg."

"It's alright, Gwenn. That's just how flamingos stand. I'm sure they all have two legs. They just can't fly."

We admired them for a moment then turned the corner, heading north on Duval. "Let's get ahead of this crowd," I said. I checked my watch. "The parade won't start for a few. We could Duval Crawl for a bit."

"Or go shopping."

We went shopping.

Gwenn had ducked into a dress shop, and I was crossing the street to grab a beer from a curbside vendor when a commotion erupted in the middle of the parade-goers. A man was pushing his way through the crowd, and people were shouting. I turned to get a better look.

Something about the guy looked out of place. Maybe it was because every other person milling about in south end of Duval Street was wearing pink, dressed like a flamingo, or was, in fact, a genuine flamingo. Or maybe it was something about his face, like I'd seen him somewhere before.

He was just on the other side of the sawhorse barriers that parade organizers set in the street to corral merrymakers and flamingos alike. It also served as a line of demarcation between the festival-goers and the protesters who were waving animal cruelty signs aloft and chanting something, but I couldn't tell you what because my attention at that moment was tightly focused on the fact that the douche bag had something in his hand.

People started shouting. "Watch where you're going." "Move over." "Is that a fucking gun?"

It was a gun. And he was raising it. In my direction.

I whirled away, started to sprint north on Duval, then made a careless—but fortuitous—mistake. Ever try running full-out while looking backwards? It's awkward. I slipped on a rising puddle of seawater streaming out of a manhole cover—freaking climate change!—and stumbled onto the asphalt.

Which saved my life.

A shotgun boomed and all hell broke loose. Men, women, and birds crashed through the barricades and into Duval Street in a pink tsunami of panic.

I'd rolled when I hit the street and was on my back when the stampede stormed over me. A panicked flamingo, wings flapping, stepped on my face with her webbed feet and kept running and squawking up the street. I could feel a scratch on my forehead where one of her claws had nicked me.

She was followed by a heavyset man wearing only a feathery lavender tutu who landed on top of me when he stumbled out of his flip-flops. He was sweaty, hadn't been using a deodorant for manly men, and it occurred to me that if I survived this I'd need a bath. With surprising agility, he rolled off, and sprinted away.

All around me birds were honking, people were screaming,

feathers—real and artificial—were flying. The street was becoming peppered with flamingo poop. At least I assumed it came from the birds. Hard to know for certain as it lacked the trademark shade of coral-pink for which flamingos are famous.

A cousin of the first flamingo who'd stepped on my face landed on my stomach and dug in with her little claws. If I didn't get out of the road soon I would either be perforated by shotgun pellets or trampled to death. I rolled over and jumped to my feet.

That's when I heard Gwenn scream: "Alexander!"

I turned and the asshole who fired the shotgun had her in a hammerlock. She must have stepped out into the street and stumbled into his grasp.

I couldn't see his right hand, but I imagined him holding a pistol or a knife. He must have dumped the shotgun. I heard a siren growing louder from somewhere up Duval. About fucking time. Where the hell were the cops, anyway? They always hung out at parades. Maybe they were too busy hunting for this guy elsewhere on the island. Him and the other Zodiac killers.

I reached into my backpack and pulled out my speargun. Then I began marching straight towards him.

I'm no hero. A hero is a guy who's scared shitless, but charges a machinegun nest anyway. I wasn't afraid. I wasn't feeling anything. I was in full zombie mode. I was going to walk up to this douche bag and shoot him in the face. It was that simple.

Out of the corner of my left eye I spotted a cowboy hat on a man walking parallel with me on the other side of the street. I cut my eyes quickly to look. It was Barfield.

I should have known. He wouldn't cool his heels at the marina waiting to see if the bad guys made an encore appearance. He'd shadowed us. And he'd correctly figured that if anything would draw the bad guys out of hiding it would be us, more specifically, me. I'd never seen him. Of course, I hadn't seen the gunman, either. So much for my extra-sensory powers.

Looking past Gwenn and the gunman, I saw a familiar couple approaching them from behind, pistols in hand.

Then it clicked. There was a reason why Paine and Kitchner hadn't called to set up a debriefing with the Coast Guard, why Barfield was so sanguine about having no role to play. They'd cooked up this scheme. They'd used us for bait. If they'd asked me to go along with the idea, I would have agreed. But I never would have allowed Gwenn to be part of it. What the hell were these assholes thinking?

But maybe our going out for a stroll threw off their plan. Maybe all three of them were staking out the Coco Plum Inn, and that plan blew up when we decided to check out the parade. I hoped that was it.

The gunman was leading Gwenn in my direction. Barfield was now flanking in from the side of the street. Unlike the cops, he didn't have a gun out. I wondered why. Paine and Kitchner had slowed their pace and were now creeping up on them. I kept my eyes glued on the gunman's. I wanted him totally focused on me.

"Let her go," I said. "You want me, you got me."

He was half pushing, half carrying Gwenn. Her eyes were wide in terror, her glasses knocked askew. Yeah, I was going to kill this fucker. It was as simple as that.

That's when I spied the pair of Wooks sitting on the curb, their heads down as if they were in a daze. The gunman and Gwenn were about to pass their position.

Anthony the Wook stood up and walked straight over to them. "Hey man, is that a gun or are you just happy to see me?"

The shooter turned on him, and Gwenn wrenched her arm from his grip and threw herself onto the pavement.

Barfield rushed in to tackle the shooter, but in a move of almost balletic grace, the gunman pivoted around Barfield's outstretched hand and grabbed him around the neck and put his pistol against his temple. Paine and Kitchner froze in their tracks.

"Walk with me, cowboy," The gunman said to Barfield as he

began backing across the street. Gwenn scrambled to her feet and ran behind me.

"Get inside!" I told her.

She grabbed the back of my shirt and hung on. Maybe she was too afraid to move. "Get away from this," I said. "Hurry."

She cried out and I heard her footsteps running across the street.

The gunman flinched slightly, his gun wavered as if he were tempted to let Barfield go and shoot me instead. But he was cunning enough to know that would be a suicide move, so he kept walking backwards.

Barfield's eyes were wide in terror. His face was beet red, the gunman's grip around his neck ferocious.

I started walking toward him again. I raised the speargun and aimed it at his right eye. "You know something about spearguns, don't you, asshole?" I said. "It was you who shot Tina Del Rio, right?"

It wasn't like in the movies where the bad guy, cornered, starts blabbing away, telling all, solving the mystery for the audience. That would have been swell, but it wasn't on today's playbill.

Both Paine and Kitchner were yelling at him. "Police! Drop that weapon! Put your hands in the air!" All the stuff we've seen in movies and on TV playing out in real life. The gunman ignored them.

Paine and Kitchner were now spread apart. The douche bag couldn't use Barfield as a shield from all three of us that way. Somebody would have a clean shot at the guy, and by somebody I mean Kitchner or Paine since we'd already witnessed my speargun marksmanship. I'd have to be right on him to hit the mark.

But he wasn't stupid. There was a narrow alleyway between an adult book store and a cigar shop, and he began backing into it, eliminating our advantage. I envisioned Bret Barfield's brains blowing out through the front of his head, his body dropping like a sack of seaweed in the alleyway, the bad guy running away.

A feeling of wild desperation gripped me. We were going to lose, and this asshole would still be around to threaten us. And Barfield would be dead. Dead while I still owed him money.

"Hey Brett, remember what you said about my poker debt? You said it was what?"

He looked at me blankly for a moment, then his eyes grew wide. He remembered. He'd called it a "drop in the bucket," the word *drop* being the operative word for the moment. He curled his knees to his chest and let gravity wrench him from the gunman's grip.

Kitchner and Paine fired simultaneously. So did I. The gunman staggered for a moment with a gaping hole where his nose used to be and blood gushing out of a wound in the center of his throat. Then he collapsed lifelessly into the alley.

I turned to find Gwenn. She was hovering in the doorway of the dress shop. I ran over and pulled her into my arms.

"You're okay, I said. "It's over now."

She was breathing hard and I could feel her heart hammering through her chest.

"I want to see him," she said.

"What?"

"I need to see him. Dead. He would have killed me. And you. I need to know he'll never do that again."

I thought that was a little crazy, but before I could try to talk her out of it she took a deep breath, stepped around me, and began marching across the street.

When we got there, Paine and Kitchner were hovering over the gunman's lifeless corpse. Paine kicked away his pistol, although he no longer was a threat, and Kitchner bent down and began looking through his pockets for ID. They didn't bother checking his pulse.

The shooter wasn't the first dead guy I'd ever seen, nor the first gunshot victim. But he was gruesome. I turned to Gwenn. Her face was ashen and she stood paralyzed, staring at the monstrosity at our feet.

Barfield was sitting in the alley, leaning against the blue clapboard siding of the cigar store. "Uh, can somebody pull this out?" My spear had ripped through his shirt collar and pinned him to the side of the house.

Paine glanced at me. "I told you. Center of mass."

Anthony the Wook trotted over along with the doe. "Doctor Strange, are you all right?"

"It's not doctor, Anthony," I said.

His voice startled Gwenn out of her trance. She turned away from the corpse and grabbed Anthony by his shoulders. "Thank you. What you did. That was very brave. You saved my life."

Anthony blushed. Then straightened a bit. "Mr. Strange, we're part of his army. It's our job."

Barfield looked up. I could tell he wanted to say something clever. But he was too shaken. I would have been, too. He took a couple of breaths then finally spit it out:

"You always get me into the weirdest shit."

CHAPTER 56

GWENN AND I rushed back to Sunset Marina shortly after the Duval Street attack. The harbormaster had called and said all hell had broken loose dockside by the *Miss Demeanor*.

Flashing blue lights greeted us as we pulled into the marina. The parking lot was jammed with county sheriff's cruisers, an ambulance, the medical examiner's truck, a CSI van, and a bomb disposal unit. Several Key West P.D. cruisers were also in the parking lot, which explained why there were no cops down on Duval Street when we needed them.

A sheriff's deputy, resting on a gurney, was being treated by medics. His shirt was off and his left shoulder was covered in white bandages. A pair of CSIs were photographing the body of a man lying on the dock by my boat. Even from our side of the police tape it was clear from the blood on the front of his shirt that he'd been shot. There were no urgent life-saving efforts underway.

Another man was shackled and sitting in the rear of a sheriff's cruiser. The doors to the cruiser were open and two grim-faced deputies were standing guard beside it. The man had black hair and a shaggy beard. We recognized him as the leader of the men aboard the Zodiac who'd threatened us on our original trip to the dive site.

Lt. Barry Taylor, who I'd met days earlier outside Tina Del Rio's office, spotted us and signaled a uniform to let us through the caution tape. Taylor was wearing tan khakis, a blue dress shirt, and a Glock, like the first time I saw him. We signed our names on a clipboard and approached him.

"Hello, lieutenant," I said. "This is Gwenn." We all shook hands. He introduced himself and gave her one of his business cards. She returned the favor.

"Guinevere G—" He stopped in mid-pronunciation, unsure how to finish.

"The X is silent," she said. "Ja-ROO."

He nodded. "Thanks. I'm sure you get that a lot. Are you representing Mr. Strange?"

"I'm his attorney-of-record, yes."

"Uh, do I need a lawyer?" I asked.

"Shoot anybody today?" he asked.

"No. I missed." I gave him a quick rundown of what we'd been thorough on Duval Street and he listened without comment, although when I described how Barfield hit the deck and Paine and Kitchner opened fire, he cocked an eyebrow. Mr. Expressive.

When I was done, he said, "Where's the speargun?"

"I turned it over to Harrison Paine. Naples P.D. has it now."

He nodded. "Good. We should have taken it as evidence the last time you shot somebody, but I guess it's a good thing you had it today."

I wasn't sure Brett Barfield would agree, but you can't please everybody.

"Now that I've done my show and tell, it's your turn." I said, nodding to Black Beard in the sheriff's cruiser. By then, I was so used to Abby Kitchner's sarcasm, I assumed he'd give me some grief, but he simply launched into it:

"Deputy Ortega over there intercepted him and his pal approaching your boat. The guy on the dock pulled a knife on Ortega and wounded him in the shoulder. Ortega shot him. Then held the guy with the beard until backup arrived."

"We recognize that man," Gwenn said. "He was on board the Zodiac when we were threatened."

Taylor took out his notebook and questioned us for a few minutes. When he was done, I asked, "What's with the bomb disposal unit?"

"They were carrying a suspicious looking satchel with them."

"Explosives?"

He nodded.

"They were going to blow up my boat?"

"Looks that way."

A CSI who was examining a late-model black SUV in the parking lot waved at Taylor then walked over holding a paper bag. "Found something that might be interesting."

She opened the bag. "Look, don't touch."

Taylor peered inside the bag. "What is that?"

I took a glimpse, but the CSI snatched the bag away quickly, no doubt concerned I would breathe on it or in some other way contaminate the evidence. "It's an underwater camera," I said.

The detective thought about that for a moment then nodded. "That woman, Silver McFadden, she was carrying a camera when she was assaulted."

"That's correct. And my guess is that when we take a look at the video on that camera, a lot of our questions about this fiasco may be answered."

He smiled briefly, but it wasn't warm and friendly.

"We?"

Up to that point, the lieutenant had been, if not friendly, at least courteous and professional, but now he'd put on his cop snark. I wasn't having any of it.

"Gwenn, how long would it take you to get a court order to have that camera returned to Silver McFadden?"

Before she could answer Taylor said, "It's evidence in a crime."

"It's private property," Gwenn retorted. "We have been assaulted and our lives threatened ever since we've arrived here. People have died. All because the Monroe County Sheriff's Office refused to take Silver McFadden seriously. You blew her off when she told you her brother's death was no accident. Now look at what we've got. How big a public stink do you want me to make about this latest insult?"

She turned to me. "What's the name of that reporter friend of yours, Agua?"

"Hermina Hermelinda Obregon."

"Yes. Let's go see her. Right now."

Of course I'd rather eat sushi than tell the *Key West Citizen* anything, but it was a nice bluff.

Before the detective could react, Gwenn pulled another ace from her sleeve: "Alexander, call Silver. Have her return here immediately. I'll begin drawing up a negligence lawsuit and we will demand this video as part of the discovery process. And I'll file a motion for injunctive relief."

She turned back to Taylor. "We *will* see this video. How painful do you want me to make it for you?"

Taylor didn't budge, so we spent the next twenty-four hours appealing to everyone we could think of: The sheriff, himself. The county prosecutor. The Special Agent in Charge of the FBI's Miami field office. The Coast Guard. Every one of them insisted on interrogating us, anyway, so we tried to trade information with limited success. But no dice on the video. It was material evidence in an ongoing investigation. We were witnesses and victims, not insiders in the investigation. And I was a reporter. They were civil, but the message was the same: Go pound sand.

But we did learn a few things:

The would-be assassin hospitalized with a spear in his leg, one David R. Bishop, no longer lived in navy housing. He'd washed out of SEAL training and had been dishonorably discharged the previous year. He simply hadn't updated his address on his driver's license.

Bishop's new address matched that of four other men, however, all of whom shared a rental house on Stock island. Two of the men were now deceased. One, Mateo Lopez, was the guy on the dock with the bullet hole in his chest. The other was the Duval Street douche bag who was shot to death by Paine and Kitchner. His name was Santiago Rollins. Both Lopez and Rollins hailed from Long Island and were believed to have been members of the gang MS-13 at one time.

The bearded guy in the back of the sheriff's car had no ID on him. Said his name was John Johns.

"He claim to be the Martian Manhunter?" I'd asked Kitchner. She pretended to have never heard of J'onn J'onzz, the sole survivor of a race of Martians who came to Earth as a kind of super cop.

"Are you ever serious?" she asked.

"Fuck with J'onn J'onzz and you'll know all about serious." I suspected Kitchner never read comic books as a kid. Probably stunted her emotional development and explained her crabby personality.

John Johns immediately lawyered up and didn't give the cops anything but his fingerprints, which showed that prior to threatening innocent people on the high seas he had been a navy diver. That fact attracted the attention of the NCIS who, Paine reported, questioned him "industriously."

They say there are three things you should never ask a journalist to do: add and subtract. Mathematically impaired though I might be, I knew that two dead bad guys plus two jailed bad guys only added up to four bad guys. And Kitchner said a total of five men were sharing a house together on Stock Island.

"Where's Numero Cinco?" I asked her after a two-hour debriefing, which was largely unnecessary since she knew most everything we'd been involved in—she'd been there for much of it. Gwenn and I were with her in a small interrogation room at the Sheriff's Office. I was surprised she was conducting the interview. Figured she'd be out on paid leave for a while after the Duval Street shooting. Standard operating procedure. Apparently, the internal review process was expedited.

Kitchner shook her head when I asked her about the fifth man.

"You know who he is?" Gwenn asked

She shook her head again.

"Should we be worried?" I asked.

That earned us a cocked eyebrow, which I interpreted as "No shit, Sherlock."

"Are we being monitored, is that why you're so mum?" I asked. Like I didn't know what the mirror on the wall was all about.

Del Rio and Forester turned out to be more helpful.

It was two days after the "Flamingo Fowl-Up"—that was the banner headline in the newspaper. Gwenn, Lester, Silver and I were having drinks in the lounge of the *Miss Demeanor.* A permanent sheriff's detail was guarding the marina. After two unsolved murders, two bad guys shot to death by cops, two other bad guys in jail—one with a very large bandage on his leg—the *Key West Citizen* was having a field day. The sheriff, up for re-election in the coming year, didn't need any more bad publicity, like, for instance, having an aging but comfortable converted fishing trawler blown up on his watch.

Gwenn and I had moved back aboard in preparation for our return voyage to Naples, and Lester and Silver had flown down at the request of the Coast Guard and the FBI. Barfield was en route back to Phoenix, vowing never to darken the streets of Key West again. "You fuckers are crazy down here," were his last words before boarding his flight.

"You get anything more out of the feds on what your brother got himself into?" Gwenn asked after Silver downed a couple of cold ones.

She shook her head. "No. I can't tell if they think he was a victim—besides being killed—or if he was in on it." She turned to Lester. "Wasn't that your sense?"

He nodded. "They did tell us they got into his checking and credit card accounts. The checking accounts show regular weekly deposits from that Trans Europa company, about two thousand each. Like he was on their payroll. Which fits with him working on a project for them. But it could also have been a smokescreen."

As soon as he said that, his eyes cut to Silver. She patted him on the leg and nodded. "I'm over it, Lester. Whatever it turns out to be, at this point I just want to know the truth."

My iPhone buzzed and it was a call from Del Rio. "Permission to come aboard," he said. I looked out the back window and he and Forester were standing on the pier.

"Welcome aboard."

"You guys on or off the clock?" I asked as they entered the cabin.

"Off," Forester said. "Where's the liquor."

They were both in suits despite the heat of the afternoon, but it didn't seem to bother them. Maybe some sort of special FBI training. Probably showered with their clothes on, too.

Forester reached into his jacket pocket and extracted an envelope. "We were never here. You didn't get this from us."

Inside was a thumb drive.

"This what I think it is?" I asked, hopefully.

"I have no idea what you're talking about," Forester said. He and Del Rio slugged down their drinks, rose in unison, and walked out, never saying another word.

"What is it?" Silver asked.

"Let's see."

I plugged the thumb drive into the USB port of my PowerBook. After it mounted on the screen, I opened the drive and saw two MP4 files inside.

I clicked on one of the two files as Lester, Silver and Gwenn huddled around the laptop. It opened to a video, and I directed the cursor over the start button and the movie began rolling. The camera was pointed at the partially exposed bow of *The Mermaid* and captured two divers, with dual tanks, loading ancient wooden chests into a sturdy diving net arrayed on the seafloor near the freshly cut hole in the side of the junk.

After four of the chests were placed inside the netting, one of the divers began tugging on the cable attached to the net that ascended upward and out of the frame of the video. In a few moments, the net enclosed around the chests and began rising in the water.

The bundle did not ascend straight up, however, and swung toward what would eventually be revealed as the stern of the ship. Suddenly, one of the chests cracked, and a stream of glassy black stones and dust began sprinkling the seabed along a line of little green plants—the mermaid's wineglasses we'd seen on the first dive.

I paused the video.

"I picked up two of those crystals on my first dive," I said. "Gave them to Akari. They were kinda like black diamonds. She was able to identify them as some sort of mineral containing uranium. Which is why they were radioactive."

"You stored radioactive rocks onboard?" Lester asked.

"Only briefly," I said.

I hit the start button again, but we were already near the end of the recording and it ended shortly thereafter as the net rose upward and eventually out of sight.

"Can you tell from the angle where he placed the camera?" Lester asked.

"Yes. It would have been on the starboard side of the shipwreck aimed in the direction of the undersea cable."

"So, Wilson wasn't filming this, himself?"

"I don't think so," I said. "The camera is stationery. It's a wide-angle lens. You notice how the camera didn't track the net as it ascended? My guess is Wilson recovered this camera sometime afterward."

"And he sent it to me." Silver said.

I nodded, unsure what the implications of that might be. But maybe the other video file would clue us in. I opened it and hit the play button.

Donald Wilson's face filled the screen. He blinked several times then began talking. "Hi, Sis. If you're watching this, I might be in trouble." He paused for a few moments and blinked again.

"The first thing I have to say is I'm sorry. For a lot of things. For how I've deceived you. For being a jerk all these years. And for being naïve. I've gotten into some trouble. I'm afraid it might not end well, although I have a plan that I hope will work. Well, I guess it didn't work or you wouldn't be watching this.

"The most important thing: You could be in danger." He took a deep breath. "Because of me. If you haven't heard from me, take this to the police. And stay safe. I know that has to be a shock. Let me tell you what's going on. Maybe for the first time in my life, I'll be completely honest with you."

I glanced at Silver. She was rigid, her fists clenched. Lester wrapped his arm around her waist to steady her. I couldn't imagine what was going through her mind at that moment. Nothing good, that's for sure.

Wilson continued: "When I was in the navy, I was never aboard the *Theodore Roosevelt*. Wasn't at the Naval Research Lab in Washington, either. I was part of a small, elite group that was tasked with implementing a naval intelligence strategy to, essentially, wiretap the internet.

"Now, especially with all your conspiracy theories, I know you're aware that the National Security Agency has been secretly wiretapping all the phone lines and internet connections for years. Edward Snowden let that cat out of the bag.

"What most people don't know is that the military, specifically Naval Intelligence, has been doing the same thing. The navy doesn't trust the CIA or the NSA. It wants its own wiretaps, and that was part of my job. Me and others, but I don't know who or how many.

"When the NSA taps undersea cables, usually that happens near shore at nodes where the lines come into the land-based systems. The navy does its work out in blue water, far from shore. So do the Russians and Chinese and others. Don't think too badly about the navy. They're trying to keep us safe. But, yeah, that was my job. To help the navy spy.

"The company I told you I was working for? It isn't real. Although what I told you about my assignment was basically true. A phone line the navy tapped was experiencing interference. It required a diver to go down and take a look, to make sure it wasn't the navy's tap that was causing the problem.

"There was a possibility that there was an accidental break, but the presumed depth of the cable precluded things like boat anchors that can snag undersea cables. Sharks were a possibility. It's a real thing. And I was very curious about that.

"But that wasn't it. It took several dives to find the break in the cable I was assigned to. But when I did, I discovered something fantastic. Not sharks—although I did have a scrape, literally, with a very nasty Vampire shark. What I discovered was a very big and very old sunken ship. It's Chinese. And it landed on an unexpected sand dune in the ocean, only about two hundred feet deep, but the sand was shifting and the cable, which was lying on top of the shipwreck, was getting stretched by the wreck's motion.

"I fixed that. It was easy…"

Gwenn said, "That must have been the claw-like thing you found."

I nodded.

"…But the real excitement was the shipwreck. And that's where I lost my way and where I was stupid. I could have fixed the cable, kept my mouth shut, and gone back to the site sometime in the future. But I didn't. I told my controller. I can't give you his name because—and I know this will sound silly, but you have to understand this was a covert operation. I never saw him in person, our communication was mostly electronic, and he had a code name. I don't know his actual name. But he told me to address him as Mr. Dark…"

I couldn't help myself. "Oh, please." I stopped the recording.

"Who is Mr. Dark?" Gwenn asked.

"A villain in a Ray Bradbury novel," Silver responded, her voice monotone.

"Also a video game character," I said. "Guess there's more than one Mr. Dark."

I pushed the play button again.

"I was excited. I told my controller about the shipwreck. That it would be an amazing historical discovery. That's about the time you and I talked on the phone, and that was uppermost in my mind.

"But I could tell something was off. My controller kept asking if I thought there might be treasure aboard. To make a long story short, he chartered a shrimp boat and some very nasty men, two of whom were divers, and he insisted that I lead them to the sunken ship. I kept asking what this had to do with Naval Intelligence, and he gave me a runaround that I didn't believe for a minute.

"I realized everything was going sideways, but I wasn't sure what to do. So, I dove on the wreck a couple of times with them, acted like I was okay with everything. On my last dive with them, I managed to retrieve this camera. You've got the camera now and the original memory card. I've stored a copy in the cloud that I'm going to show the police.

"Except for the times I went out to the shipwreck with the shrimp boat crew, I chartered a local fishing boat that Mr. Dark told me to use. After I mail this to you, I'm making one last trip out to the dive site. The charter boat captain, his name is Abner Daystrom, is picking me up here. When I get back, I've got a rental car and I'm getting my friend, her name is Tina Del Rio, over at the community college. She'll be waiting for me at her office. She doesn't know any of this yet and I'm afraid for her safety as well as yours. As soon as we're safe, I'm contacting the police, maybe the FBI—her brother is an FBI agent—and we're going to stay low for a while. I really should have called you about all of this, but, well, what can I say, the phones aren't safe.

"Hopefully, you'll never see this..."

Wilson's hand reached toward the lens and the video died.

Silver was too distraught to speak, and Lester took her below to rest. Gwenn and I looked at one another for a few moments, neither of us saying anything, processing what we'd seen.

Finally, she said, "We need to get Kitchner on the phone."

She answered on the first ring. "You want to talk on the phone?" I asked. "or do you want to meet?"

It took her a couple of beats to process that, then she said, "Larry, damn, good to hear your voice. You in town?"

"Yes, just landed," I said, playing along. "We're dying to see you."

"I'm dying to see you, too," she said. "Where shall we meet?"

I thought about that for a moment then said, "Well, since we're *dying* to see one another, let's meet at Pearl Roberts' place. You know where that is?"

It took her a few seconds to piece it together, then she said, "Be there in half an hour."

Gwenn looked at me, puzzled. "Pearl Roberts? That a bar?"

"No," I replied. "But you're going to like her sense of humor."

CHAPTER 57

GWENN AND I arrived at the Key West Cemetery ten minutes early. I borrowed Lester's new rental car—a Chevy Impala, not a go-kart this time—and parked near the Frances Street Bottle Inn.

"How'd you discover Peral Roberts' tombstone," Gwenn asked.

"It's actually the most famous one here," I said. "I ran past it—literally—when I went on a jog through the cemetery before you got here."

As we strolled to Pearl's final resting place, we passed other oddball epitaphs along the way. One read:

I Always Dreamed of Owning A Small Place In Key West

Another said:

So Long And Thanks For All The Fish

We finally got to Roberts' and her famous

I Told You I Was Sick

Kitchner and Paine showed up ten minutes late. Paine was carrying a gym bag. "We parked off Duval and walked, checking our six the entire way," Kitchner said. "I don't think we were followed."

Paine studied both Gwenn and me for a few seconds then said, "You've seen the video, haven't you."

"What video?"

"Right."

"So what was the play?" I asked. "Wait until Mr. Dark tried to kill us?"

Kitchner was chewing her lip. "Not our play, Alex," she said. I was pretty sure it was the first time she'd called me by my first name.

"Feds in charge of this now?" I asked.

"More specifically," Paine said, "The U.S. Coast Guard operating on behalf of the Department of Homeland Security, doing the bidding of Naval Intelligence."

"Still sounds like a cluster fuck," I said.

"It's worse than it sounds," Kitchner said. "That video basically exposes the Pentagon's entire domestic spying operation."

"Is that legal?" I asked Gwenn.

"Not my area, but ordinarily the U.S. military can't operate on American soil under the Posse Comitatus Act, and this particular tap is within the twelve nautical miles that defines our border. That said, I do know there is an interesting wrinkle in the Posse Comitatus Act, and that it specifically only applies to the army and the air force. Technically, the navy isn't covered. Not sure that comes into play here."

"Might not," Kitchner said. "We've been pretty much shut out of this, but from the little bit that I've gathered, the navy's pointing its fingers at the NSA, saying they were only doing their bidding, the NSA says it has authorization under a broad permission granted by the Foreign Intelligence Surveillance Act. But, yeah, they aren't eager to see any of this in the newspapers or the Huffington Post."

"That aside," I said, "from the video, it seems their agents..."

"Subcontractors, actually," Paine interrupted. "The navy made it very clear to us that there were no active-duty navy personnel involved."

"Okay, then mercenaries getting paid clandestinely by the federal government through one money laundering scheme or another, how's that?"

"Sounds about right."

"Then, these mercenaries went rogue, decided to do a little treasure hunting, and it looks like Donald Wilson and Tina Del Rio got caught up in it and were murdered."

Kitchner nodded. "Yeah, that's how we see it."

"You should have leverage over those two men in custody," Gwenn said. "Both caught red-handed in the commission of felonies, both obviously linked to all this. That video, if it gets before a jury, they'll face lethal injection."

"Right," Kitchner said. "And the murders are still ours. And that's exactly what we'll do. We'll turn them against one another until one of them breaks down and talks."

"But in the meantime…" I said.

"Yeah, in the meantime, Mr. Dark is on the loose. And we don't know who he is."

"The two men in custody, they won't give him up?" Gwenn asked.

"Not it," Kitchner said. "They don't know his real name, where he came from, or anything. Navy says the same thing. He was a subcontractor, there was a cutout who arranged everything. The cutout is missing."

"Missing."

"So they say."

"So, we don't know if he's still here, then," I said.

"That's right.

"But what about the house they shared" Gwenn asked. "Wasn't he the fifth man?"

"He was on the lease," Kitchner said. "G.M. Dark. But the two survivors, Bishop and Johns, they both say they never saw him. He arranged the place for them to stay, that's all. They also said there were more men involved than the four staying in the house. But they were on another team. They hinted our Mr. Dark might have been closer to those guys, whoever they are."

"And wherever they are."

"Yeah."

I took a few moments to digest all that. Then I said, "Hey, I appreciate you guys helping us fill in the blanks. But why is this on the down-low?"

Kitchner and Paine looked at one another. "They're watching us like hawks. They hate it that we've seen that video. We've been ordered to stay away from all of you, and to definitely not talk to you."

"So this is a risk, meeting us here."

"And making a copy of that video," Paine said.

I'd wondered how Del Rio and Forester got access to the underwater camera's memory card to make a copy. Now I knew.

"Did Del Rio and Forester know what was in the envelope?" I asked.

"They didn't ask and we didn't tell. They have deniability."

"But they knew it was the video," Gwenn said, "even if they didn't know what was on it. Right?"

"We've been through a lot together," Paine said, not exactly answering the question, but the meaning was clear enough.

Gwenn turned to Paine and Kitchner. "Thank you."

Kitchner nodded. Paine handed me the gym bag he was toting. "Figured you might want this."

"Watch your backs," Kitchner said. They turned and walked toward the cemetery's exit.

I unzipped the gym bag. Inside was a new speargun, same brand, and three new spears.

There was also a note. It read: "We tested your old speargun at the range. The shaft was bent. It consistently shot low and left. Enjoy your new toy. Remember, center of body mass."

CHAPTER 58

Gulf of Mexico

I TRIED TALKING Gwenn into taking a flight back to Naples. I argued that it would be quicker than traveling on the pokey *Miss Demeanor*.

"You're just saying that because you think it will be safer," she said.

She was right, but I wasn't going to concede the point. "What? Don't be ridiculous. The *Miss Demeanor* is perfectly safe."

"Good, then there's no reason I can't come with you."

Lawyers.

"Look," I said. "This isn't about you. It's about me. If anything ever happened to you, it would ruin my whole day, maybe even my whole week."

"Nice try. But that feels like giving in, letting the bad guys push us around."

"A few have tried."

"Yeah, and look what happened to them."

Which is how we ended up in the Gulf of Mexico on a northeasterly heading on a clear spring day, no rain in sight, no pirates on the horizon, and no Red Tide. Just me, my dog, my girlfriend, a mannequin, and a Vulcan.

Gwenn and I were on the flybridge. Fred was below in our stateroom snoozing. Mona and Spock were at their customary stations in the cabin. Gwenn had taped Band-Aids on Spock's wounds. Duct tape covered the holes in the windshield. I'd have to get it replaced when we got back to port.

Earlier, when Lester and I cruised down from Naples, we'd hugged the coastline, keeping land in sight for as long as possible. That felt like the prudent thing to do at the time. It had been the longest trip I'd taken with the *Miss Demeanor* since the hole in her hull had been patched. In fact, it had been the longest trip I'd ever taken on any boat.

Returning along that route would take longer than a straight shot north from the Keys, but heading due north would take us well into the open Gulf, far from shore. But since I'd already put some blue water cruising under my belt, I figured I could venture into the blue with confidence. After all, I'd gotten the boat's antenna repaired, so we could always call for help if necessary. And even though the route hugging the Florida coastline might feel more secure by keeping land in sight, that land was the Everglades. If we ran into engine problems there, the ratio of alligators to diesel mechanics was two-million to zero.

So, as a practical matter, I figured, a straight shot north through the open Gulf of Mexico seemed the best route. It was faster, which meant less time on the water for things to go wrong.

However, I figured wrong.

She Who Must Be Obeyed wanted to see Monkey Island, so we were now approaching the coordinates I recalled when we last stopped there, that stop required to satisfy Fred's need of a bathroom break.

As if on cue, he began whining as the island came into view. I didn't know if he really needed to go—although it had been a long time since we'd left port—or if with his exceptional sense of smell he could tell we were nearing marauding primates. Or maybe he sensed my unease.

"Freddie's got to go," Gwenn announced.

"So it would seem."

I altered course slightly toward a sand spit off the starboard bow.

I'd stored the dinghy on the roof of the trawler for this trip, but it was lightweight and would take no time to retrieve and drop in the water. I could paddle Fred ashore, let him do his business, and be back in no time. That was my plan.

However, my plan was wrong.

She Who Must Be Obeyed said, "I want to stop at Monkey Island."

"Uh, Gwenn, honey, the last time we stopped there we were attacked."

"But I want to see the monkeys."

"Can't we see them from a distance?"

"You promised."

I sighed. Maybe the monkeys found a new home since we visited last. Or perhaps they'd been recaptured and somebody already scored the thousand-dollar reward. Or maybe they'd evolved into people-loving primates and cured themselves of the fatal-to-humans Herpes B virus.

The last time I was there it was low tide and a broad stretch of sand was exposed. It was high tide now and most of the beach was underwater. And with the change in tide I wasn't sure how close we could get. I tried my best to mansplain this fact to Gwenn but got the you're-not-going-to-enjoy-celibacy look, so I decided to try a different tack. I was going to plead for Fred's safety. What if the monkeys attacked the poor defenseless puppy. And there was hardly any beach left for him to do his business on. That sort of thing. But before I could go there, the marine radio crackled. It was Abby Kitchner, patched-in through the Coast Guard.

"You guys could be in trouble," she said.

Gwenn and I looked at one another, puzzled. "Why's that?" I asked.

"John Johns, we finally got him to talk."

"What'd the Martian Manhunter have to say?"

"He said, among other things, they planted a tracking device on that floating shipwreck of yours."

"Tracking device?" Gwenn echoed.

"Yeah. The Coast Guard's sending a cutter your way, but it's going to take a while to get there."

"You have any reason to believe anyone's actually following us?" I asked.

"No," she said. "And I've no reason to believe they're not."

By then, the *Miss Demeanor's* bow was a few yards off the island. I idled the props. "If someone's coming, we can't outrun them," I told Gwenn.

Fred whined again and Gwenn bent over and picked him up. "Well, we're here and Fred's gotta go, so let's take care of him then figure it out."

That was as good an idea as any. As long as you discounted the possibility of painful disfigurement from monkey mauling and a slow agonizing death from monkey-borne maladies.

I descended from the flybridge and heaved the bow anchor ashore, then tightened the line to allow the current to nudge us parallel to the islet as I'd done last time. However, the boat was a good dozen feet away from the breakwater when the hull gently touched the sandy bottom.

"How ya feel about wading?" I asked Gwenn.

"You're making excuses."

So I climbed back topside, wrestled the dinghy off the roof of the trawler, and lowered it over the side. I held it tight against the hull as Gwenn lowered herself into it. Then I handed Fred to her.

I tied the dinghy's line to a cleat and told Gwenn, "Be right back." She nodded and didn't ask any questions.

In less than a minute, I returned from the cabin holding a .38 Smith & Wesson revolver.

"Where'd that come from?" she asked.

"Brett Barfield. He slipped it into my backpack the day we left the *Miss Demeanor* to spend the night at the Coco Plum Inn. Left a note with it, told me I might need it more than him."

"Is that why he didn't have a gun on him when he tackled that awful man on Duval Street?"

I nodded. "And I didn't discover it until later. I had it on me the whole time we were facing down that madman. In my backpack under my speargun. And I didn't even know it."

"You probably would have just shot your eye out," she said.

"Probably." I shoved it into a pocket of my cargo shorts and lowered myself into the dinghy. "Let's hope we don't need it today."

I revved up the little electric motor and pulled away from the *Miss Demeanor*. Most of the beach was now submerged on the seaward side of the island, but I hoped we might find a better landing spot on the opposite shore. We circled Monkey Island to discover even more mangroves, these growing right out into the water leaving us no place to land.

"No luck here," I said.

"No monkeys, either," she said.

"They're probably hiding in the mangroves."

Gwenn pointed to a small sandspit, slightly further eastward. "How about there?" she suggested. It was about twenty yards in length, with a mangrove-covered center, but it did have a few feet of beach. So, I pointed the dinghy in that direction and we nudged it ashore.

"Let's stay together," I said. "The monkeys can swim. They might be here, too." Fred seemed to understand. He didn't waste any time chasing shorebirds like he did on his last visit to the vicinity, simply circled three times and got down to it.

"Good boy."

Gwenn and I were holding hands. Despite everything, it was a romantic setting. Here we were, together on a quiet deserted island in the Gulf of Mexico on a beautiful, clear day. We watched seagulls circling overhead, listened to the peaceful waves lapping the shore, and observed a small canine pooping. Who could ask for anything more?

Then we heard it. The growl of outboard motors. They were faint at first but were becoming louder rapidly.

"Come on," I urged Gwenn. "Grab Fred. I'm going to pull the dinghy around to the other side of the mangroves."

The sandspit was only a few yards wide and we could see through the branches across the water separating us from Monkey Island. If the monkeys were still occupying the larger island, they were doing an outstanding job of hiding.

A center-console speedboat throttled down and approached the far side of Monkey Island and then was lost to our sight, obscured by the mangroves. We heard the engines shut off. Then all was silent.

Gwenn whispered to me, "What will he do, search the boat? Then what?"

Before I could answer, we could hear the faint crackle of the *Miss Demeanor's* marine radio. It was Kitchner again. "The Coast Guard's on the way," she said. "Give us your coordinates?"

"Fuck."

"What?" Gwenn whispered.

"Now he knows the cavalry's coming. But he had to hear they don't know exactly where we are. He'll figure he has time to find us."

I looked behind us toward the mainland. There was a stretch of brackish water about a hundred yards wide between us and the shore, if you could call it that. There was no land in sight, only mangroves and grass reaching out into the Gulf. This is where the Everglades drains into Florida Bay. We were north of Cape Sable, and if I recalled my maps correctly we should be where freshwater from the Shark River Slough, also known as the River of Grass, seeps into the ocean.

Could we retreat into the 'glades, hide among mangroves and sawgrass? Yeah, we could, but we'd be utterly exposed as we crossed the water between our little island hiding place and the shore. Or could we sit tight, let Mr. Dark or whoever it was in the speedboat, waste enough time hunting for us on Monkey Island that he'd eventually have to give up and hightail it before the Coast Guard arrived.

I patted the pocket of my cargo shorts and felt the reassuring lump of the snub-nosed revolver. Uncle Leo had taken me shooting when I was a teenager, and in that controlled environment with a long-barreled target pistol I did alright. But this was the furthest thing from a controlled environment, and the .38 with its two-inch barrel wasn't much more accurate than a speargun. I'd probably be as likely to shoot my foot as hit Mr. Dark.

We were lying in the sand, facing Monkey Island, being still. Without my asking, Gwenn placed a hand on Fred's muzzle, ready to hold his mouth closed if he tried to bark. I made a mental note, again, to write Dr. Omar Franken and ask him how to turn off the universal dog translator. That was the very last thing we needed going off now.

I strained to hear what might be taking place on the island. How long had it been since the speedboat's engines cut off? Five minutes at most? Mr. Dark by now would know we weren't aboard the *Miss Demeanor*. He would have to assume we were hiding somewhere in the mangroves. He would know that if we were, and if we were armed, he would be exposed if he ventured into the overgrown island.

Fred started wiggling in Gwenn's grasp and she scooted him under her, tightening her grip.

We heard a splash. As if Mr. Dark had thrown something into the water. Or he'd dropped into the water himself and was wading ashore. No way to know.

Oh, for X-ray vision to see through those branches and leaves separating us from the far side of the island. Then I saw the slightest motion at the top of a mangrove. A grayish brown shape.

The monkeys were home.

Which gave me an idea. I slipped the revolver out of my pocket and aimed it in the general direction of where the *Miss Demeanor* was anchored, and prepared to pull the trigger. Then I hesitated. No, with my luck I'd shoot a hole in the hull of the boat. I raised the gun into the air and fired.

And all hell erupted.

A burst of gunfire sent leaves and branches flying and bullets whizzing over our heads. Then the mangroves, themselves, burst into motion, and the screeches of dozens of rhesus monkeys split the air.

More shots. Monkeys shrieking. Then the scream of a man.

The commotion continued for about two minutes. The monkeys were caterwauling. The man screamed some more, but the gunshots stopped. Probably ran out of bullets. Then he was silent, too.

There had been something oddly familiar about the man's voice, but I couldn't place it.

We stayed glued to the sand, silent, although Gwenn unmuzzled Fred and he whined for a bit. After the monkey chatter died down, we looked at one another.

"You think it's safe to go back?" Gwenn asked.

I wasn't sure. But then Mr. Dark made that decision easy. We heard the engines of his speedboat crank up, which was a disappointment in a way. I thought, perhaps, the monkeys would have devoured him by that time. But he seemed to have cheated death. At least for now. There was always Herpes B.

In a few moments, we saw him flying across the water, back in the direction of Key West.

"Now what?" Gwenn asked.

"Let's wait a bit longer," I said. Only three things could happen when we returned: Mr. Dark could spot us and turn around with a fresh clip in his machine gun; the monkeys could attack us, too; or we could sneak back aboard the Miss Demeanor undetected and make a getaway after Mr. Dark's boat cleared the horizon.

Since the third option did not require us to do anything immediately, I opted for patience.

Eventually, the sound of the speedboat's engines faded away. We clambered back aboard the dinghy and made a cautious return around Monkey Island. I was concerned the primates might have decided to homestead the trawler in our absence. They'd tried boarding, after all, when Lester and I were here.

I looked for casualties on the little beach but saw none. Which, was a relief. Herpes B carriers or not, I wouldn't want that on my conscious.

We circled to the seaward side of the *Miss Demeanor*. While Gwenn held the tiller, I pulled myself over the gunwale and tied the dinghy's line to a cleat. Then I checked out the boat. It was clear of bad guys and bad tempered monkeys. But the bastard had searched the trawler and hadn't been tidy. The door to the cabin was wide open and Mona and Spock were lying on their backs.

At least he didn't shoot them.

The marine radio was crackling by the time Gwenn and Fred climbed aboard. Kitchner was frantically asking for our location. I thumbed the mic and told her what happened and gave her a description of the speedboat and the direction it was heading.

"You get a name on the hull?" she asked.

"No. But I think we're in the clear now. Here are our current coordinates. We'll be pulling anchor soon." I was careful not to mention our destination for fear Mr. Dark was listening in on the ship-to-shore.

On Monkey Island, a handful of the little primates slipped out of the seclusion of the mangroves to watch us as we prepared to depart.

"They're so cute," Gwenn said.

Then one of them pooped in his hand and hurled it in our direction.

It fell short.

He was a few feet from the anchor, which I stupidly had neglected to retrieve.

I was loathe to dinghy back to the island to dislodge the anchor with the monkeys hanging about. I was considering the odds of muscling it free using a winch when I noticed that one of the macaques, a baby, was holding something in its hand. And it wasn't poop.

It was a small red and black circular can.

"I'll be damned."

"What?" Gwenn asked.

"Check this out. See that monkey, the baby closest to the anchor. Take a look at what it's holding."

She shaded her eyes and squinted. “Is that a can of snuff?”

“Yeah. And who do we know who dips snuff?”

“Sonofabitch.”

“I’ve got to go get it. With any luck, that can may have prints or even DNA on it.”

We’d hung around long enough to attract the attention of even more monkeys who were now lining up at water’s edge, curious what the big primates had in store for them now.

“Alexander, you told me they’re dangerous. They have, what is it?”

“Herpes B.”

“And there are so many of them.”

I thought about that for a minute. The little monkey seemed to like its new toy, this black and red can. He held it up to his nose and sniffed, then began making unpleasant baby monkey sounds, which I translated as: “This shit will give you cancer.”

“Gwenn, let’s check the pantry. Maybe I can distract them with a snack.”

“Oh, oh! I’ve got just the thing.”

She darted into the cabin and returned a few seconds later holding a bunch of bananas. “Remember, you got these the other day at the grocery store.”

“Genius!”

There were five bananas in the bunch. I pulled one of them off and hurled it as far up the waterline as I could. All the adults in the troop raced to the banana and began squabbling over it. Poor guys probably hadn’t seen a banana since they escaped the monkey lab.

The baby monkey with the can seemed content to hang by the anchor and play with its smelly new toy.

“I’m going to try something,” I said.

I climbed over the gunwale, dropped into the dinghy, and started the electric motor. As I gingerly steered my way around the bow of the trawler toward shore, I had one hand on the tiller and the other holding three of the four remaining bananas in the air. The fourth

I'd hidden in a pocket of my cargo shorts along with an empty zip-lock bag.

I had to time this just right. If I got too close, they could swarm over me. If I threw the bananas too soon, it would take me too long to get to the anchor and the baby monkey holding the snuff can.

The entire troop was jumping up and down and screeching. It was Christmas on Monkey Island and the big ape was about to bring the gift of bananas.

Two yards from shore, I hurled the first banana up the beach like last time. About half the troop charged after it. The rest cleverly hung back waiting to see what I'd do with the remainder. I threw another banana as far as I could into the mangroves, and again, half the remaining monkeys raced after it. Then I wagged the final banana in my hand, teasing them. Just as the dinghy touched the sand, I stepped out and flung the banana into the underbrush, too. All the macaques except baby monkey with the shiny round toy scurried off.

I pulled out the remaining banana, got down on my knees in the small stretch of sand, and edged to the baby. I peeled the top of the banana off so he could get a better sniff. His eyes got big and he trotted over and reached out. I drew the banana back. He cocked his head. Then I tapped the can with it.

"Come on," I said. "Add a couple of genes and you're a human, too. You get it. It's a trade."

He did. He dropped the can and grabbed the banana with both hands and ran off into the mangroves to join his cousins.

I scooped up the snuff can with the zip-lock bag, careful not to add my own fingerprints and DNA to those of the monkey, and secured it. Then I grabbed the anchor, set it in the dinghy, and motored back to the trawler.

Back aboard, I got on the radio to Abby Kitchner.

"You are not going to believe what we just found." I filled her in on our discovery.

"So, Mr. Dark is actually Abner Daystrom?"

"Who knows who he really is?" I said. "But, yeah, that seems to be the identity he was using in Key West."

Kitchner paused. "Assuming it wasn't just some random boater who left a can of snuff on the beach."

"You like coincidences?" I asked.

"About as much as you. Let me ask, you ever take a picture of him?"

"Never occurred to me," I said.

"That's what I was afraid of. I'm going through the DMV website as we speak. Got nothing. We'll check security cameras, ATMs near Hurricane Hole, see if we can get lucky. May pester you for an artist's sketch."

"Be on the lookout for a guy with monkey scratches on his face."

"I'll put a BOLO out for him as soon as I get off the horn. Get the Coast Guard and Key West PD alerted. Maybe we'll catch him when he returns."

"If he returns."

We were still another six hours from Naples at the trawler's speed. Kitchner said a CSI would drive up and meet us at the marina, take possession of the snuff can, and find the bug that had been planted on the trawler. Odds are we'd arrive at about the same time.

When I clicked off the radio, I noticed that Gwenn had been standing behind me. She had her hands on her hips, and she didn't have a happy look on her face.

"What?"

"Is it always going to be like this with you?"

Gwenn had been threatened, manhandled, and shot at over the past several days, and the trauma of all that seemed to be taking a toll. Of course, she had put herself in harm's way by flying down to Key West and joining me. And my guess—at least my hope—was that after she had a chance to put this behind her she'd look back at it as a great adventure. But at that moment, she'd had enough.

I opened my arms. She'd either walk into them or walk away. She stepped forward and we hugged.

"Um, not to put too fine a point on it," I said, "but I think you were the one who wanted me to stay busy."

Her face was in my chest and her voice was a little muffled. "Yeah. I dated a banker a few months before I met you. I thought I'd die of boredom."

"Boredom kills."

She nodded.

"By the way," I said. "Thank you."

She looked up. "For what?"

"For insisting we stop at Monkey Island. If Mr. Dark had caught us in open water…"

She hugged me tighter.

The rest of the trip to Naples was uneventful. I was piloting the *Miss Demeanor* from inside the cabin as we cruised up the Gordon River, heading toward Naples City Dock.

Gwenn was sound asleep in our stateroom, exhausted from the ordeal.

Fred was curled up in his bed snoozing, too.

Mona was back upright, *en garde*, silent, watchful. Spock was by her side.

"We're home," I said.

THE STRANGE FILES

A Fowl-Up in Key West

By Alexander Strange

Tropic Press

KEY WEST—Donny Westhaven loved the sea. Now he'll spend eternity there.

But Donny's journey to his eternal resting place took a few detours.

They began when his girlfriend was given a coffee can filled with the wrong ashes, the ashes of another deceased man also named Donald. The Monroe County Medical Examiner's office mixed up the corpses.

And while Donny Westhaven waited on a slab at the morgue for all that to get sorted out, a lot of things happened.

- A marine biologist named Donald Wilson accidentally had his ashes spread across the sea after he was murdered.
- The corpse of Wilson's girlfriend was discovered with a spear in her stomach.
- Pirates tried to scare me and my crew off a dive site that would eventually resolve the mystery of these deaths.
- A gunslinger tried to machine-gun a boatload of people. Unfortunately for him, they were well armed FBI agents, local cops, and a private detective.
- Another group of bad guys tried to blow up my boat, the *Miss Demeanor*.
- And we found a sunken Chinese pirate ship that also led us to the discovery that the United States Navy has been tapping our phones lines.
- And a lot more.

This adventure began when a woman showed up in Naples with the unlikely story that her marine biologist brother had been murdered.

It ended when a flamboyance of flamingos stampeded down Duval Street in Key West.

Her name was Silver…

Author's Note

Mr. Dark was never found, and his real identity remains a mystery—at least to this writer. While it is clear he had posed as Abner Daystrom, no useable fingerprints could be extracted from his can of snuff. There was plenty of DNA, however. But there were no matches in the database.

Does he remain a threat? If so, hopefully the publication of this book will provide Alexander Strange and his friends some level of inoculation against further peril.

I have tried diligently to pry out Mr. Dark's real name and with whom he is affiliated. Like Alexander Strange, I have sources in the law enforcement community and count among my friends and acquaintances several former operatives of the Central Intelligence Agency, a handful of current and retired high-level military officers, and several foreign-service officers in the State Department who have been involved in counter-terrorism initiatives. Mr. Dark is known of. But his true identity is a secret.

As a retired marine three-star told me, "The world of black ops employs lots of guys like your Mr. Dark, most of them are a lot more vicious and psychotic." The general said that Mr. Dark, of whom he had heard, had also been referred to in intelligence circles as Voldemort, Moriarty, Blofeld, and, oddly, Mrs. Danvers.

Why does he use names drawn from the villains of literature? "Who knows?" the general said. "Maybe he was an English major."

Of course, there's always the chance that the rhesus macaques of Monkey Island infected him with the Herpes B virus during their mauling and that he has already died an agonizing death. Can it hurt to be hopeful?

As this was written, the United States Navy was conducting a salvage operation ten miles south of Key West to recover the black crystals found in the hold of *The Mermaid.* While the question lingers as to why and how the flagship of the pirate Madame Ching ended up on an uncharted undersea sandbar in the Gulf of Mexico, the contents of the junk's hold were revealed to be a massive cache of the mineral uraninite, the principal ore from which uranium is processed.

In its crystalline form, uraninite could easily have been assumed to be a gemstone, geologists said, which could explain why it may have been viewed as treasure. Based on a preliminary survey, it was believed that there would be enough uraninite recovered from the shipwreck to ultimately fuel several nuclear reactors—or put to other non-civilian uses. The big question is: Where did it come from and is there more of it somewhere?

The navy acknowledged that it had a program to "monitor" undersea cables as part of its national security effort, but that it was to protect data lines from foreign powers, not to spy on Americans. The Senate and House intelligence and armed services committees held closed-door reviews regarding the revelation and in a bipartisan report concluded that there were no violations of the Posse Comitatus Act.

The murders of Donald Wilson and Tina Del Rio remain officially unsolved. David R. Bishop (the guy Alexander shot in the leg with his speargun) was convicted of attempted murder without the possibility of parole for his assault on the passengers aboard the *Miss Demeanor.* John Johns (who, as it turns out, had never heard of the Martian Manhunter) pled guilty as part of a deal with the county prosecutor to a charge of aggravated assault in the beating of Silver McFadden. He is serving five years imprisonment and will face five years of probation after his release. He likely will also face Lester Rivers when he gets out. He might want to stay inside.

Alexander Strange was right in assuming that the sinking houseboat at Key West's Garrison Bight was not damaged by Hurricane Whitney. It was a flight of fancy on his part, however, to assume it had been victimized by the perpetrators of Donald Wilson's demise. It had simply rusted out due to a lack of preventative maintenance.

The video recording of the conversation between the skipper of the Zodiac boat and someone else, perhaps Mr. Dark, was turned over to the FBI for analysis. The FBI declined to comment, and an audio analysis by Tropic@Press proved inconclusive.

Alexander never saw Anthony the Wook again. He and his doe simply vanished into the streets of Key West or who knows where. Anthony, if you are reading this, Alexander wants to get in touch with you. He owes you big time for how you helped save Gwenn's life. And he has an idea he thinks you might like.

How Donald Wilson's remains got confused with those of Donny Westhaven remains a mystery.

Silver McFadden ultimately decided to place a tombstone in the Key West Cemetery to honor her brother's passing. You can see it if you visit. It's not far from B.P. "Pearl" Roberts. It reads:

"Beware the Mermaid"

Acknowledgment

I OWE A deep debt of gratitude to many people in the creation of this book. Foremost to my friend and colleague at Tropic◎Press, Alexander Strange, for allowing me to tell this story and for his comprehensive notes that made it possible.

I have written this in first person, with Alex as the protagonist, as this is his tale to tell. I am merely his scribe. Why didn't Alex write it himself? As he told me, "I'd rather crawl naked through a bed of nails than write a book."

Many of the details of this story flow from the audio recordings Alex gave me. Other sources of information include police reports and interviews with Gwenn Giroux, Lester Rivers, Harrison Paine, Sally Ann "Silver" McFadden, Akari Takahashi, and Abby Kitchner. Special thanks also to former FBI agents and now the principals of their own accounting firm in Miami, Hector Del Rio and Bill Forester.

During the course of creating this narrative I did from time to time fill in gaps not covered in interviews and notes, particularly when trying to relate Alexander's internal dialogues. He's reviewed all this, of course. When I asked him if he saw anything that troubled him in my extrapolations, he replied, "close enough for non-government work."

If I have introduced any errors, I blame it on the internet.

The names of several characters in the book and some locations and names of businesses have been changed to honor confidentiality requests and to avoid pesky litigation. It is pure coincidence if any characters, places, or businesses included in this narrative bear any relationship with the real events.

Special thanks to Edwina Mahoney, editor of Tropic◎Press, for her assistance and guidance and for her permission to use articles published by the news service, and to the mysterious Colonel Lake—and, no, I don't know his real name.

Also, thanks to all who assisted me in preparing this for publication, especially my chief editor, Logan Bruce; my inspiration and backstop, Sandy Bruce; and my talented web designer, Kacey Bruce. Also a big shout-out to my International Thriller Writers coaches Gayle Lynds, Meg Gardiner, and F. Paul Wilson for their continuing inspiration and priceless guidance. And to the many fellow writers in several critique groups who have made invaluable contributions to this effort. You know who you are.

Sidebars

Vampire Sharks:

The goblin shark, also known as the vampire shark, ordinarily is found in deep water and sometimes is referred to as a "living fossil" as it is the sole member of the family *Mitsukurindae*, which has a lineage of about 125 million years old. Its elongated snout is filled with sensors that can detect faint electrical fields, which helps it detect prey. There has been speculation that Donald Wilson may have been incorrect in his initial assumption that fish feeding off the mermaid's wineglasses growing near the undersea cable drew the vampire shark. It may be more likely that with the cable's frayed covering, it was giving off electrical signals that lured the shark instead. But we'll never know for sure.

Mermaid's Wineglasses

Appearances can be deceiving. Mermaid's wineglasses (*Acetabularia crenulata*), an algae found in subtropical waters, comprise but a single cell despite how complex they may look and their unusual size—growing to around 4 inches tall. They are highly sought after by scientists studying cellular biology.

Red Tide

While Red Tide (*Karenia brevis*) is a naturally occurring phenomenon that can be found worldwide, it was plaguing the Florida coast nearly endlessly as this was written, fed by pollution—meaning nitrogen and phosphorous from fertilizers—flowing out of Lake Okeechobee. Back before Okeechobee was dammed to allow land south of the lake to be used for agriculture, water naturally flowed from the lake all the way through the Everglades' River of Grass into Florida Bay. Groundwater from sugar cane fields and other crops now is pumped back into the lake along with their accompanying pollutants, and then the water is discharged into the Atlantic Ocean and Gulf of Mexico feeding the prolonged Red Tide algae blooms. Moreover, the fertilizer has prompted the growth of toxic cyanobacteria that has clogged rivers, estuaries, and canals and has been linked to a multitude of diseases. But we got cheap sugar, so there.

Was Einstein an Alien?

Alexander Strange is a big Albert Einstein fan. He took a course at the University of Texas entitled Einstein in Literature. One of Strange's pals, Logan Bruce, has added to the rumor that Einstein may have been a space alien and shared the observation that the Al in Albert combined with the first three letters of the famous scientist's last name sort of spell alien. Kinda. Could he have come from another planet? NASA has the answer: ***https://science.nasa.gov/science-news/science-at-nasa/2005/23mar_spacealien***

The Rev. Lee Roy Chitango

Who is the Chitango character briefly mentioned in this book? He is the most famous televangelist ever to preach in the state of Florida, and like so many of his ilk, he had, let us say, a darker side. You can learn more in *Get Strange* by J.C. Bruce.

What is a Poop Deck?

A real poop deck is at the aft of a boat and derives its name from the French word *la poupe*, or stern. Ordinarily, the deck forms the roof for a cabin below. The *Miss Demeanor's* poop deck has another history. One day Fred was asleep on the bow of the boat when a pelican landed on the overhang over the main cabin, gobbled down a fish it had captured in Buzzard's Bay South in the island town of Goodland where the *Miss Demeanor* was drydocked. The pelican then took an enormous dump on the poor snoozing puppy. This horrific event was witnessed by Alexander Strange and Lester Rivers who were sitting at the nearby bar at Stan's Idle Hour. "Guess that's why they call it the poop deck," Rivers said. Hence a redefined bit of nautical terminology was born.

Speaking of Fred

Papillons are ranked among the top-ten smartest breeds of dogs, and Fred is certainly no exception to that rule. Fred came into Alex's world when his uncle, Judge Leonard Dwayne Skousen, married his fifth wife. She was Fred's human. After a series of calamitous events (chronicled in *The Strange Files* by J.C. Bruce), Fred accompanied Alex to the Gunshine State, and they have been together ever since.

Omar Franken

Briefly mentioned, Dr. Omar Franken is the inventor of Stealth Car Wax. A self-made billionaire, he originally developed the radar-dampening polymer to help motorists avoid speed traps, but made his big bucks by selling it to the Pentagon. Alex tested an early version of the concoction and trashed it in one of his columns, prompting threats of lawsuits from Franken. But they've since patched things up. You can read more about that in *The Strange Files* by J.C. Bruce.

Rapture of the Deep

Rapture of the Deep is also known as the Martini Effect. As nitrogen dissolves into the bloodstream under pressure it can make a diver feel drunk. And the deeper the diver descends, and the pressure increases, the more drunk the feeling. The technical term is nitrogen narcosis and it can be quickly cured when the diver ascends to a more shallow depth. At its worst, however, it can lead to hallucinations and death.

The Conch Republic

The Conch Republic celebrates its independence day each April 23, the anniversary when, in 1982, it declared its secession from the United States in protest of harassment from Border Patrol agents who were conducting roadblocks to check the citizenship of people in the Keys. It lasted only briefly, but the name—and the attitude—stuck.

Ching Shih

Yes, the greatest pirate who ever sailed the high seas was, in fact, a woman. While not as well known in the West as such buccaneers as Blackbeard, Black Bart, or Sir Francis Drake, she plundered the South China Sea coast, commanding hundreds of junks and thousands of pirates. A character roughly based on her was portrayed in the movie *Pirates of the Caribbean: At World's End.*

Of Flamingos and Lizards

The first annual Flight of the Flamingo Parade and Dance Off was also the last after all the mayhem on Duval Street. But there was good news: None of the birds were injured in the melee, and the story attracted so much attention that the flamingo sanctuary sponsoring the event was overwhelmed with donations. Some interesting flamingo facts: There are four species of flamingos (family *Phoenicopterdae*) native to the Americas. They do, indeed, stand on one leg (perhaps to save energy; scientists don't know for sure) and they get their pink coloration from the beta carotene in their diet. The pink plastic yard flamingo, no biological relation, was designed in 1957 by Don Featherstone (his real name). He kept 57 plastic flamingos on his front yard at his home in Massachusetts, so, clearly, the flamboyance in front of Samantha's double-wide on Grassy Key did not set a record. The brown anole (*Anolis sagrei*) is a native of Cuba and the Bahamas but is now found all over Florida and elsewhere. Bad news: They are considered an invasive species. Good news: They eat bugs.

More Strangeness

You can keep up with *The Strange Files* at Alexander Strange's website *www.thestrangefiles.com* and in editions of the Tropic◎Press, *www.tropic.press.*

Made in the USA
Columbia, SC
10 October 2021

46424674R00207